AUG 07 2021

Telesa

When Water Burns

Lani Wendt Young

Also by Lani Wendt Young

Fiction

Telesā: The Covenant Keeper (Book I of the Telesā series)

Afakasi Woman (A Collection of Short Stories)

Non-Fiction

Pacific Tsunami "Galu Afi"

You can read more writing by Lani Wendt Young and stay updated on the *Telesā* series at her website.

http://sleeplessinSamoa.blogspot.com

ISBN-13: 978 - 1477492345
ISBN-10: 1477492348

Editor: Anna Thomson
Cover design: Jordan Kwan

Cover models: Faith Wulf, Ezra Taylor

DEDICATION

To Jade, Sade, Zion, Zach, and Bella, who allow me space to breathe, room to dance and dream. You give me the courage to write books – and then actually let others read them.

The Creation. According to Telesā Legend

In the beginning there was darkness, a great expanse, and Tangaloa-langi moved upon the face of the darkness. After a time Tangaloa-langi grew tired and rested, and where the god stood, there grew up a rock. Then Tangaloa-langi said to the rock, "Be thou split up" and hit the rock with one hand.It split open and the earth was brought forth on the one side and the sea was brought forth on the other. And the earth glowed red with fire and the sea enveloped it and water burned at its edges. Tangaloa-langi reached down, took of earth and mixed it with water, fashioning it with godly hands to make Man. And then the god breathed life on that which had been made.

"Let the Spirit and the Heart and Will and Thought go on and join together inside the Man."

And they joined together there and Man became intelligent. And Tangaloa-langi joined Man to the earth, through the creation of Woman. 'Fatu-ma-le-Ele-ele' meaning Heart and Earth.

"Let Earth give nourishment to Man and let Man always treasure her as his heart beats with the red blood of life. Let Earth be the rock man stands on to give him strength. The trees that will shelter him. The waters that will sustain him. Let Earth's fire be the heat that warms him. And in return, let Man be the protector. The guardian."

But Tangaloa-langi saw that as Man multiplied and replenished the earth, his heart grew cold and greed ate at it like the poison of the stonefish.Tangaloa-langi saw that Man trampled Earth beneath his feet and bowed Woman to his will. Earth's cries moved Tangaloa-langi. So again the god of all took pieces of earth and mixed them with water. But this time, Tangaloa-langi breathed upon this creation with the raging winds of the expanse. Touched it with the jagged fire that rains from angry skies and made a telesā. She was beautiful. Her name was 'telesā matagi.' Sacred one of storms. Air.

Then Tangaloa-langi cast a fiery net upon the waters and drew forth ocean's might. The crashing wave. The surging tide that speaks to Masina the moon. And all the living things that swim and creep in the midnight blue depths. All this Tangaloa-langi fashioned with godly hands into another. She was beautiful. Her name was 'telesā vasa loloa.' Sacred one of ocean. Water.

But Tangaloa-langi was not satisfied. Listening to the cries of ele-ele, feeling of her pain as Man's heart spurned her, rage filled the god of all things. Reaching deep within Earth's core, to where molten rock flowed and life pulsed, Tangaloa-langi brought forth fire and melded it with earth, cooled it with ocean and made 'telesā fanua afi.' Sacred one of earth. Fire. She was beautiful. She burned with all the strength of ele-ele. Her heart beat with the fire that would eclipse man's. He that had betrayed Earth. He that was meant to be the heart but had instead chosen to be the destroyer.

Tangaloa-langi looked upon what had been created and saw that it was good. "My daughters, yours is a godly trust, an eternal birthright. You will covenant to watch over ele-ele and fill the chasm left by an unfeeling Man and be her heart. You will speak with the voices of wind, water, and fire. You will stir Man up to a remembrance of his sacred partnership with earth."

Then Tangaloa-langi fashioned with godly hands a carved talisman. The Covenant Bone. Whale bone interlocked with shark tooth. Boar's tusk encrusted with shimmering iridescent oystershell, adorned with black pearl and gleaming river rock. The fierce razor-bite of the swordfish. The soulful deep green promise of jadestone. All these Tangaloa-langiinterwove to create a necklace of three distinct pieces, which was then washed in the blood of a god, imbuing it with the very essence of Tangaloa-langi.

"The Covenant Bone will unite the three elements. It will allow the gifts of many to be woven as one, making it possible for the telesā who bears it to wield the gifts of her sisters into one supreme power. For it is only when there is harmony between earth's gifts, that there can be peace. And life. There will come a time, when earth's greatest dangers threaten, that one of you will be called to unite your sisters into one Covenant. The Bone Bearer will lead you."

And then Tangaloa-langi looked upon telesā fanuaafi. "In those troubled days, you will be the one chosen to reach out to embrace man once again as the heart. So that all will be as it should. 'Fatu-ma-le-Ele-ele.' You will give your fire so that Man may live. And he will give his heart so that earth may live."

And thus did Tangaloa-langi create telesā.

To watch over earth and be the heart that Man refused to be.

ONE

Ten Years Ago, Hawaii

The little boy tried his hardest not to fall asleep, not to give in to waves of tiredness. But he was fighting a losing battle. Moonlight painted the room white. A bedraggled room with a battered chest of drawers in one corner and a single mattress on the floor with faded, torn sheets. The boy sat bolt upright with his back against the wall, one arm placed protectively over the little girl who lay asleep. Waiting. Dreading. There were hopeful questions. Maybe she wouldn't come home tonight? She had done that before. Disappeared for a few days. She would reappear giddy with repressed excitement. Her hands trembling. Talk about their luck finally changing. Show them a wad of cash. They would eat Chinese takeaway. Ice cream. She would tell them they could go to school like regular kids. But the buzz never lasted and she would revert to her usual self. The frightening stranger who screamed at them. Hit them. Berated them for making her life a living hell.

So yes, the little boy hoped they would be lucky. He hoped she wouldn't come home. Because it was better than the alternative. Because maybe she would come home lucky. With a man. And the children would have to cover their ears and hide under the sheet against the sounds that would come from the front room. And when it was quiet, the little boy would stand guard over his sister. Because sometimes, their mother's visitors would look around the apartment and discover that the exotic dancer they had left the club with had two children. A boy and a girl. A slight, thin pair with the cinnamon coloring of their Polynesian mother and the charcoal black eyes and hair of their African-American father. And sometimes, on a few frightening occasions, the visitors would display a bit too much interest in children. Yes, there were many reasons why the boy fought sleep.

There was the fumbling of a key in the front door lock, the muted laughter of a woman and the rough voice of a man. "Hurry up, I don't have all night."

The door banged open and the little boy jolted upright, eyes wide. His first move was to check his sister asleep on his lap. No, she was safe. And still sleeping. Hearing the commotion from the front room, the little boy stiffened, his eyes darting everywhere, calculating, trying to decide. There was a fire escape just outside the bedroom window. They had taken refuge out there before when their mother's visitors had been too rowdy, when the sounds of partying and sometimes even the sounds of beating had grown too terrifying. The little boy's brow furrowed as he thought about waking up his sister, shushing her questions and fears, hurrying them out to the rusty, decaying fire escape where they would have to huddle in the cold night until morning. Hoping the rickety structure would hold them. Before he could decide though, their bedroom door opened.

"What do we have here?" The man was tall and broad. His form took up the whole doorway. He smelled of beer and something else. Some indefinable odor that the boy couldn't recognize. He tightened his grip on his sister but apart from that he didn't move. He was still, so still. Like a mouse enthralled by a snake. *Maybe if I don't move, it will go away, it won't bite*? The man took several steps further into the room, peering into the darkness. "Hey, you got a couple of kids in here!"

The woman appeared from behind him. She swayed, there was no structure, no form to her body. She was a puppet missing several strings. She stared at the children with glazed eyes and the boy knew she would be no help to them. Again. His breathing shallowed and fear ran with icy cold feet into his chest. He gazed up at the man with wide eyes.

"Damn girl, how many kids you got? You're a sly whore, keeping them a secret in here."

The woman waved an airy hand, careless and dismissive. "Twins. Always getting in my way. Their useless father was no help." She turned away, pulling at the man's arm. "Come on baby, forget them, let's get back to business."

The man allowed himself to be pulled away, but the final look he threw over his shoulder betrayed his interest in the children. The door slammed shut and the little girl jerked awake with a faint cry. "Keahi?"He shushed her. "It's me. I'm here Mailani."

She sat up, looking fearfully at the shut door. "Is she home? Is there someone with her?"Keahi nodded and Mailani's lower lip trembled as tears threatened. "What are we going to do? What if it happens again?"

"Shh, we'll be fine. Come on, get up. Help me move the mattress." Together the two lugged the deadweight mattress and put it against the door before Keahi pulled her to sit beside him with their backs against the door.Mailani turned worried eyes to her brother. "This won't stop them. They can still get in. We should go outside onto the fire escape."Keahi shook his head. "No. Last time we were out there that thing almost ripped out of the wall, it's so rusted and worn. No, it's too dangerous."

Mailani didn't say anything but both children felt the heavy weight of unspoken words in the air. *Just as dangerous as staying inside.* They sat like that for over an hour. Trying not to listen to the noises from the front room. Trying not to think. They held hands and the rapid panic of their hearts beat in time with each other.

The noises from the front room had stilled. There was a rattling as someone tried the door handle. An aggravated curse as the door met with resistance. "Open this door. Do you hear me? Open it now."

Both Keahi and Mailani jumped to their feet and pushed with all their might against the door. But two skinny little eight-year-olds were no match for a grown man determined to get in. One more mighty shove and the children scattered, darting to stand against the window. The man smiled at them both, his hands on his hips. "What's the matter kids? I'm not going to hurt you. I'm a friend of your mom's. She wants us to be good friends too." He motioned over his shoulder back to the living room where the woman was passed out on the dirty sofa.

Mailani's eyes brimmed with tears as Keahi pulled her to stand behind him. "Please sir, leave us alone. Our mother won't like it if you bother us."

The man roared with laughter. "Yeah right. I told your mother that I would give her an extra twenty for a little visit with you two. You know what she said?" He leered down at them and adopted a breathy soprano voice, "Oh baby, you go right ahead. I just want you to be happy."

The little boy's face tensed and he turned to lift open the window. "Hurry Mailani, you go first."

"Oh, no you don't. I want to take a closer look at that pretty little thing. Come here." The man lunged, easily batted Keahi aside and grabbed at Mailani. She screamed and kicked her feet uselessly as he carried her back across the room and threw her down onto the dingy mattress. He put a giant hand over her mouth and his voice was low, menacing. "Shut up." With one swift movement, he ripped the front of her nightdress, exposing her thin frame with all its scars and bruises. With the moon-white birthmark of a crested wave on her shoulder. The little girl lay rigidly with her eyes shut, her fists clenched by her side. Across the room, the little boy was trying to stand. The man's blow had sent him headfirst into the chest of drawers and blood ran from the cut on his face. He looked at his sister. This was worse. So much worse than all the times before.

"Get off her!" He ran, and jumped on the man's back, wildly punching, kicking, pulling hair – anything and everything to get this man away from his sister.

The man straightened up with an angry roar. "You little brat!" He reached behind him, took hold of the boy and threw him across the room. Not content with that, he then walked over to where Keahi lay and kicked him. Again and again. In the stomach, the face, the legs, his back. The boy curled up into a tight ball but it did little for him against the onslaught of blows. Mailani was screaming. A thin high-pitched scream that only aggravated the man further. One more vicious kick and Keahi was still. Only then did the man leave him, turn aside and go back to the little girl. "I told you to shut up." He hit her once across the face. It was enough to silence her. To render her immobile. The man was deep breathing now with the exertion of his night. He unbuckled his belt and dropped his pants before moving to position himself over the inert figure of the little girl on the mattress.

Behind him, Keahi was fighting to emerge from the whirlpool of pain that held him captive, wanting to suck him down into oblivion. *No, Mailani. Have to help Mailani. Have to stop him.* He was battered and bruised. Broken ribs. Boot imprints on tender flesh. Bloodied face. Eyes swollen near-shut. But he fought on. From a wilderness away, he could hear the panting, heaving breaths of the man as he tried to do bad things to his sister. Keahi opened his eyes, spat blood and chipped fragments of teeth from his mouth. He tried to stand. He saw what was happening to Mailani. Pain, hurt, fear, rage, desperation built and exploded. And then another kind of pain ripped through Keahi's body. Pain like fire. Burning, charring, searing pain.

He shouted. "No." Fire jerked from his body, lighting up the room in blinding redness.

The man was interrupted, half-turned. "What the hell …" It would be the last words he ever spoke. A ball of fire consumed him. The man screamed, staggered, fell to his knees.

But the fire was not appeased. Flames rippled along the ceiling, down the walls, hungrily devouring the wooden chest of drawers, the mattress. The very air. The little girl. With horror-stricken eyes, Keahi watched as fire consumed his sister's body. He shouted, "Mailani!" He tried to run to her, but the heat, the flames were too much for him. The fire was moving fast, so fast. There was not enough oxygen left for him to breathe. The last thing the little boy remembered was how peaceful his sister looked as she lay there on the mattress – like a princess on her fiery pyre of death. "Mailani!"

The burning ceiling collapsed in on the boy.

Everything went black.

It was over.

TWO

Today

Simone, Samoa
Subject: The gift to surpass all others
AMAZEBALLS! I love my iPhone4. Love it, love it, love it. You rock. When I opened the package, I was almost more excited than the time I was in the elevator in the Central Bank building with some of the Manu Samoa team, breathing the same air as the dalashious Kahn Fotuali'i. Thank you!

Leila, Washington D.C.
Subject: You're welcome
As soon as I saw them, I knew you had to have one. Besides, now you can keep me up to date on all the latest from Samoa.

Simone, Samoa
Subject: Mission accepted
I knew it. You want me to spy on Daniel for you. Make sure the evil Mele doesn't sink her claws into him. *Einjo*. Don't worry, I am up to the task. I will stick to Daniel like a sweat-stained shirt. I will keep every piece of him safe. For you. And only you. (Of course.)

Leila, Washington D.C.
Subject: Whatever
Pugi. Shut up. (Like my fa'afafine slang? I'm learning.) I also know some other bad words but will save them until I see you in a few weeks. But I'm not worried about Daniel. I know who his heart belongs to.

Simone, Samoa
Subject: Body guarding duty
Who said anything about his heart?! I shall guard his body. Some parts more thoroughly than others. Do you want instant pics of us together? Visual evidence of my bodyguard efficiency?

Leila, Washington D.C.
Subject: Nupi
Shut it. There are no other words.

I had to laugh as I ended my conversation with Simone. There had been no chance to say goodbye to him before I caught my last-minute flight to Los Angeles. Actually, there hadn't been time to do much of anything before I left. After the nightmare show-down with Nafanua and Sarona, I had taken Daniel back to his house and been given the evils by Salamasina when she saw his injuries. She could barely restrain her rage when I gave her the censored and condensed version of what had happened with Nafanua's sisterhood. I didn't tell her about the dolphins. Or about the certainty that Daniel shouldn't be alive, that something inconceivable had brought him back to that moonlit shore. She was angry enough as it was. I wasn't sure who she had been more furious at – the telesā sisterhood who had abducted Daniel and stabbed him, or me for getting him marked as a target.

"I warned my son you would only bring him pain and suffering. I knew something like this would happen."

"I'm sorry Mrs. Tahi. I never meant for any of this to happen. I tried to protect him. I love Daniel. I would do anything to keep him safe."

I could have chopped my arm off in her kitchen and it still wouldn't have convinced her that I really was sorry for what had happened. She only hissed at me, "You are telesā. No man is safe with you."

There was nothing to say to that. Because in my heart of hearts, I knew it to be true.

As I left Salamasina's house, the sun had been coming up. I had been gone all night and I knew Matile and Tuala would not be happy. I rushed home to reassure my aunt that I had not been abducted by rapists, muggers, or Satan worshippers. To my surprise, she and Tuala had not been mad at me. Instead, they had sat me down to give me the news. My grandmother had been hit with another stroke. Only this time, it was bad. Very bad. She was in the intensive care unit and the family was gathering to say good bye. My uncle Thomas had called to tell me I needed to get back to Washington D.C. As quickly as possible. They didn't think Grandmother would hang on much longer. I reeled. The old lady was an indomitable force of nature – how could she be dying? Matile had hugged me, which kind of shocked me even more. And Uncle Tuala had patted me awkwardly on the shoulder.

"We are very sorry for your loss, Leila."

They talked about Grandmother Folger like she was already dead, which made me a little angry. Of course the old lady wasn't dead. And she wasn't going to die any time soon either. She was the toughest person I had ever known and she was not going to die. There had been so few constants in my life that I would not imagine living without Grandmother Folger's reserved disapproval. No, she was not going to die.

The next few hours had been a flurry of activity. Throwing clothes into a suitcase, making an emergency booking on a flight out that would leave in a few hours, everything was rush, rush, rush. I had detoured to Daniel's on the way to the airport but he had been asleep and Salamasina refused to wake him.

"I gave him a sleeping potion. He needs to rest so his body can heal."

She wouldn't even let me in past the front door. So instead, I had left him a note. And tried not to cry. What kind of girlfriend abandoned the one she loved when he needed her the most?

We had been late to check in at the airport, so farewells were rushed. At the very last minute I saw the mobile phone store with the sign screaming 'The New iPhone4 is Here! Do You Have Yours?'

It was perfect. I bought two. *Thank you, Visa.* One for Daniel and the other for Simone. Getting Matile to agree to deliver the package to Simone hadn't been a problem. She was thoroughly entranced with Simone. If I hadn't been trying so hard not to think, not to feel – I would have laughed at the inanity of it. The strait-laced, sour, forever-prayerful Aunty Matile connecting with the vivacious, exuberant, lip-sticked Simone. Oh well, life was full of contradictions and that was certainly one of them.

A rushed goodbye to the couple who had been my adoptive parents for the last year and I was through Customs and onto the airplane. Not until the plane was in the air. Not until the flight attendants had done their safety demo. Not until then did everything hit me.

My mother Nafanua had tried to kill my best friend, Jason. My mother's sister Sarona had tried to kill my boyfriend, Daniel. But instead she had killed my mother while Nafanua had been trying to protect me. All of her sisters were dead. Their life force sucked dry by Sarona in some bizarre telesā ritual. Daniel had nearly died, only some freak ocean 'thing' had returned him to me alive. There was a possibility that somewhere out there, the psycho witch Sarona was still alive. And now, my Grandmother was dying. It was a lot to process.

I hadn't slept or eaten anything for two days. I wanted to cry. Scream. Rage. Sob. Burn things.Instead, I went to sleep.

The flight attendant woke me when we landed in New Zealand, and the transit lounge was a blur of grey tiredness. On another plane to Los Angeles, the tears had finally claimed me and, once they started, I found it almost impossible to stop them. I cried because I didn't want to go back to America. I wanted to be there for Daniel when he woke up. I cried because I didn't want my grandmother to die. There were things I wanted to tell her. Things I needed to ask her. I prayed, *Please don't let her die. Please let that fierce old woman fight death a little longer. Please don't let my grandmother die.* Prayer hadn't worked for my dad but maybe a year of going to church with Aunty Matile would make God more willing to hear me. Maybe now God might know who I was?

Arriving in Washington D.C. had been a shock to the system. In more ways than one. It was winter after all, and I had just come from the sauna of Samoa. Snow was a dirty grey blanket on the city I had grown up in. I had gratefully accepted the thick coat that Thomas' wife Annette had brought to the airport for me. And now here we were, warm and sheltered in the sleek silver Lincoln town car, on our way to the hospital. I read Simone's texts again and they were a welcome warmth in the midst of a D.C. winter. A reminder of where I had come from and the people there who cared about me. I wondered if Daniel had gotten my gift yet and when I could expect a message from him.

Annette interrupted my thoughts. "Your grandmother is just hanging on. They took her off the respirator last night and she's breathing on her own, but the doctors said she probably won't make it another forty-eight hours."

Her warning gave me that unexpected pain again. The one that crept up on me, surprising me with its wistful intensity. I didn't like Grandmother Folger. And I had grown up thinking that she didn't like me either. But my experiences in Samoa had made me more able to accept my dad's constant reminder – that my grandmother's disapproval of everything about me came from genuine concern. *She just worries about you and wants you to be happy. She wants what's best for you, that's all ...*

Annette issued me with a gentle warning. "She's waiting for you. You know that, don't you?"

That made no sense. I had been nothing but a nuisance to the woman. What, did she have one last lecture she wanted to give me? "I doubt that, Annette."

A fleeting look of annoyance flashed across the older woman's carefully made-up face. "Leila, you aren't going to be difficult about this, are you? Not when your grandmother is literally on her death bed? I was hoping that your time away would have seen you mature and get over this childish need to forever battle with your grandmother. Don't tell me you still have that giant chip on your shoulder?"

Her words stung. And not because they were uncalled for. The old Leila would have snapped back with a few snide remarks. Cutting and abrasive. But the Leila who had spent months living with teenagers who rarely, if ever, answered back to an adult was better about controlling her words. Her temper. Because she had seen what losing her cool could result in. Fire. Havoc. Pain. "You're right. I apologize, Annette. It's been a long flight and I'm worried about Grandmother Folger. I hope I get the chance to talk to her. Really talk to her."

Annette's eyes were wary. Doubtful. "About what? We don't want her getting upset, Leila. Not now. Not when she has so little time left."

"No, I wouldn't do that. I just want her to know that I understand now why she was so upset about my decision to go to Samoa. And believe it or not, there were quite a few times that I actually missed her."

I could tell Annette was surprised. So was I. Who knew that I would ever admit out loud that I had missed my grandmother?

There were more Folgers at the hospital. Annette's husband, my uncle Thomas. My dad's other two brothers, Michael and Cameron. Their wives. More beautiful, elegant women like Annette. Some cousins. White on white. The Folger family was reserved and calm. Nobody was crying. Nobody looked ruffled or even unsettled. Everyone was polite and cordial. Quiet welcomes and questions about my flight. Even their children – the little Folgers – sat quietly coloring pictures in the waiting room. As usual with every Folger family gathering, I felt very brown. Very much the outsider. And now that I was a spirit woman volcano goddess in disguise, any hope of blending in with my palagi family had to be chucked out the window.

Annette ushered me into Grandmother's room. I walked to stand beside her bed, apprehensive about what I would see. But after almost a year and two strokes, Grandmother Folger looked just the same. The silver white hair pulled back into a chignon. The austere expression on her face – even now, while in sleep. Looking for all the world like she was going to open her eyes at any moment and critique my rumpled clothes and messy tangle of hair. As usual.

The only person in the room who was any different, was me.

I was not the same girl who had last simmered, listening to another of Grandmother's lectures. The resentment, the anger, the insecurity were gone. I sat beside her bed and carefully took her hand in mine, noting the frailty. I studied the lined face, wondering how many wrinkles could be attributed to her rebellious grand-daughter who had run away to an island on the other side of the world in search of a family in a land of strangers. How much had she known about Nafanua? How much had my father told her about why he had left Samoa eighteen years ago, taking me with him? What did she know about my twin? The brother I had never known? Unbidden, a tear trickled down my cheek as I remembered how agitated my Grandmother had been when I announced my travel plans for Samoa. All the times during the past year in my new home that I had thought about her. Missed her. I wished she could hear me now. I wished she could know everything I knew now that I wished I had known then.

She stirred. As if my wish had pierced the drug-filled haze she slept in.

"Grandmother? It's me, Leila."

She opened her eyes. And for the first time in forever, my grandmother looked happy to see me. "Leila?" Her voice was a bare remnant of what it used to be, weak and soft, swallowed up by the humming monitors. "Is that really you?"

I leaned closer. "Yes, it's me."

"You came back. You're alright." She tightened her grip in mine. "I was so worried about you."

"I'm fine, Grandmother. I'm alright." I took a deep breath and then rushed on, wanting to get it all out before I lost my nerve. "I came as soon as I heard you were ill. I wanted to tell you that I'm sorry. For leaving the way I did. For so many things. I didn't understand why you were so against my trip to Samoa. A lot of stuff has happened over the last few months and I've been wanting to see you so I could tell you in person, I'm sorry. For being the world's most annoying grand-daughter."

She smiled the barest of smiles and there was the hint of a softening in her faded blue eyes. A whisper. "Not annoying. Just ridiculous."

My eyes widened in surprise. "Why, Grandmother Folger, if I didn't know any better, I would say you just cracked a joke."

She grimaced, and the familiar disapproving Grandmother was back. "Ladies don't 'crack' jokes Leila." She glanced at my outfit. "Good heavens child, what are you wearing under that coat? Don't tell me you travelled looking like that?" She paused to breathe laboriously, gathering the energy to continue. "How many times do I have to remind you that denim jeans and a sweatshirt are not suitable attire for leaving the house in? Would it have been too much to ask that you brush your hair before visiting your dying grandmother in the hospital?"

I ignored the death reference and hid my grin. "You must be feeling better if you can notice my casual attire. Don't you know the grunge look is all the rave right now? Even Fifth Avenue's finest are dressing down this year."

She ignored my lame attempts at teasing and only smiled a faint half-smile before closing her eyes, fading back into sleep. A rush of happiness filled me. Relief. Gratitude. I had made it. Grandmother knew I was here. She was happy to see me. The prayers had worked. *Thank you God, and thank you Aunty Matile for introducing us.* I sat by Grandmother's side for a while longer, feeling more at peace then I had in a long while. Annette peeked in every so often to check on us. Probably wanting to make sure I wasn't upsetting Grandmother by being my usual argumentative self. (Or swiping her morphine.)

And then Grandmother shifted uneasily in the bed and opened her eyes. This time she looked agitated. Fearful. The monitors beeped alarmingly and I threw a look over my shoulder out the open door. Somebody, anybody? "Hey, it's alright. I'm here. Everything's alright. Do you want me to call for the nurse?"

"No." The sharpness of her tone caught me. Her hand clawed at mine and held me. She was breathing quick, shallow breaths and every word was a struggle. "Have to tell you. Very important. Should have told you before you left last year. Should have kept you here. Safe. From that woman."

Her words confirmed my suspicions. Grandmother had known. My dad had told her about Nafanua. There had been more behind her anger at my Samoa trip than she had revealed. I placed a calming hand on Grandmother's shoulder. "I'm safe, Grandmother. You don't need to worry about me anymore." I can set fire to this building. You really don't need to be afraid for me anymore.

"He lied. I don't know why. He lied."

"What are you talking about?" She was confused. I patted her arm and discreetly pushed the call button for the nurse.

"Your father. He lied."

"I know, Grandmother. But it's okay. I understand why he didn't tell me about my mother. Trust me, it's alright."

But she wasn't listening to me. She was shaking her head back and forth, whimpering. "No, no. He lied. After the funeral. I packed his things away. I looked through his passport. Your father. Before his trip to Africa. He went back to Samoa. Back to see her."

"What?" I couldn't believe what I was hearing. She was delusional. This didn't make sense. But as Grandmother Folger clutched me to her, I stared into her eyes and knew – she had never been more lucid.

"He went to Samoa before his last Africa assignment. I don't know why or what happened there. But two weeks later he was dead. She killed him. That witch. Your mother. She killed him. I know it. She killed my baby grandson. And then she made my son sick with her filthy island magic. I know it. She killed your father."

She collapsed back onto the pillows as if this accusation had leached her of all energy. She was spent. Her eyes closed again and the monitors settled back into their monotone hum. Calm. Unhurried. Peaceful.

Except I wasn't anything close to calm. Or peaceful. I had been dealt another gut-kicking blow. Would I ever catch a break and get a month, a week without shocking revelations? Thoughts tumbled over each other, chasing answers, chasing some semblance of order. *Dad, why did you go back to Samoa? What were you searching for, hoping for? Nafanua, what did you do to my father?* It made no sense. Nafanua hadn't said anything about seeing my father. She had been surprised to hear about his death, I was sure of it.

Or was I? How good an actress had she been really? Was it so impossible to imagine that she had poisoned my dad somehow? Cursed him with the kind of cancer that had no cure, came on with no warnings, and gave no mercy?

"Leila?" It was Annette. Concerned and curious. She was joined by two nurses who bustled about, checking the machines, checking

Grandmother Folger, insinuating messages of 'get out of here annoying girl' in their every movement. "What happened?"

"Nothing. She woke up and wanted to talk to me. She was upset. But it's nothing now." I stumbled to my feet. I wanted my grandmother to wake up and tell me more. But she didn't.

Grandmother Folger didn't wake up again. She died two days later without ever regaining consciousness.

A funeral in Potomac was a well orchestrated social event. My grandmother had left nothing to chance. Or to flights of fancy. From the hymns to the seating plan, to the choice of scripture reading to the color of the flowers on the hearse – even to the filling for the sandwiches served at the family mansion afterwards – she had it all planned. It would be elegant, dignified, and serene. Everything I was not.

The week passed in a kind of daze for me. I tried to be useful but rich people don't mourn without lots of paid help. Grandmother's stately mansion was overflowing with caterers, florists, waiting and bar staff, a sound crew, and more. Everybody had a task for preparing for the funeral of the year. Everybody knew exactly what they were doing and where they were supposed to be doing it. Everybody except for me. I was aimless. And lonely. The only thing that made the week bearable was my phone. More specifically, my messages from a far-away Simone. And Daniel. He was recovering well thanks to Salamasina's natural remedies and was already back at work in the welding shop. I'm not sure just how much work he was getting done though because I was messaging him every other minute and sending him instagram pics of everything and hassling him for the same. Being without him was like a constant ache. An emptiness. That feeling like when you've left the house and you know you've forgotten something but you're just not sure what it is. And it nags and worries at you all day. Because you know that it's something dreadfully important. Vital. And at some point in your day, you're going to need that unknown, missing something. And you would be bereft without it.

Simone was on holiday in New Zealand with his family and loved to send me photos of the scintillating scenery. Most of it seemed to be rugged and tattooed. And half naked. Clearly Simone was hanging out at a lot of beaches and making the most of his new phone. The day I got my first message from Jason in San Francisco was an exuberant fireworks kind of day. His recuperation was going much more slowly than Daniel's. Mainly because the American doctors had no clue what had been wrong with him. I had to laugh at his descriptions of the medical team that had been waiting for him once he got airlifted back to the US. Dressed in head-to-toe protective gear like spacemen, they had bustled him to an isolation unit, treating him like radioactive waste. "They think I've got some nasty new tropical infection that they've never heard of, so they're acting like I'm a plague carrier or something," he grumbled. "I don't even have a fever anymore and I keep telling them I feel fine but they're not convinced. I hate being locked up like this. I'm going to get my brothers to bust me out of here soon."

I laughed, but inside me, the truth squirmed like slippery eels, biting and gnawing to get out. When would I be brave enough to tell him what had really happened? It wasn't right to keep the truth from him. But I wasn't ready. I hid my shame and guilt in relief that he was better, well enough to complain daily about 'sadistic doctors, mean nurses, and crappy food.' I would tell him when we next met. It was not the kind of thing that you told someone over a phone, I rationalized. No, the right thing to do was to wait until we were together in person and I could look him in the eyes and confess. I practiced my apology speech in my head many times. *I broke the telesā law by telling you my secret. I condemned you to death by asking you to help find a scientific cure for my fire thing. My mother poisoned you. You were supposed to die a miserable, gut-wrenching death. I was selfish and I'm sorry. Can you ever forgive me?*

It's safe to say that I was not looking forward to seeing Jason again in person. No matter how much I cared about him and no matter how much I missed him. In the meantime, I was happy to exchange bantering, funny messages with him all day. Because there was another huge white elephant in the room of all our conversations.

Almost dying does something to a person, you know? It makes him realize that life is short. And you have to grab at every moment, every happiness with both hands. Tight. And not let go. You gotta know, I'm in love with you.

With his love declaration, Jason had placed in my hands a fragile flower of possibility. And I wasn't ready to hurt him by crushing it with the truth.

I spent some time in the attic going through boxes of my dad's stuff that Grandmother Folger had packed away into storage. I found the passport and took it back downstairs with me. The guilty Samoa stamps stared back at me accusingly. *So? Your dad took me to Samoa. Big deal. Whatchya gonna do about it?* I couldn't do anything about it. There was no one to ask. No one to confront. So I stowed it away and tried not to think about it. Being at Grandmother's house and back in D.C. was kind of painful. Everything and everywhere reminded me of my dad. I was anxious for the funeral to be over so that I could go back to Samoa. Something I suspected my Folger family would not be happy about. Something I waited until after the funeral proceedings were over with before broaching with them.

"What do you mean, you're going back there?" Uncle Thomas was exasperated and Annette handed him a glass of wine with a soothing glance.

"I think your uncle is just concerned for your future, Leila. You should be thinking about college. If you go back to Samoa, what will you do about school?"

I had done my homework. I was ready. "I have thought about college, Annette. There's a National University in Samoa and all the other seniors in my high school go there to do a university preparatory year before applying for scholarships to colleges in Australia and New Zealand." I took a deep breath before plunging into the rest of my carefully prepared announcement. "I'm going to enroll at National University and do another year in Samoa."

They both looked startled. More so because I actually had a plan. They glanced at each other before Thomas took the lead. "And where will you live?"

"National University doesn't have a dorm. My mother's relatives, Matile and Tuala, are happy to have me stay there again. I'll stay with them when I first get back but I'm going to look for an apartment to rent. I know the country well enough now to live on my own. I've made friends at school that I could probably get to room with me if I need company. I have enough money from Dad's insurance payout to support me through the year if I budget it carefully."

Thomas waved his hand at the mention of money. "Don't be ridiculous. You're a Folger and you never need to worry about finance. You have your trust fund account and I know that your grandmother would have wanted you to be well taken care of. I'll have my secretary set up an allowance for you."

Elation. Not about the money but the fact that I wasn't going to get fought on this. "So, you're going to be okay with this?" I looked at him, then at Annette and back again at Thomas. "No legal threats? No lectures?"

A tired sigh. "No. Would it make any difference? You'll be nineteen in a few months. You're an adult. Besides, my mother was very specific in her will and final instructions about you, Leila. She may not have been happy about your country choice of residence but she was insistent that we do everything to make sure you go to university. And if it means starting your degree at a Samoan university, then so be it."

Annette added her piece. "Your grandmother did say she was glad you had found some of your mother's family, that you seemed to be happy with them because she knew you often felt like an outsider here. This couple, Matile and Tuala, they have clearly welcomed you as one of their own." She studied me intently. "Your time there has been good for you. We can all see that. Can't we, Thomas?"

My uncle gave her the baffled shrug that a man gives his wife when he has no clue what she's talking about – but he knows better than to do anything else but agree. Annette smiled. "It's settled then. Leila will go back to Samoa to do a university preparatory year. But you must stay with us for a while, spend some time with your Folger family while your uncle makes the necessary arrangements."

I wanted to argue. I had been away from Daniel for two weeks already and it was killing me. But he was not all I longed for. He was not the only reason I walked with emptiness within me. The winter was burying the island fire that warmed me. I walked on tarseal and concrete and I couldn't feel Fanua. I couldn't hear her in the chill wind. She did not move upon the icy waters of the Potomac River. Or breathe in the chemical-laden soil of the luxuriant Folger gardens. I wanted to catch the first flight back, right then and there, but I knew Annette was right. I was a part of this family. Even if I was a rather surly, thug-girl part. So many of the walls that divided me from them had been of my own making. It was not they who had excluded me from the Folger fold. It was me and my hostility. Heck, I probably made a bigger deal out of being the brown one than they did. And so I agreed to stay on. For just a little while longer.

The weeks that followed were busy ones with barely space to breathe. There were extended family dinners and meetings. Trips to each of the uncles' homes. Time spent with cousins who had once been only a blur of polite faces. Annette took me shopping in New York. I think Uncle Thomas was squirming a little with guilt because he was faintly relieved that I was going back to Samoa. And so his instructions to Annette had been precise. "Buy her a new wardrobe for that university. Get her everything she needs." It wasn't easy to find summer clothes in the dead of winter but money really can buy you everything. Shopping with Annette wasn't easy either. She had never been to the other side of the equator, and it showed.

"I'm sorry, Annette. Valentino and Calvin Klein will not make sense in Samoa. Trust me. Think tropical country. Sauna heat and lots of sweat and dirt, okay? Samoa's the most beautiful place on the planet, but it's also dusty, dirty, and nasty in places."

So she took me to Gap and Banana Republic and I had to be happy with that. I think Annette was channeling the 'African Queen' and Lara Croft Tomb Raider because we ended up with lots of khaki pants, white linen tops, and breezy cotton shifts. I let her have fun with it and, I confess, I did enjoy shoe shopping for Louboutins just a tiny bit. But I had to draw the line at the felt-brimmed hat and thigh-high designer 'wilderness' boots. Next thing you know she was going to buy me a leather whip so I could hang out with Indiana Jones on weekends.

"Umm, I don't think so. My friend Simone would love those."

Annette's face lit up. "See! They're perfect."

"Not for me they're not. This is Simone. His parents call him Simon." I showed her a photo on my phone that Simone had sent me from New Year's Eve. With flawless makeup and a stunning red sequin dress. Slit up to the thigh and stiletto heels. Annette's jaw dropped.

"Oh." She put the hat and boots back on the shelf and kept on walking. "Right, I think we'll stick to the sandals and maybe a few more pairs of shorts?"

I laughed. "Okay. But Simone will be disappointed that I won't have such fabulous boots for him to borrow."

She was cool enough to laugh with me. I was starting to like Annette. And my dad's brothers weren't bad either. They liked to play cards after family dinners and I taught them the Samoan card-playing basics that I had learned from Sunday evenings with Uncle Tuala. Games like swipi and ka-isu. With a little prompting they had loads of stories to tell about when my dad was a kid, pestering his much older siblings.

"Your dad was spoilt rotten, Leila. It's true. He was Mom and Dad's golden child and could do no wrong." Michael complained.

Cameron added. "He was a sickly baby who grew up to be a scrawny little kid. Mom was always worrying about him getting sick. So he got away with everything." He mimicked Grandmother Folger. "Cameron, you let Ryan read your X-Men comics, you hear me? He was so sick when he was a baby that we need to treasure every moment we have with him. Why don't you go read to him in your room? And then as soon as Mom left the room, Ryan would be making faces at me and laughing. And he trashed my comic collection. I spent a lot of money on that collection and he never looked after my comics properly."

It was Michael's turn again. "He was definitely sly. Always getting in trouble and then finding the most ingenious ways to get out of trouble! Remember that time in high school when he didn't come home because he was making out at the back of the bleachers with that brunette girlfriend of his? And by six o'clock Mom went out looking for him and she was raging mad."

I had never heard any of these stories about my dad's childhood and I loved it. "So then what happened?"

Thomas continued the story. "Ryan saw Mom's car and knew she would be angry. So he ripped his shirt and rolled around a bit in the dirt. Then he told Mom that the reason he was so late was because he got attacked and beat up by a gang of bullies. Mom bought it, hook, line, and sinker. She drove all around the neighborhood looking for this mythical gang and even called our dad at the office to send some of his security detail down there to help her." He shook his head as everyone laughed at the memory. "Dad didn't, of course. He was more clued in to Ryan than Mom ever was. When Dad came home, he took Ryan into his study and warned him that if he ever made Mom worry like that again, he would send him away to military school."

Michael scoffed. "Not like Mom would ever allow that."

Thomas shook his head. "No. Ryan was very special to our mom." He had a sad smile on his face. "He was very special to all of us.

He was so much younger that he kind of belonged to all of us. In a way. We all looked out for him. And he was so different from the rest of us, that he was like a breath of fresh air. He brought our mom and dad closer together. And he was Mom's favorite. She had so many things planned for his future. She was so upset when he joined the Peace Corps. Mainly because it took him so far away from her. And then when he told us he had gotten married over there … well, she was devastated, worrying that he was going to live over there permanently. She was so happy when Ryan came back. With you."

There was a heavy silence as everyone busied themselves with memories. Unspoken thoughts.

"Our mom took it bad when Ryan died. We all did. It was like the sickly boy who we all worried about when we were younger had finally gotten the dreadful sickness that had always been an ominous threat. He was so young. So funny. So full of life. I still can't believe he's gone."

Thomas stood abruptly. "Believe it. Ryan's dead." He stalked out of the room, slamming the door behind him. Cold. Brutal. Final. I was shocked.

Michael spoke softly into the painful silence. "Don't mind him, Leila. Thomas took Ryan's death personally. He's the oldest, he's always felt responsible for the family. For his brothers. But more than that, he's one of the finest neurosurgeons in the country and even he couldn't do anything for Ryan. Nobody could. Not with that kind of aggressive tumor. Nobody had seen anything like it. It was horrifying."

The dinner gathering broke up shortly after that. Back up in my room, I couldn't shake it from my mind. *Ryan's tumor was like nothing the doctors had ever seen. The finest neurosurgeons couldn't do anything for him…it was horrifying.* Grandmother Folger's final words hammered away at my brain. *She did it. Your mother. She killed your father.*

I couldn't sleep after that. Long after the house went silent, I slipped out into the moonlit night. I walked through the silver shimmer of the frozen garden. My breath made little clouds of heat as I trudged away from the house and into a secluded grove of trees. I was alone. I could see Masina the moon far above me. She was alone in a pollution-laden sky. No stars. Only the red flickering of an airplane kept her company. Closing my eyes, I reached out with my mind, my soul, my heart. Searching for Fanua Afi. I wanted – needed – to listen to her speak soothing serenity to my soul. I wanted the comfort of her fire. I searched through bitter cold, fought through frozen earth, reaching down through layers of dead soil and uncaring rock, down to sluggish currents of magma that barely simmered with red heat. She was there. Far away, but she was there. I summoned Fanua Afi. With every fiber of my being. And after an endless battle, she came to me. The barest hint of flame in the palm of my hands. Not even enough to ward away the chill of that winter night. But it was enough. To reassure me that, yes, my Mother Earth spoke to me still. Even here, in this city of steel and glass, of rushed busy-ness and fervent time chasers. She was here.

I knelt in the snow and gave thanks for this small reminder of Samoa. Of who I was. And then I returned to the sleeping house. I had answered my own question. Yes, I was fanua afi even here in Washington D.C. – but my gift was only a flickering fragment of what it was back in Samoa. I thought back to all the hours of experiments and frustration with Jason and shook my head at the simplicity of the solution. If I wanted to remove the threat of my fanua afi, all I needed to do was move back to America. Embrace the Folger side of myself and be the regular girl I kept telling Jason that I wanted to be. I stared out the frosted window over the crystal night and it was like I could see two pathways stretching out before me.

I could choose. I could choose to be regular. I could stay here in America, go to a college that the Folgers picked out for me. Maybe study for a law degree like my dad. Or bio-medicine, drawing on my knowledge of plants. I could have Jason. As a friend. And maybe more? He was on this path. I could see it now. The teasing smile, the warmth of his touch, the ease with which we talked. I could go to school on the West Coast. He would give me surf lessons in the white waves of California. Take me to meet his family. I would like that. Siblings. The stifling closeness of brothers and sisters, laughter, mess, and closeness. On semester breaks, maybe I could even go with him on assignment? Be a lowly assistant for the distinguished volcano professor? With the Folger's money at my back, I would never have to work at any job I didn't want. I could even get them to sponsor Jason's expeditions. We would make a great team. I could be happy with that. Content. It would be easy. Comfortable.

And then there was the other choice. Return to Samoa. Embrace the fire goddess within me. Take up the challenge that came with being a telesā without a sisterhood. Face the risk that Sarona was alive. Be with sour-faced Matile and stern but kind Tuala. Go to university with my Samoa College friends. Simone. Maleko. Sinalei. And love Daniel. Decipher the enigma that was his vasa loloa birthmark.

This pathway was less clear. There was danger and darkness in it. Nafanua was gone. Who would teach me all else I needed to know about being a telesā? Who would I turn to for answers about this volatile heritage of mine? I didn't know if there were any more telesā matagi left in Samoa, but I was pretty sure I had burnt my bridges with them. Literally. And loving Daniel certainly wouldn't help. No, this path carried no certainty or security. It wouldn't be easy. Or comfortable.

Not too long ago, I had confronted my mother, the Covenant Keeper of the Matagi Sisterhood, and I had told her that yes, I had a choice. I didn't have to be like her and her sisters. I could choose my destiny. And here now, as I looked out over the winter of Washington, I knew that, once again, I held the key to my destiny in my hands. I could choose. Where to go and what to do. Who to love.

Choice. It was an exhilarating and terrifying thing.

Daniel Tahi, Samoa.
Subject: Missing you.
I'm so sorry about your grandmother. Are you ok?

Leila Folger, Enroute to New York.
Subject: Missing you Sick
I'm alright. I got here in time to talk to her. We made peace. In a way. In the car now with my uncle and aunt. We're on the freeway. Long drive to New York. I just stopped crying. And only because I got car sick. My uncle's a crazy driver. I'm worried we're going to crash and die. I'm an island girl now, not used to hours in a car! I had to throw up. I am now back to missing you. Sorry about the vomit reference. Too much information.

Daniel Tahi, Samoa.
Subject: Vomit vs. Kisses
I've seen you throw up before. Still wanted to kiss you after. Wish I was there to crash and die with you.

Leila Folger, Enroute to New York.
Subject: Not Happy
I have a complaint. Before the car crashes and I die. You don't kiss me enough.

Daniel Tahi, Samoa.
Subject: Not Helpful.
And this is coming from a girl who's just left the country WITHOUT ANY WARNING to fly thousands of miles away for an unspecified period of time?! Try telling me that in person. When we're alone. At our midnight pool. (Clothes optional.)

Leila Folger, Enroute to New York.
Subject: Excuse me?
Is that a dare?

Daniel Tahi, Samoa.
Subject: I will kiss you breathless.
No. It's a promise. Satisfaction guaranteed.

Leila Folger, Enroute to New York.
Subject: Fire Hazard
Stop that. It's getting hot in here. Do you want this car to flame, crash and burn?

Daniel Tahi, Samoa.
Subject: Control yourself.
Sorry. I forgot that the mere mention of my kiss often has that effect on girls. And cars. Please try to contain your excitement.

Leila Folger, Enroute to New York.
Subject: Bodyguard Duties
It will be difficult. I'll try to think about something else. Like Simone's offer to be your bodyguard. He's going to protect you against the alluring advances of all girls.

Daniel Tahi, Samoa.
Subject: Surrounded by Allure.
I feel very safe now. Me and Simone will take on the gazillions of hot chicks who want me. They are everywhere. I just saw some hiding in the bushes outside my house. Simone, help!

Leila Folger, Enroute to New York.
Subject: Whatever.
Very funny. If I was there, I would fry you with a flame ball.

Daniel Tahi, Samoa.
Subject: Bring it.
If you were here, I would hold you in my arms and never let you go. I never want to wake up after a telesa attack without you again. You could have at least put smiley hearts on your good bye note.

Leila Folger, Enroute to New York.
Subject: Sadness
I'm sorry I left you like that.

Daniel Tahi, Samoa.
Subject: Love
Don't be. I'm just teasing you. You're where you need to be.

Leila Folger, Enroute to New York.
Subject: Worried
How's your ~~chest~~? I mean, your wound?

Daniel Tahi, Samoa.
Subject: Check it out. Photo Attachment.
I opened the photo file and laughed out loud. He had taken a
picture of himself, giving me a thumbs up while lying in bed,
shirtless so I could see the bandage Salamasina had wrapped his
upper torso in. It was made of leaves and tied with finely braided
coconut rope. A sheet lay low on his hips and while he looked a
little pale he was in every other way, my Daniel. The phone
beeped, reminding me that he was impatiently waiting for a reply. I
read his message and this time, a blush of fire raced through me.

Daniel Tahi, Samoa.
Subject: My Chest.
As you can see, my chest is fine. Mama warns though that I'll have
a big ole scar there. Are there any other parts of me that you're
worried about, that you need to check out?

Leila Folger, Enroute to New York.
 Subject: Your chest.
You talk pretty scandalous for a boy who wouldn't kiss me for too
long in case he put my "virtue" in danger.

Daniel Tahi, Samoa.
Subject: You.
Getting stabbed in the chest can do that to a person. Besides, I need
ways to keep you allured. You don't have a bodyguard. And
America is full of hot surfers and scientists who want you. Not to
mention celebrities who probably stalk your every move. How do I
know that Ryan Reynolds isn't waiting for you in New York?

I tried to ignore the not-so subtle reference to Jason. If I hadn't
been trapped in a car with my uncle and aunt, I would have taken a
photo for him. Of me making a face at him and poking my tongue
out at the ridiculousness of his question.

Leila Folger, Arrived in New York.
Subject: All of You.
Don't worry. I prefer tattooed brown rugby players to mega
celebrities. I told Ryan to stop stalking me or else even his Green
Lantern costume won't protect him from my volcano fury. I don't
need a bodyguard. I'm a fire goddess who's in love with you.
Every piece of you. Even the scarred chest bits. I gotta go. We're
here. Talk later.

THREE

Six weeks. Six long weeks and I was finally on my way back to Samoa. There was so much about this journey that was familiar and yet different. The biggest difference was that this time, I wasn't running away from my life in Washington D.C. This time I was going to where I wanted to be.

And this time, Daniel was waiting to greet me at the airport. I searched him out as soon as I exited through Customs. Eager. Anxious. It had been so long. What if things were awkward? What if things had changed? What if the bond we shared wasn't there anymore? What if I had only imagined it?

I needn't have worried. There he was. Standing back from the crowd. Waiting. Staring right at me. Our eyes met. Caught. And instantly, I knew. Nothing had changed. Daniel was the same. The busy crush of the arrivals area faded to a blur as we moved towards each other. And then I was in his arms and everything in the universe was right again. That empty ache was replaced with Daniel. Strong. Solid. Strength. Warmth – more familiar and reassuring than magma could ever be. He held me close and I breathed him in with a fierce intensity. He kissed my hair, my forehead, the tip of my nose, each cheek, dancing ever closer to my lips, as if wanting to reacquaint himself with every piece of me. And then his mouth was on mine and I drowned in the perfect bliss of him. The tang of salt. The breathless flush of a raging ocean wind. The rush of adrenaline as you leap from the precipice of a rushing waterfall. He was Daniel Tahi and every part of him firmly anchored against me told me that I had been gone too long from the one I loved.

When he finally tore his mouth from mine, it was to chide me softly. "You got me breaking all the rules here, Fire Girl." That delicious smile reassured me that whatever rules he was referring to, he wasn't truly mad at me about trespassing them.

"And what rules would those be?"

"The unwritten Samoan laws on public displays of affection. We just trashed all of them. Can't you tell?"

He quirked an eyebrow at me and glanced sideways. I followed his gaze and realized we had an avid audience. The airport crowd was staring and muttering darkly about the couple entwined around each other in the middle of the arrivals area. *Shocking. Disrespectful. Disgraceful.* Immediately, I took a step back and loosened my embrace.

"Oops." I bit at my lower lip. "Sorry. I forgot that people don't do that here."

He only laughed. Low and musical. Reached for my backpack and looped it lightly over one shoulder, and then took my hand in his. "Don't worry about it. I'm not. Besides, I'm sure they can make allowances for American girls. Especially ones as beautiful as you." He bent to kiss me once more on the cheek. A whisper. "I've missed you."

Joy entangled me. Filaments of gold sunlight. Tendrils of chili red excitement. I was caught in my love for this glorious boy. And I never wanted to be free of it. I walked with him up to the parking lot and once there, away from prying eyes, I asked him, "Can I see it? Where they stabbed you? Are you really okay now?"

In answer, he unbuttoned his shirt and stood there with moonlight playing on his chest. On the ripple of scar tissue that marked where the telesā had stabbed him and then tossed his body into the ocean. Remembering that night had the fire rage sparking within me and it was a struggle to contain it. I gently traced the scars, first with trembling fingers and then with soft kisses. Wishing that night had never happened. Wishing I could erase all the pain he had suffered because of me. Wishing I could wash away even this reminder with my tears.

"Hey." Daniel raised my tear-stained face to his. "Don't cry. It's fine. I'm fine."

"No, it's not fine. You're always going to be scarred. Just like how you're always going to be a target for other telesā because of me. For as long as you love me, you're always going to be in danger."

"I'm ready for a lifetime of danger then. Are you? Because that's how long I'm going to love you." He shrugged. "I kinda like my war wound. It's a reminder for me of how together, we can overcome anything. Even a psychotic band of weather witches. Now come here."

I needed no second invitation. This time, my hands strayed over the planes of his chest and then moved to his back as we kissed. I delighted in the corded feel of his shoulders and lower to his hips. He flinched, jerking slightly away from me. "Ouch."

"I'm sorry. What is it? What's wrong? Did I burn you?"

"No. It's not you. It's me." He caught both my hands in his. Hesitant. "Remember how I said there was something important I had to tell you?"

"Yeah."

"While you were gone, I did something."

"What?" The suspense was killing me. Was this where he told me he had gotten with some gorgeous (skanky) girl? And he was really sorry? And it was a big mistake? But she was so alluring he couldn't resist?

"I got a pe'a done. I had the last stage completed a few days ago and it's still a little sore. Here." A resigned sigh as he carefully shook himself loose of his shirt. "Have a look."

"You did what?!" I pulled back, my gaze searching and finding what I had missed in the rush to be with him. There in the dim light, I could faintly see the stamped black patterning on his hips, rising from the low-lying band of his shorts. I moved us both into the glare of a parking lot lamppost and stepped back. Now I could see, peering from the edges of his shorts, the intricate markings of a pe'a, running down both legs to the knee.

"You did it. You really got one. I don't believe it." I shook my head in disbelief. "When? Why didn't you tell me?"

He ruffled a hand through his hair in that nervous gesture I knew so well. A sheepish grin. "The last time we talked about me getting a pe'a, you weren't too excited about the idea. I didn't want to upset you. Or worry you. Especially when you were having such a nice time with your Folger family." He looked hopeful that I would buy this excuse.

"Whatever, Daniel. You didn't want me to try and talk you out of it!" Worry clamped a cold fist around my heart. "Who did it? Please don't tell me they used some nasty, backwoods, rusty instruments and dirty tools. Is there any infection?"

"It's fine. Mama made sure all the tools were sterilized and she's been taking care of it ever since. She didn't want me to get it done either, you know. Which is why I didn't tell you about it. I was having a hard enough time convincing Mama that I would be okay. I got it done at home, spread out over a week."

I winced, thinking of the painful process. "How bad did it hurt?"

A shrug. "Bad. But Mama gave me some painkiller stuff to drink through it, which helped. There were three of us getting it done so that helped as well. You know, solidarity and all that. Can't give in to the pain when there're other guys around waiting for their turn, you know."He bent to fold up the hem of his shorts. "See? I told you they were fine. So, what do you think?" He mocked striking a supermodel pose. I pretended to look pensive, hands on my hips and shaking my head.

"Hmm, I'm not sure. I need to get a better look. Can you please turn around and pull your pants down so me and the whole world can get a better look at your bum?"

He pretended to look shocked. "Hey, don't even joke about it or else I will!"

I laughed with him. Relieved that his grandmother had played a part in the tattooing process, ensuring his safety. Relieved that his confession hadn't been anything to do with gorgeous skanky girls … "I'm glad it turned out alright. It's beautiful. And I know it means a lot to you. You really are that noble Pacific warrior from the legend aren't you?"

He pulled me to him in a careful embrace. "As long as you're playing the part of Sina, I'm your warrior. Shall we go? I better get you to your aunt's house before she regrets allowing me to come and get you from the airport."

In the truck, I allowed my thoughts to wander to forbidden topics. "Daniel, if you're my noble warrior like in the legend does that mean you can turn into a silver dolphin?"

His grip tightened on the steering wheel. "What are you talking about, Leila?"

"I mean that night you got stabbed. We've never talked about it. You were underwater for over an hour. You were unconscious, stabbed in the chest when they threw you in the sea. You should have died that night. But you didn't. There were silver dolphins there. They brought you back to shore. Back to me. I saw them. The ocean gave you back to me. Why?"

"I don't know anything about silver dolphins. I do know that it was a rugged night. For both of us. You were coping with a lot and maybe you saw things that weren't there. You know what I mean?"

"No, I don't know what you mean. I know what I saw. What I saw was real."

Daniel interrupted me. "Can we not talk about it? I've spent the last six weeks trying to forget that night. Can we just think about today? Think about tomorrow?" He threw me a smile. "I'm taking the day off work so we can hang out. You want to go for a picnic?"

And just like that, Daniel Tahi deflected and got us off the silver dolphin topic. And I let him. Because he was right. Sometimes, the best way to deal with unpleasant things is to blank them out and forget they exist.

Which works fine. Until they come back to bite you.

Matile and Tuala greeted me with condolences and reserved welcome. They had sent a sympathy card to the Folger family when I returned to Washington, a card that contained some precious American dollars. This gesture that accompanied every Samoan funeral had touched me deeply. It wasn't about the money. It was the fact that this elderly couple regarded me as part of their family and were reaching out across oceans and time zones to my palagi extended family with this humble gift. I had explained the custom to my American family and they had made sure that I returned to Samoa with gifts. Matile exclaimed with breathless awe at the white lace and satin tablecloth set that Annette had sent. I had approved the purchase from Saks because I knew that Matile would seize upon it as the perfect donation for the church pulpit. I was right.

"So beautiful. I will give this for the church. Just wait until the other ladies see this meaalofa. This will be a gift to surpass all others."

Tuala had met my eyes over Matile's shoulder and smiled that knowing half-smile. *You got her, Leila. You know her well!*

I was truly happy to see them again. Matile muttered darkly at my news that my stay with them would be only temporary until I found an apartment to rent, but she brightened somewhat when I told her that I would be asking Simone to live with me. And I assured her that I would be accompanying her and Tuala to church every Sunday. Of course. That was the clincher. So my request for a day out with Daniel was granted. I ate the feast that Matile had prepared and savored every mouthful. The finest American cuisine couldn't match the rich array of tastes in a Samoan feast. Especially when Matile was doing the cooking. I went to bed happy. Exhausted. But feeling like I was truly home.

The promise of the day ahead was a fiery lightness that lit up my every step. A whole day with Daniel. Just us two at the beach. Texts and Skypeover the last six weeks had been a poor replacement for the real thing. Daniel's smile. His laugh. The crinkle of his green eyes as they would dance teasingly at me. I wanted to soar and sing with the anticipation alone of the day ahead.

I had cajoled the sour Aunty Matile into teaching me how to make her banana muffins – and then earned her sniff of disdain when I 'polluted' her recipe with handfuls of chocolate chips. It was a wickedly delicious recipe and the first sampling bite had me smiling. *Yes! Not bad, Leila*, I muttered to myself as I assembled ham sandwiches and packed everything into a cooler with sliced fruit. Daniel was bringing Diet Coke and some of his grandmother's coconut buns. I was checking off my beach supplies when I heard his truck pull up out front.

A foolish smile was plastered on my face as I ran to the door. A quick goodbye to Matile, who was still ignoring me and the evil chocolate chips. And then a breathless halt on the verandah at the sight of Daniel coming up the steps. A wry smile as the thought crossed my mind – would this boy ever have an 'off' day? A bad hair day? A fat day? An I'm-so-ugly-I-don't-want-to-go-outday?

He stood there smiling at me and I hoped he couldn't hear my thoughts that screamed of delight. Love. Bliss. Adoration. *Ugh*, I was sickening. But look at him, who wouldn't be a mass of mush at the sight of him?

Khaki shorts, white t-shirt, dark sunglasses raised over his sea-green eyes. My gaze went to his legs where the bands of black patterning peered from his shorts. How long would it be before I was used to seeing him with such an extensive tattoo?

He bent to take the bag and the cooler to the truck.

"Is this everything?"

"Yup. That's it. Did you get all the drinks?"

His quick grin gave me chills. "Yes, three Diet Cokes for the coke addict," shaking his head. "You know that stuff is like nuclear waste, don't you?"

I groaned, slamming the door with an extra flourish, rolling my eyes. "Yeah, yeah, so you keep telling me. I like my insides polluted with nuclear waste thank you very much."

He laughed. And his laugh had me sighing with contentment. It had been too long since I had laughed with the one I loved.

In the car, Daniel turned on the radio as we started the forty-five-minute drive to the beach on the other side of the island. Samoa's musical answer to everything – Bob Marley –wailed *No woman, no cry*...and Daniel started singing along. I could listen to him sing forever. The drive to Lefaga beach went quickly, and it wasn't long before we were pulling off the main road and down a bumpy sandy track towards the ocean. Once in sight of the sea, we turned and started driving slowly along the parallel road past village houses and beach fale. Still he didn't stop the truck, not until we had come to the very end of the trackdid he pull up beside a thicket of mangrove trees. The nearest house was a half mile away and the little slip of sandy beach was completely empty. We both got out of the truck and I turned shining eyes towards Daniel as he began unpacking our stuff from the back. "It's beautiful, Daniel. And totally private."

He shrugged as he heftily put the cooler on his shoulder "Yeah, but the problem with that is there's no water, no taps for us to clean off afterwards, but you said you wanted to rough it today. So here you have it, nothing but sand, sea and sun and bugs and mosquitoes and dirt and sweat. Ugh."

I laughed at his lack of enthusiasm. "Oh, don't be such a spoilt baby. It'll be great. Come on." I took his free hand and pulled him with me towards the beach where we found a shady spot under a tree.

He unrolled the mat and stretched back on it with a pleased sigh. "Ah, that's better. This is how I like the beach, looking at it from the shade."

A sudden wave of shyness hit me. I hadn't seen him for nearly two months and now, here we were, all alone on a white sand beach that screamed 'romantic make-out spot for reunited couples.' I hesitated, trying to decide where to sit. What to do. I knew what I wanted to do – hold him, kiss him, hug him, and love him. Enough to make up for all the weeks I had felt an empty space inside me without him. But the immensity of all he meant to me was almost paralyzing. He smiled up at me and sat up again, holding his hand out to mine. "What is it? Come over here."

I took his outstretched hand and sat beside him. The warmth of his shoulder touching mine filled me with contentment and for a few minutes we were both silent, contemplating the silken blue sea as it lapped against the shore.

"I've really missed you." He spoke quietly. There was no more teasing in his voice this time. I turned and his eyes captured mine. They looked troubled. "I don't like being apart from you. To be honest, I don't like the way you make me feel."

"Okaaay, what does that mean?!"

"I never needed somebody like this before. You make me feel like there's something missing unless I'm with you. I thought I had it all until I met you. I had my plans, my future all mapped out. Then you came along and messed it up. You're like this massive love bomb."

I had to laugh at that one. "Love bomb?! What the heck kind of way is that to describe your girlfriend?"

He laughed with me, "I never said I was a man of poetry or anything. Give me rugby or steel fabrication and I can talk for hours. But I don't know how to talk about love. Everything you are to me, everything I feel for you, it kinda chokes me. Sorry. I'm not making any sense here."

He gave me an exasperated grin, ruffling his hair with one hand in that endearing way that tugged on my heartstrings. I moved to kneel in front of him so that I could look in his eyes. "You're making perfect sense. You're my love bomb too. Now."I pointed at the calling ocean. "Are you going to come in with me?"

He shook his head. "Nah. No thanks. You go ahead. I'll hang out here."

"Aw come on!" He shook his head in refusal again. I didn't push the issue though, knowing his sensitivity about his mother and her drowning. "Okay, I'll just have a quick dip to cool off. Don't eat all the muffins before I get back. Or else."

"Or else what?" he teased.

I didn't answer immediately because I was peeling off my sweaty t-shirt, leaving only my black bikini top. I wasn't brave enough to strip down to the bikini brief so I left on my surf shorts. I tossed my shirt down on the mat and twisted my hair up into a messy knot. I poked my tongue out at Daniel. "Or else I'll have to set you on fire."

"Too late. You already have." was his wry response. He was staring at me in my half bikini and his eyes had an appreciative glint in them.

I blushed my invisible brown-girl blush. "What? What are you looking at?"

He smiled that crooked smile and ran his eyes over the length of me, from head to toe. "You."

"What about me?" I folded my arms across my chest and wished I had kept my shirt on. Or that I had a Baywatch babe chest to flaunt.

"I'm just looking. And thinking that there's nothing quite as hot as a girl with a malu tattoo. I dare you to take the shorts off so I can get the full effect. Go on. It's not like I haven't seen you in a two piece before, Leila."

I don't know what was sending delicious chills down my spine more. His words or the way he was looking at me. I shook my head. "No. That night at the pool was different. It was dark. Swimming in the middle of the night is way different than this." I waved wildly at the postcard-perfect day. "See? Sunshine. And wide open spaces. And blue sky. And anybody can see me."

Daniel rose to his feet and took those few steps to stand a mere breath away from me. He spoke softly, "Not anybody. Just me."

He didn't touch me, but I could feel him on every raw, ragged piece of me. My pulse raged a wild battle to stay calm and I could barely choke out my dissent. "I don't have the kind of body that looks good in a swim suit."

He raised an eyebrow at me and leaned forward to murmur, low and rough against my ear. "I disagree. I've seen you, Leila. All of you. You're the most beautiful girl I've ever seen. And don't ever let anyone tell you any different."

His voice was liquid chocolate, a slow cascade over my body. Sweet and sinuous. Tugging on invisible wires of heat. And all without even a single touch. He grinned then, as if aware of the effect that his words were having on me. "Besides, I bet after all that time away in a Washington winter, you could really use a tan. Go on. I dare you. Take it off. "

And then together, our hands were on the waistband of my shorts. And I was supposed to be the fire goddess, but it was his fingers that were burning against my skin as he helped me, tugged at the drawstring and eased the slippery fabric down my hips. The next breathless instant, I was standing there in my black bikini brief. Daniel's eyes never left mine as he stepped away from me. "See? That wasn't difficult, was it?"

The sunlight was gold liqueur on my skin. I stepped out of my shorts, trying not to betray my nervousness, resisting the urge to run for the concealing sanctuary of blue ocean. Or grab my towel and skulk in the shade. Holding Daniel's words close to me, like a mantra of courage ... *the most beautiful girl I've ever seen* ... I took a deep breath and held my head high, putting my hands on my hips, trying to ignore the fact that Daniel was staring at me with an unreadable expression on his face.

"Fine. I've taken it all off. Are you happy now?"

"Yes, I am." Before I could anticipate it, he knelt on one knee in the sand beside me and traced the patterns of my malu with tender hands. His fingers were scorching fire on my skin and it was a battle to stand calm and composed as he studied my tattoo for several taut moments. "The artwork is stunning." He smiled up at me. "Your malu is beautiful, Leila." He placed a delicate kiss on my bare midriff, so fleeting that it was as if I had imagined it. And then he was standing upright in front of me and holding me captive in his embrace. "Thank you for sharing it with me."

My entire being felt like rippling blue silk in his arms. Like he was the only thing that anchored me to earth. Like he could set me adrift on the azure ocean and I would dissolve into a million strands of lightness. Joy. He continued speaking, "There were moments over the last six weeks where I worried if you were ever going to come back. If maybe, you were going to choose to stay with your American family. I'm sure you thought about it. Right?"

I nodded. "I thought about it. But only because things were different than they had been the last time I was there. Or maybe it was just me that was different. I actually felt like I belonged with them, like I was a part of the Folger family. For the first time."

"They tried to get you to stay."

"Yes. But they understood when I chose to come back. They were supportive of my decision."

"I'm glad you chose Samoa."

I smiled up at him. "I couldn't choose any different. This is where my heart is."

I pulled away then and he stood and watched me wade into the shallows lugging an inflatable tire that he had brought on the back of the truck. He laughed as I launched myself into the silken warmth of blue. "Yoohoo! This is beeeyootiful. You're missing out!"

I swam farther out until the water was too deep to stand and then pulled myself up onto the tire and lay back to soak in the sun. I was luxuriating in the chance to just be with Daniel, hang out, and do normal things with him. We had spent so little time together where we were not either fighting for our lives or fighting over whether or not it was safe for us to be together. I was determined that today would be the first of many days that would be blissfully ordinary.

I don't know how long I floated along like that, lulled by the warm sun and the gentle sway of the ocean, but when I felt a slight shiver down my spine, I sat up. *Uh oh.*

The current had taken me farther out than I had expected, further out than my second-rate swimming skills felt comfortable with. I was now closer to where waves crashed on the reef than I was to the faraway shore. I could no longer make out Daniel's shape underneath the trees.

Dammit, good one, Leila. I sat up and started paddling my way back to the beach, kicking with my legs to help spur me along. That's when I felt it. An ice-cold tingle on my skin, a sharp contrast to the silken blue warmth of the water lapping around me. I felt a presence. A something – threatening, darkening – coming towards me. My heart pounded as I clutched the inner tube tightly, wishing I was safe on shore. *Stop it Leila, just quit it, you're being ridiculous*. But not even my grandmother's favorite phrase could stop the rising terror that had me turning wildly in all directions to see what hidden threat had me silently screaming.

I couldn't see anything. The sun glinted on the diamond water. The golden line of sand beckoned. A soft breeze played in the coconut trees lining the shore. I looked back at the ocean, scanning the blue for anything out of the ordinary. All seemed well – on the surface. Then from far away, Daniel shouted, and the fear in his voice confirmed my own.

"Leila! Don't move. I'm coming. Don't move."

Daniel was running along the beach towards me, then several splashing steps into the water and he dived. Strong and sure, he surged through the water with quick, even strokes. He was a powerful swimmer and amidst my ragged fearful breathing, I heard myself exclaim in surprise. "Wow, he's a really good swimmer." He was like liquid in the water, the gaping distance between us was nothing to him and his pace never slowed. It seemed like bare moments and he was beside me in the water, one arm looped around the inner tube while he half-turned to look out over the ocean.

"What is it?" I grabbed onto his shoulder, feeling foolish in my inexplicable fear. I longed for him to laugh, to brush away my concerns as nothing but foolish imaginings. Instead, his reply was quiet and low, his eyes darting in all directions, searching.

"Just keep still. Very still. Try not to move. It's circling."

"What is? Daniel – tell me – what is it?" My question was a piercing whisper. I didn't know why I felt the need to whisper. And I already knew the answer to my question, only I was hoping that I was wrong.

"Shark. A big one."

He spoke the words I knew he would, but every fiber of his being was focusing on the water, as he twisted his body this way and that, eyes darting back and forth.

I choked back a sob. As if being quieter would somehow make us invisible to the most deadly hunter in the ocean. As if. I'd seen *Jaws*. I knew what was coming. I didn't need the theme music. The pounding of my heart was crescendo enough. I threw a searching gaze back to the shore. Was there any way anyone could help us?

The deserted beach stretched away in the blue-gold afternoon. My earlier thrill at having the day to ourselves now mocked me. We were alone. In the ocean. Too far out from the shore thanks to my day dreaming. Alone without weapons of any kind. Not that weapons ever seemed to help shark attack victims in all the horror movies I'd seen. Funny. They had neverseemed that scarywhen onelivedin the suburbs of Maryland and only sniffed the ocean twice a year. Now? Here I was with the love of my life, about to get torn to pieces in the water. I started to shake, my teeth chattering as if we were in the midst of the Arctic instead of the glorious Pacific. Daniel threw me a concerned glance, unwilling to take his eyes off the waters around us.

With one arm guiding the tube, he shielded me with his body, muttering under his breath as if talking to himself. "He's trying to decide. What angle he'll come in on. Which side will be the best point of attack. Trying to figure out which of us is the weaker. Hmm…should I take out the stronger element first? Or pick off the smaller prey? Circling. Doesn't want to let us too far. But still not worried. Knows he's got the advantage no matter what."

In the midst of my terror, I paused as confusion added itself to the mix. What the hell was Daniel talking about? Was he losing it? I grabbed his shoulder.

"Daniel? What are we going to do?" I could barely make sense because my teeth were chattering so much. I was cold in the midst of a screaming hot day. I tried to think about flames. And rage. But I knew from past experience that all the fear in the world could not make me summon fire when I was in the ocean. We were going to die. Daniel was going to die. And useless, hopeless me was going to let it happen. His voice in my ear disrupted my thoughts.

"Leila, listen to me. I need you to slowly and carefully paddle to shore. Do you hear me? Don't splash too much. Just move real slow through the water on the tube. I'm going to draw him off. Go now. Go!"

Before I could process the full import of his words and argue with them, he shoved the tube away from him and towards the shore. From nowhere, a massive wave lifted the tube and started it rushing through the water without me even beginning to paddle. I threw a terrified glance over my shoulder back to where Daniel waited in the water.

He had his back to me as he trod water and for the first time I saw it. Clearly. The dark shape in the water. Moving almost lazily as it knifed towards him. And still he did not move.

"Daniel!" the scream tore from me without thought. "No."

He turned his head, green eyes speaking to me across the water, as he stretched out his arm towards me. Another impossible wave seemedtoemanate from where he swayed in the water, rushing me further away from him and to safety. *What's happening? Where are these waves coming from?*

In vain, I tried to halt the current but it swept the inner tube along relentlessly. There was only one thing to do. I heaved my body off the tire and splashed back into the ocean. The tube swirled away in the foam, happy to be rid of my dead weight. I had no plan. No brilliant ideas. I just knew there was no way I was leaving Daniel out there to face a shark alone. But now the water wasn't my friend. I was no match for the strange current that only seemed to have one goal. To sweep me along to the shore – no matter what. Even if it meant taking me upside down with a mouth full of water.

I managed to choke out his name once before the sea swallowed me, churning me like a washing machine. Just when I thought I couldn't hold my breath a moment more, I was right side up and gasping for air. All thoughts of the shark fled as I battled the current just to stay afloat, splashing and kicking, sucking in air and water in huge mouthfuls. My grasping hands met with the runaway tire. I clutched it gratefully, my lifeline. Hanging on tightly, I took several breaths of air before wiping the hair out of my face.

I cleared my vision in time to see Daniel begin swimming towards me. Midway he stopped and shouted, "No! Get away from her. You can't have her."

He reached out in my direction again, yelling "Go, Leila! Get out of here." As he did so, another impossible wave issued from his outstretched fingers. It rushed at me, carrying me with it. I turned my head to look back at him, in time to see a dark shape close in on him. From far away I heard myself screaming. I saw Daniel spin around in the water, then he dived and the water was still. And eerily silent. No Daniel. No shark. No nothing. Just me. Hanging on to a tire. That was now scraping me along in shallow water, coral nicking at my feet. And still thecurrent wouldn't let me go. Not until it had deposited my stunned self on the shore.

"Dammit!" Viciously I kicked the tire away from me, ignoring the sting of salt on the cuts on my feet. I dived back into the water and began swimming out to where I had seen Daniel disappear. But again, a determined wave appeared from nowhere and shoved me back to shore. I battled it uselessly. Frustration at war with fear.

"Dammit, dammit. What's going on?!" I screamed at an impassive ocean. "Why are you doing this to me?"

I stood in the shallows, hoping. "Daniel?" my scream died away to a whimper. "Daniel? Please come back."

I knew I should be running back to the car. Driving to town. Going to get help. But I couldn't make myself move. I had left him behind once. I would not leave him behind again. Irrationally, I thought that as long as I kept my eyes on the ocean, there would be hope for him.

The minutes ticked by. Five and then ten, then twenty. I dropped to my knees in the shallow water, numbed beyond belief. Daniel was gone. The afternoon was fading. The last crimson rays of sunset threw their bronze spider web across the ocean. It was the most perfect of days. And I felt nothing for it. I knew with dreadful certainty that there was no way he could have held his breath for that long. Even if the shark hadn't finished him off, the water would have. Not even a splash or red water to mark his last dive. In a haze I thought dimly – *how inconsiderate of that shark, it didn't even leave me a piece of Daniel's finger to remember him by*. Then I knew I was approaching hysteria. A finger? My Daniel was gone and I wanted a bloody piece of his flesh to remember him with? I was cold. So cold. I could not believe that here I was again, sitting on a lonely beach looking out at an ocean that had taken Daniel from me. This was beyond unfair.

And then there was a splash and Daniel surged up and out of the sea several feet away from me. He was a glorious sight. With his arms stretched wide, raven red head thrown back, silver droplets on gleaming skin in the approaching dusk, he was a water god. A silver dolphin. He shook his head, sending diamond spray scattering. His eyes caught mine and his face lit up in a joyous smile. Again he dove into the water and power stroked his way swiftly to my side. In less time than it took to exhale, I was in his arms.

And he was warm. And real. And solid flesh and muscle against me. And his kiss was hot and salty. I drowned in it. And the waves lapped us in their embrace. I felt a peaceful calm sweep over me as once again the sea felt like a friend. Safe.

Effortlessly, Daniel lifted me and carried me out of the water, setting me down beside our picnic gear under the trees. He wiped wet strands of hair away from my face and wrapped a thick towel around my shoulders, rubbing my arms in response to my shivering.For several minutes neither of us spoke. Just breathed. I ran myfingers over his face, through his hair, along his tattoo, glorying in his perfection. My eyes drank him in, unwilling to believe that he was alive. Complete. Unhurt. Well, almost unhurt.There was a welt of matted red along the side of his bronzed chest.

"Daniel, you're bleeding. We've got to get you to the hospital."

"Nah, it's nothing. He didn't bite me, I got this from his skin, the impact when we collided. Agh, did you know that sharks have skin like toxic sandpaper?" He shook his head with a faint grimace as he gingerly felt his wound.

I jerked out of his embrace and leapt to my feet. What was I thinking, sitting here lapping up his hug when he'd been injured? I grabbed the first aid kit from the car and applied a dressing to his cut,ignoring his assurances that he was fine. Not until he was bandaged and we were both dressed in dry clothing – not until I was really sure that he was alright – did I ask him the questions that had been bubbling underneath the surface.

"Daniel, what happened out there?"

He sat beside me, staring out at the fast sinking sun and his voice was carefully neutral. "I'm not sure."

"I mean, what was that? You knew that shark was there? How? And when we were out there hanging on to the tire, you talked about it, like you could read its mind or something." Saying it out loud only made it sound all the more implausible. I laughed weakly, waiting for him to dispel what were surely just fanciful notions.

He shook his head. "I don't know. It doesn't make any sense. One minute I was half-asleep and then the next I could feel this thing, this presence and I just knew right away that you were in danger. Once I got into the water, the thought came so clearly to me – a shark. A big one."

He stopped and looked away, out over the waves crashing on a faraway reef. I prompted him. "Yeah, and then?"

"Then what?"

"Then you were talking about its thoughts. You were freaking me out, what was going on out there?"

He said nothing. Shrugged. I persisted. "Daniel, say something. What just happened? Those waves that came out of nowhere, pushing me to shore? Did those come from you? And then when that shark attacked you, how did you get away from it? With only that 'sandpaper scratch'? This is crazy, you were gone for over twenty minutes, I thought you were dead. It was just like…"

His anger halted my tirade. "Like what, Leila? What?" Roughly he stood and walked away from me, down towards the ocean, throwing curt words over his shoulder at me. "Just leave it, okay? Leave me alone. I don't want to talk about this. Just leave it."

I let him go, watching him walk the water's edge while a dying sun bled with orange-red light. I didn't know what had happened with him as that shark had tried to attack us, but of one thing I was sure – whatever was going on with Daniel, it had everything to do with his crested wave-shaped birthmark.

※

The drive home was an uneasy one, with neither of us breaking the silence that divided us. My unasked questions screamed, and Bob Marley on the radio was a mocking reminder of how happy we had been that morning when we had first set out on our picnic. I stole a look at Daniel sitting across from me in the darkness, hoping for some sort of sign that he was ready to talk about what had happened. Nothing. He looked like a stranger. Why was he so angry? What was happening with him and, more importantly, why was he so unwilling to share it with me?

At the house, he helped carry my gear to the front door. I stood and watched him walk back to the truck and then stopped him. "Daniel, wait up."

He turned with an impatient frown, but I refused to be daunted. Ignoring the certainty that Matile was watching us from inside the living room, I ran down the steps and took him in a fierce hug. For a moment he just stood there unmoving and then relented slightly to pat me on the back. Awkward and hesitant.

"I love you. Thank you for today. For saving me." I whispered in his ear, wishing on every star that glimmered far above us that he would kiss me. Hold me. Love me. Do something, anything to bridge the distance between us and once again be my Daniel.

For a moment it seemed the stars had heard me. He hugged me back. Bent his head slightly to kiss my still-damp hair. A whisper. "I love you too." And then he released me and firmly held me away from him. "You better go in. I need to get home."

I looked up at him, trying to decipher those green depths but he wasn't letting me in. An edge of frustration crept into my voice. "I don't understand why you won't talk to me about this. We should discuss what's happening to you so that together we can figure it all out. You keep shutting me out. This is killing me."

His whole body tensed and he took a step away from me, shaking his head in disbelief. His words knifed through me, severing our tenuous connection. "Not everything is about you. Just for once, can't you get that? I told you that I don't want to talk about what happened at your sisterhood showdown and I don't want to talk about what happened today either. Can't you respect that?"

"You're right. I'm sorry."

"I'll call you."

He didn't look back at me as he got in his truck and drove away. I watched the night swallow him as shame curled inside me. *Not everything is about you, Leila*...Being accused of selfishness wasn't exactly new for me.

F O U R

Daniel didn't call me the next day. But a lawyer called Thompson did.

"Leila Folger? I'm Phillip Thompson of the law firm Betham and Thompson here in town. Your Aunt Matile gave us your number. Can we arrange a good time for you to come in to our office please?"

"Why?" I wasn't in the mood to be polite. Daniel was mad at me and I needed to think of ways to fix the current situation. "Why do you want to see me?"

"We were – are – your mother's lawyers and have some urgent matters to discuss with you. We've been waiting for your return, and the situation with your mother's sister is getting rather urgent. Can you come in today at eleven?"

My mother's sister? That could only be one person. Sarona. She was alive. She was here. From a faraway place, I heard myself answer, "Yes, I'll be there."

I thought about her on the drive into town. Sarona. The only woman in the Covenant who registered higher on the psycho scale than my mother. The woman who had tortured me, and Daniel, and issued the death order for the boy who was my reason for living. And then tried to kill me and my mother. Okay, so Nafanua had been a flawed mother figure, but still, to give her credit, in the end she had given her life for me.

Yes, my 'Aunt Sarona' had a great deal to answer for. And I had spent many hours thinking of some of those answers.

I used to think I knew what hate was. What anger felt like. Even what vengeance tasted like on the tongue. I'd had more than my fair share of schoolyard bullying. The children who chanted 'owl face' at my deep-set eyes. The high school coven that had appointed the surly brown thug girl as their entertainment. I had tasted revenge. The warm thrill of satisfaction when you get to wreak a little payback with your fists, lash out at a jeering face. I had heard bone and cartilage give way as my fist connected with their nose. And blood. I knew what it looked like. What it felt like, warm and salty on bruised knuckles.The way it pulsed and gushed from a broken nose.

Yes, I used to think that I had tasted anger and hate.

But I was wrong. Because when I thought of Sarona and how close she had come to taking away the one person who knew me in all my demented telesā fury and still loved me – only then did I understand what a thirst for vengeance tasted like.

The air-conditioned interior of the lawyer's office was a welcome change from the sweltering humidity of a crowded morning in Apia. The receptionist showed me into a sterile conference room where a harried-looking man greeted me.

"Miss Leila Folger? Yes, of course it must be, I see the likeness." He shook my hand in a damp grip. "It's a pleasure to finally meet you. Take a seat please. We have much to get through. As the sole heir to Nafanua's estate, there are many matters that need your attention, your signature, now where shall we begin…" his voice trailed away while I reeled at his words.

"Excuse me? What did you say? I'm the what?"

Mr. Thompson paused in his paper shuffling and looked up at me in thin surprise. "You are Nafanua's chief heir. I assumed you knew that? Didn't she discuss it with you?"

A minor wrecking ball had ploughed into me, leaving me numb. I sank into a fake leather chair and tried to focus on the ANZ bank sign visible outside the window. "No. She didn't." But then, there's a lot that my mother never discussed with me.

Against my will, the past tore at my thoughts. Bitter and sour like biting into an unripe mango. Nafanua. *Leila, my daughter, at long last I have found you!*Welcoming me into her home. Standing in a jasmine-fragranced darkness as she handed me a whale bone carving. *Here, the women in my family make carvings for their daughters. A gift for when she becomes a woman. I hope it's not too late, Leila. For us to be family. To be sisters. To be friends*, she had asked me, smiling that regal smile. The one that spoke of strength. Determination. Resolve. The one that said 'no one defies me.'The same triumphant smile she had given me when I had summoned fire and it came gently, a flame nestled in the palm of my hand. When she had rejoiced, *Yes!* Nafanua. Teaching me how to dance the siva. Laughing at my clumsy efforts. Gently bending my fingers to do her bidding, follow in hers. Nafanua. Impassive as the sisterhood had tortured Daniel. Stabbed him. Nafanua. Turning to smile softly at me, *I may never have loved your father, Leila, but always remember that I loved you.* Stepping into the line of white fire that seared me. Turning against her sisterhood. Breaking the covenant that bound them all. Attacking her sisters of several lifetimes. Again and again. Until finally, Sarona had killed her.

No. I had worked so hard for so long to subdue these memories. I had successfully buried them in the weeks of dealing with Grandmother Folger's funeral and reacquainting myself with my Folger family. I had avoided dealing with the reality that my mother had been the leader of a psychotic group of environmental terrorists intent on wiping out thousands of people all in the name of 'a return to the old ways' … 'cleansing and healing the earth.' A mother who had tried to manipulate her own daughter into using her elemental powers to summon a volcano to wipe out all of Apia. A mother who finally, at the last minute, had given her life for me. Leaving me truly parentless. Alone. No, Daniel was not the only one working hard on suppressing painful memories.

Thompson was staring at me. "Miss Folger, are you alright?"

No, I'm not alright. Do I look alright to you? "Yes, thank you. I'm fine. Let's get this over and done with."

The man looked relieved. Coping with a semi-hysterical grieving girl was obviously not on his schedule for the day. "Right, well, as I said, Nafanua named you as the sole heir of her estate, apart from a few minor bequests."

"So what does that mean?"

"It means you are now the administrator of various organizations and companies that Nafanua established. They each have their own Board of Trustees so you don't need to worry about their day-to-day operations. Not unless you want to. There's a list that includes a pharmaceutical research company, a Women's Refuge Center, an animal shelter, the largest organic food supplier in the country, a cosmetics exporter, four private nature reserves and parks, not to forget the patents for thirty-seven plant-derived drugs ..."

The lawyer's voice droned on and on, listing too many things to actually bother retaining. I felt the walls closing in around me. Would he ever stop?

"... several fixed deposits and investments plus a petty cash account of 1.2 million tala, giving an estimated total value of fifty-six million tala or thereabouts." An apologetic smile. "It's not easy to calculate an exact value of the estate."

Fifty-six million tala. This seemed to be the worst betrayal of all. How dare she? How dare she off-load all her crap on me? Did I ask for it? Did I want it? Hell no. I wanted nothing from her. Nothing. All I had wanted was for her to be my mother and instead she had deceived me. Used me. And if all the pieces of the puzzle were to be believed, it was highly probable that she had infected my father with some kind of telesā cancer. She had murdered my father. All the money in the world couldn't bring my dad back. Or buy my forgiveness.

But the lawyer wasn't finished. "However, Nafanua was very specific. You are to have complete ownership and control of all her assets but there are two conditional clauses. Legally binding, but rather unusual. But then your mother was always a breathtakingly unusual woman."

Unusual? You have no idea. The man had a foolish faraway look on his face. Clearly Nafanua had held him in the palm of her hand. *Men are fools.* Out of nowhere, Sarona's voice leapt to mind. Great. Would I be haunted forever by her as well as Nafanua? Just what I wanted. To walk around with a sisterhood of crazy telesā women always in my head.

"What conditions?" Not that it mattered. There's no way in a tangled telesā hell I was going to accept anything that had belonged to that woman. But, still, before I chucked it all and walked out of there, I was curious. What wacked-up conditions had Nafanua put on her final gift to me?

Thompson hesitated. Embarrassed. "If you were ever to marry, then ownership of the entire estate would revert to an alternate heir, Nafanua's sister, Sarona Fruean."

Nice one 'mom'. Actually that one shouldn't be a surprise. *The rule we telesā live by. We can take a lover but we can never love a man. We must never share our gifts with them. They are not our equals. Men would try to control our powers, wrest them from us. No, telesā do not love the ungifted sex. A telesā's covenant sisterhood must come above all others.*

I resisted the urge to roll my eyes. "And the second clause?"

Mr. Thompson shifted in his seat uneasily. "You must understand, Miss Folger, that a client can sometimes insist on strange things and we as their lawyers can only advise them."

Like you could have stopped the woman from doing what she wanted. A lawyer giving legal counsel to a telesā Covenant Keeper? Laughable. You'd have better luck climbing a coconut tree upside down. "Yes I understand. What is the second clause?"

"If, at any time, you are to give birth to a live male child who reaches his first birthday – then your ownership will end and the estate will revert to Nafanua's sister, Sarona Fruean."

This time, pain was a bush knife that hacked at pieces of my insides, impossible to ignore. I was born a twin. I used to have a brother. But a short while after our birth, Nafanua had killed him. Smothered him. Taken him out with the trash, so to speak. Why? Because telesā are forbidden to have male descendants. *No man must be allowed to share in our gifts, wield our powers. Telesā are protectors of the earth and man is our mother earth's greatest abuser. No male child can be allowed to live.* So my mother had killed my brother, and my dad had found out her awful secret. That's when he had run away with me, taking me back to the US with him. I had grown up with a father who loved me, a grandmother who was forever irritated with me, and a housekeeper who was forever patient with me. But missing that other piece of the family puzzle.

The lawyer was still talking. "You should know that Sarona Fruean has been to see me and is threatening to lodge a caveat against the will if it goes against her. She was under the impression that she was the chief heir and was very upset when I informed her we would not be inviting her to a reading of the will." He paused with a flustered expression. I can imagine how his visit with my 'Aunt Sarona' had gone for him. No wonder the man looked like he wanted to throw up.

"The air conditioning must be faulty. It's like a furnace in here." Thompson took a handkerchief to wipe the sweat from his forehead. Jolting me back to the present. To this moment. "I apologize for the heat, Miss Folger."

Oops. My bad. The temperature in the room had leapt several degrees thanks to my somewhat violent reminiscing, and poor Thompson looked like he was about to pass out. Control, Leila. Cool it. I fought to rein in the heat that was pouring off me in waves. It's a wonder I wasn't smoking at the edges. Now that would really unsettle Thompson's lawyer day … It took a few minutes, but I did it. Calmed down. Called back the energy that had set the air molecules around me into a frenzy.

"I'm fine, Mr. Thompson. How about you? Do you need a drink of water?" *You look like you've been sitting in a sauna fully clothed. Don't pass out on me please.*

I got up to pour the man a glass of water from the jug on a table in the corner. As long as I kept my brain away from the flammable topic of Sarona Fruean, I would be fine. I could keep a hold of my rage. Thompson accepted the water gratefully and gulped it down.

"Thank you, Miss Folger. I'm fine now. Shall we continue?"

Shall we not? I wanted to get out of there. Now. I wanted to go to the quarry in the Aleisa hills. Flame. Run. Rage without repercussions. Just me and miles of forest. So I could burn Sarona a thousand times over in my mind. Control, Leila. Control. "Can we make this quick, Mr. Thompson? I have somewhere to get to."

"Oh, of course." But before he could continue, there was a ruckus outside in the reception area. Someone was giving the receptionist a hard time.

"I'm sorry, but he's in a meeting with a client. You can't go in there. You have to make an appointment."

"He will see me. Now."

The voice was one accustomed to being obeyed. I knew that voice. Before I could move, react, think – the door was flung open.

"Where is that fool? Thompson!"

A woman stood in the doorway, hands on her hips. Resplendent in a green Mena designer dress and red heels, a slash of blood lipstick and gleaming black hair hanging to her waist. Sarona.

The lawyer rose to his feet, startled outrage quickly replaced by fear at the sight of the angry woman that confronted him. "What is the meaning of this interruption …"

But Sarona ignored him. Instead our gazes locked. "You."

I stood slowly, battling the tidal wave of hatred that threatened to overwhelm me. A thought was all it would take and the entire office would be engulfed in flames. A flick of my wrist and I could hit her with a ball of fire that would send her hurtling through several concrete walls. I wanted to do it so bad that it hurt.

The receptionist's harried face peered from around her shoulder as she tried to get past the woman who towered over her in stiletto heels. "Mr. Thompson, I'm so very sorry. I tried to stop her. I told her you were in a meeting, but she insisted."

I felt the tingling in my fingertips. The pin-pricks of sparks as they raced from my fingertips to the palms of my hands. The fire was coming. And it would be oh-so-easy to let it.

I'm going to kill you, Sarona Fruean. I'm going to stand here and laugh while you scream for mercy. I'm going to watch the skin melt off your bones and smell the burn of your flesh as it roasts. I'm going to make a Sarona bonfire and dance around it. You hear me bitch? Burn and die.

But then, from somewhere far away, a baby cried. A mother shushed it softly. Jolting me out of my burn fantasy. People. The reception area was full of people waiting to share their troubles with a lawyer. A toddler broke away from her mother and ran in our direction on unsteady feet. A yelp of delight as her mother swept her into an embrace. "Baby, no. Stay here with Mom."

Dammit. How was I supposed to murder a weather witch with all these spectators? Without hurting any of them? The toddler escaped from her mother again, this time making it as far as Sarona, reaching to grab hold of the folds of her skirt in pudgy hands. Laughing as Sarona bent to take her in her arms. "What a beautiful little girl you are."

Sarona held the little girl close to her perfumed perfection and smiled at me. Cold eyes asked me, *What are you going to do now, Leila, hmm? Are you going to risk hurting all these people? Go ahead. Bring it. I'm ready.* She kissed the child, leaving a red lipstick imprint on her cheek before handing her over to her smiling mother. Turning again to face us.

"Am I interrupting something?"

"Yes you are, Ms. Fruean. As I informed you the other day, you are not a beneficiary of Nafanua's will and so cannot be party to the reading. I will have to ask you to leave." The man's courage ended there because he added a slightly desperate, "Please?"

The smile left. As quickly as it had come. Leaving a woman of steel fury. "No. This is a travesty. Nafanua cannot do this to me. I dedicated my life to our company, our Covenant. Those companies belong to me. I was always her second in the sisterhood, the heir. The money, the drug patents, the estate, everything – it's all mine. Do you hear me? Mine. This girl is nothing. She betrayed our sisterhood and turned against us. She cannot be allowed to have any of it."

Sarona's tirade had a fascinated audience. Heads turned, necks craned as everyone in the reception waiting room ogled at the spectacle of a beautiful woman losing her cool. I smiled in the face of her fury and sat back down with casual ease. All of a sudden, being the boss of fifty-six million tala seemed like something I wanted. Oh yeah. Heiress of the Covenant Sisterhood estate, that was me. Thank you Nafanua for giving me the opportunity to really irritate Sarona the Psycho. I faked a frown.

"I'm so sorry that my beloved mother cut you out of the will, Aunty Sarona. After all those years, living in her shadow, slaving as second best in the Sisterhood, taking orders, biting your tongue. Hmm, I wonder why Nafanua didn't see fit to reward your service? Is it because she suspected that you would turn against her eventually?" I smiled. "Don't worry, I'm not completely heartless. I would never forget my family. If you learn how to play nice, maybe I'll arrange for you to have a weekly allowance. I don't think it will be enough for you to afford three-hundred-dollar Mena outfits, but then, you won't have much longer to ponder your wardrobe choices." *Since I'm going to kill you. Not here. Not today. But soon. Very soon.*

Sarona's eyes flashed and outside a roar of thunder had everyone jumping. Except for me. Weather witch theatrics no longer impressed me. I had taken the very best that this telesā had to give – and survived. The next time we met in battle, I would not hold back. My fire would not waver. To protect Daniel, and for vengeance, I would summon a death strike and not hesitate. Could she sense my resolve? She backed off, regardless, dropped her gaze and turned instead to the lawyer who stood frozen in place.

"Mr. Thompson, what happens to the estate when Leila dies? Suddenly. Painfully. Tragically."

The spectators' gaze swiveled to the lawyer whose mouth opened and closed, fishlike. I almost felt sorry for him. It wasn't his fault that Nafanua had screwed over two telesā in her will and set them against each other's throats. Thompson ruffled through papers on the desk, nervous. "Well, ahem, I suppose that, unless Ms. Folger draws up a will and names an heir, the estate will pass to Nafanua's next of kin. Which would be you, Ms. Fruean." He came to an abrupt halt and his eyes darted from me to Sarona, who now wore a gleeful smile. A kind of horrible realization dawned on his face. *Yeah, that's right, Mr. smarty-pants lawyer, go on and put the pieces together. Do you get clients issuing each other death threats in your office every day?*

I matched Sarona's triumphant smile with one of my own. "In that case, I should probably draw up a will right now, right here, today. I don't want the inheritance. I would like all Nafanua's money to be placed in a scholarship trust fund." My brain was tripping over itself, trying to grab hold of a suitable beneficiary. "For ... aha, for Samoan women wishing to undertake tertiary study. Science and medical scholarships. Lots and lots of local female scientists and doctors. I think Nafanua would have liked that, don't you Aunty Sarona?"

Her eyes narrowed and her hushed tone was venomous. "You little bitch. You wouldn't do that. Nobody gives up that much money."

"Oh really?" I raised an eyebrow at her. "Watch me."

I laughed. The audience was loving it. This was better than *Days of our Lives*. And I was loving it. Sarona's hands were tied. She knew it and I knew it. The only question was, what was she going to do about it? She shot me a look of pure loathing and then walked to lean in close, to whisper words that only she and I could hear.

"Laugh while you can, little girl. Your mother begged me for mercy, and one day, so will you. So will all those that you care about. Tell me, did your father die slowly? I do hope so. I'm not as skillful with concoctions as Nafanua was. I've been wanting to tell you in case you didn't know. He came to Samoa hoping to make peace with your mother. Wanting to see if she had changed, because he said his daughter needed to know her mother. Nafanua was in Fiji at an environmental conference so I met him instead and never told her of his visit. You have no idea how much pleasure it has given me knowing that I had a hand in his death. Enjoy your inheritance. It will be your undoing."

And on that final note, she turned and left, the gaggle of spectators parting to let her pass. Thompson's shoulders slumped in a rush of relief. He moved to shut the conference room door against the inquiring eyes. "Well, that was unpleasant. But then family members can get quite emotional at times like this. I'm sure that once Ms. Fruean has had time to calm down, she will want to mend things with you. And who knows, she could be quite helpful to you? It's a very large and complex estate you know, Ms. Folger." The look he gave me had doubt mixed with uncomfortable sympathy. "And if I understand correctly, you don't have any family left do you?"

My family – or lack thereof – was none of his business. I needed to get out of there. I couldn't make sense of Sarona's parting shot about my father. Was she lying? Was she only taking blind, wild aim, trying to hurt me in any way possible? An irrational panic set in. Sarona couldn't hurt me but there were others she could target instead. Daniel, Matile and Tuala, my friends at school even. Now was not the time to sort out all the details for getting rid of my mother's money.

"Look, can we talk about this stuff more another day? I really need to get out of here. You know, go think about everything. It's a lot to process."

Thompson rushed to be placating. "Yes, of course. We can delay the rest of the details for another meeting. There is one more thing, however." He brought out a safety deposit box. "This was kept in Nafanua's bank security vault. We were instructed to release the contents to you upon her death."

Now what? A mental groan. I was already on my feet, anxious to be gone. Anxious to hear Daniel's voice. Check on my uncle and aunt. I opened the box and took out the oblong wooden container inside it. It was ornately carved and surprisingly heavy for its size. Too impatient to examine its contents, I shoved it into the depths of my backpack.

"Right, is that it? Can I go now?"

If Thompson was surprised by my lack of curiosity in what was clearly a prized possession of Nafanua's – he was professional enough not to show it. Instead, he stood to usher me out.

"Yes, of course. Thank you for coming in today Ms. Folger. I look forward to our next meeting." I almost broke into a run when we went out to the lobby and almost didn't hear his parting warning. "Oh, Ms. Folger I hope it's alright but we passed your contact number on to the Director at the Women's Refuge Center. They urgently need your approval on some key matters to do with the Center, and she will be in touch with you. I hope that's alright?"

I was out of there. I didn't bother answering.

Sarona's back. Sarona's back.

My heartbeat pounded out the chant as I ran to my Wrangler, pressing automatic dial on my phone for Daniel. Come on, pick up. Dammit, where was he? His voice mail answered. Again. I swore and threw the stupid phone onto the seat next to me as I gunned the accelerator a little more.

Sarona's back. Sarona's back.

My panic only increased when I pulled up to his house and there was no familiar green truck parked outside.

"Daniel?" I scanned the workshop – nobody– then ran to bang on the front door of the house.

By the time Salamasina opened the door, I felt ready to combust. The stern-faced woman looked annoyed to see me. "Leila, what is going on? Why are you attacking my front door like that?"

It was the first time I'd seen her since the aftermath of the Covenant show-down. I wanted to run and hide. We both stared at each other for an endless moment before I summoned the courage to speak. "I'm sorry, Mrs. Tahi, I'm looking for Daniel. He's not answering his phone and I really need to talk to him. It's important."

"He's not here. And his phone is in the kitchen on the charger."

That's not the answer I wanted to hear. I groaned. "No, where is he?"

She frowned at my rudeness. "He's gone to Savaii with Okesene to work on a steel job. They should be back this afternoon on the last boat."

He never said anything to me about going to Savaii. Did he just decide this today because he wanted to avoid me? Salamasina must have sensed my agitation because her eyes narrowed and she demanded. "What is going on, Leila?"

"I met Sarona today. My mother's sister. She's angry and she's made some threats."

"I know who she is. Who has she threatened?"

"Me." I didn't want to tell her the rest. Not as my memory jumped back to that long ago day when Salamasina stood in this very kitchen and warned Daniel that I was bad for him. *She is not for you, Tanielu. I love you and I tell you with a clean heart, this girl is not for you. You would do well to end this friendship now.*

But Salamasina knew there was more. "And who else?"

"Everyone that I care about." I felt the familiar anger build. "She knows she can't hurt me and so she's threatened to target everyone around me. But I won't let her. I couldn't take her out at the lawyer's office because there were too many people around, but I'm going to find her before she can hurt anyone else."

"And then what are you going to do?"

"And then I'm going to kill her." Speaking the words out loud vested them with strength. Power. But Salamasina only raised an eyebrow at them.

"So, you are your mother's daughter after all."

I flinched. "What's that supposed to mean?"

She didn't reply. Instead she opened the door wider and motioned for me to enter. I hesitated. "What are you waiting for? Come inside. There's something I want to say to you and I'm not going to stand on the doorstep talking where all the neighbors can see us."

She walked away into the kitchen and I followed. Wary. Great. Did I really have time for this? In the kitchen, the old woman poured us both a glass of juice and then directed me to sit with her at the table. The chill of creamy sweet soursop was a soothing breather. I sipped at it and waited for her to speak.

"When I say that you are your mother's daughter, I'm merely stating the obvious. Nafanua used her telesā gifts to kill when it suited her and you are choosing to walk in her footsteps."

"No. I'm choosing to use my fanua afi gifts to protect those I care about. There's a difference."

"Is there?" She posed the question so casually that it barely seemed to matter. "Do you know what Nafanua would do to young girls with telesā gifts who refused to join her Covenant?"

She did not wait for a reply. She continued and her voice raised a notch. "She killed them. She did not want to run the risk of them growing up to become more powerful than she was. Only our Mother Earth knows how many young women died at Nafanua's hands. Is that what you will do? Kill anyone who annoys you?"

I argued. "That's not fair. I'm nothing like my mother. This is different. Sarona has hurt Daniel before and she won't hesitate to do it again. I must protect him and if that means destroying her, then so be it."

Salamasina spoke with calm reason in the face of my emotion. "You continue to ignore the obvious because you are selfish. You lie to me and to yourself. You say you love my son. You say you are willing to kill to protect him. But do you love him enough to let him live without you?"

"I don't understand. What do you mean?"

This time, Salamasina didn't hold back and I shrank against the cold fury of her words. "The only reason Daniel's life is in danger is because you love him. If you let him go, then he will be nothing to Sarona."

I struggled for words. Angry but respectful words. "You've never liked me, never approved of me and Daniel's friendship and I'm sorry that he has been hurt because of me. But we love each other and I won't give him up. We've been through so much together already. We can overcome this too. I know we can."

"You know nothing. You are a telesā without any knowledge of her history, customs, or heritage. And a woman without her history is a fool. I'm sure that Sarona took special pleasure in torturing Daniel that day. As she will again when she carries through with her threat to hurt him again. Do you know why?" She didn't wait for an answer. "A little piece of family history that Nafanua neglected to mention to you but that had the telesā Pacific grapevine all abuzz. As a young girl, Sarona was Nafanua's special protégé. Her gifts were strong, and Nafanua had no gifted daughters of her own. Or so she thought. Nafanua went to great lengths to teach Sarona and nurture her gifts. In turn, Sarona idolized her like the mother, the big sister, that she didn't have. But when she was eighteen, Sarona made a terrible mistake. She fell in love. She wanted to get married, have a family, be with him forever – so she asked Nafanua if she could be released from her Covenant oath. She begged her as a daughter begs a mother. As a sister begs another. She was in love, she said, this boy was different from all others, special, unique. He was going to love her and treasure her always. If it had been any other telesā in her Covenant, Nafanua would probably have killed her without a second thought. But because it was Sarona, she decided to take a different approach to the problem. She decided to break her heart instead. Nafanua used her skills to brew a love potion. Not difficult if you have all the ingredients and the telesā know-how. Nafanua emptioned Sarona's lover and then arranged for Sarona to discover her with him, together in the worst possible way."

I reeled. Was there nothing my mother hadn't done? "I can't believe Nafanua did that. Was nothing or no one sacred to her?"

"I'm sure that Nafanua thought she was doing Sarona a favor. Helping a Covenant sister to snap out of what she thought would be a doomed relationship. It worked."

"Didn't Sarona suspect that the boy had been drugged?"

"Nafanua admitted it. Showed her the evidence. She wanted Sarona to see how easily a man can be swayed. But more importantly, she wanted Sarona to see what a transient thing love is. It could be faked. Manipulated. Induced. And then forgotten in a heartbeat. Listen well to this truth Leila – telesā do not love, because their earth gifts are eternal and men are only mortal. A man can only be but a passing fancy."

"Then what happened?" In my heart of hearts, I was afraid I already knew the answer.

"Sarona killed him. She could not raise her hand against Nafanua because of the Covenant but she has hated her ever since. And I'm sure that she has never again repeated the mistake of falling in love."

I didn't know what to do with this new insight, both into my mother and into the woman that wanted me dead. "What does that story have to do with me and Daniel?"

"Everything. As long as Daniel is with you, he will be a target, not only for Sarona, but for all telesā who hold to the ancient ways. I think Sarona envies you and what you have with Daniel. Maybe in you, she sees herself and the possibilities of what could have been. She hates you and the boy who you have chosen to love *against* telesā law."

I looked at Salamasina with new eyes. How much did this woman really know about telesā and their ways? "How is it that you know so much? I know your mother was a telesā but you said you were sent away when you were twelve years old. And yet, you speak of them as if you were one of them for much longer. As if you still are …"

The old woman sighed. "You forget, Tonga is very small compared to your world of America. And my island of Niuatoputapu was even smaller still, and very isolated. Even as an Ungifted, it was impossible to be truly removed from the telesā there. Especially with a mother like mine."

"What do you mean?"

"My mother is Tavake, the Covenant Keeper of the telesā vasa loloa in Tonga. She is the oldest and most powerful of all the ocean telesā, even older still than Nafanua was." A strange smile. "I have not spoken her name for many years."

I seized eagerly on this nugget of information. Surely Salamasina would know what was going on with Daniel? She would be able to make sense of the past months' events. I paused, unsure whether Daniel would be happy with me discussing it with his grandmother when it was obvious he didn't want to even talk about it with me. I decided the indirect route was best. "I had a twin brother who died when we were babies. Before she died, Nafanua told me that he was born with the mark of vasa loloa, a special kind of birthmark on his hip. Is that just a myth? Do all ocean telesā have the birthmark?"

Salamasina made a derisive sound of dissent. "Do you mean this mark?" She pulled up her right sleeve and showed me the birthmark there. My eyes widened in surprise. It was exactly like the mark I had seen on Daniel's thigh. A gleaming white shape of a crested wave. "As you can see, I have it, the supposed mark of vasa loloa but the reality that Tavake had to face was that I had no ocean gifts. Not even a hint. The mark is merely a genetic imprint found on many of us but it doesn't mean anything. It's no guarantor of telesā gifts at all."

"Oh." I tried another line of questioning, probing, seeing how far I could go with Salamasina while she was in this talkative mood. "You told me about Daniel being adopted. Was his mother telesā?"

Her eyes narrowed and there was jagged coral in her tone. "No. Why do you ask such a question?"

"Because that night when he got attacked and I helped him escape. I noticed that he has a birthmark like yours on his, umm, his thigh. And I thought maybe it could mean something."

She was quick to deny it. "It is meaningless. I have it and have seen many others carry it, others with no telesā gifts whatsoever. I hope you have not spoken to Daniel of my telesā history? You have not disrespected my wishes for privacy about this matter?" Her voice was sharp, ready to bite.

"No. I haven't. I was just curious that's all. Because Nafanua said it was a mark that my twin brother had. No other reason." I decided not to push the Daniel subject anymore and instead switched to Salamasina's past. "Is your mother – Tavake – still alive?"

"Of course." And then as if regretting her divulging of information, Salamasina frowned. "But enough about me. That is all in the past. We are talking about you. You and this infatuation you have with my son. How dangerous it can be for him. You are a telesā without a Covenant and that is an oddity. You are the only one of your kind and so there is nowhere that you truly belong. No sisterhood who can truly bind you as one of their own. Even though Nafanua welcomed you into the telesā matagi sisterhood, you were never one of them. It was a symbolic ceremony only because your gift could not be unified with theirs. Ocean can only covenant with ocean. Air with air. And fire with fire. For any telesā to unite all three gifts is something only spoken of in legend. As the only one of your kind, you will always walk alone. You will be a natural target for other Covenants, other telesā who might see you as a threat to their territory. Without a fanua afi sisterhood to stand by your side, you will always be hunted."

I slumped back in my seat. Dejected, but unsure why. I liked being a loner, didn't I? Who needed girlfriends? Especially ones who turned on you in a heartbeat and sucked the life force out of you. "Salamasina, why am I the only one? Nafanua said she had never known another telesā fanua afi in her lifetime and her mother's before her. Why?"

"There are legends that explain it, but how much truth does a legend truly contain? What is certain is that there has not been a telesā like you for centuries. Even Tavake had never met a telesā fanua afi. A fire telesā was a legend among us. There are those who doubt their essential existence. Others believe that it was the first of the three gifts to be taken away by our Mother Earth and it will only be a matter of time before the remaining gifts die out as well. It has become increasingly rare for gifted daughters to be born. Even to the strongest of the telesā. Look at your mother – by all accounts you are the only one of her many daughters to be blessed with a Gift. And my own mother Tavake, with all her powers, was still disappointed with a child who had none. The last Gifted daughter born to Tavake is many years older than I, and even then, her powers are a mere shadow of our mother's. It is a troubling thing. Even though I despise many things about the telesā culture, it is heartbreaking to think that the telesā are a dying people."

There was so much sadness in her that it was impossible not to be caught by it. Feel it "Why?"

"Because it further confirms that our Earth is sick. Dying. The respect we used to have for our traditions was closely entwined with our sacred respect for our land, our ocean, our air. All that gives us life. As we forsake our spiritual connection with the land, so too does the earth forsake us. If telesā are earth's guardians, then it is of great seriousness that telesā are increasingly few and far between."

Salamasina shook herself. "Why am I telling you these things? Leila, I know it must be lonely to be fanua afi and to be the only one. You have no parents. No family. You have never belonged anywhere. I can understand why your attraction to my Daniel would be so strong. Why it would seem so consuming. Why you would be so afraid of letting it go."

Anger prickled and burrowed inside me. "Excuse me, Salamasina, let me see if I'm hearing you right. You're saying that the only reason I love Daniel is because I'm lonely? Because I'm a loner fire telesā with no family, no sisterhood, no friends?"

A stare was her only answer. Salamasina and I were at an impasse. A chasm of difference that rested upon Daniel and the love we shared. I'd had enough bonding and soul-sharing conversation with this woman. If we bonded any more then I was going to set fire to her kitchen. *Fa'aaloalo, Leila. Respect.*

I gave her a tight smile. "Right. I think I'm going to leave now. Thank you for the juice. I appreciate the chance to have this little chat with you. I understand a lot more now that I didn't before." Like the fact that you think I'm a loser. A selfish child. And if I didn't dislike you before, I sure do now.

"I too, am glad we had this talk. I hope you will consider my words carefully. And weigh up how much does Daniel truly mean to you?"

I walked to the door trying not to snarl. Or flame. But Salamasina wasn't finished. "Leila, it will be difficult for Sarona to carry out any of her plans. She is alone, without a Covenant, and so her power will be weakened. She will need to seek out other telesā matagi and have them join her before she can hope to be a threat of any kind. And there are very few of them left. In the meantime, perhaps you should consider leaving Samoa. Go back to America. I am not without my own weapons and devices, you know. I can protect Daniel. And if needs be, there are those I can call on to take us away from here, to safeguard us against Sarona and whatever she might have planned against him. I may not have given birth to Daniel, but I am his mother. And that is what a mother does. She gives her life for her child. I will do everything to protect my son. Even if I must protect him against you."

Salamasina wasn't pulling any punches today and there were no doubts where she stood in this particular fight.

I went home and helped Matile cook dinner. I tried to lose myself in grating crisp green ambarella for the rich dessert of valu vi–fruit soaked in sweetened coconut cream – but I kept thinking about everything that Salamasina had revealed about my mother. Would I ever be able to reconcile all the different pieces of her? So caught up in my thoughts, I scraped too hard and cut myself on the sharp edge of the grater. I winced. Red stained the white mound of tangy fruit gratings.

Matile exclaimed, "Auoi! Leila,ma'imau. What a waste. Now you have to start over again. Get a new bowl. And pay attention to what you are doing."

Aunty was right. I needed to stay focused. I couldn't get lost in Nafanua's past when my present could up and zap me with lightning at any moment. *Get a grip. Focus.*If I couldn't keep my eye on Daniel today, then at least I could stay close to my aunt and uncle. Until Sarona made her first move.

I didn't need to wait very long. I was drying the last of the dinner dishes when Thompson called my phone. Nafanua's home at Aleisa was on fire. Come quick.

I went, giving Aunty Matile some jumbled story about the lawyer needing me to open my mother's house, declining Uncle Tuala's offer to accompany me. I knew who was behind the house fire and I didn't want anyone else in Sarona's line of sight. I drove fast up to Aleisa. The familiar driveway loomed ahead of me and at its distant end a red hue lit the sky. I slowed the Jeep to a crawl and shivered in the steaming humidity. The last time I had visited this house, my mother and her sisters had threatened my life and the lives of all those I loved. Nafanua had offered me the bargain that had no choices. *Join us or everyone you love will die.* Remembering that day, the way Daniel had rushed to my side after Sarona had blasted me out into the yard with a rush of storm wind, how close we had come to death. I wished I hadn't come. This was a place reeking of painful memories.

I parked beside several emergency vehicles and slowly got out of the truck. The unrestrained fury of the blaze stunned me. My mother's house was burning amidst an unruly dance of overgrown green wilderness. The skeleton of its structural frame was already apparent in the orange-red chaos. Firefighters were pumping thick hoses of water into its center but it was a useless fight and I wished they would give up already.

I knew I could still the flames, speak to the energy that raged and calm it. Convert it to earth's potential energy storage. But what use would that be? Would it bring back Nafanua's house? Would it return my mother to me? The woman I had wanted her to be? The telesā who had paused in her lightning battle against her sisters to say, *Leila, I may not have loved your father, but always remember, I loved you.*

And that's when it hit me. As I stood and watched my mother's house burn to the ground. The permanence. The finality of it. My mother was dead. And in spite of all her failings and craziness, I loved her. I missed her. I sank to my knees amidst the wet greenness of the gardenia bushes and wept. Salamasina's earlier words about being alone – being a telesā without a Covenant – resounded in my soul. For the first time since that day by the ocean-side, I mourned for my mother. I cried for the years we never had. I cried because I knew that if she had lived, we would still be on opposite sides of the telesā divide.

Because sometimes, even love is not enough to hold two people together.

The white perfume of gardenia flowers was a gentle embrace in the night. There was a loud crackling roar as the last of the central beams of the burning house gave way, crashing to the ground in an explosion of jittery sparks. I looked up, and that's when I saw her.

Sarona. Standing across from me on the opposite side of the blaze, staring at me. Smiling at my tears. Unnoticed by anyone else in the bustle of firefighting. She waved at me once before turning to snap her fingers. A whip wire of lightning seared the heavens, striking the fire truck nearest to me. It exploded, sending charred steel and wire debris flying in every direction. People screamed and ducked for cover. The force of the explosion was a wave of heat that hit me, had me tumbling backwards, shielding my face, rolling on the ground for several feet before coming to a breathless halt back beside my Jeep. It hurt. But not as much as my pride. I had let her see me vulnerable. I picked myself up, searching for the woman in green.

She was gone.

Score? One for Sarona. Zero for Leila.

And Daniel still hadn't called me. This day officially sucked.

FIVE

Salamasina

One of the most disconcerting things about being the Ungifted daughter of a telesā is having your mother grow old – and remain ageless. While an increasingly grey-haired and weathered face greets you in the mirror. As a taulasea, natural healer, Salamasina well knew all of the concoctions and ointments the telesā drank to help retain their youthful looks and yes, there were years long ago when she too had brewed them for herself. For vanity's sake. But there is an ingredient for true telesā youth that could not be sourced anywhere. Power. Fanua ola. The life force of our mother earth.

Which is why, when Salamasina answered the light knock on her door that day after Leila's visit, and saw the woman who stood there, it was like seeing a ghost from her past. A face unmarked by time. The face of her mother.

"Tavake!" Salamasina gasped and stumbled backwards.

The woman was impatient. "Aren't you going to invite me in?"

Salamasina didn't want her mother in her house. She didn't want her anywhere near her. Or Daniel. But what choice did she have? She tried to smile. Waved the visitor in. "Of course. Please, come inside. This is unexpected."

Tavake followed the younger woman into the front room. She walked with a limp and carried the ornately carved cane that her daughter had never seen her go without. Salamasina was painfully aware of the photographs that lined the shelves. Daniel, a toddler with a cheeky grin, digging in the sand. A little boy holding a rugby ball, standing next to Tanielu. Daniel and Tanielu in front of the workshop sign, both in overalls, laughing at the camera. At a sports prize-giving dinner, the whole family beaming proudly as Daniel held his trophy high. Tavake studied them all for a few minutes before she spoke. "He is a handsome young man. He has given you much joy?"

It was an odd way to start a conversation with a woman you hadn't seen for nearly twenty years.

"Yes, he has." As a polite after-thought. "Thank you."

"You have kept him well concealed from telesā. That is good."

Inside, Salamasina winced. Daniel was in love with a telesā fanua afi. The first one in living history. Somehow, she didn't think that counted as keeping him well hidden. "Yes, he has become a fine young man any mother would be proud of. And he knows nothing of his telesā ancestry. As we agreed."

"You mean, as you covenanted. A child's life for a mere promise. I think you got yourself a good deal there." Tavake turned away from her study of family photographs to frown at Salamasina's rumpled appearance. The man's shirt splattered with some unrecognizable concoction she had been working on that morning. The baggy long pants frayed and stained with mud from time in the garden. Her voice was exasperated. "You know all the earth's answers for staying young. And beautiful. At least for a time. Even for an Ungifted one. Why do you not use them? Look at you. You look so old."

Salamasina couldn't stop the laughter. "I look old, because I am old. I have walked this earth for sixty years and I'm proud of it."

A grimace from the other woman. "Does it not seem foolish to hold the answers to longevity in your own backyard and yet not use them? How does anyone trust a taulasea who cannot even keep herself youthful?"

"I have learned that there is more to life than eternal youth. And beauty that never fades."

Tavake arched a perfect eyebrow at her daughter. "Is that right? I suppose that husband of yours was your teacher. He is dead, is he not?" A muttered aside, "That was some lesson then, wasn't it? It would seem to me that eternal youth and beauty would be far preferable to endless heartbreak."

Salamasina chose not to react to the gibe. "Yes. Three years ago. Heart problems."

"You could not heal him?"

"No. Tanielu had contracted rheumatic fever as a child and the damage it left to his heart was extensive. I prolonged his life for as long as I could. Letting him go was the hardest thing I've ever done."

Tavake looked ill at ease. "I'm sorry for your loss. I can't say I understand your pain, but I'm sure it was very … difficult."

Salamasina wasn't used to compassion from the woman who had given birth to her. It was rather unsettling to see it now. "I have my son. We have each other. We are fine." She rushed to change the subject. She didn't want Tavake dwelling on Daniel. She didn't want this woman lingering here for a minute longer than was necessary. "Why are you here?"

Tavake looked relieved to be off the topic of dead husbands. Back to more meaningful subjects. "Nafanua is dead and there is a power vacuum here. What happened to her Sisterhood?"

"From what I hear, they turned against her. Her second – Sarona – cast the death strike."

"But how was that possible? What of their Covenant?"

"Nafanua chose her daughter over the Sisterhood and broke the Covenant to protect her."

Tavake's indrawn breath was a whiplash of shock. Nothing is more sacred to telesā than their Covenants, and for a Keeper to break her vow with her sisters was unheard of. More than that, it was sacrilegious. "Why? Why would she do that?"

"For reasons you would never understand." Recrimination hung in the air between them. Bitterness pooling like the ooze of breadfruit sap.

Tavake ignored the undertones and asked another question. "What of the others in Nafanua's Covenant? Have they taken vows with Sarona?"

"They've disappeared. Evaporated into thin air. I suspect Sarona invoked the right of Covenant, siphoned their power and eliminated them. So much for sisterhood. But you would know all about that."

"I did not come here to fight with you, Salamasina. I came here for information. And to warn you. And your son."

"Warn me of what?"

"Sarona has been spending time in my territory. And I think she is recruiting ocean telesā."

"But she is telesā matagi. Of what use are vasa loloa to her? She cannot Covenant with them so how can their gifts strengthen hers?"

Tavake ignored her interruption. "A truce of sorts existed between Nafanua and I. We had an understanding of territory and responsibility. She did not trespass on my authority, nor I on hers. We worked together on various endeavors over the years and helped each other seek out new sisters. When I found a Tongan telesā matagi, I would send her here to Nafanua. And whenever Nafanua came across a telesā vasa loloa, she would return the favor. For example, your son's mother, Moanasina. As you well know, she was Samoan and once her gifts came to light, Nafanua sent her to me for training. Which was very generous of her because Moanasina was unusually powerful. Even at the young age of only six years her power nearly equaled my own. I'm surprised Nafanua didn't just take a knife to her throat. You understand enough about telesā to know that the stronger the members of a Keeper's Covenant are, the more powerful she becomes. In these modern times, it has become increasingly difficult to find gifted young women. Our Mother Earth wearies of sharing her power with us and so many of our daughters are born Ungifted."

"Like me."

"Yes, like you. Nafanua knew that by sending Moanasina to me, I would then be able to add her power to mine within our Covenant. A massive boost for me. And one I sorely needed. Nafanua was an ally. I am not happy about her death. And I'm even more disturbed about Sarona's activities in Tonga."

"What exactly is she doing?"

"I'm not sure." Frustration. "She has attached herself to a science team from America that is carrying out exploratory expeditions in the Trench. The official story is that they are studying geological deposits but we know what they are really looking for. The RTG."

"The what?"

"The radioisotope thermoelectric generator that lies deep in the Tonga Trench. In 1970, America launched Apollo 13, the seventh manned mission in the Apollo space program and the third intended to land on the moon. Something went wrong with the mission and the lunar landing was aborted. The power source for Apollo 13 re-entered the atmosphere over the Pacific Ocean and ended up deep in the Trench. The RTG contains plutonium."

Salamasina paled at this news. "There's plutonium in our waters? Why wasn't it recovered and removed? Why was this allowed? How can it be acceptable for America to dump plutonium in our ocean?"

"It's a non-weapons grade isotope, Pu-238 that provided power for space shuttles through natural radioactive decay rather than through fission or fusion processes. So it's relatively safe." A grimace. "As safe as plutonium can ever be anyway. Not only that, the actual plutonium is encased in graphite and iridium, which has been doing a good job of keeping it contained. We vasa loloa have been keeping a check on the RTG and the surrounding marine life and so far, we don't think there has been any significant leakage. Of course we would prefer that the Americans remove such a dangerous thing from our ocean but they don't know exactly where it is in the Trench. And even if they did, it was always too deep for them to recover. Too expensive. Typical of them. I'm sure if they had plutonium sitting in their back yard, no expense would have been spared to remove it. We could have tried to remove it ourselves but there are limits to the reach of our Gifts and if we did recover it, what would we do with it? Where could we safely dispose of it? If we brought the RTG up to the surface, I would never hand it over to the Americans. They would only re-use it. So, the RTG has been left to rest in our Trench for more than forty years. Until now. Until this privately funded team showed up with their fancy equipment. And Sarona is with them."

"Why?"

"I believe she is searching for the Covenant Bone."

Salamasina scoffed. "The Covenant Bone is a legend, a foolish myth."

"If you were as old as I am, you would know that all legend is founded on truth. The Covenant Bone is real. Very real."

"Even if it were real, the purpose of the Bone was to unite all telesā in a common Covenant. Somehow, I can't reconcile what I know of Sarona with that purpose."

Tavake nodded. "Yes, that was the original purpose of the Bone, but in the hands of the wrong telesā, it becomes a weapon. Ancient telesā history tells of the Dark Time when the Bone was wielded as a weapon against telesā themselves, with devastating consequences. So many deaths. So much suffering. People and telesā alike lived in fear of the Bone Bearer. And when the Dark Time was ended, the Bone was separated by ocean, fire, and air into three distinct pieces and there were compelling reasons why. If the pieces are found and restored, then no telesā is safe. Not even the strongest of us."

Her words trailed away and in a sudden flash of clarity, Salamasina realized, *She's afraid. My mother, the Covenant Keeper is actually afraid.* This realization, more than anything else about Tavake's visit, was an ice lance of fear to her heart. If the most powerful telesā vasa loloa was afraid, then what hope was there for anyone else?

"I don't understand. You said you had come to warn me. What does this have to do with me? Or Daniel?"

"Your son is Gifted, possibly as much as his mother was."

Salamasina stood, her chair grating harshly against the cement floor. "No, he isn't. I have been watching him closely and there has been nothing. No signs of vasa loloa at all. He doesn't even like spending time in the ocean. He goes out of his way to avoid it."

Tavake looked impatient. "Don't be a fool. No daughter of mine, not even an Ungifted one is a fool. Refusing to accept something will not make it disappear. No matter how hard you wish it away. I only had to see your son once as a child to know that the voice of vasa loloa spoke with strength and power in him. Perhaps his Gift has not encountered the catalyst it needs to unleash. But when it does manifest, his Gift will make him a target for people in search of power. And Sarona is a telesā in search of power."

Still, Salamasina tried to dissent. "Daniel will be twenty years old soon, I highly doubt his Gift is going to show up now. He even had a pe'a tattoo earlier this year, against my wishes I might add, and even that has not triggered any vasa loloa powers. Sarona knows nothing of his birthright and even if she did, his power can only be taken if he belongs to a vasa loloa Covenant. And he's clearly not getting any invitations to join any Sisterhoods."

Tavake shook her head. "No, that's where you're wrong. If Sarona finds all three pieces of the Covenant Bone then she can take the

Gifts of any telesā, whether they be Air, Water, or Earth. Such is its power. Legend tells that one Bone piece was placed for safekeeping deep in the Tonga Trench. I believe that Sarona is using the RTG recovery team to also search for that one piece. My sources tell me that she has recruited two telesā matagi already. And two of my vasa loloa."

"I find that difficult to believe. I've seen your Gift in action and no telesā would dare to oppose you, their Covenant Keeper."

"There are always those able to be lured by the promise of great power." Tavake's curled lip was an expression of derision. "Especially amongst the young and foolish who look at their elders as a far-off weak and distant generation. They think they can defeat me? They will be sorely disappointed for I am not without my own reserves."

An icy hand of realization clenched at Salamasina's heart. "You are not here because you care about me and my son, are you? You want the power that you think he might have. You want my son."

Tavake did not deny it. "If not for me, you would have no son. He would have been put to death at birth according to telesā law. I allowed you to have him, against my better judgment, I might add. And now, it seems that decision is going to pay its dividends."

Salamasina's eyes blazed with a fierce intensity. "I will not let you harm my son. I will die first."

"I do not want to take his life, you foolish child. When the time is right, I will merely offer him the chance to covenant his gift to me."

"You expect me to believe that? Men are forbidden to have telesā power. You would never allow a man to covenant with you."

"You know nothing. There have been no new vasa loloa in Tonga or here in Samoa in all the years since you left Niuatoputapu. Do you know how many sisters I have left in my Covenant that are loyal to me? Four. Against Sarona and her gathering of five thus far. She is searching for still more to recruit. I do not like those numbers. Desperate times call for desperate measures and I am more than willing to covenant with a boy if I must. I will do whatever it takes to stop Sarona. Mark my words well, if she succeeds in whatever plans she has made for acquiring the Covenant Bone, then none of us will be safe. Not you. Or your son." Tavake was stern in the quiet house. "There is a war coming and wise leaders gather their forces in preparation. Make sure you are on the right side when the time comes. As soon as your son's Gift manifests, you will send him to me." She paused abruptly. "No, that was not said correctly. I'm asking you to please consider allowing your son to join my Covenant."

Salamasina's jaw gaped. Tavake had never asked her for anything. But then, Salamasina had never had anything that Tavake needed. "Are you asking me because I'm your daughter?"

"No. I'm asking you because you know what telesā are capable of. I'm asking you because for twelve years you lived and walked among us, you know what our purpose is, why we were born with earth's Gifts. We are protectors, guardians of our mother earth. Sarona only seeks power and control over her sisters in all their forms. I'm asking you to do this because you know it's the right thing to do."

Tavake walked with her stilted gait to the door and then paused, "This daughter of Nafanua, is she still in Samoa? Is she Gifted?"

The room was painfully quiet as Salamasina struggled with the truth. But Leila's secret was not hers to share. "She is a student at National University this year with my son. And no, she is not telesā matagi."

Tavake's disappointment was heavy in the air. "A pity. We vasa loloa are limited by our need for a proximity to water before we can draw on our Gifts. It would have been useful to have an ally who could face Sarona on her own territory."

Dread in Salamasina was clammy, cold, and slimy. Like fisting a sea cucumber in your bare hands. And watching the stranded innards spurt through your fingers. What would happen if Tavake found out Leila was fanua afi? What would she do if she ever knew that Salamasina had lied to her?

SIX

Leila

Thanks to my late night, I didn't wake up until past ten the morning after the house fire. Matile and Tuala had long left the house for work and I was alone when the phone rang. *Daniel?*

No. "Is this Leila Folger?" a strange woman asked. I sagged in my seat. Disappointment tasted like over-ripe papaya. *Bleugh.*

It was the Director of the Women's Center, the one that Thompson had warned me would be calling. She was very glad that I was back in the country. They had been waiting for me so they could discuss some urgent project they had put on hold. Could I please come in today to see her, very urgent, blah, blah, blah.

No, I can't come see you today because there's a vengeful telesā who wants to kill me and she's already burned down my dead mother's house. And my boyfriend's mother wants us to break up and she's willing to take me out if necessary. Oh and yeah, did I mention that my boyfriend can talk to sharks? And he hasn't called me. Maybe he's really busy off talking to marine life.

Those are all the things I wanted to say. But I didn't. Because didn't want another person accusing me of being selfish. *Everything's not about you, Leila.* So yeah, I told the Director I would be there. Right away.

How can you be too busy to help a Women's Refuge Center, right?

"Leila Folger?" A woman in a flowery dress came forward from behind a desk to greet me. "I'm Folole. Thank you for making the time to come and see our Center. The Director is teaching a class right now but she asked me to take you to her as soon as you arrived. We know you have a busy schedule. Please, come with me."

I walked with Folole as she made her way down a corridor and out a glass door into a courtyard. I had always imagined women's refuges to be gloomy places, peopled by depressed, frightened women but so far I was met by only the opposite. The courtyard was a haven of light and color, and the telesā in me took extra delight in the carefully tended collection of ferns, orchids, and hibiscus bushes. Children played on a swing set at the far end and the sound of their laughter followed us.We came to the open door of a classroom where a short, plump woman stood addressing a class of about a dozen teenagers who all turned curious eyes at our entrance.

"Mrs. Amani, Leila Folger is here to see you."

A huge smile greeted me. "Ahh, thank you for coming to see me." She turned to the students. "Class, this is Miss Folger, the new owner of the Center. This is her first time visiting us. Please make her feel welcome."

The students all chimed in with a perfunctory greeting. "Good morning Miss Folger." I was conscious of a sea of smiling warm faces, studying me from head to toe. All except for one young woman sitting in the back row who only glared at me and then resumed staring out the window. She looked to be about thirteen or fourteen. Thick, wiry brown hair barely restrained in a braid, with matching thick brows – and a sulky frown was the cherry on top. The brooding attitude looked vaguely familiar. Before I could try to place it though, Mrs. Amani was gesturing me to join her in the corridor.

"Come Leila, let's find somewhere private to talk. Folole will supervise the class for me." She gave the students a stern parting warning. "Everyone behave or Wednesday night ice cream will be cancelled!"

The students pretended to groan and Mrs. Amani laughed as we left the room. "We have ice cream once a week. Even us old ones look forward to the treat."

We walked down the open corridor, passing more classrooms with more students at work, this time adults. All female. All varying ages.

Noting my gaze, Mrs. Amani explained. "We run workshops for our women, to help them up-skill. Sometimes it's not safe for their children to attend regular school for a while, which is why we offer them classes following the basic national curriculum. It's more a way to stop them from getting bored. It can be stifling for them to be stuck in the Center, especially for the teenagers."

She proceeded to give me a lightning-quick tour of the Center, explaining a hundred and one details in a few minutes. By the time we came to her crowded little office, I felt like I was a walking talking expert on the Samoa Women's Refuge Center. Headache imminent. "Have a seat please. Excuse the mess. I'm always drowning in police and medical reports in this place. I was surprised to hear that Nafanua had named her daughter as the trustee and controlling Principal for the Center. None of us even knew that she had a daughter. But then, there's a lot about Nafanua that we weren't party to. I am very sorry for your loss, Leila. And to have all your mother's sisters go missing at the same time, it must be very traumatic for you."

She gave me an impenetrable look and in that instant, it hit me. This woman knew Nafanua and her sisters were not ordinary women. And she was trying to suss out whether I was like them.

"I've called you because we're having issues with security here at the Center. As I'm sure you can imagine, it's difficult to keep the Refuge location a secret in such a small island community. Ideally, women and their children could stay here and know that their partners can't hunt them down, but that's impossible here in Samoa. The next best thing that we can offer them is peace of mind, the security of knowing that they are safe here. Since your mother's death, we have had a wave of break-ins and assault incidents at the Center. We've always had to deal with angry partners looking for their wives, demanding their children, but a warning from our security guard and we never heard from them again. Not anymore. I'm not one to beat around the bush, Miss Folger. Your mother and her sisters had particular talents. These talents meant they had an impressive reputation in this country, even if it was only ever whispered about. People were afraid of them and knew better than to cross them. This worked very well for our Center. Violent partners never troubled the women who took refuge here. And the few who did? They were always taken care of. An accident here. An illness there."

Her matter-of-fact statement about the Sisterhood's violence shocked me. "Are you saying that Nafanua and her sisters would harm people – and you were okay with that?"

Steel had replaced the smiley friendliness on Mrs. Amani's countenance. "I'm saying that your mother and her sisters ensured the safety of the countless battered women who seek refuge here. If you had seen the pain and suffering our residents have endured, you would not be so quick to condemn Nafanua's actions." She took a heavy folder out of the filing cabinet behind her. "This is our paperwork on all the incidents we have had in the last two months. Everything ranging from graffiti and vandalism of the premises to threats, rocks through the windows, and the most recent – a knife attack on one of our frequent residents. A woman with a long history of domestic abuse. She's in critical condition at the hospital." She opened a file of photographs and I flinched instinctively at the array of pain displayed there.

Photographs of women with purple bruises, black eyes, stitches. Women in casts and bandages. Misery and hurt.

Suddenly, a boyfriend who hadn't called when he said he would didn't rank very high on the list of what's truly important. It hit me then, that in spite of all its greenery and cheerfully painted classrooms, the Center was a place where misery came for help. "Have you reported these to the police?"

A brisk nod. "Of course. That's where most of this paperwork comes from. Witness interviews, medical reports, accounts from the repainting, and repairs for the vandalism. But the police have always been less helpful than they could be. I cannot even begin to count how many times I have taken a woman to report an assault and had the receiving officer ask, 'Is that it? Is that your only injury? Are you sure you want to go to all the trouble of making a report for just that?" Mrs. Amani shook her head wryly. "No, the police have not been very helpful. Which is why I asked to meet with you. I would like you to approve a security detail expense in our annual operating budget. We currently have two night watchmen who are on rotating shifts, but they are elderly gentlemen who are more a fixture than a real security presence. We need a 24-hour security team of at least four guards, all of whom are able and confident to take on any threats to our residents and property. What do you think?"

"Of course I'll approve that. I don't know how to access Nafanua's funds," a wince, "because I was sort of busy when the lawyer Mr. Thompson was going over the details of stuff with me but I can get in touch with him now and clear the money."

"The money can wait, I just needed to get your approval before going ahead and contracting the security company. This won't be cheap. The annual cost is going to blow our original budget."

I waved away the warning. "Whatever it takes is fine."

We spent the next half hour going over other Center details and the time flew. Folole interrupting us with an offer of afternoon tea, startled me. Had it really been that long?

I declined food and Mrs. Amani walked me back to my car. The courtyard was filled with activity this time round. Children playing and laughing. Women of all ages feeding their babies and sitting in the shade talking and relaxing. I turned to the woman walking beside me. "There's a nice feeling here. Kind of like a closeness, a community. I like it."

Mrs. Amani beamed proudly. "Yes, we try. Our residents have been through a lot of traumatic things and for many the nightmare is far from over, but we are a family here. This is a respite. A sanctuary. Even if only for a short while. Even if …" The shadow of a frown flitted across her face.

"Even if what?"

A shrug. "Even if most of these women end up back in their violent relationships again. We try to give them the tools they need to break free from their dependent destructive cycle but they come, they stay for a while and then they go." She stopped at the gate. "And then they come back again. And we get them the medical help they need and start all over again. Until the next time. And the ones who suffer the most?" She pointed to the knot of youngsters on the swing set. "The children."

I looked, but my attention was caught by the young girl sitting at a wooden slat bench by herself. She had her iPod earphones on and she was scowling at everyone and anyone. It was the teenager from Mrs. Amani's class earlier. I nodded at her. "Who is that?"

Mrs. Amani followed my gaze and her eyes softened. "That's Teuila. Her mother is Siela, the woman who was knifed."

"Oh." I didn't know what to do with that information. "Doesn't she have any other family?"

"Siela is a sex worker – even though prostitution supposedly doesn't exist in Samoa, ha. The extended family shuns them because of it and so when things like this happen, they're on their own. Siela and Teuila are in and out of the Center a lot. This attack was the worst so far though. Her mother's boyfriend has been charged with assault but if history is anything to go by, Siela will probably withdraw her testimony. I suspect the boyfriend has been abusing Teuila as well but, so far, she's not saying anything to the counselor." Mrs. Amani shrugged dejectedly. "We see this a lot. The mother will forbid the child to speak to anyone about what's going on at home and threatens them badly enough that they will never call the police – even if their mother is getting beaten to death. Siela's neighbors called the police and the only reason they were able to arrest the boyfriend is because he was injured himself and still at the scene."

As if she knew we were talking about her, Teuila looked over in our direction. The anger in her eyes as she glared at us was a thick, malevolent thing. Mrs. Amani sighed. "Teuila has a lot of anger and very little outlet for it. But can you blame her for hating the world? She's been dealt a rough deal. All we can do is try to earn her trust. I wish there was some way we could protect her better though. Once Siela is recovered, she will take Teuila with her and she will be forced to endure the same thing all over again."

It wasn't until I was in my Jeep driving away that I realized who Teuila reminded me of. The sullen face and attitude?

Me. A year ago.

My morning at the Center had made an unexpected impact on me. I went to register for the school year at National University. Alone. Simone wouldn't be back from his New Zealand holiday until the weekend but I consulted with him via Twitter to co-ordinate my courses with his so that we would have at least a few classes together. All the while though, my thoughts were still back at the Center. While I stood in lines, filled in forms, and skimmed through my course schedule, I kept thinking about the children playing in the sandpit with carefree abandon. The women in the classrooms. I had to admit, that no matter what crimes my mother had committed in her long life – there were some things she had done right. And they were things I wanted to do as well. Unbidden, Salamasina's condemning words, *So you are your mother's daughter, after all.* In this one thing at least, I could be proud to answer yes. But how? What could I do to help?

It wasn't until my registration papers had been processed and my timetable printed that I realized how I could try and help girls like Teuila. I could set up a few basic self-defense courses and maybe even some martial arts classes at the Center. My Dad had sent me to muay thai through most of my childhood because I'd always had an 'anger management problem' and my favorite part about it had been the chance it gave me to beat the heck out of a kick bag three times a week. I never got very good at muay thai, but I always felt better after a workout session. At best, martial arts could give the girls at the Center some self-defense tips and some added confidence. At the very least, they could get a workout and feel marginally better about the crap life had handed them. Operation Kick-Butt was now commencing.

My step lightened and I was smiling as I accelerated the Wrangler out the imposing university gates. There's no way I could teach the classes but I was sure I could find people in Samoa who could. If there was one thing I had learned from growing up with rich people? It was that money could make things happen. And lots of money could make seemingly impossible things happen.

I did some online research. Made some phone calls. Googled a few things. Cleared my plan with Mrs. Amani. Made a few appointments with key people I would need to hire for the plan to work. Went to several sports equipment suppliers and spent up big, wielding my Visa card with purposeful frenzy. Sending silent prayers of thanks for Thomas' insistence on expanding my line of credit to what had seemed frightening proportions. I arranged for the gear to be delivered to the Center and then stopped at two different gymnasiums to scope things out before I headed home.

I'd had a productive day and I was a good kind of tired when I turned into Matile's driveway. Right after me, Daniel's green bomb drove in. It was piled high with welding gear and Okesene was driving but it was definitely Daniel. In blue overalls and a baseball cap.

Finally. Tension eased. Sweet relief. He was back. He was alright. So what if he hadn't called me? So what if he didn't want to talk about his conversation with a shark. Or the returning from the ocean grave thing. So what? I had spent the day with people who had real problems. I was blessed to have a gift like Daniel in my life. I slipped out from behind the wheel and ran over to the truck, suffocating him in a hug. His overalls were unzipped to the waist in the humidity of the fast-approaching evening. He smelled of acetylene. Smoke. Steely sweat.

"You're back."

He gently loosened my arms from around his neck so he could smile down at me. A tired but happy grin. "Yeah, and I'm dirty, sorry. We're on our way home from the wharf and I asked Okesene if we could just swing in here for a minute. I forgot my phone at home so I couldn't call you, and the job was a lot more complex than I thought it would be. We had to overnight in Salelaloga."

"I was worried. I thought you were mad at me."

Confusion colored his face. "Why?"

"Because of our discussion the other night. Because I kept bugging you about stuff you didn't want to talk about. And when you didn't call me, I thought you were angry at me."

He shook his head at me ruefully. "Leila, of course I'm not mad at you. I said I didn't want to think about that stuff and that was it. I haven't thought about it again. I didn't know you still would be."

I winced. What did they say about guys and their ability to think about 'nothing.' And their gift for wiping their minds clean of unpleasant conversations when they were done having them? I thought back over the last forty-eight hours and all my obsessing over Daniel and his state of mind. *Good one, Leila.* He was telling me about the intricacies of the welding job in Savaii, explaining why they had to work another day there when I interrupted it all with a kiss, pulling his face down to meet mine. I didn't care about the details. He was back. He wasn't mad at me. I could have kissed him forever but I could sense his discomfort, what with Okesene in the truck.

He pulled back gently, "Hey, I gotta go. Okesene needs to get home and I have to go to paddling club training. I just wanted to stop by and let you know why I hadn't been in touch."

I remembered all his emails about his latest sporting obsession, outrigger canoeing. "So when do I get to check out your paddling club?"His tired face lightened into a grin. "You're in luck. In a few weeks there's a big Pacific regatta. Lots of races with lots of different paddling clubs that are coming from all over. It's going to be big. There are clubs invited from New Zealand, Australia, Tahiti, Hawaii, Rarotonga, and American Samoa. Can you come watch? I'm just a novice so I'll probably come last in all my races. I'll need lots of encouragement and hot cheerleader support."

"Of course I'll come cheer for you. I'll try to be hot but it's difficult for me, you know?" I gave him a wide-eyed innocent gaze.

He just rolled his eyes at me. "Whatever!" A laugh and a quick kiss before he turned to leave. Back in his truck, he paused to ask a question before starting the engine. "So did anything interesting happen while I was away?"

I thought about the meeting at the lawyer's office. The confrontation with Sarona. Her arson attack on Nafanua's house. The tense conversation with Salamasina. My visit to the Women's Center. The plans I was already putting into action. Things that could be potentially dangerous for anyone who wasn't a fire goddess. I would definitely warn him about Sarona. Later. But he didn't need to know about the rest of it. "Oh, nothing much." I gave him as convincing a smile as I could muster. For a thug brown girl.

"Nothing much at all."

The next day was spent Sarona hunting. I wanted to find her before she found me. I drove back up to the Aleisa property. All my mother's sisters owned homes on the vast estate but each of the houses was boarded up and derelict. No Sarona there. I went to her law office in town but the glass-paneled building was empty and a 'FOR LEASE' sign glared at me. No Sarona there either. It was as if the woman had vanished from the island completely. I seethed with frustration. How do you fire blast a weather witch when you can't even find her?

The next two weeks flew by as I worked with Mrs. Amani on getting martial arts added to the Center program. I told Daniel about my mother's will and my new responsibilities but was deliberately vague about what I was doing every day at the Center. I think he thought I was giving English lessons or something equally helpful. And safe. I also told him about meeting Sarona, that she was dangerous and we both needed to be on guard. His reaction to the news that she was alive had been much more reserved than mine. A shrug. A pensive look. "I hope she stays out of my way. If I see her on the road when I'm in my truck, I'm going to have a hard time not running her over."

Overall though, Daniel seemed to be distracted. Distant even. There was something weighing heavily on his mind and he wasn't ready to share it with me. I didn't push though. Mindful of our argument the day of the shark attack, I gave him the thinking space he seemed to need. He was crazy busy with work, wanting to finish a project before the university year began. And of course, every evening he had training with the outrigger canoe club, preparing for the regatta. At the end of each day, he didn't have a lot of energy left over to push me for too many details about mine. So I conveniently left out certain things that I knew he wouldn't be happy about. Like the Center getting all its windows stoned by a drunken husband of one of the residents. Mrs. Amani calling me after waiting for police that never showed up. And my discreet use of a flame whip to take the idiot down after he had punched out the two security guards.

No, Daniel didn't need be bothered with inane stuff like that

He didn't know it, but I was stalking him. Making regular drive-by trips past the welding workshop, just checking there was nobody there who shouldn't be. Sneaking out at night when Matile and Tuala had gone to bed, so I could park at the end of Daniel's street. Watching. Waiting. Just in case. So caught up in steel work, he never noticed my Wrangler's slow drive past but I had caught Salamasina's eye several times. She had only shaken her head at me. I knew that she had not spoken to Daniel of my visit to the house. Or her warning to leave him alone. There seemed to be an uneasy truce between us. We both agreed that Daniel needed to be protected against Sarona and for now, we would each do our part. Even though we didn't like each other. Even though I was the reason Daniel needed protecting in the first place.

A new weekend came and with it came Simone. A-flush and a-flutter with stories, energy, and excitement about his holiday. "Girlfriend, it was a dream trip come true. You would not believe who I shared the same gym equipment with. Sonny Bill Williams, the New Zealand All Black rugby star. It's true. I was going to Les Mills gym with my cousins while I was over there and it was the same gym that Sonny goes to. I died. I just died. He was doing lateral raises right there!" He gesticulated wildly. "He was this close. I swear, some of his sweat droplets fell on me. Oh, I was in heaven. I can't wait until I go back to Auckland for school next year."

Simone wanted to study fashion design and had been to check out several programs of study while he was in Auckland. But his parents wanted him to be an accountant and he was at odds with them over his course choices for the year. "Why can't you do both?" I suggested. "Fashion designers need to know how to manage their money too, you know. Especially super successful ones who have their own design companies. Which will be you, of course."

He clapped his hands with glee. "Of course! Fabulous idea. I love it. Solves my inner dilemma and gets my parents off my back. Aren't you a clever girl."

Simone loved the idea of sharing an apartment with me and we resolved to start house hunting right away. Things were starting to fall into place. I could almost forget there was an angry telesā out there somewhere with my head on her hit list.

Matile invited Simone to come for dinner and he was thrilled with the chance to rifle through my wardrobe. A thrill that soon faded as he surveyed my khaki and cotton gear. A hand on his hip. "I thought you said you went clothes shopping in New York?"

I had to laugh at the look of disgust on his face as he held up a brown linen shift between two fingers, as if it were something a miserable cat had died on. "I did. My aunt Annette insisted on buying me all new clothes for the school year. They're just pleased that I'm going to university. They were worried I was going to be a bum. Or a rebel and marry my high school sweetheart and get a job at Walmart." I laughed at my own joke but Simone didn't think it was funny. He was too caught up in my new wardrobe from America.

"These have got to be the nastiest, ugliest clothes I have ever seen. Please don't tell me that you chose these bleak, colorless, shapeless sacks?"

I shrugged. "Annette did. But I don't mind them. They look fine to me. Comfortable and cool. Perfect for the humidity. And they're functional. See the khaki pants and cotton tops? I can go from school in those straight to helping Daniel at the welding workshop, not a problem. Just cover them up with overalls. They're timeless classics."

Simone's lip curled in distaste. "Classics are just another way of describing boring and old. If I was Daniel, I would set fire to your clothes on purpose. The only thing worth saving in this entire collection is this pair of shoes. Louboutins. I'm sooooo jealous." He slipped on the shoes and looked at himself in the mirror. "Daniel must love you for your mind. And the inner workings of your beautiful spirit. Because it's surely not because of what you do with your exterior."

My phone chose to beep right at that moment, sparing me from having to come up with a suitable reply. Simone rolled his eyes. "Oh, don't tell me that's Daniel now. Can't you two even have one night apart without any kissy-kissy love talk?"

I just poked my tongue at him and checked my phone, my face lighting up at the message display. "No, it's not Daniel. It's Jason."

Simone looked intrigued. In a scandalized way. "Ooooh, the hot blonde volcano man? Leila, I'm shocked. Get on with your bad self. Phone sexting two guys?"

"I am not phone sexting anybody." I busied myself with texting a reply. "Jason's a friend. That's all. He's in American Samoa but his team is coming back here next week. He wants to meet up. The Ministry of Natural Resources and Environment has requested their return because of the recent volcanic activity on the island. As a precaution." Because I summoned a mini-volcano to take out Sarona and her sisters. Because I had disrupted the natural seismic order of things. Those were things I couldn't say out loud. Even to Simone.

"Soooo, volcano man is coming back to see you then?"

"No, Jason is coming back to Samoa to work. To study volcano stuff. Stop making this more than it is."

Simone faked aggrieved innocence. "What? Who me? See dalashious wickedness where there is none? Never." He arched an eyebrow at me. "And what does the rugby god think about this thang you got going on with Jason?"

I had to laugh at Simone's code names. Even as I battled with unease at the thought of seeing Jason face to face. Soon there would be no more excuses for not telling him the truth. The whole truth and nothing but the truth. And then there was the slightly sticky issue of his love declaration. We would have to tackle that one head-on as well. "Daniel knows that Jason is not a 'thang'. Daniel knows that Jason is a friend. A very good friend. Daniel trusts me and my choice of friends." I narrowed my eyes at Simone. "I don't know why though because I'm friends with you and nobody is more wicked than you. If I was Daniel, I would be far more worried about his girlfriend hanging out with someone who keeps sending her pictures of half-naked guys on her phone."

"Nothing wrong with looking, Leila. Look but don't touch. You have to just touch with your eyes. I'm only helping you keep your options open. For when you get bored with the rugby god." He rolled his eyes. Again. "Who am I kidding? Who could ever get bored with such chiseled perfection?" He leapt across the bed, threw open the window, and struck a dramatic pose, calling out into the darkness, "Oh Daniel, wherefore art thou, Daniel?"

I chucked a pillow at him and in the ensuing laughter the Jason topic was forgotten. For now.

Nervous. Freaked out. Excited. Happy. Impatient. All those words pretty much described how I felt about seeing Jason again. It made sense though, right? I had spent two months avoiding the facts with my best friend. Too chicken to do it. Worried. What if Jason (rightfully) decided to hate me for it? What if he never wanted to speak to me again?

Just like I had been avoiding talking to Jason about the fact that, while on his death bed, he had told me (and a room full of his science team mates, nurses, and my boyfriend) that he was in love with me.

Leila, staring death in the face has that effect on a guy, you know? It makes you realize what's important, that we shouldn't waste a single moment. I love you.

And now here we were, Daniel and I. At the Amanaki Restaurant on the Apia ocean front, waiting to have lunch with Jason. He had spent three weeks in American Samoa doing volcano things and had gotten in the night before. I couldn't wait to see him. But it was freaking me out. Jason in person? Fully conscious? With Daniel by my side?

I was prepped for awkward. Tense. Possibly torturous.

What I wasn't prepared for was the woman that Jason walked into the restaurant with. Her hand in his. A petite young woman in skimpy shorts and a midriff-baring tank top that barely held her abundant curves in check. She was tiny. Even in platform heels she only came up to Jason's shoulder. Her bleached hair fell in shimmering waves to her waist and she tossed it over her shoulder artfully as she stumbled over the step, half-falling against Jason, who caught her easily in his arms. She giggled and gazed up at him. She looked like a brown Barbie doll.

I hated her instantly.

But I didn't have long to think about why because Jason had caught sight of us and that familiar heart-tugging grin was reassuring me that yes, it really was him. My surfing instructor, island tour guide, volcano expert, and self-appointed fire goddess scientist.

"Leila!"

The next minute, I was in his arms, closing my eyes against his warmth, the sun-kissed familiar scent of him. Into my hug I poured all the chaotic emotions that I had bottled up over the past weeks, trying to stifle the sour taste of guilt with the sweetness of relief and gratitude that he was okay. He drew back a little so he could smile into my eyes, kissing me lightly on the forehead. Almost at the exact same time we both exclaimed.

"I missed you."

The jinx had us both erupting into laughter and he pulled me into a fierce bear hug again. Over his shoulder I could see the Barbie doll. She didn't look happy. I was sorely tempted to make a face at her and grab Jason's butt. Just to irritate her further. But conscious of the quiet presence behind me, I ended the hug instead and stepped back to take Daniel's hand in mine.

"Jason, I'd like you to meet Daniel."

The two exchanged a quick handshake. If there was tension, I couldn't feel it. "We've actually met before, but I doubt you would remember. I was with Leila at the hospital when you were sick. You were pretty out of it."

Jason winced. "Ugh, that's one nightmare I'm still trying to forget. You know, the doctors back home still haven't been able to figure out exactly what was wrong with me? Or why I got better? All they can tell me is that I'm lucky to be alive."

My breath caught on the web of my deceit. I felt sick inside. Sensing the evaporation of my happy bubble, Daniel squeezed my hand. "It's great that you're okay. I know that Leila was worried about you. She was willing to give up everything, hoping that a cure would be found for you."

Daniel smiled at me and in his eyes I read his unspoken message. *It's not your fault. You have nothing to feel badly about here. You risked your life for him, Leila. Stop beating yourself up over this.* I smiled back at him. I love you Daniel. Can you read what my eyes, my heart, my every breath, my every fiber and particle is whispering to you?

Jason looped an arm over my shoulder for another quick hug. "I know you were there for me, Leila. Thank you."

Behind us a petulant voice asked, "Baby, aren't you going to introduce me?" The Barbie. Of course. How could we forget the Barbie?

Jason reached for her with a smile so enveloping that it stunned me. He looked utterly and completely possessed by her. I had seen that look somewhere before. Where?

"I'm sorry. This is Lesina Agiao." He held her close by his side, nestled within a protective embrace. "My fiancé."

I couldn't stop it. Shock ripped it from me. "Your what?!" Heads in the restaurant turned. Daniel nudged me warningly. *Cool it, Leila. Keep it together now ...*

Jason was oblivious to my horror. He had eyes only for the girl beside him. "Yes, I wanted to marry her right away, but Lesina insisted that we wait a while so she could meet my family and stuff like that."

"But when did you meet each other?" I glared at Jason. "I Skyped you before I flew out of D.C. and you never said anything about her." I was spluttering. "Why didn't you tell me then you had a girlfriend?"

Barbie answered me this time. With syrupy sweetness. "Jason and I met two weeks ago. I was visiting my family in American Samoa for the school break and volunteering at the National Parks and Reserves office when we met. And well, the rest just happened."

She stood on tip-toe so she could kiss Jason on the cheek and it made me want to vomit. "Two weeks? You hardly know each other. This is ridic …"

Daniel swiftly interrupted me. "Really awesome. Congratulations you two. Shall we order lunch? Jason, why don't you two go ahead? I just need to talk to Leila for a quick minute. If you'll excuse us?"

Without waiting for a reply, Daniel grabbed my hand and walked us away from the dining area and out onto the restaurant deck, out of sight of the other couple. He was incredulous. "What is wrong with you? I know you feel guilty that he nearly died because of your mom but do you think being rude to his girlfriend is going to make things better? Can't you see how into her he is?"

I winced, struggling to stay calm. "You're right. I'm sorry. It caught me off guard, that's all. He was like my best friend last year and it hurts that he wouldn't tell me about some girl he's crazy in love with."

The sentiment sounded artificial, even to me. I threw my hands up in despair. "What am I saying? He did so much to help me, but I've lied to him about what happened with the Sisterhood. I'm a crappy friend, the last person who should be getting mad when her best friend keeps secrets."

Daniel pulled me close, encircling me in his arms. "Come here." A kiss on my cheek, a whisper. "No, you're not a bad friend. You're a girl who gives everything for the people she cares about. I've seen it with my own eyes, so I'm a reliable witness."

"No, you're a biased witness." I wilted in his embrace, my head on his chest. Listening. Ah, there it was. Daniel's heartbeat. Strong, sure, steady. Constant. I smiled up at him. "I love that."

"What?"

"Your heartbeat. It always calms me. Steadies me."

A wry smile. "That's funny."

"Why?"

"Because having you near me doesn't calm me or soothe me at all. Quite the opposite." The deep timbre of his voice so close to my ear almost had a growl to it. A quick glance at his face confirmed it. He wasn't joking. His eyes glinted with an emerald intensity that sent ripples of fire into the pit of my stomach.

He bent and his mouth claimed mine with a fierce possession that surprised me. Daniel's kiss consumed me and for a moment we were the only people in the restaurant, in the world, in the universe. When we finally broke apart, it was so he could cradle my face in his hands. "Nothing about you calms me. Everything about you turns my world upside down."

"Ahh, but in a good way, right?"

A groan. "In a very frustrating way."

I didn't think I wanted to even start trying to decipher what his words really meant. Instead I blushed my invisible brown girl blush and wished we were alone somewhere. Like at our secret mountain pool. With nothing but green walls and blue sky for company.

He released me. "Come on, we better get back there. Before Jason thinks we've run away because you hate his fiancé."

Lunch for everyone else was fun. Light-hearted conversation as Jason filled us in on his latest research project. But for me, the hour was painful. Lesina had a nasal giggle and I struggled not to make a puke face every time she laughed. When the torment was finally over and we were in Daniel's truck, only then, did I let loose.

"Who wears clothes like that to lunch at a restaurant in Samoa? She looked like she'd just come straight from strutting her merchandise on Hollywood Boulevard or something."

A shrug from Daniel. "I thought she looked nice."

"Nice? Whatever. That's just because you're a guy. And whenever there's boobs involved, guys will always think a girl looks nice."

He faked a shocked exclamation, Simone style. "She had boobs? Really? No way."

I rolled my eyes at him. "Like you didn't see them. They were practically falling out of her top. They walked into the restaurant before she did."

"I didn't notice."

"And her hair. Ugh. That bleached look is so trashy."

"Hmm." A non-committal sound that meant nothing. And everything. But I was on a roll and didn't need any encouragement.

"I don't know which was worse though, the hair or the shoes. They looked like something Naomi Campbell would fall down in on the runway. This is Apia, for freak's sake. There isn't a single sidewalk or road here without cracks, potholes, and gravel slips. I bet she just wears shoes like that so she can fake an excuse to hang on to Jason." I assumed a syrupy breathless voice. "Ooh, Jason, you're soooo strong. Soooo big. I don't know why I keep falling over in these stupid shoes and rubbing my chest all over you."

Daniel laughed. "Leave the poor girl alone. Listen to you. You're a nut, you know that don't you?" He turned into the familiar driveway and brought the truck to a halt in the shade of the frangipani tree. There was nobody home, and the quiet peace of Matile's luxuriant garden was a welcome change from the dust and noise of town. He turned the engine off before giving me his trademark crooked smile. "I'm just glad he's wild in love. With someone other than my girlfriend."

But I wasn't done. Nowhere near it. "I don't get it. It doesn't make any sense. Jason barely knows her. Why would he ask her to marry him? I mean, who does that? Who wants to be with someone forever when they've only known each other for two weeks?"

He rolled his eyes and answered me drily. "I know. Crazy. It took me *at least* six weeks to know I couldn't live without you. And even then, I had to see you on fire and naked first."

"Daniel!" I didn't know whether to punch him or laugh. So I did both. He dodged me easily.

"What?" Innocent face. "Just saying it like it is. You were this vampy seductress, luring me to your midnight pool of dark desire so you could entrap me with your gleaming, wet body."

Outrage. "I did not."

"Did so. And now I'm doomed. You've stolen all of my forevers."

"What do you mean?"

Daniel wasn't teasing anymore. "I mean that no matter what future path I dream up for myself, you're in every one of them."

My breath caught on the permanence of his words. Daniel talking about forever was too much for me to handle. As if sensing that he had revealed too much, Daniel moved back to safer topics. "I'm guessing that you don't like Jason's fiancé. Even though she seemed like a very nice person." A light shrug. "Hey, I noticed she had Diet Coke at lunch. And she ordered two different desserts. Kinda like someone else I know. That's enough for you to forge a friendship on. You two could be soul sisters."

"Nowhere near it. All I know is that you are the worst person to dog on girls with. I wish Simone had been there. He would know what I was talking about."

"I like Simone, but I for one, am glad that he's not here with us right now."

"Oh yeah? Why not?" I was in an argumentative mood. Ready to do battle over nothing and everything.

"Because I'm tired of talking about Jason and his girlfriend. Because then I wouldn't be able to do this." He leaned over to kiss me, his hands slipping to twine through my hair.

Wow, twice in one afternoon. Daniel wasn't usually this generous with his kisses. I wasn't complaining though. I wasn't sure what had gotten into him, but I liked it. I angled my body so I could get maximum coverage and yelped in surprise when he lifted me easily, shifting so that I was sitting in his lap. The discomfort of the steering wheel meant I was crushed against the hard expanse of his body with nowhere to go. I wriggled, trying to get more comfortable and his kiss became even more urgent. He fisted handfuls of my hair and it got very hot inside the truck, very fast. Rivulets of sweat trickled down my back as his mouth left mine so he could breathe kisses along the edge of my cheek, down the side of my neck, the pulse point of my throat. Every nerve ending of my body was aflame with something indefinable. I wanted to incinerate his clothing and mine, remove every barrier between us. I wanted to feel the planes of his chest with my fingers. Skin against skin. Thoughts blurred to become actions. I pushed his shirt up, exploring smooth contours and ridged abs. I was careful to dance lightly over the fresh tattoo patternings but still, I wanted more. My fingers moved lower. Grazing hip-bone, the waistband of his shorts, the dip and curve that hinted of more.

That was all it took to shock Daniel out of the delicious place that we were in.

"Hey. Enough." The kisses stopped. He restrained my hands in his and carefully held them away from him. Thanks to the confined space, there wasn't much he could do about everywhere else that our bodies were touching. I shifted in his lap and he winced. A shamefaced grin.

"Umm, can you please move back over to your side of the truck?"

Innocent face. "You're the one who invited me over here." I leaned over to whisper in his ear. "And I like it right here where I am. Are you sure you want me to move?"

His answer was to lift me off his lap. "Yes. Being in a car alone with you is not a good idea. I need some air."

He opened the door and got out to lean against the truck. I scooted over and clambered out the open door, going to stand beside him. A nudge. "You're not mad at me, are you?"

A grin. "No, of course not. Just wish you weren't so damn hot." He tugged me to him, holding me against his body with fingers lightly clasped behind my back.

I slid my hands up to loop them about his neck and teased him, "Well, of course I'm hot. I am a fire goddess."

A quick look of annoyance flitted across his face before being replaced with a half-smile. "Don't remind me. What am I going to do with you, Miss Folger?"

Everything please. I stood on tip-toe to nibble at his lower lip, kiss the stubbled line of his jaw, and breathe against his ear. "Whatever you want, Mr. Tahi."

He pulled his head back out of my reach. "Leila, stop it. You're not making this easy for me. A little help here please?"

I looked up at his expression. It was serious. "Sorry. I'll stop now. Is hugging okay?"

In answer, he pulled me to him, enfolding me in a suffocating bear hug. "Yeah, hugging is definitely okay. But that's it."

Was that always going to be it? When would Daniel be willing to do more with me? I had to open my big mouth and ask him. Of course. Gently I disengaged from his arms. "When will you ever be okay with us doing ... you know ... more?"

He raised an eyebrow at me and gave me that look. The one that said, *Leila, are you nuts*? I squirmed uncomfortably but forged ahead with my line of questioning. "I mean, we've known each other for nearly a year now and I love you. I love everything that we do together and I was just wondering what the Daniel Tahi policy was on us doing more together?"

The dark expression on his face was unreadable. "We've had this discussion before, Leila. You know what happened with my parents, what my father did, and how it affected my mother. I'm not that guy. I won't be that guy. My mother killed herself because of what he did. "

There was anger in him. I could feel it. But it was directed at that faceless man who had fathered a son so long ago. "I know you're not like him." I hesitated, unsure how to proceed. Be careful, Leila. "Is it possible that maybe there's more to your parent's story than we know? Maybe your father wasn't as bad as you think he is?"

He raised an eyebrow at me in disbelief. "I'm going to be twenty years old in June. Not once has my father tried to contact me or see me. Does that seem like the behavior of a man who gives a damn about his kid? I don't think so. He never really loved my mother and he sure as hell didn't care about her son either."

His bitterness was cutting. A mental groan. A minute ago we were hot and heavy and now we were knee-deep in dysfunctional family history – how did we get here? Frantically I tried to re-route us back to my original destination. Me and Daniel. And sex.

"Okay. I understand why you would have umm … reservations about certain things, but it wouldn't have to be the same as what happened with your mom. You know, there's things we can do, precautions we can take if we, you know, go there."

He gave me a quizzical look that had the hint of a smile. "No, I don't know. Go where?"

Dammit, he wasn't going to make this easy for me. Fine. I had been through three years of Health and Sex Education at Cathedral Girls School and I could do this. Heck, if I could talk to a volcano, then I could talk to my boyfriend about anything and everything, right? I took a deep breath, "I mean, if we decide we're going to have sex, then of course we will make sure to use protection."

"Leila!" Horrified amusement are the only words I could use to describe his reaction. He was staring at me like I was proposing to work as a stripper in my spare time. "Are you really standing here talking to me about sex and birth control?"

My face burned. "Yeah, why? What's wrong?"

"Nothing." He shook his head, trying and failing to stop the huge grin on his face. "You really are an American girl, aren't you?"

"What? Where did that come from? What's that supposed to mean?" I frowned, feeling the beginning of steam building in my chest.

He held his hands up in mock defense. "Nothing. Just saying. I forget that you're not the average Samoan girl."

"Okay, now I'm getting annoyed. I don't appreciate the personal attacks on my real Samoan-ness, thank you very much. I thought we were done with that a long time ago." I pulled away out of his embrace and glared at him.

"Hey, no wait up. I didn't mean it like that. I'm sorry, it came out wrong." He gently pulled me back into his arms and raised my face to his with a wry smile. "Let me start again, please?"

I wanted to crawl under a rock and die. My first time talking to a boy about sex and it was excruciating. I shrugged, moving my face away from his gaze, choosing instead to stare at his chest. "I don't think I want to have this conversation anymore."

His voice was soft. "Don't be mad. What I meant to say was that you're the first person to ever talk to me straight up about sex. And birth control. And it caught me off guard."

"You must have had the boring sex lessons in Health Education."

"No."

"Well, your parents – I mean your grandmother – must have gone over the basics with you."

"No. She just always tells me *remember to be a good boy, Daniel.*"

"Your friends. Your guy friends like Maleko and them, you talk about it all the time."

A raised eyebrow. "We do?" He shook his head. "No, guys joke about it all the time. There's a difference. And some even boast about it. But actual straight talking about sex and contraceptives? No."

"But couples like, let me think … like Maleko and Mele, they must have talked about it when they were dating."

He laughed outright. "Definitely not. Leila, that's what I'm trying to tell you. Teenagers in Samoa don't ever have this kind of conversation. I doubt even many adults have this conversation. And people don't date in this country. Haven't you noticed?"

"Now I'm confused. If people don't date and don't talk properly about sex then what the heck do they do when they're attracted to each other?"

"They try very hard to keep it hidden. They sneak around in dark places." He faked a leery wink at me. "Like our midnight pool. Or they always go out in groups with friends. And they never, ever talk about sex before they have it. Sex is a taboo subject here in Samoa. I don't know anyone whose parents have discussed it with them. Or contraceptives for that matter."

It was my turn to be horrified. "That's ridiculous. I don't get it. Back in America we get Sex and Health Education in Middle School and my dad talked to me about it several times."

"Yeah? That's so foreign to me." He shook his head. "What did he say?"

"He was embarrassed, but he said that when I was little girl, he had reconciled himself to the fact that he would have to be both mom and dad to me, for always – and that meant giving me 'the sex talk.' *Better from me than from your Grandmother Folger!* he would say." I smiled at the memory. "I think he had been practicing what to say for a few years in advance, he was so freaked out that he would get it wrong! He told me he hoped I wouldn't have a sexual relationship with anyone until I was twenty-five but he doubted I would wait that long. He got me all these safe sex pamphlets. Then he took me to a pharmacy and made me go in by myself and buy a box of condoms. And a pregnancy test." I grimaced. "I was mortified. Which was exactly his point. He said that anybody who thought they were old enough to have sex should be old enough to accept the responsibility for those actions." Daniel stared at me with shock written all over his face and I blushed my invisible brown girl blush. "Dad would make me babysit our neighbor's kids a lot. Then when I complained about how rotten they were, he would smile and say, *you wouldn't want to be dealing with THAT all day, now would you? At least not until you're twenty-five. A moment of lust is all it takes ... sex without a condom is just stupid. I want grandchildren, but not for a while yet, do you hear me?*

I came to a halt as the memories crowded me, choked me.

"Hey, are you okay?" Daniel's voice was tender. He raised my face to his and sunlight caught on the runaway tear on my cheek. He bent to kiss it away and his lips were hot on my skin. He looked into my eyes, and it seemed as if nothing could ever break our gaze. "You're very blessed to have had a father like him."

I nodded. "Yes, I am. He was pretty cool as dads go."

He faked a frown. "Now back to this fascinating subject. I have a very important question for you. Did you ever umm …" He hesitated. "Did you ever use that box of supplies?"

"No." The idea was so far-fetched that it was laughable. "Of course not. My Dad had a very inflated opinion of my feminine charms. I never had a boyfriend and never got into any situations where a condom was required."

He gave me that quizzical grin again. "Are you sure?"

"Yeah. Why?"

"Because you're beautiful. You're from America. And we all know what beautiful girls from America are doing every weekend."

"No. What are they doing?" Now was not the time to argue that I wasn't beautiful. He was going to realize his mistake one day, why ruin his illusions now?

"They're fighting off attention from all the hot guys that are after them. You know, trying to decide which one they want to get with."

"Yeah right. Hollywood has a lot to answer for. Not every teenager in America is running around having sex with everybody else you know."

"But I distinctly remember talking to a new girl called Leila, asking her about guys and stuff and she said, *Not lately*. Leading me to conclude that she'd had tons of boyfriends in the past."

Oh damn. I forgot about that. "I never said I'd dated anybody before. It's not my fault if you jumped to that conclusion."

"Whatever, Leila!" He was laughing now. "You deliberately misled me. You knew I would make that assumption. What else was I supposed to think?"

"Okay, okay fine. So I kinda misrepresented the truth a little. I didn't want you to know that I'd never had a boyfriend before. So what?" I was sulky.

"So nothing." He had the hugest grin as he picked me up and swung me around.

"Hey!" The unexpected spin had me breathless and laughing. "What was that for?"

"I'm just happy, that's all." He hugged me to him again, a light kiss on the tip of my nose.

"Why?" Suspicious now.

"Because you're mine. And I love you."

I peered up at him. "Is that it?"

He looked embarrassed. "No. There's more."

"What?" I backed him up until he was trapped against the side of the truck, pressing into him so he couldn't move. "I'm not letting you go until you tell me."

"Okay." He took a deep breath like he was psyching himself up for something awful. "I was worried that you wanted to do more stuff with me because you were used to doing it with your ex-boyfriends. Which would make me the most boring boyfriend you ever had." He ran his fingers through his hair in that uneasy gesture I knew so well. "I hated wondering about all the guys you were probably comparing me with. Kinda feeling the pressure you know?"

No, I didn't know. I gaped at his confession. Was this boy for real? Had he not looked at me and him in the mirror lately? I wanted to laugh out loud at how ridiculous his statement sounded, but one look at his face and instead I thought fast. *Quick, Leila. What to say?* I stared in his eyes, trying not to lose myself in their jade depths, trying to let him see and feel the truth in my words. My heart. My soul. "Daniel, with my heart, with my fire – I'm telling you – there has never been anyone else. There is only you. There will only ever be you."

The fervor of my emotions summoned a single arterial current of fire that lit up the markings of my malu with a fiery red-gold glow. Without breaking our locked gaze, Daniel took my hands in his and spoke with calm surety. "Same. There's never been anyone else. There is only you. And there will only ever be you."

The afternoon breeze ruffled through vibrant bougainvillea and ginger flowers in the haven of color that was Matile's garden. In that moment, maybe it wasn't so impossible to believe that Jason could know he wanted to spend the rest of his life with Lesina. Because I knew with a fiery certainty that was how I felt about Daniel. He made me want to believe in forever.

It was time for Daniel to go back to work. To say goodbye. But before I let him go, I had to ask. One more time. "So just checking. Does this mean, you and me and umm … more, is not going to happen? Not ever?"

He shook his head at me with that lazy, slow grin. "It means, not now."

If that answer was supposed to dispel the heat that raged a war within me whenever I was with Daniel – then it failed miserably. Because there was so much delicious promise and potential in those four words that I wanted to turn the whole garden into a molten lava field.

Not now …

SEVEN

The search for an apartment proved tougher than I thought. Samoa did not have an abundance of apartments for young singles. We were going to have to rent a house. But realtors were not excited about leasing a property to two young adults.

"I don't get it. Why is it so hard to find a decent place for us to rent?" I exclaimed in frustration as Simone and I were turned away from yet another property office. We traipsed across Saleufi Street to another real estate agent.

He shrugged. "They're not used to people our age wanting to rent a house. Young people don't leave home and go live on their own in this country. Not until they get married. And even then, most couples live with their parents for ages."

"What happens when they start having children?"

"Even then. Families just share. Make space for each other. And it's the responsibility of children to take care of their elders, so it makes sense for them to keep living with their parents, look after them, contribute financially to the rest of the family. That's how it's done here. The only reason my parents are okay with me moving in to live with you is because I'm spoilt rotten. I've got four older brothers who are all living at home with their wives and kids and paying for all the bills. I told Mum I need the privacy so I can dedicate myself to my studies this year and make sure I work hard enough to get a scholarship." He adopted a studious expression. "I do hope you're not going to be a distracting influence on me this year. I have to focus. Our house will be a temple of learning. No parties. No alcohol. No boys. Nothing." He hesitated. "Maybe we can make an exception for some boys. Just the ones who will help us with our studies. Dalashious, desirable boys who like to study very, very hard. Very hard boys." A shriek of laughter. Which did not endear us to the property agent who gave us a thin-lipped glare.

I shushed him, struggling not to laugh. "We're never going to get a house if you don't keep quiet. And then you'll be stuck at home, sharing a room with your six nieces and nephews forever!"

The threat worked and he was the picture of decorum as the agent took us to view several houses not far from the university. Just when I thought we would never find a suitable property, there it was. A three bedroom, two bathroom house nestled in a tiny but well tended garden. It came furnished with all the basics, and the rent came in well under Uncle Thomas' accommodation allowance. I explained to Simone. "We can use the other bedroom as a study. You know, because this is our temple of learning devoted to the pursuit of academic wisdom?"

To the agent. "We'll take it." And before he could give us the same disapproving looks that we had been getting all day from agents all over Apia, I sweetened the deal. "I can give you six months' rent in advance."

Simone gasped alarmingly at the amount on the check but I reminded him. "I take care of the rent. You buy our food, remember?" Simone was doing me a huge favor by moving in with me because I knew that both my American relatives and my Samoan guardians would not have been happy with my living alone. We signed the paperwork, accepted the keys, and – just like that – Simone and I were officially setting up house. I took instagram photos for Annette and Thomas so they could rest assured I was safe, secure, and housed. We celebrated over Diet Coke and burgers from the McDonald's drive-through.

✺

My buzz didn't last for very long though. Daniel was not happy about my new home. He came over that night after work to help us move in and there was nothing but disapproval written all over him. He ignored my attempts to give him a tour of our little house, instead stomping away through the garden to inspect the fence at the back of the property.

There was a tight frown on his face as I came up to stand beside him. "Daniel? What is it? What's wrong?" I peered at the fence he was studying in the dim evening light, trying to see what was making him so angry.

He pointed. "That."

"Yes. That's a fence. What about it?"

"As fences go, it's pathetic. See how low it is? It barely comes up to my shoulder and it needs barbed wire along the top of it."

I was baffled. "Why?"

"Because anybody could easily climb over it, that's why. That fence is not going to keep anybody out."

Before I could respond, he turned away to follow the fence line until he came to a halt at the open steel gates to the driveway. I ran after him and watched as he fiddled with the locking mechanism on the gates, frowning and cursing under his breath.

"What is it?"

"This latch is faulty. You're not going to be able to lock this gate. Didn't you check that before you moved in here?"

Without waiting for an answer, he went back to his truck, getting in with a slam of the door. "I'll be right back." No smile. No wave. Nothing. I stood and watched him drive away, bewildered. Simone joined me in the driveway.

"What's wrong with him?"

"I don't know. He said the gate lock is busted. I don't think he likes this house." I turned to consider our new home thoughtfully. "I don't know why. It's beautiful."

"Hmm … or maybe it's not about a busted lock." Simone regarded me with thoughtful eyes. "Did you discuss moving out of your aunt's place with Daniel? Get his thoughts on it? See if he approved?"

"No. Why should I? It was a surprise. I thought he would be happy. Having my own place means we can hang out more. Do more stuff. Go more places together. I won't have a curfew. And he can come over and umm …" I stalled. Simone's knowing grin was making me feel flustered. "And we can study together."

"Uh huh. Study together. Sure." Simone drawled. He made loud wet kissing noises and cried out, "Ooh Daniel, can I study you a bit more? Ooh baby!" and then skipped out of the way as I moved to slug him lightly on the arm.

"No. That's not what I meant." I frowned and swatted at the ever-present mosquitoes that accompanied every Samoan night. "I don't get why he's upset."

Simone gave me an odd look and dropped the falsetto. "You really don't get it, do you? For a smart girl, Leila, you can be so dumb sometimes. If he comes back, you two need to talk. Now, let's go inside before the mosquitoes eat us alive."

Back in the house we busied ourselves with cleaning and unpacking but my thoughts were on Daniel and his strange mood. Where had he gone? Was he going to come back tonight?

I didn't have to wonder for very long. The green bomb roared into the driveway with tires screeching and skidded to an abrupt halt. Simone and I both stared out the window as Daniel got out of the truck, slammed the door, and quickly unloaded gear onto the front lawn. He moved with a controlled intensity and you could tell, even in the dim light, that he was angry. He ran an extension plug to the front verandah where there was an outdoor power outlet, set up spotlights, put on a welding helmet and then turned on a portable welding machine. The white sparks scattered all over the cement drive like fairy sparklers as he attacked the gate.

"What is he doing?" asked Simone.

There was a sinking feeling of dread in my chest. "I think he's fixing our gate." I bit my lip. "I think I know why he's mad."

Simone gave me a knowing sideways glance. "Finally, the lights go on ... I'm going to retire to the study, I mean, the Temple of Learning – and paint my nails. You better get your independent woman's ass out there so you can help your man transform our house into a fortress. I hope you know how to make nice and fix this. Or else you'll be joining me, singing that chorus with me ..." He broke into song as he swaggered down the hallway. "*All the single ladies! Put your hands up ... woo ooh oh ... I'm up in the club, we just broke up ... All the single ladies!*"

Sometimes Simone could be so infuriating. I walked outside to where Daniel was working on the gates. The night was humid and wet. He had unzipped his overalls and pulled them down to loop around his waist so that he was shirtless in the moonlight, his torso gleaming with sweat. Sparks from the welder splattered against his skin and I flinched on his behalf, but he ignored them with intense concentration.

I raised my voice over the burn of the welding flames. "Hey, can I help you with that?"

He ignored me. Or he couldn't hear me. I hoped for the latter. I tried again. Louder. "Daniel, let me help you."

This time, he shut off the welder and raised the visor of the helmet, revealing an impassive face. "What did you say?"

"I said, can I help you do that?"

His reply was curt. "No. The latch is done. It should lock now." He swung the gates closed and tried the lock several times until he was assured that it was secure.

"Thank you for fixing it. Do you want to come inside and have something cold to drink?"

He shook his head. "No. I'm not done out here."

"Why? What are you going to do now?"

He lifted a roll of barbed wire from the truck and carried it over to the back fence, then returned to move the spotlight so the 'pathetic' fence was revealed in all its inadequacies. He paused for a moment to wipe the sweat from his forehead and I had to force myself not to react to the sight of his chiseled, tattooed body in the moonlight. In low-lying overalls, steel-capped boots, and a welding helmet, his body drenched in sweat – even taut with anger, even radiating fury – Daniel was a magnificent sight.

"I'm going to run several lines of barbed wire along the top of this fence."

I gaped at the fence, the roll of wire, and then back at him. Was he nuts? It was going to take a couple of hours at the very least to complete a job like that. I called out after him as he lugged a metal toolbox over to the fence line. "Wait up. Why do you have to do all that?"

"I told you. This fence is too low and won't deter anyone. It needs some barbed wire along the top of it. Even then, it's still not going to be very impressive." He spat the words out like it was my fault personally that the house had such a crappy fence.

"But why now? Why tonight? It's getting late and I know you have a full day of work tomorrow. Why can't the fence wait? For another day? For the weekend?"

He paused with a pair of wire cutters in his gloved hands. "Because you've moved into this house today. Because you've decided to live here alone, in a house with a faulty gate that won't lock, a fence that's too low, and windows with rusted screen wire that any intruder with a machete can cut their way through."

"Oh. I see."

"Do you?" and then it all came rushing out. "It's not safe for you and Simone to live here by yourselves. Why didn't you tell me that you were going to do this? You didn't think that maybe as your boyfriend, I should get a heads up about this move? Ask for my opinion, discuss it with me, or something. Anything?"

"I thought it would be a nice surprise. I don't get it. Why is this such a big deal? I couldn't keep living with Matile and Tuala forever. I'm old enough to be on my own, I've got the money to do it so I moved out and got my own place, so what?"

"Leila, you don't know Samoa like I do. It's not safe for young women to live on their own. So few people do it that those who do become automatic targets. For thieves and worse. How am I going to sleep at night, knowing that you're here on your own? And no, Simone doesn't count. I grew up with him remember? He's not going to be much use if some crazy fool breaks in with a machete."

From inside the house, Simone's voice rang out indignantly. "Hey, I heard that! Stop using my name in vain, Daniel Tahi. Just because I wasn't on the rugby team doesn't mean that I can't defend myself, eh. Aikae." And then a more subdued tone. "Not that I was listening to your conversation or anything. No. Carry on, carry on. Just pretend like I'm not here."

Daniel rolled his eyes in Simone's direction. "Whatever." He took the welding helmet off and rifled through damp hair before appealing to me. "Leila, I wish that you had talked to me about this house idea before you acted on it. I'm not comfortable with you living here."

"But you know you don't need to worry about me." I pulled him with me away from the windows, away from our avid audience of one, dropping my voice to a whisper. "I'm a fire goddess, remember? Nobody can hurt me. I don't need taking care of. All this? Fixing the lock and upgrading the gate? It's thoughtful of you and I appreciate it, I really do. But I'm going to be fine. I don't need fences and gates to keep me safe. I can sleep soundly at night without them."

His face tightened and he shrugged off my hand. "Maybe so. But I need to know you have them so *I* can sleep good at night. Just humor me and let me do this for my girlfriend, okay?"

"Okay. On one condition. That you agree to let me help you."

He smiled but it was a shadow of his usual. "Sure. But since when did my opinion matter to you? It's not like I could stop you from doing what you want, even if I wanted to."

That wasn't the answer I was looking for, but I had to be happy with it. And that's how I ended up spending the first night in my own house with my boyfriend – welding, and wielding a pair of wire cutters, upgrading a fence. It took us three hours. Yes, he was half naked and yes we got very sweaty but the only time my pulse spiked was when I disturbed a big black centipede in the wet grass and had to run shrieking from the sinuous slithery crawl of it running up my leg. When I imagined thrilling, hot nights with Daniel in my own house? This wasn't what I had in mind.

Long after he had packed up his work gear and left, after I had showered and put antiseptic cream on the blisters and cuts on my hands, Simone emerged from his room to make us both glasses of ice Diet Coke with a slice of lime. We stood there by the window, sipping our drinks and studied the new and improved fence.

"It's very … shiny." Simone offered. "And it looks very painful. Good work."

I only had energy to nod. But it was his next comment that had me, "A word of advice, Leila. Men like to be needed. They don't like a strong woman who kicks ass all on her own. In future? Maybe you should try to show a little vulnerability. You know, so the Chunk Hunk will feel necessary in your life." He did that breathy, Marilyn Monroe thing with his voice, "Oh baby, yes I neeeeed you …"

"Daniel's not like that. He doesn't need a girl like that."

Simone gave me a wide-eyed look that conveyed more than I wanted to know. "Hmm, are you sure? Because that looks like twenty-five meters of barbed wire that says otherwise," and then he sashayed off to bed.

I looked out at the fence. Silver spiked lines screamed at me in the moonlight. I hoped that Simone was wrong.

The countdown had begun for university to start and time was running away from me as I tried to get things done for the Center before school caught me up in its wave of assignments and lectures. I found an instructor willing to sign up for teaching duty three days a week. Her name was Dayna and she ran her own muay thai studio in town, but she loved the idea of working with women at the Center. I liked that she was a female instructor because it would help the residents to trust her. Mrs. Amani had allocated us a prefab building at the back of the Center that was normally used as a storage space. It was a little dreary with its bare panel board walls but it would do. She asked for volunteers to help me with cleaning and set-up, and four young women were sweeping and mopping already when I showed up with a Jeep full of fight gear. To my surprise, one of the volunteers was Teuila. She kept herself distant from the other three as we worked to unload the Jeep but the sullenness was at a minimum. There was something about this girl that drew me, but I didn't know what. I had brought hammer and nails, rope and hooks so that we could hang the fight bags at strategic spots in the room and everyone got into the task of getting the bags up. I observed Teuila furtively when I thought she wasn't watching.

There was a restless edge about her. She was always moving, shifting lightly on her bare feet, fidgeting with her iPod, always looking over her shoulder, scouting her surroundings. Like she was waiting for something or someone to jump out at her at any moment. It was a cautiousness that would serve her well in the ring but probably was a nightmare to live with on a regular day.

Mrs. Amani sent over a plate of sandwiches for lunch and we took a break. The other three girls sprawled out on the floor to eat, but Teuila took her food outside, heading for a grove of mango trees at the back of the Center. After a while I followed, walking into the cool shade and then stopped short when I couldn't see her anywhere. Where was she?

"Are you following me?" Her voice, sharp and abrupt, came at me from somewhere above. I looked up. Teuila was sitting on the crook of a broad branch staring down at me with unsmiling eyes. "What do you want?"

Now that I'd found her, I wasn't sure what I wanted. Nice one, Leila. Stalk the girl and then not even know why. "Are you going to join the self-defense classes?"

A shrug. "Maybe. If they're not stupid." Her eyes narrowed. A sneer. "Are you going to teach them? You don't look like you could fight anybody."

Okay. Her social graces were even worse than mine. "No, I've hired a muay thai specialist to take the class. I'm just the organizer." *And I don't need to fight anybody, so there. I can fry them with a thought, so take that you little brat.* "You should give the class a try. It could be useful for you."

"Why? Because my mother is a prostitute and I'm a charity case living in a refuge?"

I winced. "No. Because everyone needs to feel safe, somewhere, sometimes. And learning how to defend yourself can give you that security."

"I already know how to take care of myself. I don't need some crap karate class to feel safe." She stood, light and lithe, and swung down out of the tree, landing with a soft thud in the grass beside me.

"So why did you volunteer to help today then?"

"Because I wanted to get out of school." Her stare dared me to contradict her.

I tried one more time. This was the new and improved, mature and responsible me. "I hope you try the muay thai anyway. It might be helpful. You never know."

"You're staring at me with the same pity that everybody else does. I know you've read my file and so you think you know everything about me. Get this straight, I don't need you to feel sorry for me. I don't need any help. I take care of myself just fine."

I raised my hands up in supplication. "Hey, I'm not trying to get on your case here. But yes I've read your file and yes I do feel sorry about what happened to you and your mother."

Teuila interrupted me. "I'm not. She deserved it. I'm glad she's in the hospital."

"You don't mean that."

"Yes I do."

"Your mother is an innocent victim, just like you were. And she needs our support, just like you do."

It was the worst possible thing I could have said. But even so, I could never have predicted what happened next. Teuila stiffened and her whole body radiated outrage. "I. Am. Nothing. Like. My. Mother. She is weak. And. I. Am. Strong." With each word, her voice climbed higher until she was shouting. And in fierce accompaniment there came a rushing, ripping sound. Like wind through the trees. Only it wasn't. The air was still. So still. But all around us, tree branches whipped about, strained and heaved as if being pulled by some unseen force. Wood splintered and cracked. And then leaves were raining down upon us and we were standing in a maelstrom of green.

As suddenly as it had begun, it was over. The ground was thick with foliage and Teuila was staring at me, aghast. Eyes wide. Fearful. She looked at the destruction around us and caught a muffled sob in her hands. And then she backed away from me and turned to run back to the Center.

"Wait!" I ran after her, catching at her arm. "What was that? What did you do back there?"

She shook her head. Whispered. "Nothing. Leave me alone." She pulled free and darted away, and this time, I didn't try to stop her. Instead, I went to find Mrs. Amani.

She was knee-deep in paperwork in her office and looked slightly harried when I disturbed her. "Yes, Leila? Is everything alright with the set-up? Are the girls doing a good job over there?"

"It's fine. They've been very helpful. I wanted to ask a question about Teuila? The girl whose mother is in hospital?"

"Yes?"

"You mentioned that the man who did it – the mother's boyfriend – he was hurt as well somehow? What happened?"

"Oh him." Mrs. Amani lip curled in distaste, "An obvious drug addict. I was there with Siela when they brought him into the emergency room, raving about the trees coming to life. It's so sad to see the effect that drug abuse can have on someone."

"But his physical injuries? What were they?"

"Minor. A broken wrist, scratches and bruises. Nothing like what he had done to Siela. No, he was in and out of the hospital within a few hours. Unfortunately." She scoffed. "Trying to blame everything on trees coming to life. How pathetic."

"Yes. Very." I left Mrs. Amani's office puzzling over it all in my mind. Trees coming to life – it was impossible.

Wasn't it?

It had been over a week since Simone and I had moved into our own place and Daniel still wasn't happy about it. He had started carrying out a kind of reverse-stalker operation on me, driving past the house at odd times, texting me every time he saw a 'suspicious' loitering stranger on the street. *Heads up. Man in red shorts and black shirt standing by your front fence. Lock doors.* And, *Who r those 2 guys in suits on yr verandah? I'm going to stop in and check.* I texted back, *Mormon missionaries. Dnt wori. They're harmless.* He still opted to drive in and glare at them from his truck as I gave them ice water and some of Matile's pineapple pie. When they left, he came over to demand, "Why did you invite them in? You don't know them. What if they had been serial killers?"

"They weren't. They were very nice young men from America. Besides, I didn't invite them into the house, just onto the verandah. It's a hot day, so I asked them to come in out of the sun and gave them some refreshments. That's all." I leaned over the railing to pull him close for a kiss. For a moment, he relented and everything was right again between us as we connected with slow, sweet, and perfect heat.

I whispered, "You know I would love to have you come inside so I can feed you pineapple pie. Simone's out visiting his parents. There's nobody here but us." A hopeful smile.

Which he refused. Again. "No thanks. I have to get back to work." A quick hug before he walked back to the truck.

"Daniel, why won't you ever come inside the house? Is it because you're still mad at me about the fence thing?"

He turned back with a raised quizzical eyebrow. "No."

I went to stand beside him, taking his hands in mine, trying to find the truth in the green depths of his eyes. "What is it then? Every time you stop by, you won't even step foot in the door."

"It wouldn't be right for me to go inside your house and for us to be alone in there without a chaperone."

"Are you kidding me?" One look at his face and I knew that he wasn't. "What about Simone? He was here the other night when I invited you over to watch *Game of Thrones* with me but you wouldn't come over."

"In no alternate reality could Simone count as being a chaperone. I meant an adult chaperone."

I could not believe what I was hearing. "Daniel, there are two adults present right here, right now. Me and you. There's no reason why we can't go inside the house, have a conversation, eat some pie, watch a little television. It's not like we're going to be having sex in there." I stopped as an awful thought occurred to me. "Wait up, is this about what happened the other day? About that conversation we had? Do you think I'm going to jump you or something? Are you not coming inside the house because you don't trust me?" I was getting angry now.

Daniel sensed it and shook his head. "See? This is why I didn't want to get into it. Because I knew you would react this way. You always do."

"What way? How do I always react?"

"Exactly like this. Whenever I disagree with you, immediately you take it personally and you go on the offensive. We can't discuss anything if all you want to do is fight with me."

The truth in his words stung. Enough to make me bite back the angry words that had been my first reaction. Deep breath. "You're right. I'm sorry. Let's start again. Can you please explain to me why you think it's a bad thing for us to be alone in the house together?"

He smiled to show me he knew I was making an effort. "Samoa is a small place with some unwritten rules for stuff like this. For couples. And for girls especially. I don't want people thinking certain things about you."

"I don't care what people think about me."

"But I do. I care what people think of you. There's safety in a good reputation. And I want that safety for you. Especially if you and Simone insist on living here alone." And then he grinned, and the teasing Daniel that I loved was back. "Besides, it's not you that I don't trust. It's me."

He got into the truck before I could decipher that comment. "What do you mean?"

A crooked smile, a stare filled with meaning as he looked me up and down, lingering on the glimpse of skin at my waist where my too-short t-shirt failed to meet my shorts. A stare that had me feeling flushed and foolishly happy. He spoke slowly, dragging out every word. "I mean, that I'm not worried about you ripping MY clothes off. I know my limits, Leila."

And with that parting shot, he reversed out of the driveway. Leaving me very alone. Very flustered. And very hot.

After two weeks of flatting together, Simone and I had learned something very important. Neither of us could cook. Which made eating a bit of a challenge. Like the night I attempted chop suey. We both stood there in the kitchen and stared at the glutinous black gloop in the pot.

Simone gave a theatrical wail, "What did you do to our dinner? It looks like something a dog threw up."

I poked at the mess viciously. "I don't know. I followed the instructions on the packet."

"I thought you knew how to cook? I moved in with you thinking that you were a good cook. Your Aunty Matile makes the best food on the Samoan planet."

"It doesn't mean I absorbed her cooking mojo by osmosis or something. I lived in her house, I didn't take a chef's course with her. Besides, you can't talk. That koko rice you made last night was disgusting. I thought all fa'afafine were supposed to be amazing cooks?"

Simone gasped and then hissed in outrage. "Stereotypical much? How dare! So because I embrace my feminine mystique, therefore I must be an expert domestic slave? I am so offended."

I knew him well enough now not to care about his dramatic state of being offended. Instead I regarded the mess that was supposed to be chop suey. Sadly. Sighed. "I really wanted to eat chop suey."

A big sigh from Simone. "Me too."

There was only one solution to this epic culinary fail. We chucked the chop suey in the rubbish bin and went to Aunty Matile's house to scavenge for dinner.

Yes, Simone and I were going to Restaurant Matile for meals quite a lot. Which Tuala and Matile didn't seem to mind. I quickly realized that she was making extra food in anticipation of our strategically timed visits. We were decent enough not to over-do it though, so we alternated with eating out and had found a few favorite food options. Monday was leftovers from Sunday toona'i from Matile's, Tuesday was steak at the Hotel Millenia, Wednesday was pizza from Giordano's, Thursday was High Tea at Plantation House, and tonight we had invited Daniel to join us at the Amanaki Restaurant, which was our favorite dinner spot. He was checking into a two-day training camp the next day in the build-up to the big paddling regatta, so I was happy for the chance to spend some time with him.

It was another steaming hot night in Apia as we chose a table and gave our orders to the waitress. Mine was the usual sashimi appetizer followed by oka, raw fish marinated in coconut cream with little chunks of cucumber and tomato. The owners of the restaurant also owned several open-sea fishing boats, so they always had the freshest fish in town. Tim, the head barman, knew us so well by now that before we could order drinks he sent over tall glasses of Diet Coke brimming with crushed ice.

Daniel raised his eyebrows at our drinks. "I think these are a sign that you two come here way too often."

Simone rolled his eyes at him. "Pugi. No, it's a sign that they love us here and we need to come here way more often." He blew a kiss at the tall, dark-eyed bartender who always had a frank, easy smile for us.

While we waited for our food, I pestered Daniel with a barrage of questions, eager to make sure that I understood what was happening when we went to watch him at the regatta. He would be racing in the individual events as well as in team races.

"Double-hulled outrigger canoes were used by our ancestors who navigated the Pacific ocean in search of new lands to settle. We use single-hulled boats, called va'a, for racing now. It's different from rowing, we sit in line facing toward the bow of the canoe, in the direction that we're paddling towards," explained Daniel. "All six paddlers have different roles. The steerer is the skipper and he sits in the last seat of the va'a, seat six. The most experienced paddler is usually the steerer."

I asked, "So is that what you are? The steerer of the va'a?"

"No. Are you kidding me? I'm new to the sport, remember? I'm a number one, the stroke. I set the pace for the team." He faked a flex, "That means I've got a high level of fitness and endurance."

Simone interjected, "And I thought you were the stroke because you were good with your hands. But fitness and endurance is very helpful too."

"Just ignore him, Daniel." I frowned at Simone's cheeky smile, "He's had too much caffeine."

The food came, and Daniel kept talking – this time about the setting up of the race course, which he was helping the Pualele club president with. It sounded like a rather complicated operation that involved orange buoys and GPS measurements and a compass and such stuff. I tried to stay interested but my brain always shut down when it came to the mysteries of measurement and distances and, finally, he gave up with a wry grin.

"Okay, your eyes glazing are over. I'll shut up now. I can see that you're not willing to be a supportive girlfriend and at least pretend to be fascinated by my sporting passion." He faked an aggrieved look, which I merely rolled my eyes at.

"Of course I'm fascinated by outrigger canoeing. What girl in her right mind wouldn't be? A bunch of half-naked guys, sweat dripping off their tattooed muscular bodies as they stroke their way through the water – totally fascinating stuff. Right Simone?"

"Oh girlfriend stobit! You're getting me all excited and the regatta hasn't even started yet." A shriek of laughter, which had several other diners looking over our way in irritation. Simone ignored them. Of course. "Daniel daahling, we L O V E outrigger canoeing. And the only reason why we are coming to the regatta is so that we can cheer for you. We will have eyes only for you. I mean, I don't know where Leila's eyes will be, but I bromise you, my eyes will be only on your glistening muscles."

I mouthed a curse word at Simone's treachery, and Daniel laughed. "Thank you Simone, I knew I could count on you. Can you make sure my girlfriend doesn't get distracted by all the other rippling muscles tomorrow? I'll be busy paddling and she might run off with some hot paddler."

Simone adopted a serious expression and patted Daniel's arm reassuringly. "Einjo. You can count on me baby. If necessary, I will even sacrifice myself for you. If some enticing paddler boy tries to lure Leila away from you, I will throw my body on the line and offer him everything I have, just to keep him away from her. You see the lengths I'm willing to go to for you?" Another burst of laughter added extra emphasis to Simone's declaration.

I didn't bother to argue, just poked my tongue out at both of them. "Like Simone will be anywhere near me. As soon as he sees something he likes, he'll abandon me. I'll be the lonely idiot girlfriend cheering for her boyfriend while he's surrounded by adoring female fans."

"I have adoring female fans? Where? I'd love to meet them."

"I bet you would" I threw some fries at him and he ducked, his easy smile deflecting my aggrieved tone.

Simone shook his head at us. "Untidy. Children please, try to behave yourselves. You're embarrassing me."

Daniel stood. "I hate to break this up, but I've got early training tomorrow and I need my beauty sleep. You know, so I can try to look good next to the paddlers from Hawaii."

In the parking lot, Simone took my keys and went ahead, leaving me and Daniel alone in the moonlight beside the green bomb. He leaned against the car, took my hand in his and gently pulled me to him, further into the shadows. I went willingly, gladly. In his arms was always where I wanted to be. He nuzzled his chin against the top of my head as I burrowed into his warmth. His strength. There was a cool breeze blowing in from the harbor, and his skin felt cool to the touch. I closed my eyes and placed a kiss on the bare skin of his shoulder before he held me away slightly so that he could raise my face to his. His voice was soft in the darkness. "Did I tell you how beautiful you look tonight?" I shrugged, ridiculously pleased. No matter how many times I heard him say it, a part of me would always react with disbelief. That he loved me. That I was beautiful in his eyes.

We stood there for a moment that lingered on the edge of perfect. Everything in my life was going so well. There had been no signs of Sarona. There was no telesā sisterhood stifling my every thought. I was doing good things at the Center. My fire gift seemed to have settled down and I wasn't always struggling with erratic power surges – some days I even forgot I was a telesā. Best of all though, Daniel was happy with me.

From somewhere in the dark parking lot, a car horn blared. Simone yelled at us. "Hello, I'm waiting!"

Perfect moments. They're rare, few and far between. Hold them close when you find them. They will give you strength when the storm comes.

EIGHT

It was a perfect day for the beach. Sunny, but with the sauna-like heat swept through by a brisk breeze coming in off the diamond sea. The road running along the Mulinu'u coast was lined on both sides with cars and it took me a while to find parking, with Simone impatient beside me.

"Hurry up already. All the good ones will be taken by the time we get there."

"I won't even ask what kind of good ones you're referring to, you skanky thing."

It was the biggest outrigger canoeing event thatSamoa had hosted, with teams from as far away as Hawaii and French Polynesia. Daniel's first race was up next. The men's individual event. There were twelve single-man boats at the start line and my eyes were only on him in the bright yellow Pualele t-shirt. I was apprehensive for him. He was naturally fluent on the rugby field but here on a glistening blue ocean, he was a newcomer. The whistle blew, bronzed arms flexed, dipped and the boats darted away, gliding through the water. Daniel was focused with intense concentration on the course ahead of him as he powered through the water.

I exhaled with relief as he skimmed across the finish line in second place after the paddler from Hawaii. I waited for him as he came up the rock steps to where I stood on the seawall. "You were amazing out there."

He smiled with unrestrained pleasure and my heart missed a beat at the golden glory of his happiness. "It felt great to be on the water.

Once I got my rhythm, it was like I could keep paddling forever. But hey, that paddler from the Hawaii team was on fire out there. He didn't even look like he was breaking a sweat." He looked around at the milling crowd of people. "Where is he? I want to congratulate him." He took my hand in his, "Come with me, let's go find him."

"Sure." I would have walked barefoot through the Sahara desert as long as Daniel's hand was in mine. We made our way slowly through the crowd as people smiled and congratulated Daniel until we came in sight of the red-shirted team, gathered around their canvas shelter.

"There he is. I think that's the guy." Daniel's hand slipped from mine as he quickened his pace towards a paddler standing somewhat removed from the others. A slight figure with his back to us, who unlike the rest of his team, was wearing a full t-shirt instead of a singlet.

"Hey, nice win out there man," Daniel said with an open smile.

The boy turned. My first gut impression of him was – danger. He seemed to be all tattoos and piercings. His neck and forearms spoke their inked patterns abrasively. He was shorter than Daniel, smaller – about the same height as me, lean and lithe, with skin the color of burnt sugar. Black hair cut razor short. An awkward scar pulled at his right eyebrow that sported a gold corner piercing and as he moved forward to shake Daniel's proffered hand, my eyes were drawn to the banded tattoo that covered the length of his forearm. Not so much the tattoo but the scarred markings of skin underneath it. I puzzled at it. It seemed this boy was inked strategically to conceal scars. Lots of them. I gave myself a mental shake and forced my eyes back to his face, to his unsmiling eyes as he accepted Daniel's congratulations with a curt nod.

"It's not like it was a difficult win. None of you have had much experience have you?" He spoke with a strong American accent, which for some reason I found annoying. Never mind that until a few months ago, I had spoken with the same marks of America. I prickled defensively at his coldness. Why was he being so unfriendly?

Daniel seemed oblivious to the boy's coldness. "You're a natural on the water. You been paddling long?"

A casual shrug. "Long enough."

"I take it this isn't your first competition then?"

A smirk that grated on my nerves. "Nah. You're looking at Hawaii Waka Ama Junior champion for the last three years." He jerked his head towards the regatta oceanside. "This? This ain't a competition. It's a massacre. Pathetic."

I barely restrained my snort of disdain at his arrogance and instead merely rolled my eyes. Daniel chuckled, "I'm new to the sport so I'm just glad to be getting a chance to compete."

"Yeah, I could tell you were fresh to the water."

I couldn't resist throwing in my two cents worth. "I'm surprised your team even decided to come here for this regatta – seeing as how we're so pathetic and all."

He turned to me, his lip curled in sardonic disdain. "And you are?"

Before I could reply, the race marshal announced the next event. An announcement that had Daniel moving. "Oh, sorry, Leila, I gotta go. We're up next right after this one and I have to get stuff ready. Be back right after, okay?"

A fleeting kiss on my cheek and he was off. My gaze followed him, lingering on the play of light on his body, the restrained power in his every movement. Would I ever tire of looking at him?

Beside me, the tattooed boy laughed, a low, mirthless sound. "Oh, so that's who you are."

I turned back to him, impatient to follow after Daniel and find the best vantage point to watch him compete. "Excuse me?"

The boy was staring at me with that scarred eyebrow raised slightly. Like Khal Drogo from *Game of Thrones*. "You. You're his chief groupie. The leader of his fan club."

His words cut at me. Because they hinted too closely to the truth. "What are you on about?"

He spoke slowly, carefully. "You. I asked who you were and yet, I see I didn't need to. You're his bitch."

I reeled, unused to the direct coarseness of his language and grasped for words to respond. For one wild moment I envisioned flaming his sneering face with a mini-fireball and that thought more than anything, forced me to speak calmly, "What is your problem?"

A casual shrug, a jerk of his head in Daniel's direction. "Nuthin. Just sayin it like it is. He's the golden pretty boy, the one all the girls drool over, and you? You're his lucky chosen flavor of the moment."

I gaped at him. This complete stranger who stood there calmly tossing insults into the wind. The sane, reasonable me said to walk away from this fool, he wasn't worth my anger. But the Leila who could burn people's faces off with a thought took charge. "Just shut it. You have no clue what you're talking about."

A smile flashed across his face, he leaned forward and dropped his voice suggestively. "Oh, I get it, you two are in love! You're deluded enough to believe that aren't you?"

"Where do you get off? You talk to me for all of two seconds and you know everything about me?"

He faked a yawn and folded his arms. "Sure do. Age old story, maybe you've heard it before? Girls everywhere worship hot stud. Hot stud bestows his favors upon one …" he stopped to look me up and down, the rake of his eyes had me squirming uncomfortably "one plain and worshipful girl. Fireworks explode in her universe. Then hot stud realizes life is boring with only one girl to hang on his every word, so off he goes to broaden his

horizons, leaving behind one very sad, broken-hearted little girl."
He faked a mournful gaze but still that charcoal dead look in his
eyes betrayed a lack of any emotion.

I tried not to show how much his words cut at me. Yes, they cut at
me. Because – no matter how much Daniel told me he loved me,
how many times he held me, no matter how many times he chose
me above all others – that still, small voice whispered *Why? Why
would he love you? You are not worthy of this boy, of this love ...*
My gaze went to search through the thronging crowd, searching to
find Daniel. The one who held my happiness in his hands. He
stood on the seawall with the wind whipping through his hair, the
burn of the sun highlighting his every muscular imprint. The boy I
loved. The boy who loved me in all my fiery weaknesses.

My face hardened, my voice was laced with poison as I spoke to
this boy who dared to assume he knew anything about me. "Screw
you."

And with that I walked away without looking back. Without
waiting to see how he would respond. Praying that I wouldn't run
into him again – or else I might lose it and set fire to his sneering
face.

The individual events continued to be won by the paddlers from
Hawaii, the women's team events were dominated by the local
club, Pualele, and finally it was the closing event – the men's team
500m. The sun was now high in the sky, people were tired, hot,
and ready to go home. Sweat soaked the back of my shirt, and I
found myself wishing for the coolness of the mountain pool.
Maybe me and Daniel could go there after this? My musings on
swimming with Daniel, ok, let's be honest – my musings on
kissing Daniel in a mountain pool – were interrupted by the
marshal's whistle. The race had begun. Daniel's boat had pulled
out into the lead ahead of the Hawaiian team and the crowd went
wild at the possibility that we might actually beat the visitors in
this one. But the lead was only a slight one. The red-shirted
paddlers worked in determined unison, furiously trying to catch up.

Would they be able to overtake before the fast-approaching finish line was reached? Suddenly, there was a murmur of disbelief from the spectators. The red boat was veering to the right, towards the lead blue boat. The steerer was maneuvering the boat like a missile, directly at the side of the va'a.

"What are they doing? Crazy fools are going to cause a collision."

The lead paddler of the blue boat yelled out in warning at the red team, a warning that was ignored and the canoe continued on its collision course.

"That steerer is deliberately trying to get them off course!" exclaimed Simone beside me. "It's that paddler who beat Daniel in the single canoe event. The hot one with the tats."

I frowned at Simone's treacherous observation before taking another look at the Hawaiian boat. The steerer was a dark, lean figure, a glint of a smile on his face as he directed their boat closer to the blue team. My breath caught at the vision of the impending crash. *What was he doing?* I couldn't stand to watch. I wanted to send a flash of fire at the red boat, enough to blow them out of the water. Enough to incinerate that maniac in the steerer seat. At the very last minute, the blue boat veered sharply to the right to get out of the way. A decision that took them away from their course to the finish line. Enough to allow the red boat a clear route to the win. They cheered and raised their paddles in celebration as they coasted over the line. The crowd booed.

There was an unwilling note of admiration in Simone's voice, "Wow, that was sly. They totally planned that, screwed our team over."

"What a total jerk." I exclaimed.

The teams were out of their boats and swimming to shore now. I ran towards the rock steps where a crowd waited for the paddlers. I had to push and shove my way through to the front where an altercation was taking place.

Daniel and the other five Pualele paddlers confronted the lead Hawaiian paddler. "What was that? You almost caused a collision, you cheated."

The crowd buzzed in angry assent. The lean boy ignored them. He shrugged his shoulders and opened his arms in careless dismissal. "What? That was standard race tactics. There was no contact between the boats. It's not our fault if you couldn't handle the race pressure and chose to veer right. There was nothing illegal there. If you had more international race experience, you would know that you were just beaten. Fairly." Another shrug. "Better luck next year." He turned to his team and made a comment that had them all laughing.

Another paddler on Daniel's team – a bulky boy called Pita – overheard the comment and he didn't like it. He took a step closer towards the Hawaiians, "What did you say?"

The leader laughed again and stared down at the shorter boy for a moment before raising his voice to ensure the gathering crowd could hear him. "I said, grow some balls, then maybe you won't be so chicken next year and run away from our boat."

Pita snapped, went straight for the jeering boy's throat. He never made it. In one quick movement, the Hawaiian had him in a chokehold that swiftly changed to a ground slam as he expertly maneuvered the heavier boy into a position face down in the dirt. The situation then went from bad to worse as one, two, three, more and then everyone was in on the scuffle. Some, like Daniel were trying to separate red- and yellow-shirted paddlers who were now locked in mutual chokeholds, while others were eagerly joining in with punches and blows of their own. The lead Hawaiian boy was in the thick of the action. A knee to the gut of another boy, an elbow to the face of another. He fought with expert skill, lightning-fast movements that belied his experience and always there was that smile his face. A taunting, laughing smile that provoked angry reactions on all sides, but still the boy fought on and apart from a cut of red on his cheek, he was fighting unmatched. Even the untrained eye could see that this boy was a professional fighter. I hated watching as one and then another Pualele paddler was taken out by the Hawaiian. He paused in between punches to shout.

"Come on! Bring it, is that all you got?"

I cast a furtive glance over my shoulder but nobody was paying any attention to just one more girl in the throng of spectators. Daniel was some distance away, still struggling to separate two other paddlers and Simone? Simone was standing on the seawall cheering excitedly. "Einjo! Hmm go baby! I love it."

No, nobody was paying any attention to me. Nobody would notice if I did something. Anything. Like shut this arrogant fool up. I sidled through the crowd until I was directly opposite the Hawaiian captain. He stood jeering at a wary crowd as he spun a paddle with practiced ease, wielding it like a war club. I breathed, focused, and summoned fire. Just a little bit. Just enough to flick at the boy's hands like a fiery whip, enough to make him cry out in surprised pain and drop the paddle. I was fast enough that nobody even saw my attack. Or so I thought. Because as the boy stood there holding his burnt hands he looked up and directly at me.

"You…"

And then I couldn't resist giving in to some of my murderous rage from our earlier encounter. Even as I acted, my internal rational radar was screaming at me, *Don't do it, Leila! Just walk away* … I would have so many times in the coming months to regret not listening to that advice.

Taking advantage of the boy's momentary burn I stepped forward and tripped his feet out from underneath him, using one of those nifty hook-twist-pivot-swing moves that Dayna had showed the girls in their very first class. He never knew what hit him. One minute he was staring at me in shock – the next, he was flat on his back, stunned. I grabbed the paddle from the ground and hit him in the abdomen. A sharp, quick blow with the handle. The boy lay gasping for air, curled up in pain on the ground, as the watching crowd cheered. I was high on adrenaline. It felt amazing. *I wonder if this is what the Rock feels like when he's kicking butt in the ring*? I couldn't resist leaning down with a triumphant smile to whisper so only he could hear, "Yes, it's me. And I'm nobody's bitch, so don't you forget it."

I wish I could have recorded that moment for posterity. Or YouTube. That moment as arrogance was replaced with total shock. That moment when a neon sign lit up in this arrogant boy's brain – *I just got my ass kicked. By a girl.* Ha.

And then I quickly melted back into the brawling crowd, searching for Daniel.

It didn't take long for the fight to be over. The Pualele captain, the one they called 'Pres' swiftly waded into the throng, his height and build making it an easy task for him to put a stop to the action. He pulled Pita away from one of the Hawaiian paddlers, snapping out orders to the others.

"That's enough! Stop it. Daniel, help get these fools out of here. Pualele Club, all of you, back to the tent. Now."

Then he turned and issued a curt command to the Hawaiian team captain, who was slowly getting to his feet. "And you, get your team under control before I call the police."

The captain smiled that irritating cocky smile and raised both hands up in surrender. "Fine, fine. We didn't start this, but hey, we're happy to finish it." He jerked his head at the rest of his team. "Come on boys, we're leaving. These amateurs are sorry losers. They can't handle knowing we're way out of their league."

The crowd parted for them as the red-shirted boys pushed through, back to their base where they began packing up gear and throwing it onto a big flatbed truck. I made my way through the crowd to Daniel's side. "Hey, are you alright?"

The slight edge of panic on his face cleared when he saw me, as he pulled me close. "There you are. I was worried about you. You didn't get caught up in any of this did you?"

I thought about barbed wire fences and reassured him, "No. I was watching from over there. It was such a crazy mess and I didn't want to get anywhere near it. I'm just glad you're alright."

It was the right answer because he smiled and brought my hand to his lips, a lingering kiss on my fingers. "That team from Hawaii sure knows how to finish a regatta on an explosive note. I hope they don't bring their attitude to the prize-giving function tonight. Come on, let's find Simone and get you out of here."

As he carved a path for us through the crowd, I felt the burn of eyes at my back. I turned to find its source and saw the captain of the Hawaiian team standing on the seawall staring directly at me with an inscrutable gaze.

Still high on happy adrenaline, I thought about giving him the finger. But decided to just smile instead. Victorious. Triumphant.

Gloating. It's so immature. But oh so fulfilling.

"Are you crazy? You can't go to a party wearing that!" Even the neighbors could probably hear Simone's exclamation of horror as he stared at me with one hand on his hip and eyebrows raised in disdain.

"Why not?" I looked down at my white linen blouse and navy denim skirt. My sandals. "What's wrong with it? Daniel said it was a semi-formal function and this is what I wear to church with Matile and Tuala. This is as formal as I get." I felt for the bun at the nape of my neck self-consciously. "I thought I looked quite nice. See, I even put my hair up, I made an effort."

Simone was disgusted. "You look awful. I will not be caught dead with you. If you don't change then I'm going without you."

I laughed. "Don't you think that will be a bit difficult seeing as how I'm the one driving – oh, not to forget – you don't have a car? You're stuck with me, Simone."

He didn't reply because he was too busy going through my closet, muttering under his breath. "Honestly, I don't know how we can be friends when you don't have a single fashionable bone in your bony-as body. Now, there's got to be something decent in here somewhere …"

I rolled my eyes and made a face at his back and his voice snapped at me from the closet depths. "And don't you go being cheeky at me girlfriend, eh? I have eyes in the back of my head." There was a sudden squeal of satisfaction. "Yes, I knew we could find something worthwhile in here."

He emerged from the closet, tugging at a familiar bag. "What is this huh? Why are you hiding it all the way in the back there?"

I frowned at everything that bag reminded me of. "No, those aren't really my clothes."

He ignored my protests, threw the bag on the bed, opened it and grabbed at handfuls of vivid fabric. "No freakin way. Mena and Tav designer labels? Where did you get all this stuff? And more importantly, why haven't you shared it with me?" He threw a hurt, angry look in my direction as he pounced on a fuchsia tube dress painted with frangipani flowers. "Mine! This one's mine. You can't have this one."

"Umm, nobody's fighting you for any of this stuff. You go right ahead and have that one. In fact, you can have the whole bag. They were gifts from Nafanua last year and they're not my thing. I think I only ever wore one of them to be honest."

My mind jumped back to that night of celebration when Nafanua had taken me to dinner at Aggie Grey's Restaurant. The night I had met Jason. The night my mother had told me how proud she was of me. Simone jolted me out of my reverie.

"Hello, earth to Leila? You're an idiot, you know that right?" He had already stripped off his own shirt to wriggle into the fuchsia shift and paused mid-shimmy to reprimand me. "You wear such ugly clothes all the time. The most stylish thing I've ever seen you wear is your SamCo uniform – that's how bad your wardrobe options are. Those denim shorts to your knees and the faded t-shirts? Even the linen potato sack dresses your aunt in America bought? They do nothing for you." Noting my hesitation, he softened his tone, " I'm sure your mom would want you to wear the clothes she bought for you. Right?"

Without waiting for an answer, he turned back to the assortment of clothing spilled out on the bed and started shifting through it. "Ah, here, this one screams 'Don't hate me because I'm beautiful.' Just not as loud as my dress. You already have a man so you don't need to shine too much. Put this one on."

I resigned myself to my fashion fate. "Fine. But the only reason I'm not fighting you on this is because we're already late and I don't want to miss Daniel's performance. Give it here."

I took the red two-piece outfit and changed quickly. The top had a scoop neck that was lower than I wanted it to be but at least it wasn't strapless. Or backless. The skirt was silk-screened with scarlet hibiscus flowers and fell in soft folds to just above the knee. I gave a twirl for Simone's benefit. "Happy now?"

"Yes. Much better. That speaks to me of elegance and restrained sensuality." He chucked a pair of black heels at me. "Add these. Now you at least have a chance of keeping Daniel. Because next to me in this dress, ooh la la, I will be stealing everyone's boyfriend tonight!" He struck a runway pose and I made all the appropriate exclamation mark sounds. And finally, he deemed us ready to go.

The regatta prize giving was being held at Sails Restaurant. A stunning venue that opened out to a deck over the ocean, lit with candles and fairy lights. There was a band playing when we arrived and I quickened my pace up the entrance steps, dragging Simone after me. "Come on, Daniel could be on soon."

"I'm going as fast as a girl can go in these shoes," he grumbled. At the entrance to the restaurant, he caught at my arm. "Wait. We have to make our entrance."

"What?"

"Our entrance." He studied my appearance with a critical eye, "Couldn't you have at least put some makeup on?" He whipped out lipstick from his neat red purse and applied it expertly. "There, now you look more like a friend of mine. Let's go. Put your shoulders back, stick your chest out. Don't you know anything?!"

I grimaced and followed after him as he sauntered into the crowded restaurant. All the paddling clubs and their supporters were out in full force and the place was packed. Thankfully, the open-air setting and cool ocean breeze saved it from being too uncomfortable. Still, I was ill at ease, searching everywhere for the only reason that I was there in the first place. Daniel. He found me first. An arm slid around my waist, making me jump.

"Here you are. I thought you were never going to show."

I turned with a welcome smile of relief as he enfolded me in his embrace, a light kiss on my forehead before he pulled back to study my red ensemble. A low whistle. "Wow."

A nervous smile. "What? Do you like it?"

"Like it? I love it." His hold on my waist tightened and he pulled me to him again, this time taking several steps back into a sheltered spot behind some palm plants. "Come here." He kissed me again, this time tasting my lips. The noise of the crowd, the band, the smoke, the laughter and chatter, all of it, everything faded to nothingness as I gave in to everything that was Daniel. The salt-sweetness of his mouth. The light play of his tongue on mine. The slight scrape of his newly shaven cheeks. The way he anchored me to earth with his hands on my hips, the delicious burn of his fingers as they caressed against the glimpse of skin where my top just edged my skirt. All too soon, the kiss ended and he pulled away to whisper against my ear. "I love it, almost as much as I love you in denim shorts and a sweaty tee, welding in my workshop. Almost."

I smiled up at him. "I think I would prefer to be in shorts and a tee, welding in your workshop right now. It would be more comfortable than this get-up that Simone forced me into." Someone in the crowd bumped against my back, which made Daniel frown. He pulled me closer and maneuvered us so that now I was the one with my back against the wall. And he was pressed in close, sheltering me.

Daniel grimaced. "At least at my workshop we would be alone." He raised an eyebrow at me. "Simone chose this outfit? I'm glad he didn't put you in something as bare as the outfit he's wearing." He motioned with his head over to where Simone was dancing in the center of the dance floor with a trio of boys I vaguely recognized from the regatta earlier that day.

I faked a frown. "Oh, and what would you have done if I had worn that dress Simone's got on right now?"

"I would have taken my shirt off to cover you up with it."

"In that case, I'm sorry I didn't switch dresses with Simone." I teased. "I can never get enough of seeing you shirtless, you know."

"I would have taken off my shirt, covered you up, then thrown you over my shoulder and taken you to my welding cave." Daniel's tone was teasing but the kiss he gave me was filled with taut promise. The world was spinning. I slipped my hands up around his neck and clung to his hard strength, wishing that this moment could go on forever.

All good things always come to an end. A voice called out over the loudspeaker. "And next up we have one of the Pualele Club boys taking to the mike. Daniel, where are you bro? We need your silky smooth voice up here on the stage."

He gave me a wry smile. "Gotta go. Wish me luck. And don't let anyone kidnap you before I get back, okay?"

Still trying to catch my breath, I could only nod, watching him as he made his way through the crowd. It would be his first time performing in public – apart from church and school, and I knew he had to be apprehensive. I was nervous for him and joined the crowd in clapping and cheering as he joined the band on the stage that had been set up under the stars.

He took the mike with a wave out to the crowd. "Thank you, everyone. And thank you to the band for letting me up here." A teasing grin for the audience, "Be nice to me. This is my first time."

The crowd laughed, some calling out. "We love you, Daniel!"

"This song is going out to the lady in red at the back there. The girl who holds the key to my forever in her hands."

Daniel started singing, the first few lines of 'I Can't Help Falling in Love' by Samoa's all-time favorite band, UB40.

I had never heard him sing a contemporary piece before and I was captivated. So caught in his song that I never noticed the man holding a beer bottle who swayed and stumbled at my side. Not until he bumped into me. "Oi, shaman. Shorry babe." He was drunk, his voice slurred, but he smiled when he saw me. "Pretty girrrl. Hi babee. You wanna dance?"

I shook my head, wishing he would stumble away somewhere else. "No thank you. I'm waiting for my boyfriend."

The drunk didn't seem to hear me. Instead, he tried to hug me in a sweaty embrace. "I like you babee. Let's have some fun." His hands were everywhere. Grabbing my butt, groping my breast. His beer breath hot in my face as he tried to plant a slobbery kiss on my lips.

I reacted. Without thought. A lightning flash of flame from my raised hands hit the man in the face and he yelped, releasing his hold instantly. His beer bottle fell to the ground, the crash of breaking glass swallowed up with the noise of the crowd, of the band. He half-fell against a table, and the group standing there pushed him away, snapping at him to "go home … alu i le fale, you drunken fool!"

I stood there frozen, worried that people had seen the flames but everyone seemed to be caught up in the performance. Daniel was now singing a Bob Marley song and half of the place was singing along with him.

"Whew." A sigh of relief, but it was short-lived because standing there in the half-darkness of the crowded bar, I felt a coldness. A prickle of unease, as if there were a centipede crawling up my back. Someone or something was watching me. I turned and saw him standing a few feet away, holding a bottle of Vailima beer, staring at me. The boy from the regatta. The one with the piercings and scars, only tonight he wore a black silk shirt and slacks. How long had he been standing there?? What had he seen? And why was he looking at me like that?

I raised my chin defiantly and stared right back at him. He must have interpreted that as a signal that I wanted to talk because he walked over to me.

His first words were teasing. "So your pretty boy can sing too, ay Leila?"

I was in no mood to play. With anyone. But especially with arrogant boys who saw too much. Eyes narrowed, my voice was a hiss. "What do you want?"

A careless shrug. A heavy American-accented drawl. "Nuthin'. Just bein'friendly." His eyes raked me up and down. "Don't you look nice tonight."

I glared. "Wait, how did you know my name?"

He looked bored by the inanity of the question. "Samoa's a very small place. Ask and it shall be given. Simple." He held out one bandaged hand. "My name's Keahi."

I ignored it and folded my arms. I hoped I had hostility stamped all over me. I hoped the very air radiated with chemical aggression. "What do you want?"

A wry smile transformed his face as he opened his arms expansively. "This is me apologizing. I'm trying to be friends here. You know, make peace. For today."

"I don't want to be friends. You've apologized. Now go away and leave me alone." I turned away from the boy who had me on edge even when he was apologizing. I didn't trust him, didn't like him, and didn't want to be anywhere near him.

Still he didn't leave. Just stood there, smiling that irritating smile. I tried snapping. "What? Now what do you want?"

"Aren't you going to apologize to me?"

"Excuse me? What for?"

"Let me see, for doing something to burn my hands. For taking advantage of my gentlemanly respect for women so that you could knock me down and then almost break my ribs with that blow to the abs. Lucky for me I've got rock hard abs of steel. But see the bruises you gave me?" He pulled up his silk shirt to mock a sorrowful shake at his abdomen stamped with more ornate Pacific markings. Even in this dim light though, I could see the scar patterns that sat just beneath the tattoos, giving them a slight disfigured edge. And I noticed – but didn't want to – the taut muscle and contoured abs, the curve of his hip as it dipped down to something else.

He looked around to make sure nobody was listening. He needn't have worried because the whole place was captivated by Daniel's singing. He turned back to me and the smile was gone. "What did you do to that drunk?"

"What do you mean?"

"I mean, what did you just do to that guy who was groping you? I've been watching you and I saw the whole thing."

"Nothing. An intoxicated man groped me and I pushed him away, that's all."

"That's not what it looked like to me."

"I don't care what it looked like to you, that's what happened."

"And what really happened today at the regatta?"

"You mean when I kicked your arrogant ass today?"

His eyes narrowed and his tone was steel. "I mean, when you did something to that paddle so that it burnt my hands. What did you do?"

I shook my head and tried to walk away. "I have no idea what you're talking about. Why don't you leave me alone. I'm trying to listen to my boyfriend's singing."

His hand shot out and grabbed my wrist in an iron grip, "You're not leaving until you tell me what happened today."

The suddenness of his attack had me gasping. I knew my eyes flashed fire. "Let go of me. Trust me, you do not want to make me angry."

He ignored my warning. Instead he yanked at my arm, pulling me after him as he walked a few steps out of the restaurant and onto the grass. Not wanting to cause a scene, not wanting to disrupt Daniel's first performance, I allowed myself to be pulled outdoors, but inside my rage was simmering. Outside, the moonlight painted Keahi's charcoal eyes near silver as again he asked, "I want to know what you really are."

I wanted to incinerate this disturbing boy with his tattoos and pierced face, this boy who reeked of danger. "For the last time, I'm warning you. Get your hands off me."

"I want to see what happens when you get mad. Come on, Leila. Show me."

Cold dread. He knew something. Suspected something. "Nothing. I don't know what you're talking about."

He shook his head. "I saw you just now with that man. But more than that. I felt you." He leaned closer and I shrank back from his accusing gaze. He was standing so close now that I could taste his breath. The air was layered in his scent. It tasted of chili. Subdued vanilla. Overlaid with smoke. This boy called Keahi smelled familiar.

He smells like me ... telesā fanua afi.

As the familiarity hit me, Keahi winced, stumbled backwards, with his head in his hands. "Argh." His cry of pain ripped unwillingly from him.

My anger was turned to confusion, "What's wrong? Are you okay?"

The boy swayed, turned, and lurched a few steps away before tripping to fall to his knees in the rock garden.

"Hey, are you alright?"

I moved to kneel beside him but again he cried out. "Aargh, get away from me. It hurts. Get away from me."

Ignoring his command, I touched his shoulder, "Let me help you. You don't look well ..."

And that's when I saw it. The boy's tattoos – on his arms and neck, all of them – were glowing in the black night. Glowing red. Like blood. Like fire. I fell back away from him. "What are you? Who are you?"

The distance between us seemed to help because he shook his head and staggered to his feet, still with one hand to his head. "What did you just do to me?"

"I don't know." We stood there in the moonlight with an ocean of questions between us.

"Leila?" We both turned at the voice. It was Simone, a fuchsia vision. He stood there with a hand on one hip, studying us both. "Hmmm, am I interrupting something exciting? And forbidden?"

I smiled with weak relief. "Simone, there you are. I was looking for you."

"Yes I can see you were looking reeeally hard for me. Out here in the dark. Because I always hang around in dark corners with dop bad boy honeys." He batted his eyelashes at Keahi, who looked like he didn't know how to react to being confronted by a beautiful boy in a tube dress. "I'm Simone, dahling. And while I would love to talk dirty with you out here in the darkness, I really need Leila to come with me inside, right now."

Simone grabbed my arm and pulled me inside. He didn't stop until we were both inside the privacy of the girl's bathroom. Two other girls were touching up their makeup when we walked in but Simone dispensed with them immediately.

"You two, leave. Now. Before I scratch your eyes out. This ladies room is now occupied."

He locked the door behind them before turning to confront me. "What the hell were you doing getting busy outside with that boy when your man is singing his little heart out to you on stage?"

Simone was so mad that he looked like he wanted to rip my hair out. I was almost afraid of him. "It's not what you think. Nobody was 'getting busy' outside and dammit, Keahi is not a 'dop hot boy'. I would sooner spit on him than get near him, okay?"

My outrage seemed to appease Simone somewhat. "So if you weren't getting up close and personal with that Hawaiian hottie, what were you doing outside with him?"

I struggled to find an explanation that would make sense. "He wanted to apologize about the fight at the regatta today."

Simone still looked puzzled. "Apologize for what?"

"He was rude to me. He called me Daniel's bitch and said all this stuff about me and Daniel …"

"Get out, he did not! Why didn't you tell me that before? Girlfriend, you know I got your back. Did you tell Daniel?"

"No."

"No? Are you out of your freakin' mind? Let's go tell him now so he can work that fool over. Ooh, I can't wait to see Daniel fasi him." Now he was gleeful.

"No, I don't want any trouble. I don't want Daniel to know. Promise me you won't say anything to him. I'm not letting you out of here until you promise me."

I put on my serious, angry face and finally Simone relented. "Fine then. You're the boss. But I still think you should tell Daniel. It is so hot when two honeys fight." He had a faraway look in his eyes. "Just think, their shirts would get all ripped up and they would get all sweaty and dirty rolling around on the ground."

"Simone!"

He pouted, unlocked the door, and flounced out. "Fine. I won't tell Daniel."

"Tell me what?" It was Daniel. Standing in the walkway outside the bathrooms, a frown of worry on his face. "Leila, there you are. I've been looking everywhere for you."

Simone rolled his eyes at me behind Daniel's back as he pulled me close. Relief as he kissed me on the forehead. "I was getting worried. What's Simone talking about? What are you not going to tell me?"

He looked from Simone to me and back. Simone only shrugged, miming a 'my lips are sealed' motion before flouncing back out to the dance floor, throwing over his shoulder. "You're on your own with this one, Leila."

A reassuring smile up at Daniel. "Nothing. I loved your singing babe. Heck, everyone loved it. They couldn't get enough of you.

You were awesome." I pointed out to the dance floor. "Come on, do you want to dance?"

But Daniel would not be distracted. "Later. What's Simone talking about? Did something happen when I was on stage? I knew I shouldn't have left you on your own."

I could see he wasn't going to let this go. "It's nothing. While you were performing, some drunk guy fell on to me and was a little free with his hands. But I pushed him away and that was it. He carried on stumbling into everyone else in the bar."

Daniel's face hardened. "Where is he? Who was it? Point him out to me."

"No, it's alright. It's done. He was just drunk and didn't know what he was doing. I handled it already. It's fine."

"No, it's not fine."

The unusual shortness of his response had me taken aback. "Why isn't it fine? I can take care of myself you know. I'm a fire goddess remember …"

Daniel interrupted abruptly. "Dammit Leila, would you stop saying that? I'm sick of it. I'm sick of this."

People around us were turning to watch. This was not the place for this conversation. I took Daniel's hand and pulled him away from the crowd, outside and away from the curious onlookers, down the beach beside a grove of coconut trees. "Would you just calm down? I don't understand. What's going on here? What are you sick of?"

He stared at me for several minutes, frustration at war with my plea for calm. "I love you and I am going to spend the rest of my life loving you, but do you know how it feels to know that your girlfriend can incinerate you on the spot? That she can summon a volcano or literally make the earth move beneath your feet?"

Horror and hurt choked me. "Don't you know that I would never hurt you? Everything I am, everything that I have, all that I can do – it's all nothing if I don't have you." I held out my hands helplessly. "This power, gift, curse, whatever you call it – I didn't ask for it. I am a telesā without a sisterhood. My only covenant is with you. My fire is for you, always. To protect you and the ones that I love. Keep you safe. I would never hurt you. Please believe me."

"You still don't get it, do you?" Daniel raged, and the ocean wind whipped his words about. "I don't want you to safeguard me. I'm not a pathetic little boy who needs protection. I'm your boyfriend and I need to know you trust me to take care of you. And I don't want you to be 'Leila the Fire Goddess' who goes around kicking ass all over town." He nodded his head. "Yeah, that's right, I heard about what happened today at the regatta when I wasn't looking. When I wasn't with you." He mimicked her words, "When you told me, 'Oh nothing happened. Don't worry about me, I'm Leila the fire goddess.' You lied to me. Again. What? Did you think I wouldn't find out? That nobody would tell me?"

The onslaught continued. "Of course I heard about it. The boys just *loved* telling me about how my girlfriend jumped in and knocked down the captain of the Hawaiian outrigger team with some kind of Jet Li martial arts techniques. And you know what they loved even more? They were crazy-loving it when I told them, no that couldn't be right, because my girlfriend never said anything about fighting anybody. My girlfriend doesn't know any Jet Li stuff. Because if she did, she would have told me. Because I'm her boyfriend and that's what people do when they love each other. They trust each other. They take care of each other. But you wouldn't know anything about that, would you? Because you're *Leila the fire goddess.*" He shook his head at me. "No, I can't do this anymore, Leila."

His tirade came to a sudden halt and we were two people standing beside a black ocean, divided by far more than the breeze that blew in from the velvet night. Now his voice was soft. "You've never really let me in. Last year when we first met, you threw up so many barriers, you hated everybody and didn't give people a chance. Then, just when I thought we were connecting, you got your powers and you shut me out of your life. I was out again, like that." He snapped his fingers. "And then you let me in." A smile at the memory. "We went to hell and back together, Leila. We literally shouted at death in the face. So why can't you be honest with me now, about something as minor as a sleazy drunk? Or tell me why you felt you had to get involved in that fight at the regatta today?"

"I didn't want to worry you, Daniel. It was nothing. I didn't want you to get hurt or upset, so I just dealt with it."

"You can't keep doing that. You can't attack guys who beat me in an outrigger race. Or spare me the gory details when some drunk guy mauls you. You can't keep hiding things from me or lying to me about the bad stuff. You can't keep protecting me. I get that you're a fire goddess, Leila. I get that you're always going to be stronger than me. But I'm still a man. Your man. And if you can't give me that much respect, then this isn't going to work."

My shock turned to fury. "You're damn straight this isn't going to work. This is rubbish. This is about your over-inflated male ego getting bruised because I'm not some frilly, pouting girl who runs squealing to her boyfriend every time someone so much as looks at her funny. I will not pretend to be weak just to make you feel better."

Daniel's face was incredulous. "That's not what I said."

I didn't give him the breath to continue. "Yes, I'm protective of the people I love, so what? You're forgetting a crucial detail here. You died. I saw a gang of demonic spirit women tie you up, torture you, and then kill you. And I couldn't do anything to stop them. All of my powers, all of my fire goddess mojo and all I could do was watch. Because of me, you died. And I'm always going to live with that. I don't know what brought you back to me, but I've got you, so yeah, I'm never going to stop trying to protect you. And you can't stop me."

Daniel started backing away, shouting. "Oh yeah? Well look at me now. You see this? This is me, walking away from you. Walking away from the protection detail. Because I don't need a psycho bodyguard. I need a girlfriend." He walked away down the gravel driveway, throwing once over his shoulder. "So you come find me when you're ready to be that girl."

I didn't wait to watch the darkness swallow him up. Red rage ripped through me. I stamped my foot and threw a flaming fireball at the empty beachfront, screaming. "Damn you to hell, Daniel!"

The flames skittered harmlessly onto wet sand and died. I stomped away to the Jeep, texting Simone furiously. 'Can we go now? I'm at the car. I wait 4 u ther.'

Leila never looked back. Not in the direction where Daniel had disappeared. Not at the beachfront where they had been standing. Not even at the restaurant. And so she never saw the boy who had been standing in the shadows of the coconut grove, listening. Watching. Keahi lit a cigarette, the red glow dancing on his sardonic smile, catching on the glint of gold at his raised eyebrow as he watched Leila get in her Jeep and slam the door with another curse word.

Today was a day of firsts. I had started at a new school three different times in the last two years but this time was different. Here now, today, at the National University of Samoa, was the first time I was starting at a new school with ready-made friends. Simone in full pulili mode led the way from the Jeep, wearing one of my ruffled off the shoulder TAV tops, a skintight pair of black jeans, and red platform heels. Sinalei struggled to keep up in the puletasi her mother had made her wear. Maleko was checking his hair one last time in the mirror, "Wait up guys."

As the only one with my own car, I was resigned to the fact that I would be providing the official taxi service for everyone, especially as Maleko and Sinalei were en-route so I couldn't very well say no, could I?

"Hurry up Leila, we're gonna be late and all the good ones will be taken." Simone waited impatiently for me to grab my bag and lock the Jeep.

Just then, Daniel's truck turned into the parking lot and Maleko let out a whoop, "Uce!"

Just great. My smile faded and I quickened my pace to the admin block. Because today marked another first. The first time I would experience running into an ex-boyfriend who had effectively dumped me. This was the first time I would rather face an angry horde of telesā than see Daniel. I almost ran in my haste to get as far away from the parking lot as I could, Simone and the others following behind me.

Ever clueless, Sinalei asked loudly, "That's Daniel. Why aren't we waiting for him?"

Simone rolled his eyes and heaved a dramatic sigh. "Because we're not speaking to him today Sinalei. Must we spell it out for you?" He turned mid-step and spoke slowly, as if to a child. "This week, Daniel is a dumb ass. Next week, he will go back to being Leila's Chunk Hunk and we can delight in his gorgeousness, okay? Right, Leila? We're just gonna be mad for this week right?"

I ignored Simone and kept walking. "You all can talk to Daniel whenever you want to. I have nothing to say to him."

I stalked off to find my first lecture, but my brain was crowded with a swarm of thoughts. Chaotic fruit bats battling to escape. I didn't know how it had all gone wrong. Only a few days ago, life had been a series of almost perfect moments. Daniel and I had been talking about forever. And now? I had been doing lots of thinking since that anger-filled night, trying to see things from his perspective, but I couldn't shake the certainty that Daniel was being a class A jerk. Looking back, I could trace the progression though. Starting with his refusal to talk about our close shave with that shark or anything to do with the night the ocean had saved his life. To the whole stupid fence and gate thing. How idiotic was that? I should have seen the barbed wire for what it really was. An insecure boyfriend's attempt to assert some measure of control over a girlfriend he obviously felt threatened by. But then, what boy would be able to handle a girlfriend who could incinerate him with a thought? I shouldn't be angry at him for deciding he couldn't handle it, right? I shouldn't. But I was. Because he had convinced me that what we had was strong enough for even the most explosive of volcanoes. That together, we could face anything and everything.

Everything, it seemed – except for a fragile male ego.

The first day of lectures was relatively painless. Simone was in three of my five classes, which meant they were guaranteed to be interesting, no matter what. Every so often I ran into other familiar faces from Samoa College. Some less appealing than others. The lissome, beautiful Mele was in my English tutorial. Lucky me. We both ignored each other. Sinalei and Maleko were in my science lectures and it was a relief to have friends to sit with. And Daniel was in my other two core subjects, but it didn't matter because so were two hundred other students and he was just a boy across a crowded lecture theatre. Yeah, so he was a boy impossible to miss, even in a plain t-shirt and shorts. Beauty cut in perfect lines of supple stone. But I was working hard on the ignoring him part. And not doing too badly. I would have made it through the entire day without even talking to him if the unexpected hadn't happened.

The unexpected being Keahi. The boy from the regatta. Sitting at a table in the canteen courtyard with a group of other students. Talking. Laughing. Looking for all the world like he belonged there. I stopped short in my tracks with a Diet Coke and a half-eaten donut in hand. Too startled to be composed. Wondering how I could flame him without about fifty students noticing.

I went up to him. "It's you."

He didn't betray any surprise. "Yeah, it's me. And ooh look, it's you." he replied drily.

"Are you following me?" I demanded.

He turned and raised that pierced eyebrow at me with a pitying look. "Baby, I hate to break it to you, but you ain't got nuthin' worth following."

He said it loud enough for the others to hear, and they laughed. Of course. Because that's what self-important boys with grating, deficient personalities and meager intellect like to do. Belittle girls in front of as large an audience as possible. Probably to make up for their inadequacies in every other area that counted for anything. I didn't back off. Instead, I raised my voice, inviting even more listeners. Loud. Firm. Authoritative.

"You followed me at the bar the other night, harassed me, touched me, grabbed me – even after I told you several times to get away from me. And now you're here at my university. I think that counts as stalker behavior."

People everywhere in the courtyard were staring now. I had just called him out for sexual harassment and being a stalker. Take that, you cinnamon chili stick. You walking advertisement for the perils of ink addiction. Ha.

To his credit, he didn't even look embarrassed. Instead, he smiled that sneering grin and threw a side comment at the other boys. "Excuse us. If I don't deal with her now, she'll never leave me alone." More laughter. He stood up and looped an arm casually over my shoulder, taking me with him away from the rest of the lunch crowd so that we stood out of hearing distance but not so much that everyone couldn't still see us.

My skin crawled at his touch and I shook his arm away. "Don't touch me. Ever. I just want to know why you're following me. And the other night at the club, what was that all about? Were you sick? What is wrong with you?" Still he said nothing, only kept staring at me with that same sneering smile on his face.

"Are you listening to me? I said, why are you here at my school? Why haven't you gone back to Hawaii? I heard all the teams left in the weekend. Keahi? Say something. Why are you staring at me like that? Are you listening to me?"

His response had me gaping. "No, I don't give a shit what you were saying. I was looking at your lips and imagining kissing you."

Stunned, I took an involuntary step back. "Excuse me? What did you say?"

Keahi shrugged. "I'm wondering what it would be like to kiss you. Do you taste of vanilla and a hint of chili? Because that's what you smell like."

Fear tiptoed with icy feet through my tightening chest. "I don't know what you're talking about."

"Oh, I think you do." Keahi smiled and leaned in closer, much to the avid interest of the lunch spectators. "I think that when I kiss you, all your tattoos will glow red like fire. I know mine will. Shall we try it? Right here. Right now?"

With his closeness came that same familiar fragrance I had tasted the other night. *Don't panic. Don't panic. Don't freak out.* Because with panic and freaking out comes fire and heat. I needed to get away from this boy. Now. I backed away. "Stay far away from me. You hear me? Don't come near me again."

But this strange boy wasn't ready to let me go. He grabbed my arm and pulled me against him so he could whisper. "I've always wanted to kiss a fire goddess." The ice cold feet were now a stomping avalanche of fear suffocating me.

"I don't know what you think you saw that night – but you're wrong. You're insane. Get away from me."

Who was this boy? Why did it feel like he knew me? The earthy, simmering, always-ready-to-erupt me? And why did he stir up such bone-crushing terror? Terror tinged with something else. I fought against fear, fought for control of my fire before the entire courtyard exploded with a lava jet plume. I was fighting a losing battle, when I saw him. Daniel. *Oh no.* He strolled into the courtyard with Maleko. Almost immediately, his eyes leapt to where we stood and took in the entire scene. Keahi. My arm captive in his. The fear on my face. Instantly, his face darkened and he walked over with purposeful strides. Keahi hadn't seen him.

Seeing Daniel gave me the jolt I needed to re-assert control on fanua afi. I yanked my arm away from Keahi's grasp. Fierce. "I'm out of here."

"But I'm not done talking to you," he warned.

And then Daniel was there.

"What's going on here? Are you alright, Leila?" Daniel's body was tense with anger, and the air was a finely strung wire waiting to snap. Beside Keahi's slight build, Daniel looked even bigger. More threatening. Solid. Immovable. Unbreakable. I wavered, longed to move into his arms and wilt into their strength. But I was not, and would not, be that girl. The one who needed barbed wire fences and gates. The girl who got her boyfriend dragged into conflict situations where he could get attacked. Tortured. Killed. I held fast to that image, that memory of his inert body, electrocuted again and again by the telesā matagi, the glint of the knife as it stabbed into his chest, the stillness of the water after they threw his body over the side of the boat.

I held fast to all those things, held my head high and drew strength from my mother earth fanua. "I'm fine, thank you. I was just leaving."

I turned to go, ignoring the cut of pain in Daniel's eyes. It would have worked though. The defusing would have succeeded. If Keahi hadn't opened his taunting big mouth. "Hi Daniel. Leila and I were just talking about you. She was telling me all about how your over-inflated male ego can't handle the fact that she's not a whimpering … no, that's not it. What words did she use exactly? Hmm, that's right. You can't handle it that she's not a simpering, squealing girl who needs her boyfriend to protect her every time someone as much as looks at her funny. Did I get your words right there, Leila?"

My words wielded as weapons by this taunting stranger. Could this day get any worse? Outrage. "I did not say that … how did you know that?!" I turned to Daniel, who looked as if he'd been slammed by a pack scrum. "He's lying, I never told him about any of that."

But Daniel's defenses were up. "No, you're right Leila. You're not a girl who needs a boyfriend to protect her. You do just fine on your own, don't you?" He threw a glance at Keahi. "Or maybe I was just the wrong kind of boyfriend."

"Daniel, no – wait!" But he was gone. Striding across the courtyard in the painfully brilliant sunshine.

I looked back at Keahi. The laughing, the broken smile on his face, the raised eyebrow. All of it. "You lied. There's no way you could have known those things. Unless …" my voice died away.

"Unless what?" He leaned against the brick wall, arms folded, clearly loving every minute of the encounter. "You should be more careful when you're having deep and meaningful screaming sessions with your boyfriend out in the open. You never know who could be listening."

I glared at him. Anger, hate, rage, frustration, hurt. "Why? Why are you doing this to me? Why won't you leave me alone?"

"That's just it." Keahi shrugged. And for the first time, his tone was no longer teasing. "I don't know why I can't."

Defeated. I walked away. And this time, Keahi let me go.

The days blended into one another. Days of torture catching glimpses of Daniel at a distance, trying to still the smile, the leap of my heart, the catch of my breath every time I saw him. Listening to Simone lecture me about girls who are "awful witches to their poor boyfriends for no reason. You know what happens to those girls, don't you, Leila? They end up lonely, haggard old bags talking to their imaginary friends. Watching *Game of Thrones* re-runs and believing that Khal Drogo is going to come alive again. Why can't you fix this? Why can't you apologize?"

So maybe I was watching a few too many episodes of *Game of Thrones*. Big deal. So what? The brutal violence distracted me from the anger I harbored. For Keahi. For Daniel. For the world in general. No, more specifically – all boys in general. I couldn't understand them and I wasn't sure that I wanted to.

Simone had it all wrong. I had tried to fix it. I had called Daniel after the courtyard show-down. Apologized. Explained what had happened. And he had listened. A silent, cold presence on the other side of the line. And when my explanations had run out of steam he had assured me that no, he wasn't mad at me. Anymore. No, he didn't hate me. But he didn't think it was a good idea for us to be together right now.

"I think we should take a break from each other."

"A break?" My voice squeaked. The chocolate ad jeered in my head. *Have a break, have a Kit-Kat.* Why in hell would I want a break?

"Yeah. Some space. I think we let things get too intense between us, way too fast. So much happened last year. Maybe we need space so we can get perspective. So we can breathe."

What was he talking about? I couldn't breathe now, listening to this rubbish about space for breathing. This couldn't be happening. Me and Daniel weren't some *High School Musical* teenagers who squabbled and split up over petty things like lip gloss and basketball. We had stood strong against a matagi sisterhood. We were tougher than this. We were forever. This could not be happening.

But it was. "Last year, you needed time out from me. And everything. I love you more than life and I'm always going to love you this way, but I'm asking you, Leila, if you love me? Then please, give me some time out."

I couldn't argue with that. Reason it away. Or make sense of it. All I could do was agree. For the first time I understood the meaning of that stupid saying, *If you love someone, set them free...*

Daniel was hanging up on me now. "Hey, I gotta go. I got work to do. We'll catch up sometime."

I clung to that word 'sometime' like a life raft. The possibilities in it. Last year, Daniel had waited for me. Loved me from a distance. I could do the same for him. Couldn't I?

In the meantime, I threw myself into my work at the Center, attending the self-defense classes after university lectures, pretending to be Dayna's assistant so I could have an excuse to hit things. The numbers grew every day as word spread about the skills we were learning and most classes were maxed out at twenty-five people – young and old – all Center residents and their children. The space quickly became cramped, and Dayna moved sparring sessions outdoors with bag work inside. Mrs. Amani had agreed that the Center needed a proper gymnasium, and I met with Thompson about accessing Nafanua's funds for a building project. We contracted an engineering firm to do the plans, and they would break ground in another month. In the evenings, I volunteered in the homework tutor classes, helping girls with their English assignments (but wisely stayed away from math problems).

The work at the Center was invigorating. Addictive even. I liked seeing my mother's money – the proceeds of her telesā gifts – being utilized for good. I liked spending time with the Center residents. So many of them had lived through hell and were grateful to have a month, a week, a day without fear. Conversations with them made me realize that I had lived a rather sheltered life. Folgers didn't get out in the regular world much. Even brown thug Folgers. I quickly discovered that Mrs. Amani had been painfully correct about the children being the most vulnerable victims. Time and again, I saw another woman check out of the Center to go back and live with her abusive partner, taking her children with her. And everyone hoped they wouldn't need to come back. But chances of that were low.

I kept tabs on Daniel. Of course. But it wasn't easy. I rarely saw him at university. I drove past his house every night though. And casually meandered along his street after school every day, pretending that I wasn't staring at the workshop. At his house. Maleko reported that Daniel had quit playing club rugby for the Moata'a team and instead spent all his spare time paddling. So I took up outrigger canoe stalking in the evenings. I went for runs on the Apia seawall, scoping out the Pualele boats as they did their sprints in the harbor, knifing through the blue-jet water. Always hoping for a glimpse of the boy who wanted a break from me.

I saw a lot of Keahi though because every other minute of the day, the boy was in my face. He was enrolled in all the same classes as me. Smoking in the corridor when I walked to my next class, lurking in the library aisles without any books, sipping a soda across from me in the courtyard at lunch. He never tried to make contact or talk to me. He was just everywhere I turned. Just present. Just there. Staring at me with those charcoal eyes and taunting me with that sneering smile. Simone hated him.

"There he is again, giving you those creepy eyes. He makes me glad we have a barbed wire fence." Simone shivered. "We need to call him out." He yelled out across the lecture theater, "What are you looking at? You see something you like over here?" He stood up and lifted up his flirty top, flashing Keahi with his boob top. "You wanna piece of this? Baby, you couldn't handle all of this."

The class laughed, but Simone failed in his bid to embarrass Keahi, who only puckered his lips and blew Simone a kiss.

"What a jerk." Simone exclaimed with disgust. It was easy to agree with him.

I had a much harder time agreeing with Simone later that day though when he brought home his new friend.

"Leila, remember I told you about my awesome Accounting Studies tutor who's helping me with my project? Come out and meet her."

I walked out of the room with a welcoming smile that died as soon as I saw the girl standing in our living room.

"Lesina."

Barbie didn't look too excited to see me either. "Leila."

Simone was excited. "You two know each other! No way. My two favorite people have already met. How? Where?"

He looked back and forth, waiting for one of us to fill in the gaps. Lesina spoke first and her acting skills were epic because even I almost believed her. The relaxed smile, the cheerful ease, the friendly tone all added up to best-friends-are-us. "Leila is best friends with my fiancé Jason. I knew all about her before we even met a few weeks ago. Jason told me so much about her that I knew we would be great friends. And I was right. We met and just clicked right away, didn't we, Leila?"

I forced a smile. "Yes. We did. I was so … so … surprised to meet Jason's fiancé but happy. Happy. Because I could see how happy he is and together you two are just perfect and happy. Really happy. So happy." Did I just use the word happy six times? "I didn't know you worked at the university."

Leila nodded, "Only part-time. My real job is with an accounting firm in town but the university was desperate for help with their tutor program because there's a shortage of qualified people who can teach accounting. I was only too glad to help. Working with teenagers is a joy of mine."

Ugh. Was that a dig at my being seven years younger than Jason? "You don't seem very old though. But then, it's so hard to tell." *With all that muck on your face.* "I would never have guessed you're an accountant. And a teacher." Isn't all that peroxide seeping into your brain doing bad things to it?

She smiled. Sweetly. "I'm afraid I was a bit of a genius at school and graduated early. Flew through an accelerated program at UCLA with a full scholarship."

Of course. You would be a genius. Jason was a freak genius and all freak geniuses got married to each other. And lived happily ever after in genius land. And had little freak genius babies. I wanted to smack her. Or at least kick her out of our house.

Simone was clueless about the undertones though. "I've asked Lesina to stay for pizza dinner with us."

There goes fun pizza night. "You have?"

"Yes. And guess what? Lesina has agreed to model for me at the Independence Fashion Awards." Simone was gleeful.

I was confused. "Huh? The what?"

He rolled his eyes at me. "You never pay attention to anything I say, do you? I told you last week, I'm entering some of my designs into the Fashion Awards being held during the June Independence Week celebrations. Lesina has signed up to be my first model."

I wanted to say 'this vertically challenged, over-boosted, busting-out pip-squeak is going to model clothes in an actual fashion show?' But I didn't. Instead I gave my best plastic smile. "That's great."

Lesina was puzzled. "Wait, isn't Leila modeling for you as well, Simone?"

Simone laughed. Way too loud for my liking. I mean heck, the idea of me modeling stuff on stage couldn't be THAT ridiculous, could it? "Are you kidding? She hates dressing up. My designs are couture and there's no way Leila could handle them."

How dare he dismiss me? I could model couture crap just as much as the next girl. As much as Barbie could. "Oh Simone, you're exaggerating. Of course I can handle your designs. I love dressing up." I laughed airily and 'confided' to Lesina, "He's always stealing my clothes every time we go out. And I swear he will kill me in my sleep one day for my Louboutin shoes."

Simone arched an eyebrow at me in disbelief – which I ignored. I stuck one hand on my hip and tried my best to look fashion weary. "I would love to model for Simone but unfortunately I'm just too busy with my work at the Center."

"Yes, how unfortunate. For all of us." Simone remarked drily. "Okay ladies, let's order pizza. I'm starving."

Lesina stayed for dinner. And for another two hours after that. She and Simone loved the same music. Lusted for the same Hollywood celebrities. And hated the same fashion trends. I listened to them laugh and talk and laugh some more and sourly reflected that they would make far better friends than me and Simone. Although I had to admit that maybe, just maybe Lesina wasn't so bad after all. Once she took the stupid shoes off and relaxed over pizza and Diet Coke with us, she seemed more natural, more approachable, more likeable. I still didn't want her marrying Jason though. There was something not quite right there.

After she left, Simone confronted me. "What the heck was all that earlier?"

"What was what?"

"All that rubbish about you loving fashion? And why don't you like Lesina?"

I protested. Weakly. "I do like her."

"Yeah right."

"No, I do. It's just that I feel she's a little fake sometimes, you know? Don't you get that feeling like she's not being genuine? Not really herself?"

"No, I don't get that at all."

I tried again. "How about her hair then? It's so over the top. And all that makeup she wears? It's so overdone."

Simone shook his head at me, "Now you're just reaching. What's makeup got to do with anything? You don't wear any and I still like you. No, there's something else going on here. Admit it, you're jealous."

"I am not!" I was aghast. And wounded that he would think that of me. "Why would I be jealous of her?"

He rolled his eyes heavenward. "Oh, it's so obvious. Because she's engaged to Jason the Volcano Man and you still have a secret crush on him."

"No, I don't." And as I said the words, I knew them to be true. Yes, there may once have been sparks between Jason and I, but that was in a long ago other lifetime and they were overshadowed now by the depth of what I shared with Daniel. Because even though Daniel was 'taking a break' from me right now, I was still bound to him. By love. By fire. And by some other unnamed thing that even I could not explain. I took a deep breath. "I mean it, Simone. I don't have any feelings like that for Jason."

"So why don't you want him to be with Lesina then?" he demanded.

"I can't explain it. There's something not right about their relationship. I can sense it but I can't express what it is that makes me feel uneasy about them. About her."

"Well, I like her. And she's helping me with my accounting project. And she's going to model for me. So she's going to be hanging out here a lot from now on. Don't you dare be mean to her, you hear me?"

I nodded and then thought of something else that was bugging me. "Why didn't you ask me?"

"Ask you what?" Simone was getting exasperated, his patience wearing thin.

"Ask me to be a model for your show?" I sulked. "You asked her but you didn't ask me."

Simone threw his hands in the air. "Leila, getting you to wear a MENA dress is like forcing you to endure the worst kind of torture. Have you even looked at any of my designs? You've been so busy with your work at the Center that you've hardly been home. I'm not making t-shirts and denim shorts here you know. I didn't ask you because I knew you would hate it. And I didn't want to force you to do something just because you're my friend."

I felt guilty. Simone was right. I hadn't been paying any attention to what was a very big deal for him. This would be the first Independence Fashion Awards show for Samoa, there were designers entering from overseas, and it would be the first time for Simone to showcase any of his creations. "I would love to help in any way I can. I'm sure I would suck at being a model, but I can do anything else that you want done. Like, umm … I don't know. What do fashion designers do anyway?"

Simone laughed. "Come on, I think it's time you had a look in our Temple of Learning. Now, don't freak out, okay?"

I followed him to the third bedroom, the designated 'study.' Which I hadn't set foot in since we moved into the house. Or studied in for that matter. He opened the door with a flourish, "Ta dah! Don't touch anything, you hear me?"

I gaped. 'Creative chaos' was the only term that captured the mess confronting us. One wall was covered with sketches and fabric swatches. Another with pages ripped from magazines, pictures of clothes, clothes, and more clothes. There was a sewing machine on the desk in the corner and rolls of fabric, coils of ribbon, an industrial glue gun, staplers, and even a hammer and nails, a bag bursting with feathers, jars filled with shells and seeds. And everywhere on the floor was bundles of siapo tapa cloth, dried pandanus leaves, coconut shells, and more.

"Where did you get all this stuff?"

A shrug. "Oh from here and there. My mum got me the machine and all the other equipment. She's being very supportive – but quietly, because my Dad doesn't like me wasting time on the fashion fantasy. If my designs do well in the Independence Show then maybe my father will see that I can make a true career out of it."

I couldn't believe I'd been so oblivious to what Simone was working on. *Bad friend, bad friend* ... chanted its way through my head. "This is amazing. I'm so excited for you." I took several careful steps into the mess, peering closer at the sketches pinned on the wall. "Are these your designs for the show?"

"Yes. I'm exploring our Samoan myths about teine sa. Some people call them telesā. They're spirit women of legend that have power to curse those who defy them and even possess people. I'm walking a dangerous line here because teine Sa are a taboo topic, you know?" His excited explanation came to a halt at the sight of my face. "What is it?"

Simone had hit me with a wrecking ball of the unexpected. "Telesā? Your fashion collection is inspired by telesā?"

"Yes, have you heard any of the legends?"

A weak smile. "Oh, a few. I had no idea you would choose to focus on such a … forbidden subject for your first collection. Are you expecting much controversy?"

"I don't know what to expect but I'm hoping I can shake people up a bit at least. Telesā are fierce, passionate, and strong women so I want those elements reflected in my designs."

He showed me several sketches, vivid slashes of color with intricate detailing. I was impressed. "Wow, these are stunning." I pointed to a red and orange creation. "That one especially. It's almost like these telesā could be representative of some of the earth's elements, you know? This one with the blaze of reds, it reminds me of a volcano eruption. And this other sketch with the brown pandanus leaves? If you added some green to it, that would be earth and foliage and it makes me think of lush rainforest." For some reason, I thought of Teuila from the Center. "And I know the perfect girl who could model that one."

There was a gleam in Simone's eyes, "Leila, aren't you a surprise. Telesā as earth's elements, I love that concept. Now, I feel an irrepressible creative frenzy coming on. You have to get out. Go on. Leave the Fashion Temple."

I laughed as I backed out of the room. "Fine. Just remember who your best friend is that helped inspire you when you're a world famous designer."

Just before he shut the door, Simone paused, "Hey, Leila? Thanks. And to show my gratitude? I'm going to let you be one of my models in the show. Oooh, lucky you!"

The door slammed before I could argue, and Lady Gaga cranked up on the stereo. Simone was now in his creative 'zone' and should not be disturbed.

Simone's warning had been justified because Lesina did start spending way too much time at our place. Jason was away in Savaii at Matavanu Volcano during the week so Lesina spent most evenings with Simone. It turned out that she was more than a genius accounting freak. She could also sew. So she was allowed into the Fashion Temple and put to work assembling Simone's visions. But even more useful (in my opinion), Lesina could cook. She made ginger shrimp with coconut cream sauce and I almost forgave her for having the most irritating giggle in the entire universe. She made perfect chop suey, and I decided that the girl wasn't related to Jessica Simpson. But it wasn't until the night that she baked chocolate pie – decadent with a hint of koko Samoa, a delicate melt-in-your-mouth crust, butter cream icing, and a sprinkling of toasted grated coconut – that I finally stopped calling her Barbie in my mind. And I apologized to her face. For being a 'little reserved' when we had first met.

She took it good naturedly. A shrug. "Hey, that's okay. I understand. You and Jason were friends before I came along and you probably thought I was going to trample all over that friendship." She confessed with a sheepish grin, "I was jealous of you before we even met. Jason talked about you all the time, being the toughest, bravest girl he'd ever known. It made me feel very inadequate. I'm glad we're getting to know each other. And I know Jason is happy we're hanging out."

I felt very mature and reasonable being able to talk to Lesina like that, but all the girl bonding was making me a little uncomfortable so I escaped to the Center right after dinner, leaving Simone and his helper sewing coconut shell links together in some sort of space age gladiator woman outfit. At least at the Center I didn't get requests to be a mannequin. *Just try this on for me, I need to see what it looks like on a person ... Just let me borrow your legs for a minute, what do you think, Lesina, are these thigh-high coconut sinnet boots too much with the feathers?*

Yes, the Center with its physically demanding workout classes was proving to be my favorite place to hang out.

Until the day I showed up for a class with Dayna only to find she
had scored herself a new assistant. Keahi was leading the juniors in
warm-up exercises outside on the lawn while Dayna was
overseeing a sparring session indoors. I walked over to her and
hissed, "What is he doing here?"

She was surprised at my antagonism, "Who? You mean Keahi
Meredith? He's great. He's been coming to my gym since he
moved here but he's been doing muay thai since he was a kid.
Fought professionally back in Hawaii as well."

"But what's he doing *here*?"

"I put up a flyer at the gym asking for volunteers who wanted to
help with our classes here at the Center and he signed up. What's
wrong?"

"Nothing. I just wish you'd asked me first."

She looked around us at all the activity. "I'm sorry. We've got so
many people signed up here now that we need all the help we can
get."

"But don't you think that having a male instructor is going to freak
some of the women out? After all they've been through?"

"No. The opposite. Having a class with a male who's interested in
helping them learn how to defend themselves could be a positive
experience."

I couldn't argue with Dayna's reasoning. What could I do to get rid
of him? I wasn't about to tell Dayna that I didn't want this boy
around because he smelled like chili and vanilla. Instead, I waited
until the warm-up session was finished and then walked over to
where Keahi stood outside. "What in hell are you doing here?"

His eyes narrowed, "I could ask you the same thing. I thought this
was a self-defense class for a Women's Refuge, not for spoilt rich
girls from America."

"I'm here because my mother funded this Center. And because these self-defense classes were my idea. Not that it's any of your business. And don't lie. You only signed up because you knew I would be here. And I am not a spoilt rich girl from America."

"Correction. I signed up because Dayna said she needed help. I used to volunteer at a youth center back in Hawaii so this is nothing new to me. And as for the other stuff, do you come from a rich family? Are you from America?"

I shrugged. Refused to answer. Which was answer enough. He sneered. "So it all fits."

I stamped my foot. "But I'm not spoilt."

He raised that scarred eyebrow at me, the one that reminded me of Jason Momoa. Even when I didn't want it to. "Stamping your foot and having a tantrum? I'd say that was classic spoilt brat behavior."

Before I could react, Dayna called Keahi over to help her demo a new combination and he walked away from me with casual ease. Smiling. The only thing stopping me from cursing – screaming, breaking something, storming out of there – was my desire not to be mistaken for a spoilt brat.

He was at the next class on the following day. And the one after that. And, much to my disgust, the students loved him. Everyone wanted to be in his warm-up group. Everyone wanted to have him as their sparring partner. Even Mrs. Amani was impressed with him.

"He's so good with the class. He has a natural rapport with them, you know?"

I did know. I observed Keahi with the class, and he was a different person. The sneering attitude was gone. Along with the arrogance and barbed sarcasm. Instead, he was friendly and helpful, never overstepping the line between instructor and student but always interacting with the class with relaxed confidence and professional ease. He was patient with them and funny. Even Teuila was hanging on his every word. And no one could fault his martial arts skills. I waited until one day, after a grueling session had ended, after everyone had streamed out of the room, sweaty and exhilarated, and then went over to confront him. "I don't get it."

"What don't you get?" The condescending grin was back.

"You. When you're with the class and everyone else, you're not an egotistical, abrasive maniac."

"So?"

"So I want you to tell me why you're so rude to me. Why do you keep trying to push all my buttons?"

He moved closer towards me. "We both want something then. Sparks fly when I push your buttons, Leila. I want you to tell me why."

I stepped backwards to get away from his closeness, the impenetrable directness of his gaze – and bumped into one of the kick bags. It bumped back, tripping me a little off balance so that I stumbled against Keahi and his hands came up to steady me against him. His touch burned. And not in a 'you're so hot and I want you' kind of way. No. In an electrical spark and fizz kind of way. Without even looking down, I knew that my malu was highlighted in blood-red lines because the tattoos on Keahi's neck and arms were doing the same thing. We both jumped apart at the same time.

He looked as freaked out as I was. "There it is again. Did you feel that?"

I knew there could only be one possible answer but I wasn't about to share it with a boy I didn't trust. "I don't know. I have to go."

He called after me, "Leila, wait."

But I didn't look back.

The next day, Mrs. Amani invited Keahi and I to stay after class for Wednesday night ice cream. We both took our food outdoors and there was no shortage of children wanting to sit beside Keahi at the long trestle table. They were all jostling for a chance to pester the exciting visitor with questions about everything from his tattoos to his pierced eyebrow and whether or not he had ever killed anyone in the ring. Or met the legendary Dwayne Johnson, 'the Rock.'

I rolled my eyes. Whatever. These kids were mistaking Keahi for somebody important. I studiously ignored him and his table, instead focusing on the rapport I was trying to build with Teuila. The young teenager was an enigma. I knew there was something different about her, something ethereal. Possibly telesā. But it wasn't air, fire or water. So what was it then? I called her to sit with me at a table as far away as possible from the others so we could have some privacy.

"Teuila, I wanted to ask you about the other day when we were outside under the mango trees."

"What about it?"

"Has that happened to you before? That thing with the trees?"

She glanced around us, apprehensive about a possible audience. "A couple of times. At first it was just small stuff. Like when I was sad, plants would …" she halted and looked embarrassed. Muttered. "Give me stuff, like flowers or fruit. Or plants would act out how I'm feeling.It sounds dumb, I know. I thought I was just imagining it. Then something big happened. One night my mum was having a party with some friends. It was really noisy and I didn't like them. Her friends. I was mad. But only because I was scared, you know? I've seen what always happens when she gets drunk with her friends. So I got mad and went outside to get away from them. I was out there and the breadfruit tree in our backyard – it snapped in half and fell on our house. And then all the other trees started moving their branches but there was no wind. It was terrifying. That cut the party short real fast. I still hoped it was an accident. Until the night my mum got attacked. Then I knew all that stuff with the trees wasn't an accident. It was happening because of me."

She stopped and her gaze went to a distant, faraway place ...

Teuila didn't like her mom's new boyfriend, Toma.But then, that was no surprise. She didn't like any of the men her mother brought home. Usually none of them stuck around for very long and Teuila supposed she should be grateful her mother was better at repelling men than keeping them. This latest one had been coming over regularly for a few weeks now though. Long enough to notice Teuila. Long enough to make her lock her bedroom door every time he visited. Lock the door and resolve not to open it no matter what sounds came from outside it. She was doing her homework with the iPod on loudwhen the ruckus from the next room got so bad it couldn't be ignored. Her mother screamed. Teuila gripped her pen tighter and turned up the volume. The bedroom wall shook as something thudded against it. Something. Or someone. Teuila shut her eyes and wished she was somewhere else.

Wishes are for fairytales. And Teuila didn't live in one.

The struggle had moved into the living room. Noise. Strident, harsh noises. Breaking glass. Splintering furniture. Toma was cursing. In between the thudding sound of blows. And her mother was still screaming. Begging.

Teuila took the earphones off.She was shaking now. Heaving huge gasping breaths. *Don't do it. Don't open the door*...Teuila's survivor voice shouted at her. But what kind of daughter doesn't open the door when her mother is being beaten?

She stood, slowly slid the lock aside, and opened the door just the slightest bit. Toma had his back to her.He stood over her mother who was sprawled on the sofa. He had their kitchen knife in his hand – the one they used to hack at stubborn mutton chops – and he was stabbing at her. Again and again. Siela was still struggling. Fighting. Kicking. But not very effectively. Again he raised the knife, and blood spattered over the wall.

Shut the door. Go back in the bedroom. Shut the door. The
survivor voice was very loud now. Teuila told the voice to shut up.
She looked around for something, anything that she could use as a
weapon. But there was nothing on hand. The house was a dingy,
sparse place. All she had was her pen. Teuila gripped it tightly,
ran, and plunged the pen with all her might into Toma. She had
been hoping for his neck, but instead she got his back. He arched
his back, bellowed with rage. Surprise. He turned.

"What the hell? What is that?" He reached behind him and jerked
the makeshift weapon from his back. Redness stained his shirt. He
stared at the pen in disbelief and then at Teuila. "You are going to
regret that."

Toma getting stabbed with a ballpoint pen was like a raging bull
being stung by a wasp. A tiny prick of pain that only made him
very, very mad.He came at Teuila with a manic light in his eyes.
Siela lay in a bloody heap behind him.

Teuila ran. Out the back door and across the overgrown yard
towards the tangle of trees that edged the property. On the other
side of those trees was a busy main road. If she could make it that
far, Teuila hoped a car would stop for her. Or run over Toma. Both
options were fanciful notions. She would have had better luck
wishing for her fairy godmother to show up with a pumpkin
carriage.

Toma caught her midway through the trees.Caught her and threw
her to the ground. She had all the air – and wishes – knocked out
of her. She lay there gasping for breath. Toma knelt over her,
triumphant. He drew back his fist and hit her in the face. Pain
looked like a sharp burst of light and fear tasted like the iron
saltiness of blood. Teuila knew what was going to happen next. It
wasn't the first time she had tried to interrupt her mother and one
of her boyfriends. It wasn't the first time she wished she had
stayed inside the bedroom. Kept her door locked and the iPod
turned on full blast.

And so, while Toma did what he wanted to do, Teuila did what she
always did. She went to that beautiful, distant place in her mind.

Where golden sunlight fractured on green leaves. And the long grass was warm against her skin as she lay under the shade of a mighty tamarind tree. There were hibiscus flowers in her hair. And the sweet taste of mangoes on her lips. A light wind set the branches dancing and the gentle call of the manumea bird resounded through the trees. Teuila was happy. Safe.

Yes, Teuila visited her idyllic forest retreat often. Only this time, something was different. This time, the vast tamarind tree seemed to be reaching down to her. And the liana vines around its trunk were moving. Writhing. Twisting.And the peaceful sky sullied dark and ominous. No. This wasn't her happy place. Confusion. Someone was screaming. "Help me!" And it wasn't her.

Teuila was jerked out of her trance-like state. Toma was still on top of her. But he had been pulled back on his knees, and around his neck was wrapped a thick layer of vines. His face was turning purple as he tugged vainly at the chokehold. And then Toma was yanked off Teuila in one abrupt movement and smashed into the broad trunk of the tamarind tree. But once seemed not to be enough. Again,Toma was whipped about, shaken, and rammed against a tree. And then, every tree, every bush and vine in the little gathering of forest all seemed to come to writhing, seething life. Pressing in on their captive.

Teuila was horrified. She sat up and scuttled backwards on the ground, eyes wide at the sight of a man being pummeled and shaken. By a forest. *No, this is impossible. This isn't happening.* Teuila stumbled to her feet. Turned and ran back to the house. Fearing with every step that something green and powerful would grab her as well.

Teuila was living in a fairytale where trees attacked people. And it was terrifying.

"Teuila, are you okay?"

Teuila was zoned out. She only shook her head when I tried to prompt her for more. So I tried a different approach. "You know I'm happy to give you a lift to the hospital to visit your mum."

Her reply was vicious. "No. I told you I don't want to visit her."

I persisted. Because I'm stubborn (and dumb) like that. "But your mother has been in the intensive care unit for nearly two months now. And Mrs. Amani says you haven't gone to see her once. Whatever bad stuff has gone down between you two in the past, don't you think you should put it aside for now? I'm sure she would love to see you."

And that's when Teuila lost it. She pushed her chair away from the table, hard. It fell to the ground with a crash. "I said no! I hate her. You can't make me go see her. I hope she dies in there." Her voice rose to a shriek as she swept her plate off the table, glass breaking on the concrete. "Do you hear me? I hope she dies!"

People were looking at us. I jumped to my feet, "You can't mean that ..." I started to say, but Teuila wouldn't let me finish.

"Yes I do. You don't know anything, about me or my mother. Just leave me alone." She turned and ran from the courtyard

I tried to go after her, "Wait, Teuila come back."

But Keahi beat me to it. He was up and walking after her. "You stay here. Let me go talk to her."

I didn't argue. I was happy to let him. I had no clue how to deal with an angry teenage girl who wished her mother was dead. *Or didn't I?* I watched as Keahi caught up with an angry Teuila in the parking lot. At first, her reaction to him was heated. She looked as mad at him as she had been at me. But after a few quiet words from Keahi, she calmed down and they both sat on a garden bench, deep in conversation. I cleaned up broken glass and fought my irritation. Teuila frustrated me. Couldn't she see that people were only trying to help her? Every time I felt like I was making progress with her, something like this would happen and blow my expectations out of the water. I sneaked another furtive glance in her and Keahi's direction. Maybe she was going to blast at Keahi now. And punch him in the face? That possibility immediately made me feel less depressed.

But nobody was punching anybody out there. Instead, they were both laughing and walking back towards me. Teuila surprised me and spoke first, "I'm sorry for blasting you like that."

I hid my shock with an apology of my own. "I'm sorry for bugging you about your mother. I'll get off your case about that from now on. I promise."

"Thanks. I'll see you guys tomorrow in class." She went back inside the center, heading in the direction of the dorms. Smiling.

I watched her go, with disbelief. Asked Keahi. "What was that?"

The Momoa eyebrow. "What was what?"

"That. It takes me days, no weeks, to get her to trust me enough to talk and smile and there you are chatting for all of five minutes and she's laughing? Joking with you? What did you do?"

"Nothing."

But I was not about to let this go. "I mean it, Keahi. How were you able to get through to her? What did you say?"

"Let's just say that I know where she's coming from."

"What does that mean? Come on, talk to me. I need to know this stuff."

Keahi shrugged. "Fine. Teuila hates her mother because she's a selfish whore who cares more about her next drink than about her daughter. She hates her because she keeps hooking up with men who beat her and her daughter. And most especially, she hates her mother because she didn't do enough to protect her kid. I'm guessing that the guy who stabbed Teuila's mother probably raped Teuila as well. All I did was tell her that I would teach her how to kill a person. So if she wants to kill her mom and the man who hurt her then she can meet me tomorrow after school. I'll give her a few lessons, show her some essential kill moves. And you see?" He pointed in Teuila's direction. "She's all smiles and happiness now. That's all she needed."

I was horrified. What the hell had we done, bringing this nutcase into the Center and exposing teenagers – no, make that, children – to his psychotic philosophy on life? "I cannot believe you said that to her. Teuila has lived with violence her whole life. What she needs now is healing. Counseling. A nurturing, caring environment where she can grow and get past this horrible stuff." My voice rose to a somewhat desperate shriek. "And instead, you tell her she needs to learn how to kill people?! Are you out of your mind?"

There was a dangerous fire in Keahi's eyes as he leaned towards me, whispering through clenched teeth. "No. I've never made more sense. You want to connect with Teuila and kids like her? Then you have to realize that hate is a legitimate reason for living. It's okay to hate people when they've done nothing but lie to you and treat you like their personal punching bag. Hate is how we cope. Hate is how we survive."

His rage had me flinching. "You shouldn't be coming anywhere near these kids. You have no clue what you're doing."

He sneered. "And you do? You make out that you're the misunderstood, misfit girl, all alone in the world. When the truth is, you're a spoilt rich kid with not one but two trust funds. Yeah, I've asked around. I know your story. The worst thing that's ever happened to you was finding out that the mother you thought was dead was actually the richest businesswoman in the country." He mocked, "Oh no. What a tragedy. And let's not forget that you've got the fire power of a freakin' volcano at your fingertips. You wanna know the real reason you can't connect with Teuila? Because you have no clue what suffering is. You've never been hungry. Or terrified for your life. You've never had to switch off out of your mind while somebody is beating the crap out of you. If you don't like it somewhere, you can swipe your gold card. Or write a check for a million dollars. People like Teuila? Like me? All we've got is our hate. Don't try to take that away from us."

And with that, he turned and stalked away. Somebody had just gotten slammed with a double-barreled kick in the gut. And it hurt like hell.

✳

I didn't sleep much that night as I mused over everything Keahi had thrown at me. By morning I had decided I could no longer delay the inevitable. Keahi and I needed to talk. About lots of fiery stuff.

I went to the Center right after my last class and headed for the makeshift gym, walking in on Keahi attacking the workout bag with unrestrained fury. I hoped it wasn't my face he was imagining as he kicked, punched, and elbowed. He looked like he'd been at it for a while. His torso was flushed and glistening and his black silk muay thai shorts clung to his thighs with sweat. He had earphones on and didn't hear me come in so I stood back for a while and studied him unawares.

Keahi was a world of difference from Daniel in so many ways. Daniel had a face and form that could feature on the cover of GQ magazine and there was only a single scar that marred his chiseled perfection. Nobody could call Keahi beautiful. Striking and memorable – yes. Gloriously beautiful – no. He was smaller. Leaner. And his body told more stories. His torso and legs all bore the faint ridged scar tissue that spoke of horrific burns a very long time ago. Those weren't his only scars either. There were dark markings on his back that looked suspiciously like stab wounds and more stitched scars on his legs and arms. It was difficult to tell their origin because of Keahi's obsession with ink. Angry tattoos screamed at me from his back, forearms, and the top half of his chest. Even his neck had something confronting to say. No, Keahi was not beautiful. But his body had an arresting magnetism about it that I had difficulty ignoring. Like now.

The workout – or more aptly, the kill session – ended with a roundhouse kick and I could tell that he had seen me standing there when he executed his spin. He took the earphones off and walked to pick up a towel from the corner, swiftly drying himself before putting a shirt on.

I didn't realize that I was so obviously staring until he threw me an irritated glance. "What? Aren't you done staring? Oh I know, you want to be horrified a little more, is that it?" He pulled his shirt off over his head again and walked towards me, arms outstretched, daring me to look. "Here you go, the freak on display. Get your stare on." He paused a few feet away and slowly spun around. "Take a good look. You had enough yet?"

He was angry. Again. But underneath the defiance and aggression I now saw something else. A kid like Teuila. Who had been to hell and back. He wasn't going to scare me away anymore with his bad boy routine. I didn't flinch or avert my eyes. "No. Turn around again. I want to see the markings on your back."

He looked a little taken aback. Seeing I was serious, he narrowed his eyes at me, folded his arms across his chest and turned. There was a taut silence. I took those few steps forward and raised a hesitant hand to the longest jagged scar down his shoulder, bracing myself for the inevitable crackle of energy when we touched. I asked, "What's this one from?"

"Got knifed in a nightclub. There were three of them and I was careless. Should never let anybody get behind you."

I moved my fingers down to the dark, almost circular, mark on the lower plane of his back. "And this?"

"Gun shot. Different night. Same club. Hurt like hell."

"Sounds like you shouldn't spend so much time in nightclubs."

"It was my job. I worked security for clubs for two years. Knives and guns were an occupational hazard. I always carry a knife on me now."

I was surprised. "But you're so young. How could they let a kid work security at a club?"

He turned to face me with a wry, joyless smile. "I haven't been a kid for a very long time. Can't you tell?"

He was standing too close to me now. And it made me uneasy. *Don't be stupid, Leila. You can fry him with a thought. He's got nothing for you to be scared of.* I tore my gaze from his and chose a scattering of pebbled scars on his chest, just below his neck. "What about these?"

They seemed insignificant in the face of the war field that was his torso – but he shifted uncomfortably. He didn't want to answer me. "Cigarette burns."

I flinched at that. "Ouch. How did you get those? They must have been really deep to leave scars like that."

The walls had gone up in his eyes. "You meet a lot of nuts in foster homes. I was young. I wouldn't let anybody do that to me now."

The unspoken threat sent a shiver down my spine. I could tell he wanted me to change the subject, move on to a new set of scars, but I wasn't going to be scared off. I stared into his eyes, daring him to tell me the truth. "How old were you?"

Challenge issued and answered. "Nine." I was appalled. But I hid it, pointed to another stitched mark on his abdomen. "This one?"

He caught my hand in his. "Hold up. No fair. If we're sharing secrets here then you should at least trade me some of yours. This body is basically an open book. How about you, Leila?"

He was still holding my hand, cradling it against his midriff and I wanted to snatch it away to safety. Away from the hot wetness of his skin. Sweat. Steam. Fire. "What about me?"

His gaze burned me. "What secrets are you going to share?"

"I don't have any. Boring spoilt rich girl, right here. No secrets." I fought – and failed – to keep the sarcasm out of my voice.

He raised the eyebrow at me. "In that case, you won't have a problem with answering my questions. We'll trade information."

"Fine." I pulled my fingers away from his and went back to studying his scar map. I pointed to a rough patch of skin on his shoulder. "This one."

"Dirt bike crash. Abrasion."

A discoloration above his hipbone. "That one."

"No way." He shook his head. "It's your turn to reveal something."

"Okay. What do you want to know?"

"How old were you when you first started setting stuff on fire?" His question caught me off guard. I guess I expected something else. I looked at him but he was all serious intent. He really wanted to know.

"It didn't start until recently. Last year. Just after I moved here."

"How did it start? Did it just explode out of you one day?"

"No. It was a gradual thing. I was getting these heat attacks, temperature spikes, awful dreams. One night there were singe marks on my sheets. But no fire, no exploding until …" I came to a halt, embarrassed.

"Until what? Go on." Keahi was hanging onto my every word, so eager for my answer that it was a little scary.

I took a deep breath and tried to be careless and nonchalant. "Daniel and I were kissing. It was my first time – kissing – and things got very hot and then I kinda exploded. It's just lucky that Daniel didn't get hurt."

He had a distant look in his eye. "Yeah. Lucky." His body had gone all tense again. I was standing so close to him that I could feel that invisible wire of strain twisting tighter and tighter.

"Hey, so I answered your question. Now, back to explaining the war wounds." I was skirting around the obvious and instead, pointed to his scarred eyebrow. "That one's my favorite. Where did you get that?"

His eyes crinkled into a smile. "From my sister."

In that instant, there was a happy, carefree expression on his face, so much so that he almost looked like a different person. Aha, I had discovered something important. Keahi had a sister. And he loved her very much. Enough to distract him from being the usual antagonistic boy who radiated raw energy and anger. I pounced on this new insight. "You have a sister?"

"I did. She's dead."

Ouch. I was wrong. This was not a happy topic at all. "I'm sorry." He was back in his moody place but I wouldn't let him stay there alone. "What was her name?"

"Mailani. She was my twin."

I caught my breath, eyes wide at this revelation. There was nothing else he could have revealed that would have hit me with more incisive impact. Keahi had been part of a perfect whole. He had been a twin. Like me.

He continued, oblivious to my surprise. Raising a hand to his jagged arched eyebrow. "She gave me this. We were seven. She had this stuffed toy that she took everywhere with her. A blue whale. She loved that thing so bad. I stole it off her and threatened to drown it in the toilet. Get it, drown it?" He laughed softly at his own lame joke. "I was holding it over the bowl, telling her 'I'm gonna flush! Say goodbye to Baby Whale!' and she was screaming at me to stop. Then she grabbed a glass paperweight and threw it at me. She had terrible aim. I should have stood still. But I ducked and so the paperweight hit me right on the face. The glass shattered just over my eye. I needed fourteen stitches. I was lucky not to lose my eye." He laughed. "She felt soooo bad. She stayed with me the whole time at the hospital, kept crying and asking me to forgive her. She even told the doctors that she could donate her eye to me. *You can take my eye. Please give him mine. I can wear a pirate patch. I don't mind.* Even though it was totally my fault for messing with her, she took the blame for it all." He stopped and gave me a sad smile. "We did that a lot. Looked out for each other. She was my best friend." We were both silent for a moment.

I hit him with another question while he was in a confessional mood. "Why did you stay in Samoa after the regatta finished?"

"Because of what happened that night when I touched you. And afterwards, when you argued with your boyfriend? That fire thing?" He took a deep breath and said simply, "I stayed in Samoa because of you. My turn, where does your fire come from?"

"From earth. I'm what Samoans call telesā. The palagi would call me an elemental. I can channel the energy in the ground into heat and fire. Tap into magma. Talk to volcanoes. Summon earthquakes. That's all."

"Oh, that's all, huh? Nothing too flash."

"I told you what I am, now trade me a battlefield secret."

"A what?"

I gestured at his body. "You know, your war wounds."

He smiled. And that dangerous glint was in his eyes again. "So my body is a battlefield? Well, it's certainly seen a lot of action."

I rolled my eyes at his crude joke. "Whatever. Your burns. The ones all over you. The ones you're hiding under those tattoos. What happened to you?"

I had saved the worst for last and his body tensed as he answered me. "I was in a fire when I was eight years old. The apartment block we were living in burned to the ground. I had second- and third-degree burns to a lot of my body. I was in a burn unit for a long time. Had lots of skin grafts. Some plastic surgery. Most girls run screaming from the room when I take my shirt off."

A rush of gratitude filled me. Keahi had entrusted me with a piece of himself and I had a feeling that he didn't do that very often. "Thank you."

"For what?"

"For not lying to me." I gestured to the burn scarring. "I forget how deadly fire can be. How much pain it can inflict. When I flame, it always makes me feel so happy. Complete. Sometimes it's a struggle to stay in control of it and not give in to its destructive force." I asked the question that I had been puzzling over ever since the night at the regatta. "Have you ever flamed?"

There was a long pause taut with tension. Like we both stood on the edge of a cliff that called for us to jump. And then Keahi made his choice. "I've flamed only once. I'm the one who set fire to our apartment. I killed the man who was trying to rape my sister. I killed our mother, the woman who sold us to him for the night for twenty dollars. And I killed my sister. The only person who ever meant anything to me. I've been surviving on hate ever since."

A shock wave rolled me in its airless grip. Tumbling and battering at my every thought as I tried to process this revelation. "I'm sorry." I sounded like a broken record. Sorry was such an inconsequential word.

Keahi shrugged. "Don't be. I don't need your pity. Hate is a useful drug. It's what made sure I survived the foster system. It's what drove me to the local muay thai gym and kept me fighting in the ring and on the street. Hate is my best friend."

"The fire thing has never happened to you again since then?"

He shook his head. "Nothing even close. I woke up in the hospital and thought maybe I had imagined it all. Never had any more fire episodes after that. Not until the other night outside the club. Not until you. My tattoos lighting up like that? That red glow? I've never had that happen before. And then later when I followed you and saw what you did after Daniel left the beach? You threw a ball of fire at the ocean." He paused to stare into my eyes and this time there was something more than anger in them. Curiosity? Hope? Fascination? "You can do things with fire. Controlled things. Are we the same? Am I telesā? Can I learn how to control it like you can?"

My words were whispered. "I don't know. I'm new to this. I didn't know there were telesā in Hawaii but I guess it makes sense.

There's a telesā Covenant in Tonga and there used to be one here, so why wouldn't there be telesā in Hawaii?"

"Can you teach me? Show me how to do what you do with the fire?"

"I guess. I've never taught anybody. My mother Nafanua was my teacher. But she's gone now.And even if she were alive, there's no way in flaming hell that she would help you." A wry laugh that had no humor in it. "Male telesā are an abomination so the women kill them. I was a twin too and my brother was Gifted with ocean so she killed him. You're lucky you weren't born to a telesā mother."

His reply was harsh, "There's nothing lucky about the mother I had."

Ouch. Stupid use of words. I tried to fix it. "You're right. You got a pretty raw deal where mothers are concerned."

He accepted the peace words and offered some of his own. "I guess we both lucked out with mothers." And then the impossible happened. We were both smiling at each other. We had found common ground at last. Bad mothers. "I'm sorry about what I said the other day. I guess maybe you aren't such a spoilt brat after all."

I laughed. "You say that like you have a bad taste in your mouth. You don't say sorry very often, do you?"

He laughed with me. "I do too. I apologized to you at the regatta night. You're just not very good at accepting apologies."

I did my best Simone fake-offended face, "Excuse me? Your apology sucked. You showed me your abs, like they were supposed to be your 'get out of jail free' card. You call that an apology? It was offensive."

A lazy shrug, a hand rubbed over his ridged sides, "What can I say? Magic abs. They always worked for me before."

Pointedly, I ignored the abs, which were getting far too much air time and instead stuck my hand out. "I'm calling a truce. I'll stop hating you if you stop provoking me on purpose."

He took my hand in his. Held it long enough for our connection to ignite, sending a bolt of pure energy rippling through me. I tried to pull away but he wouldn't release me. "Truce. And you'll teach me how to control these powers and use them?"

"I'll try." I focused on the flare of power surging through me, directed it, and smiled in satisfaction when Keahi jerked his hand from mine and stumbled backwards.

"Ow! That hurt." He stared at me accusingly.

Over his shoulder I saw Teuila walking across the lawn towards us. "Your student is on her way over here. You better get ready." I warned him before leaning forward to whisper, "Maybe if you're nice to me, I'll teach you that little zap trick in your first fire lesson."

I expected a glare but got a wicked smile instead. "So we're friends then? My apology worked." He flexed, lifting his arms so he could slowly run his hands over his head, angling his body to better catch the light. Classic body builder pose. He pointed downwards in the general direction of the fabled six-pack and mouthed the words at me, "It's the magic abs. They work every time."

Magic abs, my ass is what I wanted to say – but Teuila had arrived and I was trying to set a good example for the youth of today. So I went to punch the stuffing out of a workout bag.

And tried not to think about abs.

Teaching Keahi was much harder than I thought it would be. I took him up to the deserted quarry at Aleisa, the best place for setting people on fire. But unlike me, Keahi couldn't – or wouldn't – flame. Not completely anyway. His fire was an uncontrollable, chaotic thing that erupted from him in flashes. A scattering of sparks from his fingertips. A line of fire that abruptly seared from his chest. Erratic flickers of red heat that refused to be directed or channeled. But even more strange, it was a fire that he could only summon when we were in skin contact. Standing alone, he couldn't even generate a glimmer of fire, but if I held his hand, then it would burst from him. Wild. Untamed.

"Dammit, Keahi. Focus. You have to clear your mind of everything and feel for fanua afi deep beneath your feet. Listen for her. Let her speak to you and through you. Again."

"I'm trying" he shot back at me through clenched teeth as he stood in the midst of grey stone and tried to make something fiery happen on his own. Nothing. He cursed. Loud and frustrated. Picked up a handful of gravel and threw it at the quarry wall.

"Well, that's mature." I didn't bother trying to keep the derision from my voice. We had been at it for two hours now and I was hot, bothered, and regretting ever agreeing to do this. "Look, maybe you're not meant to manipulate fire the way I do. Maybe sparks are all you're ever going to make."

He snarled, "Or maybe you just need to be a better teacher and give me more."

Before I could react, he ripped off the remnants of his singlet, walked to me, grabbed my hand, twisted and pulled me into a restraining lock. Body pressed against my back, one arm held me in a chokehold, the other locked my hand at my back. It all happened so fast that I was caught by surprise. He spoke and his breath was hot in my ear, "Now, fire goddess let's see if I can make more than sparks."

"Let me go." I struggled. Kicked. Fought. Against his heat. Sweat. Skin. Smell. But he had me well locked. Pain knifed me as I tried to free myself. "You're hurting me. This isn't funny." I couldn't breathe properly in his choking embrace. Rising panic choked me, with it came rage. And with rage, came fire.

Keahi felt it. He laughed as I strained against him. As together we both burst into flame. He released me then, to raise his hands to the sky in wonder. Delight. Amazement. I stumbled away from him, turned and let loose. "You animal!" I ripped a ball of pulsing fire from the air and threw it at him. It hit him square in the chest, lifting him off his feet, throwing him ten meters back, slamming him into the rock face. If he had been flesh and blood, every bone in his body would have shattered.

But he was magma. Fire. And so he picked himself up slowly, shaking his head and still with that mocking laughter. "Well, that's mature." He didn't have a chance to say anything else before I hit him, again and again, with a volley of incendiary spheres. The force of each one pushed him back a little more until he was pinned against stone. He called out, "You got me. Now what are you going to do with me?"

Every fiery piece of me throbbed with fury. I wanted to detonate the entire quarry and wipe him from the planet but I didn't think that would work. Not against a telesā fanua afi. I heaved one more cannonball of power at him and spat, "I was trying to help you. How could you do that to me?"

"What? It worked didn't it? We came out here so you could show me how to flame like you and we found out what works." He shook himself free and walked to stand in front of me, two beings of liquid fire, face to face. Who knew when such a thing had last occurred in the entire history of telesā? Staring at someone who was just like me was a disconcerting thing. Keahi reached to caress my cheek with fire. "This is what works. You and me. Us, together."

I hit his hand away. "There is no us. We are not together. I was willing to help you, but not anymore. You can't hurt people like that and expect them to still be your friend."

"I will do whatever it takes to control this fire thing. I've seen what it can do and I will make it mine."

"You'll have to do it without me then." And then I tried something I had never done before. I spoke to the flow of energy that linked

Keahi to fanua afi and called it to me, summoning his fire, effectively switching his off. It wasn't difficult, because his control on it was so tenuous. Weak. His fire left. Leaving him standing there in flesh form. And very naked.

He looked down and then back at me, incredulous. "What happened? What did you do?"

To his credit, he didn't even seem bothered that all of Aleisa forest could now see more than just his magic abs. "You turned it off somehow. Nice one." A shrug and he moved towards me, "But not a problem, we can just flick the switch again."

"No, we can't." I threw a whip wire of flame that held him at bay. He leapt back. "Hey!"

I ran to my Jeep, sheltered on the opposite side of it and quickly extinguished my flames, grabbed the lavalava I always carried in the back seat and wrapped it around myself. I was in the driver's seat and had the engine revved before he even realized what was happening.

"Hey! Where are you doing? You can't leave me here like this."

I reversed, the wheels spinning gravel angrily. "Yes, I can. Watch me."

He shouted, "But I'm butt naked. And I can't flame on without you."

I paused the Jeep, "Exactly. You can't do this without me. You should have thought of that before you put me in a chokehold."

"How am I supposed to get home like this?"

I smiled. Sweetly. "Start walking. The closest houses are five miles that way. Maybe you could hitchhike. Try flaunting the Magic Abs."

And with that final suggestion, I drove off. Before I gave in to my original inclination to drown him in a volcano.

I berated myself the entire bumpy drive back to town. *Stupid, stupid Leila.* I had been too quick to trust Keahi. His motives for wanting fire control were questionable. The lengths he was willing to go to for fire power were dangerous. How dumb was I to trust a boy who said "hate is a legitimate reason for living ... hate is how I survive." It bothered me that he couldn't flame without me. Did that mean we were linked in some inextricable way? Was that a fanua afi thing? Or just a Keahi and Leila thing? I didn't like the sound of that. I needed to talk to someone about this. And there were only three people who fit. One of them was on a break from me. The other was his grandmother, who hated me. Which left only one other person I could talk to about fire and volcanoes.

Jason.

The sun had well and truly set as I drove up the rugged road to Fagali'i village, swerving to avoid potholes and people who didn't know that roads were for cars. The chitter of flying foxes feasting in papaya trees filled the night as I pulled up to the house where Jason had once carried out his molten heat tests on me. It seemed a very long time ago now, almost like a different lifetime. My heart sank a little to see Lesina's pert little blue two-door Getz car parked beside Jason's red truck. I had hoped to catch him alone, but I had driven all this way so I may as well follow through.

Lesina opened the door at my knock. A smile. "Hey, Leila. This is a surprise."

"Can I talk to Jason please? It's kind of important."

"Of course." She welcomed me in, calling out, "Jason!"

He walked from the kitchen with a plate full of pizza. His face lit up when he saw me, "Hey, stranger. You're just in time for dinner. Wanna join us?" He pulled me close for a quick hug.

"Thanks Jason. Sorry to bust in on you two like this, I probably should have called first."

"Nah, don't be silly. I haven't seen you in ages. I've wanted us all to get together but work has been crazy. Lesina tells me she's spending heaps of time over at your place with you and Simone though." He looped an arm over Lesina's shoulder and gave her that consuming, brilliant smile. "I'm glad. I hoped you two would be friends."

"We got over our shaky start, didn't we Leila?" she grinned at me.

"Your girlfriend won me over with her chocolate pie. And because of her, Simone is not going to fail accounting. Lesina is a very good teacher." It pained me to admit it, but it was true. "And Simone is exploiting her sewing skills as well."

"Aha, that's right. I heard about this amazing fashion show. And Simone's collection that's inspired by telesā mythology." Jason gave me a look loaded with meaning. "Did you have anything to do with it?"

I was quick to deny it. "No. Definitely not. That was all Simone's idea."

Lesina added, "But she's going to be one of the models with me though, aren't you Leila?"

Jason whooped with laughter,which I did not appreciate. "You? Model?"

"Yes, and what's so funny about that?" I demanded.

Lesina leapt to my defense. "Don't be rude, Jason. Leila's going to be an amazing model."

He shook his head at both of us then said generously, "I'm sure she will. I look forward to seeing both of you supermodels in action." Then he killed it by adding, "Just don't let Leila wear high heels, that's all. She'll be a menace to everyone within a five mile radius."

I remembered that night by Aggie Grey's pool and had to laugh. Lesina was mystified so I hurried the conversation along to the real reason why I was there.

"Jason, is there a chance I could talk to you about something work related? Umm, privately? You know that special project you were helping me with last year?" I stared at him meaningfully and finally, he got the hint.

Awareness dawned. He stood. "Of course. Why don't we go for a walk outside? Lesina, do you mind if I have a quick chat with Leila?"

Her face was open and friendly. "No. You two go ahead. I'll wait here."

I followed Jason outdoors to the back yard where a panoramic night sky greeted us. Bold, brilliant, and beautiful. The inevitable hum of mosquitoes accompanied us as we strolled away from the house. Jason looked worried. Tense. "What is it Leila? Has something happened with your powers? When you were back in the US, you said it had been reined well in under control, you weren't having any trouble. Is something wrong now?"

I rushed to allay his concern. "No, there's nothing wrong with me. Since I've been back, I haven't had any trouble with controlling the fire. Okay, that's not exactly true. I have had a couple of unexplained flare ups but only with one particular person and only because there's something weird about him. So it's, technically, not me having a problem, it's this other person. Only it's affecting me and my powers so I guess it is my problem as well. But he has a problem too. And together the problem is worse, I mean it's better but worse as well and ..."

He listened to me babble for a minute before raising his hand, "Stop. Just stop. I can't understand a word you're saying. Simple sentences. What in heck is going on?"

I took a deep breath. "I've met another person like me. But he's a boy and he's unstable and dangerous. We're connected somehow and I don't like it and I don't know what to do ..." And then it all came out. I told him everything about Keahi, starting from the regatta and up until that afternoon. "I don't want to be linked to this boy. Why am I triggering the reaction in him though? Why do you suppose he can't flame on his own?"

Jason looked pensive. "I'm not sure. But I don't think you should worry that you're his trigger. He flamed out of control when he was a child and that had nothing to do with you. Clearly, he's got the same mutated gene that you do so there must be some other reason his power hasn't manifested on its own since then."

Two of Jason's words sidetracked me. "Excuse me? Are you calling me bad words? I've got mutated genes as in I'm a mutant freak?"

"No, you idiot. You've got mutated genes as in you're a step above the rest of us in the human race. It's not an insult, it's a compliment. Quit being your reactionary self and listen." He grinned to sweeten the delivery of the reprimand. "Remember those blood samples I took from you last year? My geneticist friend got back to me with the results. You're not quite human. But we already knew that, right? Telesā are a genetic aberration and my friend is very interested in meeting you. But don't worry, I didn't tell him anything about you. You're not going to get kidnapped by some *X-Files* mutant investigation team."

I was still not happy about being classed as a mutant. "Telesā are not genetic aberrations. We're guardians, chosen by our Mother Earth and gifted with her power. It's a spiritual elemental thing. Not a genetic thing."

He held up his hands in mock defense. "Whatever you say. I'm a scientist who's only interested in cold, hard fact. Us rational types don't get into matters of the elemental spirit world." He grimaced, making a 'woo hooo spooky' sound. "We'll agree to disagree. Back to the issue of this boy, Keahi. I'm wondering if maybe, his inability to flame is linked to the trauma of his initial fire experience?"

"Like maybe he blew it all out of his system when he was a kid and so he melted down like a nuclear reactor and he's all flamed out forever?" I liked that idea. It meant Keahi wouldn't ever be a threat. Just a sparkly nuisance that I needed to keep at a distance.

But Jason crushed my excitement. "No. Like the horror of that first experience was so awful that his subconscious hasn't allowed him to flame. If his mother and his sister died in that fire he caused, then he's probably carrying around a lot of guilt, which might be causing him to repress his – gift – as you call it."

"So why would being with me make his fire possible?"

Jason hazarded a guess. "Because you annoy the heck out of him?"

"Be serious."

"I thought I was," he teased.

Eyes narrowed, I resorted to threats. "You know I can burn all that sun silk blonde hair off your head, don't you?"

Laughter. "Fine. Look, this boy's issue sounds more like an emotional one than a scientific one. I'm not a therapist so I'm making wild assumptions here. Maybe his subconscious feels safe with you. Maybe his mutant Gift thing recognizes yours and so they want to talk to each other. I don't know." He gave me a sideways glance. "Maybe Keahi just thinks you're hot and he wants to set the night on fire with you."

"And those would be your purely scientific hypotheses?" I demanded, with my hands on my hips.

"Yes, they would." He quit teasing me. "Look, if he makes you feel uncomfortable, then stay away from him. And be careful. If he tries anything violent on you again, then I say flame the hell out of him. What does Daniel think about this?"

"He doesn't know anything about Keahi being a fire telesā."

Now Jason looked angry. "Why not? Leila, a boyfriend needs to know this kind of stuff. Why haven't you told him?"

"Because we're on a break." I rushed to deflect his questions. "Because it's complicated, that's why. His ego is having trouble coping with a girlfriend who can generate volcanoes. And because I don't want to talk about it."

Jason knew me well enough not to push it. "Fine. I'm just going to say one more thing about Daniel. It takes a special kind of man to love a mutant genetic aberration – or a fire goddess – with all her strength, power, and beauty, knowing that you're never going to be her equal. Daniel's that guy. Don't mess it up by shutting him out. Because you're not only a fire goddess Leila, you're a person who needs to love and be loved, just like the rest of us." He backed away with his hands up in surrender. "And that's it. That's my lame attempt to be a relationship guru."

"That's it?"

He paused as if weighing up something heavy. Difficult. "No. There's one more thing. Something I've been wanting to talk to you about for a while, only we haven't ever been alone until now." He threw a cautious look back at the house. "Last year when I was sick, I meant what I said to you at the hospital. You're very important to me, Leila and I don't want you thinking that I go around telling girls I love them for no reason. Yes, I was heavily drugged and having a near-death experience – but I meant what I said. Even when they airlifted me back to the States, that whole time I was in hospital, I kept thinking about you and planning how I would come back to Samoa as soon as they let me out."

Here, now, was the conversation I had been dreading for months. I didn't want to hear this. I wanted to combust and evaporate into a puff of smoke, anything except have this conversation. I tried to interrupt but he wouldn't let me. "No, hear me out. I was in love with you and plotting a million ways to make you fall in love with me too. And then you started messaging me about Daniel. And I realized that you were trying to tell me that your heart was already taken." A wry grin that tore me up on the inside.

"It broke me. I loved you, and it broke me, Leila." A simple statement of fact without recrimination or bitterness. "But I didn't give up. I took the American Samoa assignment because I knew it would bring me back here. Maybe I was still hoping for something. And then I met Lesina and it was like she took all the broken pieces of me and joined them back together. I wasn't looking for it, I didn't expect it – but love found me. Lesina found me, and she makes me crazy happy."

There was that look again. That lost and drowning in love look. It reminded me of someone, only I couldn't put my finger on it. Seeing it on Jason made me uncomfortable. I wondered, did Daniel and I look at each other that way?

He continued, 'I'll always love you though, as a friend, and I hope I can be that for you. The big brother you never had, maybe? Which is why I'm glad you came to me for help tonight."

Shame and hurt twisted inside me. Jason had always been honest with me. Generous with his friendship, quick to trust and accept. He deserved so much more than I had given him. "I'm sorry Jason. About hurting you and about a lot of other things." It was my turn for confessions. Haltingly at first, I told him the truth about what had happened to him and it was a relief to finally have the full story out in the open. I cried. "Can you forgive me?"

He pulled me into his arms, enfolded me in a familiar embrace that always reminded me of gold-dusted sunshine, moonlit surfing lessons and late-night calculus lessons. "Forgive you for what? Having a vengeful, cruel, and power-hungry mother? You didn't hurt me. You saved me. We don't get to choose our parents. But we do get to decide what we will do with the examples they gave us." He carefully wiped away my tears and kissed my forehead. "You're not your mother. Or her sisters. Don't let their choices define you."

We walked back to the house and I stayed for pizza dinner with him and Lesina before driving home with a smile on my face and some measure of peace in my soul. Feeling like I could handle the Keahi situation. Feeling more hopeful about me and Daniel. *It takes a special kind of guy to love a fire goddess ... Daniel's that guy. Don't mess it up by shutting him out.* Jason was right. I looked back over the past month and knew I had made some mistakes. The question now was, how was I going to fix them? How was I going to convince Daniel that what we needed was not a break – what we needed was each other.

I was having a wonderful dream. Me and Daniel were at our Secret Place. Our mountain pool – location unknown. We were alone. (Of course.) And he was saying all the things I wanted to hear.

I've missed you, Leila. I never want to be apart from you again. I don't want a break. I don't want a Kit Kat. I want you.

And then he was kissing me. And it was perfection. And I knew he wouldn't say no to me this time. (Yay for dreams!) But then a voice called. *Daniel. Leila.*

Daniel stopped doing delicious things to me and we both looked around. Who was daring to interrupt my dream? Maleko was standing there on the other side of the pool. He looked super happy, like he was bursting with some super news. *Daniel, I've been looking everywhere for you. You've got to come with me, quickly. The coach for the NZ All Blacks just called. You've been selected for the team! You're going to be an All Black, can you believe it?*

Yes, yes that's wonderful news. Can you go away now so we can get on with this delightful dream? But Daniel didn't look like he wanted to keep kissing me. He pushed me off his lap and jumped to his feet, leaving me in a forgotten heap. Excitement. *Yes! My dream has come true. I'm going to play for the best rugby team in the world. Goodbye Leila. I must go. It was nice knowing you.*

He didn't even look back at me as he waded across the pool and did the whole 'high-five, we're so bad and cool, slapping hands and doing the secret rugby brother's handshake' with Maleko … The two of them set off through the tall grass, leaving me with snatches of their conversation. *This is it uce. Fame. Fortune. Girls. A Nike commercial. Sonny Bill Williams, step aside.*

For a moment I was rigid with shock. Then I scrambled to my feet and yelled after them. *Wait up! You can't leave me here. You can't go be an All Black. You said you loved me. You said your life was incomplete without me. You said I was your love bomb!*

Nobody came back. Nobody answered. I was standing all alone, beside a chilled mountain pool in a green blanket of white ginger flowers. I was going to cry now. What a complete let-down this dream was turning out to be. And then someone spoke from behind me. *Leila.* It scared the heck out of me. I leapt to the side with a scream.

It was Keahi. Wearing a pair of muay thai boxing shorts. He was smiling. *Here you are. I've been looking everywhere for you, my love.*

Huh?

What are you doing here all alone? Why are you sad?

Oh no. It was the nice, kind Keahi. His voice was tender and sweet and I tried not to sniff as I wiped away a runaway tear. *I'm not here alone. I'm with Daniel.* He gave me the raised eyebrow thing. We both looked around and confirmed that no, Daniel was nowhere to be seen. Which made more runaway tears escape. *He was here. But he had to leave suddenly because he got called to be an AllBlack. And now he's gone after fame, fortune, and girls. He's going to be the next Sonny Bill Williams.*

And the whole situation was just so desperately sad that I caved. Burst into tears. And it seemed to be the right thing for Keahi to take me in his arms. Hold me against him. Hug me. He ran his hands lightly down my hair and kissed my forehead. *It'll be alright. Don't cry. I'm here.* He took my face in his hands and raised it to his so he could look into my eyes. *He was never the one for you. He never truly loved you. How could he? He is vasa loloa and you're fanua afi. Like me. We're supposed to be together forever. You are fire and wonder, passion and mystery. Better than koko Samoa chocolate cake with whipped cream. Now that I've found you, I'll never leave you. Not even to join the All Blacks.*

It was very comforting to be held by Keahi. And what girl doesn't like to hear that she's wonderful, passionate, and mysterious? And more desirable than the All Blacks? I wasn't sure if I believed the bit about being better than chocolate cake and whipped cream, but hey, I wasn't about to argue. Not right now. Not when Keahi was looking at me so intensely with those charcoal ember eyes. I felt myself start to get mad. At Daniel. He was supposed to be here with me right now, dammit. And instead he was off, chasing fame and fortune. (And girls.) Why couldn't he see what Keahi was seeing? I leaned into this enigmatic boy with a little sigh. Keahi's grip around me tightened. The tattoos on his neck and shoulders began to glow. My malu simmered red in response. Things were getting hot around here.

Leila! Now who was interrupting? Keahi and I both looked around. It was Simone. Standing there next to us with his hands on his hips and outrage on his face. *Leila. What are you doing? You stop that right now. Get away from that boy.* Aww heck. I rolled my eyes. Would I never get to be the boss in my own dream? Who was going to show up next? Mele? Mr. Raymond? I shut my eyes tight, wishing for Simone to disappear. But his voice kept calling me.

Leila. Leila. Get up. Leila!

I opened my eyes. Simone was standing by my bed, shaking at my shoulder. This wasn't a dream anymore. There was an urgency in his tone that frightened me. "Leila. Wake up. You gotta come see this. Wake up."

I sat bolt upright. "What is it? What's wrong?" I looked around fearfully, wondering what was lurking in the messy room, the closet, the house.

Simone stood beside my bed. He shook his head at my fear. "Nothing's wrong." He stepped back and looked at me suspiciously. "I've been trying to wake you up for ages. You were asleep with a huge smile on your face. What were you dreaming about?"

The slightly demented dream rushed back and I flushed with embarrassment, glad that Simone couldn't read minds. "Nothing. I wasn't dreaming. Just really tired that's all." I checked the clock on the bedside table and groaned at the time. "Simone! It's only six in the morning. Way too early. What did you wake me up for?"

"Stop whining. Get your lazy butt out of bed and come with me."

"I'm not dressed." I looked down at my boxer shorts and skimpy singlet, but he only waved at my sleepwear ensemble with a dismissive gesture.

"Who cares. It's six in the morning, there's nobody looking." He waited impatiently for me to stagger after him out through the living room. He threw open the front door with a dramatic gesture. "Look."

"Look at what?" Grumpy and rude, I pushed past him, muttering about annoying flatmates and then came to an abrupt halt. The complaints died in my throat as I was consumed by color. Fire. Wonder.

We'd had a visitor during the night. And whoever it was, they had left a gift. Flowers. An exuberant wealth of fire colors. Red and orange hibiscus. Scarlet ginger. Crimson heliconia. Garlands of bougainvillea and frangipani were draped along the railing. You couldn't see the tiled floor for all the scattered teuila petals. A single potted plant – a rare burgundy orchid – sat on the outdoor table and a note was tucked into its branches.

Clapping his hands with delight, Simone pranced across the verandah to carry the cream-colored envelope back to me. "Daniel is sooooo romantic, so hekka vela!"

I couldn't help my smile. Or the sting of happy tears. Standing there, enveloped in the lush scent of frangipani, it was so easy to believethat Daniel loved me. He wanted me back. I didn't know what had changed his mind, but I didn't care. The last few weeks of painful distance and emptiness without him – it was all swept away in a blaze of tropical blossoms. Still dazed, I took the envelope, opened it, and slid out the card. On the front was scrawled – 'I'm sorry.'

Simone, reading over my shoulder, cheered with a kind of muffled yelp. "He's sorry. And he didn't even do anything wrong. Oh he is just too perfect." He threw me a dark glance, "Girlfriend, do you even deserve this boy?"

I didn't answer. Because I was reading the words inside the card.

No more chokeholds, I promise.

No magic abs in this apology.

Just all the colors of the fire you light in me.

Forgive me?

All of my delight was washed away in a cold deluge of realization. The flowers weren't from Daniel.

Disappointment was bitter and biting. Eyes narrowed, I walked off the verandah, searching everywhere for a sign of the boy who had left this splendor of blossoms as his apology. The front gate was still locked. Simone came to stand beside me. Puzzled. "What's wrong?"

"Nothing." I turned to stalk back into the house. "Daniel was right. That fence is way too low."

Simone called after me. "What are you talking about? Girl, where are you going?"

I came back outside with the broom and a garbage bag and set to work, sweeping up all the petals. Simone was angry now. He came after me and grabbed the garbage bag out of my hand. "You stop that right now. This foolishness has gone on long enough. Whatever you two were fighting about, he's apologized. He wants you back. I am not going to let you still be mad at him."

With gritted teeth I explained, "The flowers aren't from Daniel. They're from Keahi."

A freight train of different emotions raced across Simone's face as he tried to decide which to pounce on first. Confusion. Anger.

Shock. He went with anger. "I knew there was something going on with you and that boy. Right from that first night at Sails when you were outside getting up close and personal with him. I cannot believe you are choosing that freaky stalker over Daniel."

And now I was getting annoyed. "I'm not choosing him over Daniel. How could I possibly'choose' Keahi over Daniel, anyway, when Daniel took himself out of the picture. He broke up with me. He wanted a break from me." It was the first time I'd confessed that to Simone. I don't know if it was my anger or the threat of my tears that was more convincing to Simone, but he backed down.

"So what are all the flowers for then?" He asked suspiciously.

And so I had to come clean. To an extent anyway. In the most neutral of terms possible, I told Simone about Keahi volunteering at the Center and that we'd had an argument during a training session because he had been too rough.

Simone looked pensive. His gaze took in the abundance of blossoms. "So this is how Keahi apologizes…I didn't think he had it in him. Flowers. A note. An orchid plant. It's not what I would have expected from someone like him."

I sniffed, misery at war with curiosity. "What do you mean? What would you have expected?"

A shrug. "Oh, I don't know. A crate of beer maybe?" He ran his fingers lightly along the orchid flower. "There might be some potential in this boy worth exploring…"

I followed his gaze. "The flowers *are* beautiful. And he did go to a lot of effort to set this all up." Even if it did edge on the border of creepy stalker behavior.

I don't think Simone liked my tone of appreciation because he quickly changed the subject, placing an arm around my shoulders, "Why didn't you tell me that Daniel had broken up with you?"

I gave him a helpless and hopeless shrug. "He said he would spend the rest of forever loving me but he needed to have a break from us because he needed to think about stuff. He wasn't happy about the way I was keeping secrets from him and doing things on my own. He said I wasn't being fair to him. At the time, I thought he was being an egotistical male jerk. But now, I'm not so sure."

Simone gave me a slight shake and turned me to face him. "Listen here, we are going to put our heads together and come up with a plan to fix this. Daniel loves you. I know he does. Everybody knows he does. You messed up but we can fix this." Excitement was making him jittery. Uh oh. I could tell Simone was going to pour his heart and soul into bringing about a Leila and Daniel reconciliation. And pity the poor fool who dared to stand in his fabulous way.

"Thanks Simone. What would I do without you?"

He waved a careless hand, "I shudder to imagine." He went to the door, "Come on, the first step is to make you a dress. One that defies the laws of physics, logic, and everything else that has laws."

"You go ahead. I'll come in soon. Let me finish cleaning up the flower explosion."

He went inside and I started to gather armfuls of color when the phone rang. Simone yelled, "Leila, it's for you." He opened the door to hand me the phone with a distracted look on his face. He was in design planning mode and hated being disturbed.

I took the phone and walked across the verandah. "Hello?"

"So am I forgiven?" His voice was caramel smooth but with a raspy catch to it like coconut rough.

I faked distance. "Who is this?"

A low laugh. It sent a thrill of electricity down my spine without my permission. Which annoyed me. "It's the boy you left standing naked in the middle of the Aleisa bush yesterday. The same boy who spent most of the night picking flowers in the dark for you. It wasn't easy you know. I bumped my toe on a really big rock. And I got bit by my neighbor's dog while I was stealing frangipanis."

I caught my laugh in time and forced sternness into my voice. "Good, I'm glad. I hope it hurt. A lot."

"A little bit. Not as much as you got me hurting while I wait for you to forgive me." He paused, "Hmm, maybe you don't like flowers?"

My smile was soft, unbidden, and blushed with the myriad of color that enveloped me. "I do. I love flowers."

"Does that mean I'm forgiven?"

"It means I'm thinking about it." I breathed in the sweet scent of frangipani and placed one pink-tinged blossom in my hair. "I'm still mad – but it was a beautiful thing to wake up to. Thank you."

"You're welcome. In flowers and not much else, you're a beautiful thing to wake up to."

There was tenderness in his voice, something I had never heard before. I didn't know how to respond. And then something made me look up. *Wait up…that means…*

Keahi was standing outside the front gate, leaning over the metal frame. Looking right at me while he spoke on his cellphone. Catching my gaze, he raised an eyebrow and gave me that slight, enigmatic smile. And then he cut our connection, slipped his phone into the back pocket of his jeans, turned, and walked away. A moment later, the roar of an engine,and a gleaming black motorbike went past.

I stood there with a frangipani in my hair and watched Keahi drive away.

I'll give him this much. The boy knew how to leave a girl speechless.

The next day, Simone and I were ready with a plan. Operation Reignite Daniel. Luckily I only had one lecture, first thing in the morning, and then would have the rest of the day to put the plan into action. With a little help from Simone and the others. I raced to catch my class. The last person I wanted to see was Keahi. Which is why it made warped sense that he would be the first person I ran into when I got to the university. Only he wasn't alone. Walking through the parking lot, with my mind on my assignments, I almost bumped into the couple leaning against one of the cars, making out with an almost frenzied intensity. Keahi – and Mele?

My surprised brain registered who the girl was entwined around him, almost at the same time as they both recognized me and pulled apart. Mele's eyes shot daggers at me as she pulled her shirt down and back into place while Keahi only smirked at me. I backed away. "I'm sorry. I didn't see you two here."

Keahi called me back, "Hey, Leila wait up. I want to talk to you." He dismissed Mele with a jerk of his head, "You go on ahead to class. We'll catch up later."

She didn't like it, but she obeyed, reaching up first to kiss him on the mouth with a stamp of possession that only amused me. *Don't worry Mele, I don't want him. He's all yours.* She gave me one more vicious glare before strutting away.

I waited for her to be out of earshot before I spoke. "I didn't know you were friends with Mele."

"I'm not."

"Oh, so you just swap saliva with random girls in the parking lot every day then?"

He was dismissive. "Only if they're pretty and put out."

I was disgusted. "You're sick."

"And you left me butt naked in the forest, miles away from anything. I'd say that counts as sick and twisted." This time, there was an unwilling gleam of admiration. "You're a bit feisty aren't you?"

"And you're cruel." I nodded in Mele's direction. "Tell me, do you even know how to be friends with a girl? How to treat her with respect? You jumped me and put me in a chokehold so you could force my Gift to ignite yours. Even with the flowers, I don't think I'm ever going to trust you again."

"You're exaggerating. You weren't really angry the other day. You were just scared because you like what happens when we collide. Something happens when we're together – it's something big, powerful, and exciting. I've got something you want. And it's freaking you out."

I could not believe the magnitude of his delusions of grandeur. "You're unbelievable. Insane. You've got nothing I want. Or need. Your pathetic flickers of fanua afi are laughable. Your power is nothing compared to mine." Wrath ripped through me. "I can speak to volcanoes, move the earth beneath your feet, carve a chasm of fire through this parking lot, and turn this whole school into a raging inferno. You have no idea what I'm capable of."

He didn't look freaked out at all. Rather, his eyes lit up eagerly, "Exactly. But you saw what happened yesterday. You're the catalyst for my flame power and we would make the perfect team. Imagine what we could do, together."

"You're not listening to me. There is no way I would team up with you to do anything. You're on your own. Go spit out some sparks and light a candle somewhere."

I turned away from him, but he wasn't done. "Is this about your pretty boyfriend? The one who dumped you for being a fire goddess?"

"He did not dump me. We're on a break." Even as I said them, I knew the words sounded lame.

His face twisted in a mocking grin. "Is that what he's called it? Haven't you seen that movie, 'He's just not into you'? I guess you gotta tell yourself whatever makes you sleep easy at night." And then the grin was replaced by serious intent. "Just remember this, Leila, I have no problem with doing a fire goddess. None whatsoever. Remember that when you're ready to be with a real man."

There were no words adequate to express what I was feeling. I walked away instead, struggling to contain the vortex of heat that roared inside me. Keahi was wrong. About me and him. About Daniel. And tonight, I was going to prove it.

Evening was creeping in when I drove up to the workshop. Daniel and Okesene were working overtime, both welding a pair of gates out front. Both of them cut off the welders and raised their visors when I approached. I was gratified to see that they looked a little stupefied by my appearance. Simone had gone all out to transform me into a girl who was worth paying attention to. The white elei printed two-piece sheathe dress set off my tan nicely, and Lesina had woven white gardenias into my hair, which was then left free to tumble in dark waves down my back. There was a silk band of white fabric loosely tied around one arm. I worried that I looked like I had stepped out of a bridal catalogue but Simone had been vehement, "No, white is the new black. It's sensual and sexy in a virginally contrasting way. And in the moonlight you will be a vision of light. Like Masina, the moon goddess!" So here I was, trying my best to be sensual and sexy. A mental wince. Even the words made me feel icky.

Okesene's face broke into a huge smile, "You look beautiful, Leila."

"Thank you." I carefully stepped over steel beams and made my way over to stand in front of Daniel, who wore a distant expression.

His voice was curt, "So where are you going dressed like that?"

I smiled bravely up at his coldness, "To see you."

He was confused. "What about?"

"I want to ask if you'd please go for a ride in the Jeep with me. There's something I want to show you."

He refused, "Thanks, but we're really busy over here and I can't leave."

Okesene jumped in, "I can handle it, boss. You go."

Daniel looked irritated but I took his hand anyway, giving Okesene a grateful smile, "Thank you. Come on Daniel."

He allowed himself to be escorted to the Jeep but then pulled his hand away once we were out of Okesene's sight. A sigh. "Look, Leila, what's this all about? I thought you understood we're having a break from each other."

"Yes, I know that. But all I'm asking is that you go on one drive with me. That's all. Please?"

"Fine. But we need to hurry back. I've got a lot of work to do." He climbed into the Jeep and slammed the door shut. He wasn't enthusiastic, but he had agreed and that was enough for me. For now.

I got in the driver's side and produced the blindfold. "Here, put this on."

He was incredulous. "What? No way."

"A while back, you took me for a drive in your truck and you asked me to wear a blindfold. And I did it. Even though I was new to Samoa and had no idea where you were taking me, or even what kind of person you were. I went with you because I had spent the night talking to you and crying on your shoulder, because I trusted you. Now, I'm asking you to do the same for me. Put the blindfold on and trust me."

I couldn't gauge his expression in the dim light inside the Jeep, but wordlessly, he tied the blindfold on.

"Good, thank you." I started the Jeep and drove in silence to our destination. Samoa College. It was deserted, as I knew it would be, looming shadows in the night. As I drove in the gate, I waved at the security guard who had been generously persuaded to act as my accomplice. He waved me past, giving me the thumbs up sign. I parked the Jeep and went to help Daniel out, warning him, "Remember, don't take off the blindfold until I say so."

"You're so bossy." I thought I heard him mutter, but I ignored him. I was too busy scanning the area, checking that everything was in place. Yes it was. It was a still night, without any wild winds to knock over my props.

I guided Daniel to a particular wooden bench underneath the flame trees, savoring the chance to hold his hand in mine, to have him close to me. "Here, sit down."

He had a frown on his face as he sat uneasily on the bench, "Where are we? Can I take this off now?"

"In a minute, wait up … … now."

I reached up and helped him untie the blindfold. He looked around trying to find his bearings as I looked up at the trees and focused on one hundred coconut shell candles, sparked, and then lit them with a single thought. *Yes, it worked!* His eyes caught on the fire of a multitude of candles suspended from the branches of the flame trees that lined the Samoa College driveway. Around us on the ground, lining the tarseal driveway and standing on all the wooden benches were more candles and lanterns, casting their warm glow. There was a round table on the grass with two chairs draped in white elei print fabric, set for dinner with sparkling crystal ware, a bowl of fragrant white frangipani for a centerpiece. A silver ice bucket with cans of Diet Coke. A three-tiered dessert platter of sweet treats specially ordered from the High Tea team at Plantation House. We were standing in a fiery wonderland of scarlet blossoms mingled with gently swaying buds of flame, and his face broke into an unwilling smile of awe. "It's amazing. How did you do all this?"

I thought about working all afternoon with my trio of helpers – Simone, Maleko, and Sinalei – perching precariously at the top of a ladder and clambering through tree branches to tie on candles, but there's no way I was going to ruin the fairytale effect. I grinned up at him, "Magic?"

It felt so right to be standing there with him that I almost forgot what I was supposed to say. What I had rehearsed many times in my mind. "There's a hundred coconut candles up there. And another hundred or so candles and lanterns all around us. That's a lot of candles, but nowhere near as many as all the memories and meaning that this place has for me. I know our old high school is kind of a weird place to take you on a date, but Samoa College will always be precious to me because it's where we first met and where our friendship grew." I pointed to the assembly area. "Over there is where I first saw you conducting an assembly. Up in Ms. Sivani's classroom is where I first hated you on the debate war field … So many firsts, our first touch, our first laugh, our first time cutting grass on Hard Labor Detention together, and our first explosive kiss. It all happened here." As the memories flooded, I fought to contain my emotions. *Don't cry, don't cry*. I took a deep breath and kept going. "We talked about telesā for the first time and you asked me a question. You asked me, 'Leila, if you were a telesā, would you choose me?' Do you remember that?"

He nodded, his expression unreadable. I prayed for the courage to say everything I needed to say. "I chose you then. But not as telesā. As Leila Pele Folger, a girl who loves you and needs you to love her back. And then I hurt you but I didn't understand how or even why you were so upset with me. You told me that you didn't need a bodyguard, you wanted a girlfriend, someone to walk with you, who would trust you with her heart, her strengths, and all her weaknesses. You said to come back when I was ready to be that girl."

I paused to carefully remove the bandage on my arm. Slowly because the skin was still so raw and painful. I bit my lip, wincing a little at the sting as I peeled the last piece of cloth away. His eyes widened with shock to see the tattooed band. "I got this done today. I designed it myself. The patterns in this tattoo represent many of the reasons why I love you." I moved closer to show him each inked marking in the flickering light. "This is the flame tree flower. A year ago, you stood on this bench and did an impromptu strip tease for me in the middle of lunch hour, in front of hundreds of students – because you wanted to make me smile. Every time I see flame trees, I think of you and how you make me laugh. You stole a piece of my heart that day."

"This is the origami ninja star you gave me the day you described me as mysterious, instead of 'hostile social recluse,' which is what I usually get tagged as. That's the day you took me to the pool in the mountains, blindfolded so that you and I would know that the only way I can ever go back there again is with you. You treat me with respect and wonder, like I'm special and unique. You make me feel like a Pacific princess."

"This sphere is for rugby. Your strength, power, speed, and courage on the field. And off. The way you took care of me after the fight at the game. The way I always feel safe with you."

"These lines and flame marks are for your welding. How you work hard to support your family and balance school with your job and your sport. The fire and passion of your commitment to the values you hold, even when I try to jump you and persuade you to change your mind." I nudged him and he laughed with me at that one.

"The crested wave is what you promised you would be to me. The water that keeps me real, focused, and in control. It's for the day you risked your life for mine, rescuing me from that shark. Your willingness to give everything for the ones you love."

I stopped, too choked with tears to carry on with the rest of the tattoo designs. "What I'm trying to say, is that I'm sorry for shutting you out and thinking I could make all the decisions for us. I'm ready to be that girl. To walk by your side, no more secrets, no more lies. You already had my heart but I'm ready to entrust you with my fears. I don't know what the future holds for us. I'm afraid of what can happen to you and to us whenever some psycho telesā like Sarona finally catches up with us. But I know that as long as we are together, I can endure anything."

"I love you, Daniel. I'm asking you please, will you choose me?"

He slid his hands around my waist, drawing me to him, careful not to touch my new tattoo. It felt so good to be in his arms again. He looked closely at my arm band taulima and asked with that crooked smile, "Is that my name written on there?"

"Yes. I probably should have asked you first, right? Or at least made sure you wanted to still be with me. World's dumbest girl – gets her boyfriend's name tattooed on her body, when her boyfriend is on a break and doesn't want to be with her." I was only half joking, painfully aware that he had yet to answer my question.

"So does my name tattooed there mean that you belong to me? Or do I belong to you?"

"How about both?"

"I like the sound of that. You didn't have to do all this, you know. You could have just shown up at my workshop in a t-shirt and shorts, given me the same speech and gotten the same response."

"Overkill?"

He nodded, "Yeah. But I love it. It's so you. Not one candle, but a hundred. The table setting, the dinner, the flowers, all of it. It's so you. When you do something, you go all out and leave nothing to chance. You're an unstoppable force of nature, you know that?"

"I wanted to overwhelm you so you would have no choice but to take me back. Did it work?"

He brushed his lips against my cheek. A whisper. "The answer is yes. It's always been yes."

Yes. A pyrotechnics display, a volcanic eruption, an entire spangled night sky and one hundred candles – could not come close to the joy inspired by that single word.

The rest of the evening was a magical dream date come true. We sat and dined under the stars with flame flower petals drifting down upon us in the night breeze. The fish steaks I'd ordered from Amanaki Restaurant were cold by the time we got to them but we didn't care. He fed me dessert and laughed when I bit into a chocolate éclair and whipped cream spurted onto my face.

I wiped at my cheeks and asked, "Is there any cream left on my face?"

He looked, "Yes, come here, let me get it for you." Before I knew what he was doing, he had leaned in and licked at the side of my bottom lip. My insides were a pool of melted chocolate. And the pyrotechnics and volcanoes I mentioned before? They were all going off. Madly.

He pulled back. Grinned. "Got it. It's all gone now."

I stared at him with my mouth agape. He had to shake me out of my fiery daze. "Umm, Leila? You're burning holes in your dress."

"What?"

He pointed to my legs where my malu had lit up, glowing red through white fabric, searing patterns into my dress. "No, not the dress! Simone is going to kill me. Quick, quick." I looked around wildly and then grabbed the ice bucket and dumped the contents onto my lap. Stupid move. The icy deluge was a shock. I screeched and leapt to my feet, dancing about, "That's cold!"

Daniel laughed – which I didn't appreciate. "It's not funny." I used a napkin to try and soak up some of the water. "Do you know how long it took for Simone to get me to look like this? He will be so mad at me if I ruin this dress."

That wasn't quite true. Simone's actual words to me before I left the house had been triumphant, "If Daniel doesn't rip this dress off you in a passionate frenzy – then I have failed." Thinking about that had me flushing.

When the meal was finished, Daniel and I talked. True to my word, I told Daniel everything. About my work at the Center, about Teuila and my suspicions, about Keahi and our disastrous fire lesson. He listened intently. He didn't like some of it but there was nothing but happiness in the hug he gave me when I was done. "Thank you. That's all I wanted, for you to be open with me about everything that's going on in your life. That wasn't so hard, was it?"

"No." I grinned back at him and then got serious. "Now it's your turn to talk. Can you please tell me about your ocean experience? What's been going on with you?"

"I knew there was a catch. Can't get anything for free around here." He replied lightly, but when he saw my face he hurried on, "Okay, I don't remember anything from the sisterhood showdown, honest. Just getting stabbed, and chucked overboard and then waking up on the beach with you holding me. The naked you."

"Don't sidetrack."

"Just saying. A guy's got to treasure those naked moments, you know?"

"Daniel, back to the subject at hand!"

"Alright. Since that day, I've been having a lot of strange dreams. About the ocean. And you." He hastened to add, "You're not naked though."

"I'm glad to hear it."

"But the thing that's been freaking me out is the voice. At night, I think I hear a voice calling me from the ocean."

"Who's calling you?"

I could tell he didn't want to answer me. "Daniel? Who do you think is calling you?"

He shrugged. "The ocean." He gave me a dark look as if daring me to contradict him. "I know it sounds weird. But some nights, the ocean is talking to me. It's crazy isn't it?"

"You're talking to a telesā fanua afi. If anybody knows impossible, it's me. If you say the ocean is talking to you, then it must be." I hesitated, speaking very carefully, unwilling to shatter the bubble of trust that we found ourselves in. "That day on the beach with the shark, did you really hear its thoughts?"

"I think I did. I was asleep when something told me to get up because you were in danger. And then when I ran to the water, I felt a presence of some kind. Menacing. And then I was caught in its intentions. Not so much words, but distinct images and feelings like I was seeing what the shark was seeing and planning. It was terrifying."

"Where to now?" I asked him in the candle-lit night.

He smiled down at me, "What do you mean?"

I chose my words very carefully. I was tip-toeing through a bed of prickly sea-urchins here, my desire to help Daniel find answers in opposition with my promise to Salamasina to keep her secrets. "I think we should tell your grandmother what's happening to you."

"No, I don't want to worry her. Ever since my grandfather's illness and then after he died, she's been carrying a heavy load. I don't want to add to it." He was adamant and I could see he was not going to be moved. I tried once more, this time with white lies.

"Nafanua and her sisters told me once that there was a sisterhood of ocean telesā in Tonga. Perhaps your grandmother knows something about Vasa Loloa. She might be able to tell us what's going on with you."

"Or she might think I've got some mysterious illness that she needs to try and cure with her medicines." He shook his head. "No. I saw how she suffered when she couldn't heal my grandfather. The days she spent trying to save him. The guilt and pain she still carries. I won't do that to her."

I didn't know what else to do to try and change his mind, so I left it. A weak smile. "Okay, let's just figure it out together then, shall we?"

He hugged me. "Sounds like a good plan. And in the meantime, don't ever go swimming again. I came so close to losing you that day. I don't think you and oceans mix."

We laughed together but his words had hollow truth in them. I was fanua afi, and maybe me and vasa loloa were never meant to be together?

TEN

Daniel and I were together again. The world could have been hit by a comet and it wouldn't have mattered to me. All was right between Daniel and I, which meant I could endure anything. Which was a useful feeling to have because it was time for me and Lesina to start practicing for the Independence Fashion Awards.

"You never said anything to me about daily practices, Simone!" I accused. "This is stupid. Why do we need to practice for two hours every afternoon? All we have to do is put the damn clothes on, walk up and down, and not fall over. How hard can that be? Why do we need to practice for that?"

Simone was not in the mood for petulant models. He had ensembles to complete and deadlines looming. He glared, "This is not some bush fashion show, you hear me? There is choreography to be learned and change techniques to be mastered. This is an international fashion event and you will do as you are told. Or else I will never speak to you again. And I will cut all your hair off in your sleep."

"Somebody just got told off!" Lesina laughed before taking pity on me. "Come on, I'll help you. We can do this."

The practices were being held at the show venue, the Sinalei Reef Resort, which was a thirty minute drive from town and we all crushed into my Jeep. There were five of us who would model Simone's collection – me, Lesina, Teuila, and two other fa'afafine friends from school, Rihanna and Mariah. They were both more beautiful than the originals but after listening to them croon all the way to the Resort, I concluded that neither of them could sing. I seethed in the car, feeling like I had been conned. I would have to cut back on my hours at the Center until this show was over and scramble for time to spend with Daniel. When Simone had talked about a fashion show, I had imagined a handful of models walking down a makeshift stage, a few people clapping politely, and then lots of cocktails afterwards. End of story. But this? Choreography and routines and change techniques? This was something entirely different.

Sinalei Resort was set on acres of stunning landscaped grounds that overlooked the beckoning ocean and some of my tension eased as we walked through jubilant foliage. Heliconias, orchids, and hibiscus were only a few of the flowers that lined the walkways. We were directed to the main restaurant fale that opened out to a swimming pool. We were late, and the practice was already in full swing. The passion and fever of Pacific band sensation, Te Vaka, was the music that the models were walking to. And dancing to.

"We have to dance as well?" we asked Treena, the show director, an imposing woman all dressed in black. (If you've ever wondered who wears head-to-toe black on sweltering tropical afternoons, then wonder no more. Creative Directors of Pacific fashion shows do. And somehow they don't sweat.)

Treena looked at us like we were infants. "Yes. And act. This is a Pacific production that will integrate design, art, music, and dance. It begins with a contemporary interpretation of the Samoan creation myth and continues to the ava ceremony and more. We need all the models to participate in the dance acts so there will be daily practices until the show."

Great. Just great. Modeling for Simone had taken a giant leap from a vague nuisance to a nightmare. Like I didn't have enough to deal with in my life. He was so going to owe me for this. Big time. We went to join the other girls who were milling at the back of the stage and my disgust only intensified when I saw that my least favorite person was one of the models. Mele.

Another skinny, skanky reason to hate being a model at the Independence Fashion Awards. I couldn't sulk for too long though because the organizers quickly put us to work. There were dance numbers to be learned and runway tips to be absorbed. Simone came back to check on us and I was about to hiss my complaints at him until I saw the look on his face.

Absolute delight. "Leila, isn't this amaaaaazing? It's like a dream coming true." He waved his hands around. "All this is really happening. Did you know that my fashion idol will be one of the judges? Lindah Lepou, the groundbreaking creator of Pacific couture, is going to be right here, looking at my designs." He grabbed my hands in his. "Thank you so much for doing this."

That shut me up and put an end to anymore resentful thoughts. This was Simone's dream. A fierce, fabulous opportunity and I was going to be happy to be a small part of it. Even if it killed me.

It was the mantra that sustained me in the next two weeks as life in our house was consumed by fittings, feathers, shells, and the endless whirring sound of Simone's sewing machine. Lesina crashed at our place most nights as she and Simone sewed later and later. And then Mariah and Rihanna basically moved in as well because they were doing all the appliqué and embroidery work. They wielded glue guns with wicked glee and played their namesake's songs constantly. Super loudly. Endless suffering for the rest of us.

 I was appointed driver, errand girl, and general doer of all random tasks associated with preparing a couture collection. I was the mannequin, maker of Diet Coke cocktails, cleaner of coconut shells, sorter of seeds, and cutter of pandanus leaves. From the front door to the Fashion Temple, our house was devoted to creativity. Which meant it was a mess. None of us was paying much attention to school. I wasn't going to the Center at all except to pick up Teuila for fittings. Even Lesina had taken an official 'leave of absence' from her office – so she could sew feathers onto strips of tapa cloth.

Every afternoon at three, work stopped so we could pile into the Jeep and go to practice at Sinalei Resort and then get back at seven for dinner and then back to work. I wondered if designers made all their own clothes AND modeled them in the big shows and made the mistake of asking Simone that question.

"I mean, this is exhausting, Simone. You've got us all making the clothes but we're also supposed to be the models too. And dance and shake our bootie and do ava ceremonies and everything."

"Salapu! Shut up Leila, you're not being helpful," was his unhelpful response.

Daniel stopped by every night, usually with something delicious from Salamasina's kitchen. He still wouldn't come inside the house but he would sit on the verandah with me while I ate sticky sweet coconut buns or a piece of mango pie. Simone was worried about us not fitting our clothes on the night and so he didn't approve of the desserts. "Daniel, would you stop bringing that girl food to eat? She's going to get fat and then I am going to do emergency liposuction on her before the fashion show, do you hear me?" We both just rolled our eyes at his stress and I ate another piece of pie, just to spite him.

Jason joined us on the weekend. Lesina was able to escape from her slave driver boss and the four of us went out dancing – with Simone's strict instructions ringing in our ears as we left. "Don't you be back late. Lesina has more sewing to do and Leila needs her beauty sleep." Muttering, "That one needs all the extra help she can get …"

"We love you too, Simone!"

The nights out with Jason and Lesina were more fun than I expected. It made me happy to see Daniel and Jason getting along so well, my two favorite people in the world. I still wasn't completely at ease with Jason and Lesina's engagement but had resolved to put it away in a cupboard marked, '*stupid feelings that I can't explain.*'

As the date for the show drew near, so did Simone's agitation, and we all tried to be patient. He had worked incredibly hard on this collection and we wanted for it to be a success. I didn't know much about fashion, but to me, his Teine Sa designs were breathtaking. I only hoped that the judges thought so too.

We all went out to the Resort early on the day of the show. Daniel rode with me in the Jeep and we picked up Teuila from the Center on the way. He helped us unpack and then gave me a gift before he left us to prepare.

"What's this?" I asked as I opened the package to reveal a small bottle of golden liquid.

A rueful grin. "Just something small. It's coconut oil with moso'oi flowers. I made it. Grandmother taught me when I was a kid and now I have to make it for her to use with her medicines."

I unscrewed the lid and a divine perfume filled the air, the blend of the yling-ylang flower steeped in hand-pressed coconut. "It's exquisite. I love it. Thank you."

"I heard Simone talking about how you have to oil your skin for the show as part of your taupou costume, so I thought I'd give you this. I figure you'll be nervous."

"You figure correctly!" I interrupted with a laugh.

"Yeah, so maybe having this, something I made with my own hands, will be kinda like having me right there with you on stage. Reminding you that you're the most fiercely beautiful woman I've ever known. You're going to be amazing up there."

He kissed me, light and fleeting, and then left. I watched him go and wondered if I would ever be worthy of a love like his.

I was walking through the gardens towards the changing area when someone called my name, "Leila, wait up."

It was Keahi. The last person I expected to see on this side of the island. "What are you doing here?" I wasn't smiling, but neither was he. He had a distracted look on his face.

"I came with Mele. But I knew you would be here. I need to talk to you."

"We've done all the talking we need to. Sorry. I'm busy." I kept walking.

He ran after me, but was careful not to touch me. "Leila, it's important."

I was cold. "No. What's important is my friend's first ever collection is being launched in another half an hour and I'm supposed to be backstage, getting my outfit on. Go away."

He called after me, "A woman came to see me. She knew about my fire power and she wants to train me."

He had my attention now. I stopped in my tracks, shocked. "What? Who?"

"Sarona Fruean. Do you know her?"

Do I know her? Was he kidding me? I glared at him. No, he was serious. Even the arrogant sneer was missing. "Yeah, I know her. A little too well. I don't get it. How did she know about you? What did she say?"

"She said she's telesā and she showed me some of what she can do." He was impressed, you could tell, and that annoyed me. "She said she can teach me how to unlock my powers and she wants me to join something called a Covenant?"

I scoffed, "That's impossible. She's lying to you. She doesn't know anything about fanua afi and you can't join her Covenant because you're both different elements. She can't do anything with you. Besides, she believes that crap about male telesā being an abomination. Stay away from her. Your Gift is so weak that she could wipe the floor with you."

Keahi didn't like my derision. He replied angrily, "She seems to think that I have a lot to offer and at the moment, she's the only option I've got."

A wild shout interrupted us, "Leila! What do you think you're doing? We're waiting for you." A very harassed, very angry looking Simone was standing outside the dressing room tent.

I winced, looked back at Keahi, "I have to go. We can talk later. You can't join Sarona's Covenant. She's dangerous."

"When can we talk then?" Keahi wasn't going to let me be until he had a commitment. "I have to give Sarona an answer and right now, that answer is going to be yes."

Idiot. Sarona was going to chew him up and spit out the pieces. "Later, after the show. Meet me then and we'll talk. I have to go."

I ran to join Simone, accepting his lecture with meekness. "I'm sorry. I'm here now."

Keahi and his hook-up with Sarona would have to wait.

The tent set up for a dressing room was a madhouse with too many divas crowded into a small space. Models grappled with clothes. Stylists battled with hair, designers fretted with nerves. Simone had staked out a section for us at the back and I made my way over to where the others were getting dressed. Every model was in the first item – a creative dance number that portrayed the Polynesian creation myth – which required that we wear shifts sewn entirely with oiled ti leaves. Simone helped me into mine and then went to arrange Lesina's hair, leaving me to coat my skin with the sun-fragranced oil that Daniel had made for me. I smiled a secret smile to myself as I rubbed handfuls of the thick liquid onto my legs and arms. Daniel's hands had made this gift and thinking of that gave me a slow burning happiness within. It really was like having him right there with me.

The creation dance was a joy for me. The siva always connected me to fanua afi in ways that defied poetry, with music tugging on my soul and lingering on my skin. The dance was over too soon, and then it was a mad dash to the changing tent so we could dress for the fashion section. I had to have a quick hot shower to wash off all the coconut oil because my outfit called for extensive bodypaint, so it was a frantic rush for me to get into costume. There were eight other designers presenting collections that night, and it was fascinating to watch the myriad of colors and fabrics flow past.

And then it was time for Simone's 'Sacred Woman' collection to be launched. Each of us represented some facet of the telesā legends. Rihanna was the Aute, the red hibiscus that young girls were warned never to wear in their hair, for fear of inciting the wrath of telesā. Teuila was the Forest, the reputed home of the telesā spirit women. Lesina was the Bird, for many legends spoke of how telesā could take on the form of different birds and animals. Mariah was Water, for many pools and rivers were sacred to the telesā. And I was Fire, for the passion, power, and fury that telesā were so often associated with. Co-incidence? Or maybe Simone was picking up on all the fire vibes in the air around me? The design was far more revealing than I was used to. There was a brief shift skirt that skimmed my thighs and a thin band of fabric for a top, both entirely embroidered with red lopa seeds. Flowing from the back of the shift was a train of siapo cloth. Every inch of my bare skin was painted elaborate tapa patterns in red and gold body paint. Even my malu designs were highlighted with the paint. The key piece in the ensemble though, was the headdress inspired by traditional taupou and adorned with shimmering pearl shell.

Simone had just finished applying all of my body paint when there was lots of chatter and soothing noises from a group of models huddled in the corner. "What's going on over there?" he asked.

Rihanna confided, "One of the models for the Island Flava collection is a wreck. Her boyfriend dumped her just before the show." He rolled his eyes, "She's being such a drama queen. I think she's been drowning her sorrows in Vailima beer all night."

Just then there was a shriek, and the gaggle of girls parted as the center of their attention stood up. Mele. Her makeup smeared and her taupou headpiece askew. She pointed at me. "This is all your fault."

Me? What? Everyone in the room froze and looked at me. Mele staggered forward with a glass of something in her hand, "You did this. I saw him talking to you outside. You always ruin everything."

Girls stared at me accusingly. I was a boyfriend stealer. The lowest of the low. And flashing 80% of my gold-painted body in a skimpy outfit that Lady Gaga would be happy to wear did not help my case. I cleared my throat nervously. "You've got it wrong. I didn't take your boyfriend. What would I want him for? I already have one."

Mele laughed a shaky laugh that ended in a sob. "Just rub it in, why don't you?" She swayed and addressed the rapt crowd, "You all know who her boyfriend is, don't you? The beautiful, the perfect, Daniel Tahi. The one with the perfect six pack and the perfect smile and the perfect voice and the perfectly sweet everything." She veered back to me, took several steps so she was in my face, "Doesn't all that perfection just make you sick sometimes?" And then her shoulders slumped and more tears came, "I used to have a sweet boyfriend. A long time ago. His name was Maleko. And then you took him away from me. Just like you took away Keahi. Isn't Mr. Perfect enough for you? Why didn't you stay in America where you belonged, you afakasi trash!"

Mele's eyes flashed. Before I could react, she threw the contents of her glass all over me. Alcohol soaked what little fabric I had on and smudged the body paint patterns on my midriff and chest. Then, as if that wasn't enough, she ripped at my sheathe top with both hands. There was an awful tearing sound, and the pitter patter of seeds scattering on the floor as hours of embroidery came apart. Instinctively, I grabbed at what was left of my bra. "My top!"

At the same time as Simone wailed, "My design!"

There was a stunned silence. Even Mele looked horrified by what she had done. Everyone looked at me to see what I would do next. My blood boiled for Simone's work, ruined. Through gritted teeth I said, "You are so lucky I don't hit girls."

And then Simone pushed past me, yelling. "But I do." He clenched his fist and threw a mighty right hook at Mele's face, knocking her backwards. People scattered as she went down. Simone stood over her spread-eagled form, still yelling, "You ruined my design. Do you know how long it took me to make that?"

The room was in an uproar. Rihanna and Mariah restrained a cursing Simone – who looked like he wanted to start stomping his high heels all over Mele's face. "Just leave it. Come away." Mele was crying and holding on to her bleeding nose. Her friends ran to kneel beside her, trying to help her up, while giving me and Simone dirty looks at the same time.

Into this chaos walked Treena. "What is the meaning of this? We have a show to put on. Everyone, just get a grip." She pointed at Mele, issued an order, "Get that girl out of here. I don't want blood getting on any of the clothes. Simone, you've got five minutes to get your collection backstage. You're on next." She looked around, "Well? Don't just stand there, people. Move it!"

Someone bundled Mele away. Someone else swept up my lopa seeds. Simone was hyper-ventilating. "What am I going to do?" He pointed at the remains of my outfit, "You were supposed to be the finale. You can't go out there with your top ripped to pieces and your body paint all messed up. We don't have enough time to repaint you. This is a disaster. Ohmigosh, somebody just set me on fire so I can burn with shame." He was crying now – but the angry kind of crying where he kept pausing to yell more swear words at the departed Mele. A volley of Samoan curse words so vile that (thankfully) I couldn't translate them.

His desperate plea for fire gave me an idea. "I've got an idea how to fix this." I started taking off the mangled remains of my top. "Didn't you say that the key piece in this ensemble is the headdress and the shoes? So all the other bits don't matter?"

He nodded, still agitated. "Yes, but you can't go onstage topless. I've seen mangoes more impressive than that chest."

I forgave him the insult – he was in the middle of a crisis. "Don't worry, I won't be topless. Not really."

From the stage, we heard the MC begin reading the introduction for Simone's collection. Rihanna screeched, "Oh no, that's us. We have to go. What are we going to do?"

I was the final design, there was time for what I had in mind. I pushed Simone towards the others, "Go with them. I'm coming. Don't worry, I'll fix it."

Simone was not convinced. He wrung his hands, "Leila, how are you going to fix it? You don't know anything about fashion. I think I'm going to throw up. I can't handle this."

"No." I grabbed his hands in mine. "You have fought so hard for your dream. You've worked your butt off to put this collection together. Your parents are out there in the audience and they are going to be so proud of you. Your talent deserves to shine tonight. You can do this." I looked at the others, who looked as freaked out as Simone. "Right ladies?"

Teuila was the first to answer, "Leila's right. We look amazing and it's all because of your vision Simone. Let's get out there and show Samoa what teine Sa look like."

Hearing the youngest among us speak with so much confidence was the boost everyone needed. Mariah and Rihanna led the way with their signature catwalk strut, and Lesina gave Teuila a quick hug before they followed suit. Simone and I were left alone. He looked a little bit more calm now, "Thanks, Leila." A dejected frown. "But I still don't see how you're going to fix my fire design. It's trashed."

I gave him a look loaded with meaning, "Just trust me, okay? I may not know anything about fashion – but I know everything about fire. And telesā."

Before he could react to that, I darted after the other models. Te Vaka music pulsed as the first design in the Teina Sa Collection took to the stage – Rihanna as the 'Sacred Woman of the night.' He wore a floor-length black cloak made from layers of tufted, dyed pandanus fibres and as the spotlight came on, he was sitting in front of a shell-encrusted mirror, with his back to the audience, brushing his lustrous long hair. Affixing a red hibiscus flower above his ear. There was an eerie silence as the MC read the script.

Don't brush your hair at night. Don't gaze into mirrors, admiring your beauty. Don't wear a red flower in your ear. The teine sa is a jealous and vindictive spirit and will curse you. Punish you for flaunting your beauty.

The drums beat a sudden rhythm. Rihanna slowly rose to his feet, picked up a shell, and smashed the mirror. The shattering glass jolted the crowd and there was complete silence as Rihanna turned, loosed the cape and dropped it to the ground with a dramatic swirl, revealing the blood-red gown he wore beneath it. A simple sheath, the beauty was in the detailing as the entire gown was made of overlapping layers of dyed coconut matting that clung to his body as he walked the length of the stage and back. There was a fragile pause from the audience, as if they were unsure how to respond – and then the decision was made and they erupted into applause. I felt myself relax. *Yes!* It was going to be great, I just knew it. I wanted to stand there and watch the rest of our team do their thing, but I needed to get myself sorted out.

I darted out a side door into the moonlit garden, a quick sweep to check that I was alone and then I ripped the rest of the ragged top off and used the wet fabric to wipe away most of the smudged body paint on my midriff. I hesitated when I got to the brief skirt but then gave myself a mental shake. *Do it, Leila. Nobody will see anything important anyway. Do this for Simone.* Quickly, I slipped off my skirt and briefs so I wore nothing but the elaborate head-piece and the shoes. Now for the tricky part. I took a deep breath, trying to still my racing heart. The night breeze danced over my skin and a rush of fragrance assailed me, golden mosooi flowers and the hint of coconut. *You're the most fiercely beautiful woman I've ever known. You're going to be amazing up there tonight.*

Happiness, love, and gratitude bubbled and spread through me. Warmth, heat, fire. A careful thought and I captured it, shaped it, and wrapped it around me. A sinuous red coil at my breast and another draped about my hips. Now I was dressed. In pure fire. Another thought and the markings of my tattoos lit up the night with their crimson glow – the malu on my legs, the taulima band on my arm. There was no mirror to check how I looked but I hoped the overall effect would be worthy of Simone's collection.

The announcer began reading the introduction piece for my entrance and the music changed to an insistent island drum beat. It was my turn. *Here goes nothing. Whatever you do, don't fall over and set fire to the stage.* I hurried back inside and up the narrow stairwell. Simone was standing stageside and the first to see me coming. His eyes widened in shocked approval, the excited smile told me that my creation met with his approval – and then I was center stage. Every light had been extinguished in preparation for my iridescent body paint so my fiery appearance lit up the night. There was an explosion of sound as people applauded, shouted, and cheered. I think that meant they liked it. I was glad for the darkness, which meant I could see no one, just the stage lights marking out the runway.

It was harder than I thought it would be to maintain control over the swirls of flame that swathed me, willing the rest of my body not to ignite, all while striding the length of the stage in heels and a two-foot-high headdress.. I executed the poses that Simone had spent agonizing hours trying to teach me and then returned to center stage. It was time for the designer to take his victory walk. The crowd roared again as Simone joined me onstage and then the other models filed out to line up behind us.

Standing with me but edging away from my fire, Simone gave me a sideways glance and muttered, "I take it back. I've never seen mangoes as impressive as that." Then he flashed a gleeful smile as we walked the length of the stage so he could take his bow.

Simone's collection was a triumph, winning the Supreme Award, and his Forest Woman creation – modeled by Teuila – taking out the Most Original Art Piece as well. The media was on hand to photograph him and his proud parents. He got to meet his fashion idol Lindah Lepou, who wanted to discuss his 'exciting future.'

With the show out of the way, the party began in earnest. There was an impressive lineup of Pacific music artists performing, with at least two hundred people enjoying the music and dancing under a radiant night sky. At first we all danced in an exultant group with Simone but then Daniel pulled me to him and away from the others. For a long while it seemed to be just the two of us, caught in the flow of the music, and I gave myself over to the sheer thrill of moving my body in unison with his. Daniel on the dance floor moved like he did on the rugby field – assured confidence, skill, and graceful ease that belied his strength. I could have danced with him to the fiery edge of earth and back. The music slowed and he melded me to him. Ragged breath. Sweat. Exhiliration. Adrenaline. A murmur, "You made me wild tonight."

Bemused, "Why?"

"I wasn't sure what I wanted to do more – grab you off that stage and yell at you for walking out naked like that. Or lock you in my truck where nobody else could see you and then cover you with kisses. You were stunning."

Thinking about the two of us locked in his truck was making it difficult for me to concentrate. He had to repeat his next question twice, "How did you get away with using your fire power in public like that?"

"What? Oh, I told everyone some scientifically impossible story about draping kerosene-soaked cloths all over me and then setting them on fire and hoping for the best."

He raised a doubtful eyebrow at me, "And they bought it?"

I waved at the crowd around us, "I think everyone did, except for Simone. But it's a party, nobody cares about the science right now." I remembered then to correct him, "And I wasn't naked, I was basically wearing a very conservative two-piece swimsuit. But I was terrified though. And I'm never doing any modeling like that again."

He looked happy to hear it, "Good. Because I want to be the only guy you set on fire." And then right there, in the mad crush of the dance floor, he kissed me. Everything faded as I drowned in the swirling ocean of emotions and feeling that Daniel always inspired in me. And then Simone was tugging at me.

"That's enough you two. Daniel can you be a dahling and go get us some drinks? I want to talk to Leila for a minute." He batted his eyelashes at Daniel who bowed to his request.

"Your wish is my command, O Supreme Award Fashion Maestro. I'll be back."

Simone watched him edge his way through the dancing crowd and then pulled me to join him at a table closer to the restaurant where we didn't need to battle so hard against the thumping bass. "Thank you for what you did, saving the collection like that. I know that fire had nothing to do with kerosene or whatever other lame story you're telling people."

I opened my mouth to protest, but he gave me the *talk to the hand* flick of the wrist. "It's alright. You don't need to tell me how you really did that. Just hear me out, I know there's a part of you that you keep hidden and sometimes that's for the best. But other times, we need to embrace what sets us apart. Not everyone will approve, some will be afraid of us, but when we unleash the fierceness within – then we fly. You were definitely fierce tonight." He gave me a quick hug and wrinkled his nose. "Eww, girlfriend you are all sweaty and nasty. And you know that top is see-through when wet, don't you? Just letting it all out tonight, are we?"

"What?" I glanced down. Ugh. Simone was right. My white linen top, which had seemed like such a classic, elegant choice an hour ago, was now sweat-soaked and skanky ho' personified. Immediately, I folded my arms against my chest and stood up. "I've got spare clothes in the Jeep. Can you please tell Daniel that I've gone outside to get changed?"

Simone waved me away. "Don't worry, I'll take care of him until you get back."

I bolted to the parking lot, unwilling for any more people to see my 'nasty, sweaty' self. I had parked far away from the main entrance, under a sheltering of trees. The night air was cool on my skin. It was good to be out of the party crowd. Alone.

Except, I wasn't alone. As I rifled through my bag, I felt – rather than heard – a presence behind me. I swung round with a muffled yelp, searching the darkness. "Who is it? Who's there?"

The shadows moved, a lean lithe shape detached itself and strolled across the grass. Keahi. Silken smooth in stone-grey suit pants and a white shirt unbuttoned at the throat. "It's me."

"What are you doing creeping up behind me like that?"

"I wasn't creeping. I saw you leave the party so I followed you out here. You said we would talk after the show, right? It's after the show. Here I am. Let's talk."

Painfully aware of my see-through top, I hugged my arms across my chest. "Now's not a good time. I only came out here to get something from the Jeep. I have to get back in. Daniel's waiting for me."

He smiled. That lazy, knowing, and incredibly irritating smile. "Ah yes, I noticed that you and Pretty Boy have kissed and made up. How sweet."

"Yes, we're together. Not that it's any of your business." I raised my chin defiantly. "Now, excuse me, but I have to go."

Before I could move, Keahi took another few steps closer, "I was watching you two together and I saw something very interesting."

"What?" Hostile.

"When Daniel touched you, kissed you, none of your tattoos lit up. Not like when I touch you." As if to emphasize his point, he leaned forward and ran his fingers along my arm. The taulima burned in immediate response. His voice was triumphant, "See? He can't make you do that."

I jerked away from him. "Yes he does. Daniel ignites things in me that you could never understand but I control them so we can be together."

Keahi was undeterred. "Sounds boring. Who wants to be with someone when you can't let loose and be yourself with them?"

He was crowding me now, but I refused to panic. "Quit it with the mind games, alright? What do you want?"

"I don't want to take up Sarona's offer. You entice me, Leila. I can't stop thinking about your fire … and my fire. And what they would be like together."

With one eyebrow arched and coal black eyes glinting, I knew he intended to invest the word 'fire' with all kinds of added meaning and even as I fought not to, my pulse leapt to respond. My breath caught in my chest and noting that, a slow smile worked its way across his face. "Yeah, you've been thinking about the same thing haven't you?"

"I don't know what you're talking about." Curt, cool, and calm.

He smiled again and slowly started unbuttoning his shirt. Inner turmoil made me blunt.

"What are you doing?"

He shrugged as he continued, stripping off his shirt and then moving to unbuckle the belt at his waist. His corded chest screamed at me in the moonlight, the jagged scars only seeming to accentuate the restrained power of lean muscle and sinew. He shook his head, feigned innocence mocking me. "What? You don't think I'm going to incinerate a perfectly good suit, do you?"

Before I could react, he had unzipped his pants. Dropped them and stepped out of them in one swift movement. I spun my gaze away. Stared fixedly at green trees, black sky, and brown earth. But all I could 'see' was him. Burnt into my mind. The lines of his abdomen, as if painted on with liquid silver. The curve of his hip as it dipped inwards. "Dammit Keahi, what the hell is wrong with you? Put your clothes back on. What are you playing at?"

From somewhere to my right came his lazy drawl that always seemed to be mockery laden. "I'm not playing. Not yet anyway. I told you – I've been thinking about fire. Yours and mine."

"What about it?" I kept my eyes locked on the forest night.

He sighed. "Aww, would you please look at me? Didn't yo mama teach you that it's rude to ignore somebody when they're talking to ya? Come on, look at me." His voice had adopted a fake southern twangy drawl. Maybe that worked for him on other girls – along with the magic abs – but I wasn't falling for it.

"This conversation's over. I'm leaving. I've seen more than enough of your damaged scarred body." Desperation was making me cruel and I regretted the words as soon as they sliced through the air, remembering the raw pain in his eyes when he had first shown me the remnants from his childhood trauma.

His voice was harsh. "No, we've only just started." And before I could think, before I could act, Keahi had pulled me to him with a ferocity that left me breathless, and captured my mouth. His lips were scorching coals against mine. I fought him. With my mind and my heart, I resisted. But my core – that hot place that sang to molten rivers of lava – screamed to be one with the fire that Keahi's body hinted of as he pressed his hard length against me, forcing me against the side of the Jeep. Fanua afi rejoiced to feel the presence of another that answered her fiery song and I was losing the battle for control. Keahi's tattoos began to burn with a heat that ate through the thin fabric of my clothing so that skin met skin in agonizing, tantalizing patches. If I had been any other girl, I would have cried out in pain. But I was telesā fanua afi and my skin welcomed the burn even as my mind screamed *No. Don't do this.*

I felt his heat and it sent a shudder of swirling lava current through my entire body. I welcomed it because Keahi was right. I did want to know what it would feel like to be enflamed and be with another person. To give in to my fire and be able to touch. Feel. Kiss. Truly be myself without worrying that I would injure someone. The thought of being able to lose control was intoxicating. And then it happened. Fanua afi took over me. Keahi kissed me and I kissed him back. His mouth, his tongue, his heat was all I thought of.

In his kiss I could taste the red burn of chili encrusted in the rich sweetness of melted chocolate. I breathed in his scent and it spoke to me of vanilla. Because fire is warmth and comfort. I closed my eyes and I could see the red passion of the ginger flower. Because fire is beautiful. The ink of my malu began to burn, searing patterns of red joy into my legs, my thighs. The ink made by my mother's hands.

You are telesā fanua afi. You are Pele. The creator and destroyer of lands. Embrace who you are. Revel in the birthright that is yours. Fire is warmth. Fire is beautiful. Fire is power. Fire is you.

"No!" I tore my mouth away from his and pushed my hands against his chest. "That isn't me. We can't do this."

This time he listened. Loosened his grip on me. "What's the matter, Leila? Fire too hot for you?" His eyes gleamed with some unreadable emotion andthere was the hint of a smile at the edge of his lips. "Come on. Flame up. You know you want to. Let it all out and let's have some fun. I'll go first, shall I?" He stepped away, sparked, and burst into flame. He was getting better at this. I could tell.

He stood there smiling at me, his arms folded across his chest, legs apart. I could not stop myself from being awed by the sight of another person like me. On fire, like me. He was beautiful. His flames lit up the night, calling to me to respond. The edges of my fingertips prickled with that itch, that tingle to flame and I fought to suppress my desire. Forced myself to speak with coldness. "You're using me again. As a trigger. A catalyst. Only this time, instead of a chokehold, you're trying sex. I don't like being used. For fire. Or for sex."

He laughed, low and musical, "Why are you fighting us? We are the same, you and I. And fire should be with fire."

"We're nothing alike. And we most definitely should not be together."

"Whatever. You say no Leila, but your body? It says yes. I've kissed a lot of girls and I know when your lips are lying."

I wiped my mouth with the back of my hand wishing I could erase the taste of him, the memory of him. Of us. Of me and what I had felt like when he was kissing me. I looked down at the remains of my dress, the fabric splattered with charred holes. "You idiot. Look what you did to my clothes."

He shrugged. He was blowing flame bubbles into the air and didn't even look at me. "You should have taken your clothes off before rubbing yourself all over me then."

"I did not rub myself all over you. You were kissing me, not the other way around." I stopped abruptly as he spun around and threw a ball of fire in my direction. A missile that would have hit me if I hadn't leapt out of the way at the last second. "What are you doing!?" I looked wildly over my shoulder to where the fireball had landed and was enveloping a small gathering of teuila plants. "Are you nuts? You could have hurt me."

His reply was venomous. Gone was the lazy drawl. "Don't lie to me. I hate liars. I've been lied to all my life and I'm not going to take it from you too."

I was too bewildered to be angry. "What are you talking about?"

"You're lying, Leila. You want me. I know you do. You could search the whole world and never find another person who burns the same way you do. I've always thought I was the only one cursed like this. And then I found you."

He came to an abrupt halt and in that moment, I saw the boy who had set fire to the world so he could save his sister. But had killed her. The boy who used hate to survive. The boy who walked alone.

I chose my words carefully. "Keahi, I don't want to be with someone because they burn like I do. I want to be with someone who loves me for me. Yes, there's a spark between us but it's a literal spark. It comes from the fanua afi Gift that we share. But that's all it is. I'm sorry."

A voice interrupted us. "Leila! Leila, where are you?"

Daniel. He had come looking for me. Wildly, I looked from Keahi in flames and back down again to my singed clothing. What to do? It was too late to do anything because Daniel came into view. His gaze took in everything. Keahi in full fire mode, me with bedraggled charred clothing, and behind me the still-burning evidence of Keahi's attack.

Daniel's reaction was instantaneous. "What are you doing? Get away from her!" Without hesitation, he charged at a fiery Keahi and tackled him with all the fury of a two hundred plus pound rugby player. Caught off guard, Keahi was knocked to the ground, his flames dimmed but still alight. Still enough to burn. Still enough to harm.

"Daniel, no. Get off him." I shouted as I ran forward to try and pull Daniel away from a stunned Keahi. "What are you doing? He's burning at magma temperatures, you're going to get burned, who does that? Who tackles a fire god? Oh no …" My voice faded as the air filled with the smell of burnt cloth and burnt flesh.

Daniel slowly raised himself to a seated position, ignoring the burns on his face, chest, and arms. He shook his head at me "I'm fine. But he's not going to be by the time I'm finished with him." He pushed me aside and walked over to where Keahi was pulling himself to a standing position.

Keahi saw him coming and laughed. "Oh yeah? And just what are you going to do to me?" He flexed his shoulders and lit up his hands again, summoning flame from his feet to … But before fire could reach his upper torso, Daniel had reached him. Reached him and hit him in the face. "This." A blow so swift that I barely registered it. Fist smashed against flesh. Bone jarred against bone. Keahi's head snapped back and he fell to the ground.

Daniel stood over him. His voice was low and venomous. "Stay away from my girlfriend. Don't ever hurt her again. Or I'll kill you."

Keahi lay in the dirt, all flame knocked out of him as he shook his head dazedly, bringing a hand up to wipe the trickle of blood from his cut lip. His nakedness screamed at me in the night. He made no attempts to cover up. Or to fight back. He just lay back in the grass and laughed some more. His voice dripped with satisfaction.

"I wasn't hurting her you fool. I was kissing her. And she was loving it."

Daniel didn't even blink. Didn't even entertain a question, a thought, a fleeting moment of doubt. Only shrugged dismissively and turned away, throwing back over his shoulder. "You're pathetic." His trust, his complete confidence in me, cut me with guilt. With far greater hurt than if he had attacked me. He walked over to me and took me gently in his arms. His voice was soft. "Hey, are you ok? Did he hurt you?"

I shook my head, my words muffled against his shoulder as he held me close. "No, I'm fine." Over his shoulder I could see Keahi sitting up, staring at us with a sardonic expression. He caught my gaze and rolled his eyes, his face contemptuous. I pulled away and checked out Daniel's injuries. His shirt was burnt through in several patches and blistering flesh showed through. The skin of his forearms was burnt raw. "But you're not. Come on, let's go inside the resort and get you some first aid."

He winced, "No. I'm not going back in there. Let's just go. I want to get out of here. Mama has lots of medicine at home that will work much better anyway."

We got into the Jeep and I texted Simone that we were leaving, so he wouldn't worry. I drove fast up the mountain road, threw him a glance in the dim light. "Are you okay?"

"I'll live. It's not the smartest thing I've ever done, but it was certainly the most satisfying." A low laugh had me shaking my head.

"You're crazy, you didn't need to do that. You know he can't hurt me." Because I'm a fire goddess. I wasn't dumb enough to say the words out loud but they hung in the air unspoken. I could sense rather than see Daniel tensing in the seat beside me. I rushed to soothe the tension. "Thank you for coming to rescue me."

"You mean even though you didn't need it." His voice was bitter.

"That's not what I meant. What you did tonight was brave and good and I loved it. I love you." It sounded empty even to me. We drove in silence for much of the way back to town.

"Turn right up here." He pointed to an unfamiliar side road. Curt and cold.

"Why? I thought we were going straight to your house."

"No. I don't want to go home. Take this road."

I stole a glance at him in the darkness. He was staring out the window, his profile harsh and carved in granite. I gave up arguing with him and made the turn.

"Now where?"

"Just follow this road. I'll tell you when to pull over."

It was a deserted road. Long sections of fenced plantation lots broken here and there by the distant lights of a sleeping house. He pointed to a section of trees coming up on the left.

"Pull over up there."

I obeyed, bringing the Jeep to a stop on the overgrown grass. I turned the engine off and the lights cut off, leaving us in darkness. Moonlight.

"Umm, now what?"

But he was already out, slamming the door behind him. I got out, but he wasn't waiting for me. There was some sort of trail through the trees and he seemed to know where he was going.

"Daniel, hey wait up. Where are you going.?"

"Come on. Follow me."

Okay fine. Nice, loving, gentlemanly Daniel had been replaced by mean, cold, and abrupt Daniel. I was in no position to argue with him though. Not after all that had happened tonight. Not when I had let some other guy kiss me. *And don't forget, you kissed him back, Leila.* Yeah, I wasn't going to fight Daniel on this. I ran after him.

He walked with quick surety, and my curiosity was aflame. It was obvious he knew where he was going. He's been here before. Where in heck are we?

And then I didn't have to wonder anymore because we had broken through a thicket of ginger plants and there it was. My midnight pool. Silver glistened over the low waterfall as it danced over black water. Ringed with bottle-green ferns.

"Hey! It's my pool. We must be close to Matile and Tuala's house." I peered through the forest, trying to get my bearings.

He still didn't look at me. Instead he pointed off to the right. "Yeah, it's through the trees that way." He jerked his head back in the direction we had come. "That's the road I always use to get here. Me and the village boys would come swim here after school sometimes when I was a kid."

"But why are we here?"

"The water. I want to be with the water."

In one swift motion he pulled his shirt over his head, wincing slightly as he threw it to the side. Time came to a crashing halt at the sight of his chiseled body drenched in starlight. He was beautiful.

He waded into the waist-deep water and splashed cooling water onto his burns, making a face at the sting. Shame. Guilt. Sorrow. Daniel was hurt. I did this to him. I had betrayed him tonight and now he was hurt. This was all my fault. I walked over to join him in the water, standing behind him and slipping my hands under his arms to gently, carefully embrace him. I lay my head on the curve of his back. He was still. Rigid. His skin was cool against my cheek and I closed my eyes as all the tension of the night's events seeped away. Replaced by the calm peace, the 'rightness' that Daniel inspired in me. With him, I was whole. With him, I was home. We stood like that for a long moment before he spoke.

"Why were you out there with Keahi?"

"He followed me from the party when I went to get a change of clothes. He wanted to talk about Sarona. And he asked me again about training him. Helping him." I answered truthfully, wishing I could see his face, read his expression.

Daniel moved my hands away so he could turn to face me. We stood close enough to touch. The burnt remnants of my thin dress were a poor shield against him. Every nerve ending could feel him. Wanted him. Longed for him. Even now. Even though he was angry with me. I looked up into his eyes and what I saw there frightened me. There was something fierce and taut in him tonight. Something I had never seen before. He stared down at me and when he finally spoke, his words resonated with restrained fury.

"Did he kiss you?"

I took a step back in the water and straightened to meet his eyes as best I could. This was Daniel. The one I loved. And I would not lie to him. "Yes."

"Do you want him?"

My reaction was immediate. "No! I don't even like him. He's arrogant and rude and a jerk and I don't trust him." I took a deep breath, choosing my words very carefully. "But I'm not going to lie to you. The fire in me, the telesā in me, it responds to him, to his fire. I don't quite know how to explain it. I think it's because it's excited, I mean, glad to find another person who has the same gift. But no, I don't want him."

There was a slight softening in his face. Did he believe me? I whispered in the soft darkness. "Daniel, I love you."

"I don't like the way he looks at you."

"Like what?"

"Like he knows you in ways that I don't. Intimately. Like he's got you naked in his mind."

"I don't know what's going on in Keahi's mind and I don't want to know. All I care about is what's going on in *your* head." I stood on tiptoe so I could kiss his cheek. "And in your heart." His arms went around me to clasp me tightly against him. I looked up at him. His eyes were storm ridden. He was still angry.

"What if Keahi's right? What if he does know you inside out? In some twisted fire telesā way? What if you two are supposed to be together? Fire and fire, or some shit like that."

"No. Don't even say that. I love you. I didn't know something was missing until I met you. Right here in this pool, a long time ago, you stood right here and you told me you would be the water that calmed me. You told me we bring out the best in each other, and you were right. You're everything I'm not. You're what I need. You're the better part of me."

"I hate seeing you with him. I don't want anyone else to touch you, Leila. Or kiss you. You're mine."

And then he was kissing me.And it was angry and intense. His embrace was rough, his mouth on mine was searching and impatient. In one swift movement, Daniel hoisted me up, with legs around his waist, and carried me several steps, so I was seated on a rock shelf on the side of the rushing waterfall out of reach of the foaming splash. There was an urgency about his movements that I had never encountered from him before. His breath caught as he stared at me in the deepening twilight.

He smiled. The anger was gone. A gentle smile that caressed my soul with its love. His voice was soft in the silken evening. "You're more beautiful than I dreamed you would be."

Slowly, carefully he reached with one hand, almost as if in worshipful awe, to touch me, and then to kiss me, in places I had only ever dared to dream about. He pulled away one strap of my top so he could kiss the naked skin of my shoulder, pausing only to give me a searching look, 'Is this ok?' My smile was answer enough and then nothing separated us but water.

That's when the world changed. Irrevocably. Irredeemably. Daniel's tattoos began to burn, to light up with an eerie blue glow.

"Daniel?"

"What is it? What's wrong?"

As he looked at me questioningly, I caught my breath, eyes widening as I stared at his body. All his tattoos, all of them were glowing with the same blue fire. Through the rippling water I could clearly see the markings of his pe'a, the banded sleeve that marched up his arm and spread over his shoulder, even the patterns on his lower leg – all shimmering with iridescent blue. "Your tattoos, what's happening to them?"He held up his arms and looked at them in astonishment. "I don't know."

As we both stared wide-eyed, the water around us began to bubble and swirl as if a mini tornado was building up. Fear caught at me as it always did when I was in water, away from my power source. The earth that gave me fearlessness and unbridled power. "Let's get out of here." I slipped off the shelf, stumbling over rocks as I moved towards the safety of the poolside. But he didn't follow me. Instead he stood there in the center of the pool, raising his hands in wonder, regarding his glowing blue markings. I spoke his name sharply, but it was as if he did not hear me. "Daniel!"

The pool was now a raging broiling mass of white as the water churned, and in its heart stood Daniel. He smiled. But not at me. At the water around him. As tendrils of liquid began to rise from the churning surface, snaking its way around his body, along his outstretched arms, like silver ribbons of mercury. I couldn't believe what I was seeing. The pool heaved with some unseen force and the water lifted like a platform of white surf, lifting Daniel with it so that he stood a few meters off the surface.

I screamed his name and this time he turned his head to look at me. But it wasn't Daniel. Not the Daniel I knew. Not the Daniel I loved. His eyes glowed with the same blue light as that which highlighted his every tattoo, and ropes of water were coiled around his arm. He raised the hands that had caressed me, that had traced the outline of my face with love, and shook them, as if trying to loosen the ropes. They responded to his motions and from that slight impatient shake of his hands, a whip-like wire of pure water lashed the surface of the pool. It reached to the earth on which I stood, lashing it with deadly force, ripping up rocks and plants as it scythed along the ground only inches from where I stood. I was too stunned to move, and shattered fragments of rock sprayed against my face. If there was pain , I didn't feel it. I just stood and stared at the one I loved.

Telesā vasa loloa.

The shock on his face mirrored my own. "What the hell? Leila, I don't know what's happening. How to stop this …" He held his hands up at me with a helpless look on his face and even that despairing movement was not without consequences. In answer to his motions, the pool of water heaved again and a wave emanated from where he stood, rushing toward me, knocking me down, swirling around me as it pushed through the surrounding forest.

I fell to my knees, buoyed by the rushing water, grabbing for a handhold at bushes, rocks, plants, anything. I could hear Daniel calling me.

"Leila! Are you alright? Leila!"

I shook my head in his direction ruefully, steadying myself against a tree, calling out "I'm okay. Fine. Don't worry about me." *Worry the freakin' hell about yourself and what in heck is going on with you*, was my silent scream. From my secure place against the tree, I could see him still raised several feet above the ground, still trying wildly to shake off the coiled ropes of water. The panic on his face was an all too familiar sight – it mirrored my own the first few times my fanua afi gift had begun to manifest. Daniel was afraid. Out of control and afraid, and I knew all too well what that felt like.

I shouted over the roaring water. "Daniel! Listen to me. Stop moving. Just stand still and breathe."

He looked over at me, confusion at war with terror in his eyes. "What? What do you mean?"

"Stop moving, stand still, and breathe. Count to ten, or twenty or whatever, just do it! Look at me. I'll count with you. Look at me, look in my eyes, and we'll count together. Do you trust me?"

He nodded, responding to the authority in my voice. "Yes. I trust you."

"Good. Don't move. Breathe. Look at me and count with me."

He stopped thrashing about, stopped shaking his arms, and stood still. From his raised position above me, his eyes found mine, caught, and held, and together we started counting. One, two, three …

I gazed at him, this boy that I loved with every fiber of my being and I willed him with everything I possessed – to calm. To gentle the power of the Gift that raged within him. To soothe it and subdue it.

Her malu shimmered and glowed a fiery red as she called on the perfect strength of earth to speak with a mother's love to this son of the ocean. Daniel and Leila counted, their voices in unison, and gradually the wild waters around Leila receded. The water platform Daniel stood upon began to sink until he was again standing in chest-deep water. And still they counted, their gaze locked. Forty, forty-one, forty-two … and the pool's surface was once again a glass mirror, broken only by the silver splash of the

rocky waterfall. She walked to the edge of the pool and he took those few steps forward out of the water until they were standing face to face. Together, their voices dropped to barely a whisper. Sixty-five, sixty-six, sixty-seven ...

And then it was over. They were two people standing beside a forest pool. Two wet, half-naked, and somewhat bedraggled people. The counting died away but still Daniel stared down into her eyes, unwilling to break the lifeline that bound them. They did not touch, but she had never felt so close to him. Something had happened to him. And neither of them would ever be the same again. They were bound now by more than love. More than trust. They were bound by their mother earth, fanua.

He spoke softly in the darkness. And there was tiredness and remnants of fear in his words. "Thank you."

Wet and chilled, she wanted – needed –to hold him. Reassure them both with the comfort of closeness. But she was afraid to touch him. Afraid of what that might generate. And so a thought summoned fire. Just a gathering of it in the palm of one hand. A flick of a wrist and tendrils of flame slowly encircled them so they stood within a gossamer-web of ruby red and orange. Ripples of energy that danced about them like a thousand fireflies.

And thus they stood beside a black pool, under a solemn night sky. The patterns of her malu glowing ember red and his pe'a answering with ice blue fire.

A daughter of earth, fanua afi, and son of the ocean, vasa loloa.

E L E V E N

There was only one logical course of action for us to take after that. We went to speak with Salamasina. "She's the only person with any kind of answers for you, Daniel. There are things in your past – in her past – that you need to ask her about." I didn't even need to worry about breaking any confidences because as we sat by the poolside, surveying the wave-stricken damage all around us, Daniel had to agree.

It was long after midnight when we pulled up beside the weather-beaten house. Daniel went in to wake his grandmother while I waited in the quiet kitchen, unsure if I should be present when he had this talk with her. She came out of the bedroom with questions in her eyes but one look at the both of us and her shoulders slumped. She sank into a seat at the table and asked us with dejected eyes, "It's finally happened, hasn't it?"

Daniel and I exchanged glances. "What do you think has happened, Mama?" he asked her gently.

"You are vasa loloa." There was so much sadness in her words that Daniel moved to embrace her.

"Mama, don't be sad. I'm alright. Something has happened to me, but I'm alright. I'm hoping though that you can explain it? I've always known that I was adopted. Was my mother telesā?"

Salamasina closed her eyes and breathed deeply in Daniel's arms, as if seeking strength in her son's closeness. "Come with me." Sensing my hesitation, she nodded at me, "You too, Leila. This involves you both."

She rose to her feet and walked out of the house, carefully making her way across the tarsealed road, half-lit by a flickering temperamental streetlight. We followed – up and over the stone seawall that lined the roadside and then down to the beach. There was a half moon casting her diamonds upon the black ocean and the tide was coming in, each wave lapping in a little further than the one before it. Salamasina did not stop until we stood at the very edge of ocean where feet sank a little into wet sand. The old woman breathed deeply of the salt breeze and gazed out to the oceanscape, searching, searching. "Where are they? Ah, there. Look, what do you see? My eyesight is not what it used to be. Tell me, what do you see out there?"

We looked where she directed and saw them. Betrayed by the silver flash of their fins as they leapt, danced, and played far out by the reef. I exclaimed, "Dolphins! I see dolphins."

Salamasina nodded her head and there was the same heavy sadness in her face. "Yes, dolphins. They have always been intermittent visitors here, but lately, they have been this shoreline's constant companions." A raise of her chin. "And if you could see further still, you would see the whales. The local fishermen speak of them. At least six of them are out there. Never venturing very far away from this beach. Do you know why they are here?"

Moonlight glinted on the tears on her cheek as she spoke the truth that had been dancing on the waking edge of possibility. Ever since I had believed in the certainty of Daniel's death – only to have him returned to me, battered and bruised, but alive. Returned by a school of silver dolphins.

"They are here for you, Daniel. You are telesā vasa loloa as your mother was before you. She gave her life to protect you from telesā law. There are reasons why Tanielu and I did not tell you the truth of your heritage. They are the same reasons that we left our home on Niuatoputapu and came here to start a new life. All your life I have watched and prayed that you would not inherit your mother's Gift. You have reached manhood now, and I had thought you had escaped the curse of the ocean, but now, I see it is not to be. I hope you can forgive me for keeping your past a secret. What I have done, I did for love."

Daniel moved to take Salamasina in his arms. "Mama, please don't cry. I have never doubted you and Papa's love for me. I am blessed to have you for a mother."

For a moment there was only the sound of the ocean as mother and son embraced. And then Salamasina moved to sit on rocks by the water, motioning for us to join her. We sat where wet black crabs scuttled to hide, and listened as she told her story. Which was also the story of Daniel. And the story of the one they called the Wild Child.

TWELVE

Salamasina

She remembered that day as if it were only yesterday. The day she had first met a wild child called Moanasina.

Salamasina had already been removed from the sisterhood by then, but like everyone else on Niuatoputapu Island, she had heard of Moanasina before she even arrived. Her mother had been a teenager who concealed her pregnancy from her family and friends. When she gave birth, she had abandoned the baby in a village stream, and passing children had stumbled across the newborn in time to save her life. Moanasina's father was rumored to be Tongan. A waiter at a local resort. Either way, neither parent had wanted her and Moanasina had been raised by various families in the village. Looked after by many but loved by none, she was a child who did not speak. A child who spent all her time in the ocean. Frolicking with dolphins. Throwing rocks at the children who caught a ponderously large turtle and tried to drag it to shore so they could tease it. Kill it. Cook it. A child who sabotaged the fish traps that the village boys put out overnight.

When she was six years old, Moanasina summoned a tidal wave to destroy a Japanese fishing boat that was fishing illegally in Samoan waters. They had harpooned a whale, and the little girl had responded to its distress cries. From many miles away. Four of the fishing crew had been killed. Discreetly and swiftly, Nafanua had arranged for the child to be sent to the Tongan vasa loloa sisterhood as the best place to receive the training she needed to control her gift. A gift that was deadly and terror filled.

But when you looked at her, you could not see it. She was a pale, thin thing. Just a frightened little girl who never spoke. She spent all her time in the ocean with a school of dolphins that were always close by. She ran away from the Covenant every other day. Away from her lessons. Away from the stifling company of sisters she did not know and did not want. And every other day, the telesā would hunt her down and bring her back. Punish her, hitting her with a coconut frond salu broom. She would stand there, biting her lip, never crying out as the salu cut her legs with the fire of a hundred biting red ants. And afterward, she would wait and watch for an opportunity to run away again, swimming far out to sea with her dolphins. Her only friends. Her only family.

Until the day she met Salamasina. Salamasina was in the forest, gathering plants for her medicines, when there was a crashing through the undergrowth, the panting heaving breaths of a person running. Far off in the distance, there were shouts of people coming in pursuit.

"This way! I saw her go this way."

Salamasina didn't have to wonder for very long what was happening for, in the next instant, a little girl broke through a stubborn tangle of ilovea vines, coming to an abrupt halt at the sight of the woman carrying a woven basket of roots. The girl's t-shirt was ripped, her lavalava skirt disheveled, and her face dirty with tears and sweat. They stared at each other as the sounds came closer. The girl threw a hunted look over her shoulder and then looked back, her eyes darting everywhere, searching for the best route of escape. Salamasina could tell this child of the ocean was a stranger to the bush. She gazed with fear at the shadows of the trees and there was disdain as she shifted her bare feet awkwardly in the grass. This child was not at ease with fanua. Against her will, Salamasina smiled. Salamasina hated the telesā vasa loloa sisterhood, the women who had raised her and then rejected her because she was not truly one of them. She knew who this child was – the most powerful vasa loloa in many generations. She should hate her. But as the girl darted to the other side of the clearing and tried to rip a path through the ilovea vines, Salamasina only felt kinship.

"Quickly, hide in here." She pointed to a hollow at the base of a tamaligi tree, in amidst the giant roots. "Hurry!"

The girl regarded her with suspicious eyes. *Why should I trust you?* they asked.

Salamasina was impatient. "I know this forest like no one else. You have nowhere else to hide. Get in there, now."

Indecision warred with fear and then the girl hurried over to crouch down into the hollow. Salamasina grabbed the basket of roots and dumped it on top of her, quickly arranging them so that the girl was well concealed.

Just in time, as the pursuers broke into the clearing. Three young telesā, beautiful and haughty in the surety of their position as vasa loloa. They halted when they saw Salamasina, who had resumed digging for choice roots with her knife. The eldest of the group threw her a question. "We are hunting for a young girl, a disobedient girl. Did she pass by here?"

Salamasina ignored her for a moment, concentrating on a stubborn root. The telesā shifted on their feet and the leader reprimanded her, "Woman, I asked you a question. Did you not hear me?"

Salamasina paused and looked up, shading her eyes in the afternoon sun. "Yes, I heard you."

Again there was an expectant silence in the clearing, enough so you could hear the call of the wood pigeon and the distant constant roar of the ocean. A second telesā jumped in. "Well, if you heard her, then answer the question. Don't you know who we are?"

The older telesā gave a sneering laugh. "I know you. You're Salamasina, one of the ungifted ones." She turned to her sisters, "She used to be one of the Covenant until they realized she was no true vasa loloa and they gave her away to the old healer in the village. Her true calling, digging for roots in the dirt where she belongs."

The other two joined in her laughter. Salamasina slowly rose to her feet and their laughter dimmed.

"So roots-digger, you know then who we are and what we can do to you if you don't speak up and answer our question?"

Salamasina spoke and her words were carefully measured. "Yes, I know who you are and what you can do." She lifted the bush knife in one hand and tapped the blade gently against the palm of her other hand, regarding first the blade and then the women who stood opposite her. "I also know that you are a long way from the ocean. The nearest water source is five miles from here. Too far away to be of any use to you." A smile. "So here we are. The three of you vasa loloa and me, the roots-digger. With a knife." With casual ease, Salamasina swung the bush knife, arcing it over her head like a fire knife, spinning it from one hand to the next, the steel blade glinting in the sun as she swung it lightly from one hand to the next, confident and at one with the blade.

The telesā looked at each other and some unspoken agreement was reached. The leader spoke, "We don't want any trouble with you. We are seeking a runaway from our sisterhood, a young girl. A skinny little thing. Have you seen her?"

Salamasina brought the spinning blade to a halt and pointed off into the distance behind her. "That way. She came through here and ran that way. Not too long ago. She is a very little one and it will not be difficult to catch up with her."

The leader gave her a slight nod before turning to the others. "Quick, we have wasted enough time with this one. Let's go."

The trio ran across the clearing and into the bush in the direction pointed out by Salamasina. But before the leader went after the others, she stopped to look back at the older woman. "I will not forget your insolence. One day, soon, we will meet again and next time roots-digger, it will be on my terms, and you will pay respect to vasa loloa."

Salamasina shrugged. "I look forward to it."

As soon as the women were out of sight, the clump of roots and leaves shifted and the little girl peered out. Still fearful. Questioning. Salamasina brushed away the debris and helped her to stand. "It's alright. They've gone. You can come out now."

The little girl stared and her silent eyes asked, *Why? Why did you help me?*

Salamasina spoke gently. "I have no love for the vasa loloa. And as you just heard, they have none for me. Now come, let's be away from here in case they realize we have misled them and they return." Quickly, she gathered up her pile of roots and leaves, gently replacing them in her basket before walking across the clearing in the opposite direction from the telesā. The little girl watched her walk away, not following. Still wary. Still hesitant.

Salamasina paused. "Are you coming? Or do you want to wait for your sisters to come back? It's up to you." She turned and continued on her way through the brush.

The little girl made her decision and went after her, not walking too close though. Just keeping a safe distance away. Ready to bolt at any minute. Salamasina continued talking, ignoring the girl's silence.

"I hope you haven't bruised these ginseng roots. It took me a good two hours to collect this many of them. And these mangosteen leaves are from a secret tree that only I know the whereabouts of. They are the key ingredient in a treatment for migraine headaches. Not many people know where to find mangosteen trees on this little island …"

Somewhat calmed by Salamasina's prattle of plants, roots, and medicines, the little girl moved closer to her so that eventually they walked side by side. After a while they came to the edge of the forest and before them was sand. Rock. And ocean. They stopped at the sight and Salamasina glanced down at the little girl beside her. She was a child transformed. The wariness and suspicious fear was gone, replaced by relief and a joyous lightness. Her eyes feasted hungrily on the gently lapping waves on the shoreline. The distant crashing white surf where ocean communed with coral reef. Salamasina saw her joy and felt only sadness. All her life she had wanted to feel that way about the ocean. All her life she had longed to commune that way with the blueness that surrounded their island so she could be truly her mother's daughter. So she could be one with her vasa loloa sisters. But it had never happened. No matter how hard she tried. No matter how much she wished it. Where her sisters spoke to the ocean like a friend – a mother, a lover – she had only ever seen it as an impassive and unpredictable force.

She sighed. "You're Moanasina aren't you? The wild child they brought here from Samoa? The vasa loloa they cannot tame?"

The little girl nodded and her eyes were troubled.

"Why do you keep running away from them? It's obvious you're one of them. Why do you keep rejecting your sisterhood?" Salamasina tried not to let her hurt and bewilderment show but it was hard. This child had what she had always longed for and yet – she didn't want it. That cut at her more than she thought possible. After so many years, she had thought she had well and truly gotten over it. That she had successfully 'moved on.' But here now, with this child, this unwilling vasa loloa, all the hurt came rushing back. She repeated the question and this time her tone was harsh. "Why don't you want to belong?"

The little girl had taken several cautious steps out onto the sand, eyes searching in every direction for pursuers. Her body was poised to make a run for it. But she paused. Turned back to Salamasina and spoke. Every word was awkwardly voiced, as if unused to being sounded. "Because I don't need a family. A sisterhood. Because I already belong. With them." She pointed out to the playful ocean. Where a pod of silver dolphins danced. She smiled at Salamasina. "Thank you."

And then the little girl ran across the golden sand, into the frolic of white surf and dived into the ocean, surfacing again to swim with powerful strokes out to where her true family waited. One larger dolphin took her onto its back and together the pod moved away from the shoreline, farther and farther out until Salamasina could no longer see them. She thought that would be the last time she would ever see the little girl.

She was wrong.

Two weeks later, Salamasina had dropped her guard. She was no longer avoiding the ocean or watching out for the vasa loloa. Rumor had it that the wild child was still not found. Salamasina smiled a secret smile every time the villagers spoke of it. She was glad the little girl had escaped. She imagined how frustrated that would make Tavake the Covenant Keeper – that a mere child had defied her – and Salamasina was happy. She hoped that Moanasina had gone far away over the ocean and would never come back.

Salamasina was at the rock pools to gather seaweed. She was alone. As dusk was beginning to creep in, turning azure blue ocean into purple-black gloaming. And that is when they came upon her. The same three telesā vasa loloa led by the threatening one, the one with the sandy brown hair who had grown up in the Covenant at the same time as Salamasina. The one they called Vahalesi.

"See, sisters? Ungifted ones do more than dig for roots. They scrabble for seaweed and shells. What have you got there, Salamasina?"

Slowly, Salamasina rose to her feet, trying not to betray her fear, cursing her foolishness. She was out on the beach alone with three telesā vasa loloa. She had her knife but that was a small comfort. She knew too well what vasa loloa could do with the full might of the ocean at their backs. She stood and faced them, tall and proud. She would not run. She wouldn't give them that satisfaction.

"You know Vahalesi, it's funny how much you loathe root-diggers as you call us, and yet you are happy to use our medicines and drink our elixirs for youth and beauty. Goodness only knows what you would look like without them."

The other two laughed and Vahalesi shut them up with a look of loathing. "Oh, you think it's funny do you? Well, do you want to know what amazes me?" She took several steps forward. "It amazes me how much disrespect you have for us telesā when you know how much we can make you suffer."

Swifter than thought, a single flick of her wrist, and Vahalesi held a coiled whip wire of water in her hands. Summoned from the darkening ocean beside them, she wrapped one sinuous end around her wrist. "You need to learn some respect. You need to be reminded who we vasa loloa are. By the time I'm done with you, roots-digger, you will beg me for mercy."

Before Salamasina could react, Vahalesi wielded the wire with deadly accuracy and lashed her across the face, narrowly missing her eye but tearing into her cheek. Salamasina cried out at the searing pain. But Vahalesi was only just getting started. She waved the rippling, silver wire of water over her head and then coiled it around Salamasina, pinning her arms to her sides, stinging at her flesh. She yanked viciously and tugged. Salamasina was forced to the ground, landing with her face in the sand, all the air knocked out of her.

For a ragged moment, she couldn't breathe, couldn't feel. She tasted blood and sand in her mouth. She spat, trying to raise her face from the ground, trying to stand but unable to move because of the suffocating grip of the water coil. Vahalesi pulled at the ropes and jerked Salamasina so she was lying on her back, so she could look up at her jeering face.

"So roots-digger, you still want to laugh and make jokes about vasa loloa now, ah? You still think you can defy me?"

Vahalesi didn't like it when Salamasina refused to answer. The ropes coiled tighter, cutting into her arms, pressing like a heavy weight into her chest. Salamasina winced at the pain, but that was not enough for the telesā vasa loloa. She summoned another whip wire of water that curled up out of the ocean, coiling, dancing, rippling to Vahalesi's command. This one wrapped itself around

Salamasina's throat. Choking her. "Now what do you want to say to us, roots-digger? Hmm?"

Terror gripped Salamasina as her need for air became a burning, raging need. She twisted her body this way and that, uselessly fighting to get free as her vision began to cloud.

Vahalesi laughed at her distress. "What was that? You want to say something? Here." She relaxed her grip on the coils at Salamasina's neck and leaned closer to her face. "Are you ready to beg now? What did you say?"

Sweet air rushed into Salamasina's lungs as the chokehold eased. And with it rushed fury. She swore viciously as she spat in Vahalesi's face. Blood, sand, and spit.

Too late, Vahalesi recoiled in disgust as the others joined her in her outrage. It was unheard of for anyone to dare speak to a vasa loloa in such a manner. Vahalesi slapped Salamasina's face and then stood to kick her again and again. In the face, the stomach, everywhere – screaming maniacally, "You dare to insult me!"

"Kill her, Vahalesi," the others chanted. "Kill her now."

Their cries were only a dim blur now as the stranglehold resumed around her neck, as the kicks and blows intensified. But just before she slipped into unconsciousness, the blows ceased. The chokehold abruptly released. And there was screaming. Only, it wasn't her doing the screaming. Dimly, Salamasina realized that she was no longer being restrained, the water coils were gone and instead the air was filled with a rushing, roaring sound. She struggled to her feet, blocked out the pain in her face, her arms, her ribs. The sight before her was awe inspiring.

Standing on the sandy shore a few feet away was a little girl in worn, wet rags. She stood staring, expressionless, at three swirling whirlwinds of water, three tall columns of water and in each one, a woman was held captive. In each one, the churning water viciously spun and battered at a woman who kicked and struggled for release. Their resistance was futile though as the water held them prisoner as if in the midst of a spinning washing machine. And still the young girl stood and stared at them with uncaring eyes. In that moment Salamasina was afraid of this child, this vasa loloa who was powerful enough to use the ocean against her own sisters. Her breath caught in her chest, a pain-wracked breath as she winced. She had at least one cracked rib, she was sure of it.

"Moanasina, what are you doing? Let them go."

The girl turned to her with an impassive face. "Why should I? They were going to kill you. I heard them. And besides, do you know how many times they beat me when I was in their stupid sisterhood? No." She turned her attention back to the water prisoners. "I'm waiting."

"For what? What are you waiting for?" Salamasina limped over to stand beside her.

Moanasina smiled. A secret, knowing smile. And pointed out across the bay. "For my friends. There they come."

Salamasina looked and fear knifed through her. One, two, three dorsal fins cut through the water, moving with deadly speed. She grabbed at the younger girl's arm. "No, don't do this. Let them go, please."

The wild child only looked puzzled at her pleading. "Why? If they truly are vasa loloa then they will speak to the sharks and will not be hurt." She turned back to the ocean, nodded her head, and the water whirlwinds dissipated instantly. All three of the telesā fell into the water, blueness swallowing their screams. Black fins circled them.

"No." Salamasina knelt in the sand beside the little girl, wincing as every movement sent serrated blades of pain through her body. She put her hands on Moanasina's shoulders and forced her to look her in the eyes. "They are not like you. They are not as strong as you are. They will not be able to communicate with those sharks. Please don't do this. It doesn't matter what they have done to me, or to you – you do not want their blood on your hands. Stop this now, before it's too late."

Moanasina ignored her, staring out over her shoulder to where, one by one, the telesā were re-surfacing, spluttering, and splashing, disoriented from their mad spinning in the whirlwinds. Vahalesi was the first to attain some measure of control, gazing wildly about her. And so she was the first to see the sharks. Her scream was angry and panicked. Salamasina watched in horrified fascination as Vahalesi struggled for some control. Over the ocean. Over the situation. She seemed to be trying to summon waves, something, anything, but nothing happened. She was too flustered, too afraid. And as the three dark shapes moved in lazy circles around the panicked women, Salamasina was afraid for them. She turned back to Moanasina.

"Stop this now."

To her surprise, there was a cheeky smile on Moanasina's face and her reply was flippant. "Oh, I'm just playing with them. You didn't really think I would force my friends to eat them do you? I only want to scare them a little. Show them what it feels like to be afraid. Teach them a lesson. Don't worry, I won't let anything eat them."

Salamasina breathed a sigh of relief. "Whew. You had me worried there." Now that the threat had been removed, she stood up, her body wilting and reminding her how sore she was. "Ow …"

A sharp voice from behind them startled them both. "What is the meaning of this?"

They turned and Salamasina's heart sank at the sight of the group of women who now stood on the beach. A group of women led by Tavake. The vasa loloa Covenant Keeper. Salamasina's mother. Well, at least she had been her mother until Salamasina had failed the telesā initiation testing when she had turned twelve. Then the woman who had been her mother had given her away to another. Because she was ungifted. *Not even cursed. The opposite of blessed. Just a nothing. A nonentity. I may as well never have been born.*

Again Tavake asked, "What is happening here? Moanasina, what are you doing with this woman?" If she recognized Salamasina, she gave no sign of it.

The little girl looked defiant. "She's my friend. I'm helping her. Those telesā were hurting her and I stopped them."

A telesā standing to Tavake's right, tapped her on the arm, pointing out to where Vahalesi and the others still trod water, trying not to move too much as still the sharks circled. "Look there."

Tavake looked and her eyes narrowed. "Is that your doing, Moanasina?"

The girl nodded, and the lack of remorse on her face had the other telesā hissing. "Make her call her creatures off, Tavake, before they harm our sisters. This foolish child really has gone too far this time, trying to harm one of the sisterhood." There was a murmur of angry assent from the group, like an angry humming hive of bees. If looks could maim, Moanasina and Salamasina would both have been flayed where they stood. But Tavake only rolled her eyes and shook her head at their panic.

"Be still. Those fools are in no danger." She raised an eyebrow at Moanasina and the child shifted her feet awkwardly at the searching gaze. "The sharks are there for visual effect only, aren't they, Moanasina?"

The others looked disbelieving, but Tavake waved away their concerns with an impatient gesture. "I have spoken with them and no kill command has been issued. The question is though, why did you deem it necessary to frighten them? And prove yet again to all of us that these idiots are undeserving to be called telesā vasa loloa. The first hint of danger and all their training is forgotten. They are reduced to blithering babies. Leave them there. Perhaps then they will know better than to break their sisterhood vows and raise their hands against another telesā."

The other women objected. "But Tavake, these are not telesā vasa loloa, well not really. One is a child who hasn't even entered the

Covenant yet. And the other?" A sniff of disdain conveyed more than words what they thought of Salamasina. "Is an Ungifted."

"Exactly. What telesā targets children who are meant to be our pupils and women who were once within our sisterhood? No. Leave Vahalesi and the others where they are."

The coldness in her tone was chilling. It matched the evening wind that came in off the darkening ocean and the emptiness of the blackening sky. By now the women thrashing in a shark circle had caught sight of their Covenant Keeper and were screaming for help. Their cries limped across the water, tired, afraid, and pitiful.

The other telesā objected. "But Tavake …"

She ignored them. Instead, she addressed Moanasina, and the gentleness in her voice was disarming, "So tell me Little One, why do you keep running away from the Covenant? We want to be your family. Your sisters. Why won't you let us?"

In that moment, Moanasina's armor slipped and she looked like a frightened, lonely child. Like she might burst into tears, and Salamasina's heart ached for her. She stepped forward and placed a comforting arm on the little girl's shoulders. It had been many years since she had spoken to her mother but compassion gave her strength. "Moanasina has not felt welcome in your Covenant. Some of the telesā have been unduly harsh with her and she feels more at home with her ocean family."

If Tavake was annoyed that Salamasina had spoken without her permission, she did not show it. "Is this true?" she asked the little girl.

Moanasina nodded.

"I want you to come back to the Covenant. This time it will be different. I have been away travelling and out of touch with the situation. You will live with me and I will take over your training personally. You will have no instruction with any other telesā." She smiled. It was a beautiful smile that spoke of hope, love, and joy. All the things that Salamasina had never had. 'Moanasina, you have a blessed future ahead of you. With the right training, your gift could be the one we have all been waiting for, the one spoken of in prophecy. Come with me back into the Covenant and I promise you, no one will hurt you." She held out her hand, but Moanasina did not move to take it.

"I don't want to come back to the Covenant. Vahalesi and her friends will be there."

Tavake smiled again. "No, they won't be." She turned to look out to the shivering, crying women in a black ocean. Softly, barely whispering, she spoke to the ocean creatures. "I release you."

Moanasina's eyes widened in panic. "No, what are you doing? I told them to be on guard." She turned and ran to the water's edge, her eyes, her whole body concentrating on the sharks. Muttering under her breath, she stamped her foot in frustration. "No, stop it. Stop it I say! Listen to me." She looked again at the Covenant Keeper who only stood there with her arms now folded, relaxed, waiting. Waiting. "Why aren't they listening to me? I summoned them. They aren't listening to me anymore."

Tavake shrugged. "I gave them permission to be true to their nature. You are not the only one who can speak with sharks. They are doing what they do best."

Realization trudged with heavy footsteps of dread in Salamasina. "No …" She looked. All the gathered telesā looked.

The sharks had stopped circling. The dorsal fins had disappeared. For a moment there was nothing but a silken velvet cloth of ocean where three women swam fearfully. And then the screaming began. The wild thrashing in the water. Moanasina cried out, "No, please don't!"

Salamasina pulled the girl close to her, covering her eyes, but knowing it would be little use trying to shield her. Moanasina shared a mental link with the ocean predators and no amount of blocking would stop her from feeling, seeing, experiencing everything they were as they ripped the women apart. She was thankful for the darkness at least, shadowing the water that surely must be blood filled. There were two, then one, then the women were no more.

Moanasina fell to her knees on the sand, retching. Salamasina was angry and her anger gave her courage. "Why did you do that? Can't you see what that did to her?" She pointed to the child who now rocked back and forth without tears, a vacant gaze out to the ocean. "She's just a child."

Tavake arched an eyebrow. "Exactly. A child with far too much power. Who thinks it's fun to summon great white sharks to just 'scare' people she doesn't like. She's playing with gifts that she barely understands, gifts that can bring life or death to those around her." She pointed out to the bay where sharks continued to churn white surf as they fought over the leavings of their victims. "She needs to see vasa loloa's creatures for what they really are. They are not her pets or playthings. These ocean gifts are not to be wielded lightly. This child needs telesā training and if you care for her at all, then you will make her see that what we offer her in the Covenant is her best option. Her only option."

Salamasina didn't want to hear the truth in her words. "I could look after her. She could live with me. I would teach her."

Tavake sighed, and in that moment she looked older than Salamasina had ever seen her. "And just what would you teach her exactly? How to make cough medicine? Cures for back pain?" She smiled, not unkindly. "You are my daughter and I have watched your talent for healing flourish. I know that many owe you their good health, their mended bones, and even their very lives. There is no denying that our mother fanua speaks to you with the richness of her living bounty. But you are no telesā vasa loloa. And Moanasina does not belong with you."

Tavake moved to kneel beside the girl who wept silent tears on a desolate beach, "Come, let us go now."

Moanasina's question was anguished. "Why did you do that? I was never going to let my sharks hurt them."

"They were never *your* sharks, my child. Even though you and I may speak with them, vasa loloa's creatures are not ours to control. We may befriend them, swim with them, hunt with them, and even live with them for a time – but they are not our tamed animals ready to perform at our bidding. And we must never forget that some of them, like the Great White shark, though we may swim with them, they are never far removed from their basic nature. They are wild. The most lethal killers of the ocean. It was a grievous wrong on your part to call them here today if you were not prepared for them to kill. Let this be your first lesson. When telesā vasa loloa use their powers unwisely, death is the result. The ocean gives us these gifts so we can help people, and protect our earth. Not attack the Ungifted and bully small children. When you are one of us, you will be able to bring much good to many lives. You will be a champion and protector for the ocean that nourishes us all."

She gripped the carved handle of her walking stick firmly and rose to her feet. Moanasina rose with her. But before they walked away, the little girl slipped away from Tavake and ran back to hug Salamasina fiercely whispering.

"I will see you again one day. I don't care if you are Ungifted. We will see each other again."

Salamasina watched the telesā vasa loloa leave before making her painful, bruised way home. She had ointments and bandages that would heal her injuries, but she knew the memory of this day would never fade.

Time passed. Salamasina met a man called Tanielu Tahi. Love blossomed, grew like the enduring, red burn of the torch ginger flower. They were married. Tanielu had a welding business and catered for all the fencing and boat repair needs on the island. Salamasina continued with her calling as a healer. They were happy. Salamasina's heart was at peace and wanted no more reminders of vasa loloa. Of what she could have been. They lived their lives separate from the resident telesā sisterhood. As separate as one could be on an island as small as Niuatoputapu.

But every so often, Moanasina would visit her. They would talk, but nothing too detailed. She was vasa loloa and Salamasina was Ungifted, what was there to say? Tavake had been true to her word. She took over Moanasina's training personally and people said that the Wild Child would be the inheritor of the Covenant one day. Moanasina never spoke of it on her visits, but she had never been much of a talker. Sometimes Moanasina would just sit in Salamasina's garden, watching her at work with her medicines. She would listen to the older woman, let her prattle on – about her beloved husband, her plants, her babies.

Yes, her babies. Salamasina and Tanielu wanted nothing more than to have a family but it was not to be. Three times they were blessed with a pregnancy, and three times Salamasina miscarried. In spite of all her knowledge, all her efforts, none of her babies made it to full term. And each time, Moanasina knew somehow and came to visit her friend. Still not speaking a word. Just to hug her, cry with her – and then slip away before her absence was noticed.

The years passed. Moanasina stayed with the sisterhood and made her Covenant with them when she was old enough. She was their most powerful weapon when it came to marine conservation and protection, but she never truly felt like she belonged there. She hated many of their rules, felt suffocated by their closeness. By the sisterhood. Because in her heart, in her soul, Moanasina was still that wild child who preferred the company of dolphins to people. Salamasina was the closest thing she had to a sister. A mother. A friend. She allowed no one else in.

Until she met Ryan Grey. A marine biologist from New Zealand who came to study the abundance of sea life in Tonga's pristine waters. One day he came across a dolphin caught in a fishing net and was battling to try and save it. Moanasina heard the dolphin's distress cries and went out to find it. There they were, the two of them. Both champions of the ocean. Was it any wonder they fell in love?

For the first time, Moanasina had found another human who spoke her language. And Ryan Grey? Love for this dark-eyed girl with the wild edge to her every movement swept through him and over him. They were inseparable. She joined him on his boat and they spent many days at a time out in the ocean. She helped him with his research, led him to all the best locations for gathering the information he needed. Ryan had a taste for music, and on moonlit nights he sat on the deck of his boat and played wordless love melodies for the girl who swam with silver dolphins in a sea that trembled softly with black diamonds.

Those who knew Moanasina saw her change. A gradual but consuming change. Salamasina had never seen her so happy. At peace.

Her happiness was dangerous. Salamasina tried to warn her. "You must put an end to this relationship before it's too late. You are covenant telesā, Tavake's second. You are putting this man's life at risk. And your own."

But Moanasina did not listen. Love is like that. It makes lovers feel invincible. Like they can take on the world. And overcome all. It was obvious to Tavake that Moanasina was in way over her head with this man. But what made it worse was that the telesā suspected Moanasina was using her gifts to aid his research. Tavake took her aside. Warned her. Pleaded with her to end the liaison. Send the man away before telesā law was invoked.

And then the inevitable happened. Moanasina went to share the news with Salamasina. Running into her backyard garden with feet of lightness. Joy. Laughter. Pausing first to look somewhat suspiciously at the older woman.

"Salamasina, are you expecting?!"

An embarrassed laugh. "Yes. At my age? Something of a shock, I know!" She patted her belly with careful pride. "But a miracle that Tanielu and I are both so grateful for. I'm only about six weeks along and already showing." A rueful shake of her head. "I think she will be a very big miracle baby."

Mindful of all that Salamasina had endured in her years of trying for a child, Moanasina's eyes softened as she hugged her friend with delicate care. "Yes she will. And she will have the best mother any child could hope for."

Salamasina smiled, "Thank you." She drew Moanasina to sit with her in the shade of the sweeping mango tree that ruled the yard. "Now, tell me what news brings you here with such a happy smile and a light heart?"

"It is wonderful news. The best news." She stopped and held the healer's hands in hers. "I'm pregnant too. We will be mothers together. Our children will grow up together."

Cold dread darkened the day. "No, please say you are joking. You are being foolish Moanasina."

Still smiling. Still unaware of the oil slick of horror pooling in Salamasina's chest. "No, I'm not teasing you. It's true. I'm going to have a baby. Ryan doesn't know yet. I'm going to tell him tomorrow. It's his birthday and this will be the most precious gift." Can anyone be more absorbed than a teenager in love?

"Have you forgotten who you are? What you are? You are telesā. Our children can never grow up together."

Moanasina was defiant. Stubborn. "This is my baby and I will say what will happen to him."

Salamasina reeled. "Him? You are carrying a boy? How do you know this?"

She smiled a secret smile and patted her still-flat midriff. "My water brothers and sisters have spoken to him. They have told me so. My baby lives, breathes in water within me. And already he speaks to the dolphins. They can hear his thoughts, sense his feelings. He is vasa loloa like me. I can't see him, but at night I dream of his face and he will look just like his father. Just like Ryan. He's going to be so happy. We have talked about how much we want to have a family. We just didn't think it would happen this soon."

Salamasina wanted to shake her. Slap her. Snap her out of the fantasyland she was living in. "You fool. Don't you know what telesā do to male babies? Don't you know anything of telesā law?"

"What are you talking about? You should be happy for me that I have found someone who makes me as complete as Tanielu does for you." The younger woman's eyes were filled with confusion. "Why aren't you happy for me?"

"Telesā law forbids male offspring. Men are not allowed to have telesā gifts. When your baby is born, the Covenant will kill him. And if you continue to give of your gifts so openly to Ryan's research, then they will kill him too. There is no future for you with this man. Or this child. I'm so sorry."

"You're lying. That can't be true. Telesā are protectors of life."

"Are you sure about that? Have you forgotten that day on the beach? Tavake didn't think twice about killing Vahalesi and the others. She eliminated them so she could make you stay with the Covenant. Do you really think she will allow you to leave the sisterhood? To be with this man, to live life as a wife and a mother? Tavake will never let you go. You are too powerful. Your Gift is too great an asset for her." Salamasina was soft with compassion. "I'm so sorry. It can't work. Not for you and Ryan, and certainly not for your baby."

It didn't seem possible for the day to still be so rich with beauty and lushness. For the air to be sweet with ripe mango, golden sticky sweetness. Not when a young woman in love was struggling to accept this most dire of news. The two women were silent for a long while as Moanasina stared at the distant blue of the horizon. Finally, she stood. "I must go."

"What will you do?"

"I'm going to tell Ryan everything. And together we will figure it out." She tried to look braver than she felt.

Salamasina winced. Telling Ryan Grey about the telesā would break even more laws. But then, Moanasina had already passed the point of no return. She hugged the younger woman fiercely close. "Be careful. If there's anything I can do to help, you will tell me?"

She watched Moanasina leave and felt very useless. It had been a long time since she last wished for telesā power. But she wished for it today. So she could stand beside Moanasina when she faced her greatest challenge.

Moanasina meant to go to Ryan as soon as she left Salamasina's garden, but she was met on her way by another. Tavake. The Covenant Keeper waited for her in the Dolphin Cove.

"Can we talk?"

Moanasina gazed out over the beckoning blueness, to where flashes of silver called to her – tempted to refuse. To run. To leave. To go and never look back. But Tavake was the one person she could never evade. As the Keeper, Tavake was the crucible for the sisterhood's combined Gifts, even Moanasina's. There could be no hiding from this woman.

"What do you want to talk about?"

"I know you are with child. I know it is a boy. The ocean has spoken it to me."

Moanasina didn't try to deny it. "What are you going to do?"

"I have allowed you much leeway. More than any other vasa loloa in our sisterhood. But this foolishness must end. I can no longer excuse you from telesā law. When the sun sets on this day, I will kill Ryan Grey. But I will spare your life and that of your son. You will leave this place and find temporary refuge elsewhere." She waved a careless hand out to the ocean. "There are any number of scattered atolls you can live on. You will wait out the duration of your pregnancy, and when your child is born, you will give him to another woman to raise. You will return to us and resume your rightful place as my Second. Our mother ocean needs you. Our

Covenant needs you. None of the sisterhood need know that you birthed a male child. It will be as if all this had never happened."

Her command brought Moanasina to her knees in the sand. "I beg of you, please, spare Ryan's life. I'll send him away, give him up. I'll never see him again. Please. Spare his life and you will never again have to doubt my commitment to vasa loloa. I covenant to you on my sisterhood, that I will give everything that I am to our ocean mother. Just promise me you will let Ryan and my son live. Please."

Was it compassion that moved Tavake? Or judicious leadership? Either way, she relented. "See to it that Grey has left our Tongan waters before nightfall. And remember Moanasina, you can keep no secrets from me on the ocean. I will know if you lie to me. If you try to run from me. I will find you. I will know if you make contact with this man again. And any time I so choose to change my mind on this? I can seek him out on any of the many oceans of the world and kill him." A chilling smile. "How convenient that he is a marine biologist. He will always be within easy reach."

And with that final reminder, Tavake turned and left the beach.

Nobody knew what was said on Ryan's boat that afternoon between him and the girl he loved. What is known is that Moanasina said goodbye to the one man who spoke her language and understood her communion with the ocean. The man with chipped emerald eyes and a crooked smile who sang to dolphins in the moonlight. That afternoon, lies were told in the name of love. There was anger. Hurt. Betrayal. And before the last rays of fire bled from the horizon, Ryan Grey smashed his guitar on the gleaming wet rocks that encircled the harbor and then cast off, setting sail for the open sea.

Moanasina stood on the silent shore and watched him go, wishing with every fiber of her being that she could summon him back. But love gave her strength. To say goodbye and to safeguard the secret of the child she bore. Ryan must never know about his son. Both their lives depended upon it. Not until she was certain of his departure, not until his boat had long disappeared into the silken night did she give way to her grief. Salt tears mingled with ocean as she took to the water, calling to the majestic grey bulk of a whale to carry her far away from Niuatoputapu. To an island where she could grow a son, far away from the eyes of the sisterhood.

People love gossip. And the more tragic, the better. The whole island buzzed with the news. Moanasina's lover had up and left her. Packed up his boat and sailed away without looking back. And Moanasina was missing. Nobody knew why. But Salamasina thought she knew. She was certain that Ryan Grey had done what many men do when they hear their lover is with child. He had abandoned her.

Tavake breathed a sigh of relief at Ryan's departure. Moanasina's place in the sisterhood was intact. A broken heart is much easier to heal than a broken covenant vow. She looked forward to the day when Moanasina's son would be born, for then the most powerful member of her Covenant would return.

The months passed and Salamasina's pregnancy seemed to have escaped the curse that accompanied the first three. Hopes, wishes, and dreams for the child that would be blossomed with the swelling of her belly.Tanielu fashioned her a wood rocking chair 'to rock our baby to sleep,' he said with a proud smile. Salamasina put aside her work in the garden and started sewing clothing for the little one that would come. They were happy times. Days of expectant waiting, light with the promise of the joy that a child would bring.

It was in the final weeks of Salamasina's pregnancy when she arrived. Moanasina.

She came to Niuatoputapu one storm-filled night in a canoe without paddles, carried by an ocean current that moved to her command, accompanied by the silver dolphins. She was already in labor by then and Tanielu had to carry her from the canoe to their home. Lightning overhead illuminated her pain-wracked face.It was a long and difficult birthing, one that even all of Salamasina's medicines could not gentle. Moanasina needed her ocean mother's strength to help her through the delivery but she would not allow them to take her to the water. She was adamant that she did not want to give birth in the ocean because she was afraid the sisterhood would sense her.

"No!" A tortured scream. Moanasina grabbed Salamasina's hand in a vise-like grip, her eyes wild with anguish, "No, we have to stay away from the ocean. The vasa loloa must not know of my son's birth. Please, no ocean."They heeded her pleas. What else could they do? And so the delivery was far more painful than it should have been. Far more gut wrenching and drawn out. Her son was born in the early hours of the morning. A child of the dawn. He was beautiful. But he had the mark of vasa loloa and Moanasina wept to see it.

"Please, I beg you, take my son and make him yours. You are the only woman I want to entrust my child to." She pointed to Salamasina's own swollen belly. "In a few days your child will be born. You could give birth to twins and no one would question it. You are Ungifted, the sisterhood does not care about your children. Please."

They agreed. Of course. Moanasina was like a daughter to Salamasina, the little sister she had never had. They promised they would love her son as their own, raise him side by side with their child. Moanasina did not linger. She held her son for only a moment, whispered tender words of farewell and then she slipped out into the rain, leaving him in Salamasina's arms. They tried to call her back and Tanielu would have gone after her, but all the night's excitement brought on Salamasina's pains and his wife needed him. Another baby would be born that day.

Unlike Moanasina though, Salamasina's delivery was brief and, unlike Moanasina, her baby did not survive. Tanielu held his daughter in his arms and wept.

"Where is she? I want to hold my baby?" Salamasina asked, exhausted.

"I'm sorry Salamasina, she's here but she's gone."

He handed her a perfect child. She was a frangipani blossom ready to wilt if held too close. So soft. So small. So still."I'm here, Little One. Mama's here." Salamasina cried, but it was no use.

Tanielu buried their daughter beside the frangipani tree in the yard. There would be no twins. Only Moanasina's child. They named him Daniel.

In giving them both up, Moanasina had ensured the safety of the man she loved and the child she carried. But she was not yet done. She removed the carved bone neckpiece she wore that Tavake had given her many years ago upon her entry to the Covenant. She left it at Tavake's doorstep with one final message. *I said I would give everything that I am to our ocean mother. Know this – I will always be watching. Remember your promise.*

It was the most perfect of mornings when Moanasina climbed to the rugged cliff-top on the nearby island of Tafahi. She paused for a moment at the peak, to look out over the vast expanse of ocean to the blue strip where earth meets heaven. She invoked the ancient right of telesā, to gift one's soul to that which gave her strength. She prayed that her ocean mother would accept her Gift.

And then she leapt to her death on the jagged rocks below.

Moanasina's body washed up on the Niuatoputapu shore the next day with the early morning tide. Battered, bruised, and broken. Salamasina wept at the news. The sisterhood prepared the body for burial but gave each other sideways glances, wondering who would replace Moanasina as the Covenant Second?

Tavake raged. She was livid with anger at this final act of betrayal and the ocean beat with fury upon the island's rocky shores. But it was a useless anger. With her death, Moanasina had severely weakened Tavake's Covenant and by gifting her power back to vasa loloa – she had ensured that she would never truly be absent from her son's life.

Or from Ryan's.

It was fitting revenge against the Covenant Keeper.

Five months later and Salamasina was bathing her son outdoors in a giant tub that Tanielu had made for him. She would fill it with water first thing in the morning and let it sit in the sun to warm. By mid-morning, the bathwater was perfect for a little boy to splash in. Daniel loved the water. Salamasina was careful and never took him to the ocean, but bath-time was always his favorite time of day. A shadow covered them and the baby gurgled with delight at the appearance of a visitor. Salamasina turned.

Tavake.

Startled, she leapt to her feet, snatched Daniel from the water and instinctively held him close. Tanielu was at the workshop. She and Daniel were alone with the Covenant Keeper. Fear choked her. *My son, I will give my life for you but it will not be enough. No. It will not be enough. Not if Tavake wishes to take more.*

Neither woman spoke for a taut moment. And then Daniel wriggled against Salamasina's tight embrace, annoyed at being confined. Gurgled with that delight-filled sound that babies have and smiled at the strange woman.

"He's beautiful." Tavake smiled at the baby, who responded with more excited wriggles.

It was not what Salamasina expected. Noting her surprise, Tavake gestured impatiently. "What? You think that because I am telesā I cannot find joy in a child?"

Her words cut in ways that Salamasina knew she had not intended. Her reply was laced with the sting of the vaofefe biting grass. "You never found any joy in your own child so, yes, I find it difficult to accept that you would take any in your grandson."

She put emphasis on the words 'your grandson' as if to say, *See Tavake? This is MY little boy. Isn't he perfect? He's my son. Son of the Ungifted. Not telesā. Not Covenant. No.*

Tavake sighed tiredly. "You're wrong. All my daughters have given me happiness. But a Covenant Keeper carries much responsibility on her shoulders. She must make difficult decisions to preserve her sisterhood and abide by many laws not of her making. Not of her choosing. We keep Covenants. We very rarely make them. A strong leader cannot afford to have emotions …" an impatient shake of her head. "Never mind. One day maybe you will understand why a mother would choose to close the doors of her heart. To love, to feeling. Because sometimes it hurts less that way."

She gestured towards the laughing little boy. "May I hold him?"

Salamasina wanted to scream a refusal. But that would only set alarm bells ringing. Carefully she wrapped Daniel in his towel, concealing his tell-tale birthmark. A crested wave.

"Be careful." The voice was gruff, but hands were gentle as she gave Moanasina's child into the hands of the woman who could issue his death warrant.

Tavake held Daniel with an awkward delicacy, as if afraid he would shatter. "Hello little one." The baby responded with eager delight, kicking, waving his little hands everywhere, smiling. He caught a strand of Tavake's hair in his fingers and tugged at it, moving his fist to his mouth. She stopped him with a gentle touch. "No, no. Don't do that. Such a strong little boy. So perfect. Faka'ofo'ofa. So beautiful. Look at his eyes. Green like emerald oceans. Unusual eyes indeed for a Tongan baby, don't you think?" She looked at the other woman and there was nothing innocent in her question.

Salamasina shrugged helplessly. Her heart fragmented into a thousand pieces. *My son. My Daniel.*

Tavake tickled the little boy and smiled as his peals of laughter rippled through the garden. Laughter danced like butterflies in the breeze. "Tăpuaki, such a blessing. He will bring you much happiness, Salamasina. I pray you will always find joy in your motherhood." She placed a soft kiss on his forehead, breathing in his sweet baby scent before returning him to the other woman. "Thank you for letting me see him. Hold him." A wry smile. "A gift for an old woman." The words sounded strange coming from a woman who defied time and looked like she should be Salamasina's sister.

Salamasina clutched her baby fiercely, wishing Tavake would leave them. But she was not done. The light left her face. Tavake's eyes were wet river stones of severity. "But he will also bring you much heartache. Listen to my words, daughter. If you want this child to live, you and your husband must take him, leave Niuatoputapu and never return. It is not safe for him here."

She knew. Tavake knew. Salamasina rushed to protest, to deflect, but Tavake waved away the lies impatiently. "Save it. There will be time enough for deception later, and I only hope you will be practiced at it enough to safeguard your family. The path you are choosing is a dangerous one. The boy's future is inevitable but you can try to keep him with you for as long as possible. If you love him – he must never know the truth of his birth. Never speak of telesā to him. Or to others. Do not forget, there will be telesā wherever you go throughout the Pacific. Always be on guard. Always keep him close."

Salamasina secured Daniel's wrapping around him a little tighter and wished she could erase the mark that screamed out his heritage. Tavake shook her head. "I don't need to see the mark of vasa loloa on his body to know that he will be Gifted. As Covenant Keeper, I can sense him. The ocean is strong within him, as it was in his mother. That is why you must leave here. There are those who would move heaven and earth to ensure that this child never reaches the Gifted year. Or worse, there are those who would seek him out so they can take his Gift. Treasure this child while you can Salamasina, for it is most likely that you will not have him long."

Tavake turned to leave. Salamasina watched her go with tears streaming down her cheeks. "Wait!" A deep breath. "Why? Why are you doing this? Why are you letting us go?"

The smile Tavake gave her had no joy in it. "In spite of what you may think of me, I have never killed a baby. And I'm not about to set a precedent now." A careless shrug. "Think of this as my gift to you. Because of the Covenant, I could not be your mother. But here now, I can ensure that you enjoy the gift of motherhood, even if only for a short time. Farewell. You will understand when I say that I hope we never see each other again."

And so Tanielu and Salamasina left their home, the island where they had both grown up, knowing that they could never return there. They moved to Samoa and Tanielu established his welding business. Salamasina made sure not to display her skills with healing too openly. They lived a simple, quiet life with their son and they were happy. When Daniel grew to boyhood, they told him Moanasina had been their daughter – and in some ways that was true – Salamasina had loved her like a daughter, a sister, a friend. Daniel was a son who gave his parents much happiness.

It was a happiness that Salamasina did not take for granted, for she knew it could be taken from her at any time. The possibility of Daniel's Gift was forever looming in the background, like the ominous distant roar of the waves beating against the reef in front of their house.

THIRTEEN

The sunrise was beginning to burn the horizon when Salamasina came to an end. "Not a day goes by when I have not given thanks for the blessing of being of your mother. Tanielu was so proud of you, as am I."

Daniel was silent as he stared out at the crashing surf on the reef. He looked so very weary and my heart went out to him. This had been a night of intense revelations for him. I reached for his hand, trying to will him some of my strength. Salamasina sighed at our clasped hands. "That is why I did not want you two to be together. It was nothing personal against you, Leila, but I knew of your ties to telesā and I feared that you would be a catalyst for Daniel's Gift." The look she gave me was accusing, and I shifted uncomfortably. "And then when you revealed that you are fanua afi, it was like a nightmare coming true."

"Grandmother," Daniel interrupted with an embarrassed laugh. "Please. I wouldn't use that word to describe the girl I love."

Salamasina rushed to explain. "No, you don't understand. There is a telesā legend that speaks of fanua afi and the purpose of telesā. It is the telesā creation story and you both must hear it so that you can know why it is that I wish my son had never met you, Leila."

Ouch. I tried not to show how her words wounded me. This was my boyfriend's mother after all. And Samoan culture was all about fa'aaloalo, respect for your elders. So instead, I clasped Daniel's hand tightly in mine and listened as Salamasina told us the creation myth – according to the telesā.

And when she was done, Daniel voiced the same question that I had. "Mama, I understand that these old stories are very important, and we can learn many useful things from them but honestly, I don't see what that creation myth has to do with me and Leila."

"It is not just any story. It is the arcane knowledge that has been handed down from telesā mother to daughter since the creation. Telesā speak this knowledge to their daughters before they can understand its mysteries. They whisper it to their babies as they nurse at their breast, soothing them to sleep with the familiar words. They tell it to them as they search the forest for the plants that will heal. And the plants that will hurt. They recite it as they teach them how to unleash their gifts, how to speak to wind and water. They sing it together as they dance the siva, as they speak of earth's mysterious beauty through their dance. No, it is not just a story." The old woman paused and pointed at me. "Why do you think your mother Nafanua was so quick to embrace you? So eager to have you join her covenant, even against the wishes of her sisterhood? She knew of the prophecy. Ancient telesā have long spoken of the telesā fanua afi who would come and set to right the balance, awaken this people to a remembrance of their debt to fanua. In you, Nafanua saw the answer, the power that would restore telesā to their rightful place as the guardians, the protectors. What she conveniently forgot to take into consideration was the rest of the prophecy. That for the prophecy to be fulfilled, a man was required 'he who would give his heart that earth may live.' The prophecy is about sacrifice. A sacrifice of gifts, of life, of heart so that the land might live. I will not let my son be that sacrifice. Do you hear me!?" She shook her fist vehemently inches away from my face and I cringed against the force of her anger. "You must choose another. You must let my Daniel go. I tell you, let my son go." And then she crumpled, her energy spent. She turned to Daniel. "Please? Surely you can see why it is a mistake for you two to be together?"

Both Daniel and I sat in stunned silence, trying to process all that Salamasina had just hit us with. And then the boy I loved spoke with firm conviction. "Mama, I don't want to hurt you, but Leila is the girl I love. She is my heart, my earth. I know nothing of legends or prophecies. But I know that without Leila, I am nothing. And together, we can endure anything."

Salamasina gave up trying to convince us of anything after that declaration. But she did tell us about her visit from Tavake the Tongan Covenant Keeper and her concerns about Sarona. "Now that your Gift has manifested, Tavake is going to want you to join her. She assured me that she would not harm you, but still, I worry for you, my son. I worry for both of you."

As we walked back to the house , Daniel held my hand in his and I tried to share the same faith that he had, *together we can endure anything.* More than anything, I wanted that to be true.

Simone and I were so exhausted from the fashion show spectacle that it took a full three days for us to recover. It took another week for us to clean the house of its two weeks' worth of creativity, until we could inspect our domain and agree that it finally resembled its original self. What a relief. Maybe now, life could go back to normal. Whatever that was. School, my work at the Center – everything had taken a back seat to the show and I was looking forward to the ordinary and mundane. I should have known better. There is no room in the telesā world for the 'ordinary and mundane.'

I got a phone call from Salamasina in the early morning, before the neighborhood dogs, or even the chickens were awake. The insistent beeping burrowed into my sleeping subconscious, waking me. What the hell?

"Leila? Daniel's missing. He's not in his room, or anywhere in the house or the workshop, I can't find him." She choked on the words.

Daniel. I didn't hesitate. Falling over the mess in my room in my haste to get dressed, I was out the door and in the jeep within minutes, remembering at the last minute to leave a scribbled note for Simone to explain my absence. I knew the route to the ocean-side house in my sleep and I drove on auto-pilot. What could be wrong? I pushed a little harder on the accelerator, gripping the steering wheel firmly, trying to stifle the rising tide of panic that threatened to drown me. Too many thoughts. *What if it was Sarona? What if she had taken Daniel? What if she had rounded up some more psycho* telesā *matagi? What if…* The ten minute drive felt like an eternity. I pulled up beside the faded welding shop sign. Salamasina was waiting for me on the porch, with all the lights on in the house. She was pale and drawn, her hair a wiry mess as she stood there wringing her hands.

"I don't even know how long he's been gone. I always get up at five and when I walked past his room I saw that his bed was empty and the back door was open. His truck is still here. Oh, where could he be?" In that moment, she didn't look like a proud, mean woman who had threatened me to leave Daniel alone. She looked like a very frightened and rather frail grandmother.

I walked her back into the house, trying to calm her. "I'm sure he's alright. Maybe he's gone for a run? Or just a long walk?"

"No." She shook her head in agitation. "He would have left me a note, or said something about it last night. He knows I worry about him, especially since Tavake's warning about Sarona. What if she took him?" She sunk her face into her hands and gave in to her tears.

"We'll find him. Don't worry." I patted her on the back, my mind racing to think of all the possible places that Sarona could have taken Daniel. She had a house at the Aleisa property. I could check there first, although that would be a far too predictable spot to take a victim. Maybe I should go to the same beach the Covenant had taken us to last year? I refused to let my terror overtake me. Daniel needed me to be calm and composed. Plan with care and precision how to approach this. Through my fervid thoughts, something Salamasina said caught my attention. Something about nightmares…"What did you say?"

"I said that I should have known much sooner that something was wrong. Every night for the past few weeks, he's been having terrible nightmares and waking me up with his shouts and thrashing about. But last night, there was nothing, no noises at all and I just slept through it. I should have checked on him. I should have known he wasn't in the house." She sobbed piteously.

Nightmares. Immediately I was reminded of my fear-filled dreams from the year before. So real. So life-like. The dreams that had led me to the secret pool. I thought of Daniel's birthmark, sharks and dolphins and I knew where he might be. I leapt to my feet. "I think I know where he is. Come on."

I ran out the door, down the porch steps and across the road to the seawall with Salamasina following closely behind me. "Where are we going?"

"To the ocean. I think he's somewhere on the beach."

We stood at the top of the seawall and gazed down the beach in both directions, right and left. The sun had begun to pierce the horizon with pinpricks of orange gossamer thread that embroidered the shadowed beach with filaments of light. I couldn't see Daniel anywhere. A long distance away to the right was an outcropping of rocks, leading to a sheltered cove. A good place to start? I set off running.

 If only I had some kind of telesā radar, some way of sensing if there were any in the shadows waiting for me. I called his name in a hushed kind of whisper.

"Daniel? Where are you?"

And then I heard him. "Over here." His voice came from the faraway silver strip of beach that beckoned from beyond the rocks. "Come quick. But be careful."

His voice seemed to catch on something unseen. I was afraid and fear made me hot. Tendrils of smoke rose from cindered patches on my singlet as my agitation ate through my skin, my clothing. I sprinted to the rocks and clambered over them

"What is it? What's wrong…" the question died in my throat as I jerked to a standstill on the beach.

A beach that was cluttered with sea creatures. The bulk of a dolphin lay heavily at the far end of the sand, arraigned about it were turtles, the black triangle of giant sting rays, the silver glint of fish as they threshed and flapped in the shallows and all about the sand. And sitting in the midst of them all was Daniel. Clothed in the usual ragged pair of shorts, the muscled plane of his back was criss-crossed with vicious red welts. He looked up at my approach with an expression of bleak despair.

"They're dying. And I can't help them. I don't know what to do."

I ran to kneel by his side, navigating squid, jelly fish, and *whoa, is that a shark?!* "Are you alright? What happened?" He raised his arms to hug me with a fierce intensity. That's when I saw his chest. Scourged with the same lacerations and purplish swelling bruises. "You're hurt. We've got to get you up to the house where Salamasina can take care of you."

"No, I can't leave them. It's my fault they're stranded here. They're dying. They keep coming to me and I can't make them stop."

"What do you mean?" I sank to kneel beside him in the wet sand, "How is this your fault?"

"I couldn't sleep. Something was calling me. I could hear my name so I came down here to the beach." He looked up out over the ocean and his eyes had that same faraway look which had transported him on that day when the water had leapt to his desire. Daniel was there with me but he wasn't. Flies buzzed around his lacerated body but he didn't see them. He saw nothing but the ocean and the sea creatures that surrounded us. A cold fist of fear clenched me. I wanted nothing more than to get him as far away from the ocean as possible, back up to the house where his wounds could be tended to, where we could assert some reason on this strangeness.

He turned his face away from me and in the splintered dawn I saw tears glisten and glide on his cheek. Daniel was crying. The fist of coldness clenched tighter and I could barely breathe. The boy who had risked telesā wrath to stand by my side, endured lightning torture, and been to hell and back at the hands of a power-hungry Covenant sisterhood – now sat here on a beach littered with dead and dying sea life – and wept. His tears pierced me with a pain that I never knew was possible.

"I wanted to see if I could make it happen again. What happened at the pool that day. You know, that thing with the water?"

I nodded, willing him to go on. *Don't shut me out now Daniel. Tell me everything. Let me in to your personal nightmare.*

"So I tried focusing, thinking about how it felt at the pool when the water was responding to my thoughts, my movements and it worked." His face lit up for the briefest of moments. "The ocean was moving to my thoughts, it was – well, I don't know how to describe it." He shook his head at the memory and I filled in the gaps for him.

"It was magical?"

"Yeah, that's it. Magical." He studied his chafed hands thoughtfully. "Like something sleeping inside me all this time is finally waking up."

"Then what happened?" I prompted. "How did you get hurt?"

"I was doing stuff with the water when all the fish went nuts. Out of nowhere, everything started to throw themselves on the shore, swimming all the way up until they beached themselves. And their thoughts. It was like a frenzy, I couldn't make sense of their language anymore. They weren't scared or angry. They were happy. Joyous. To see me. To hear me." He shook his head, frustration blazing in his sea-green eyes. "I tried to stop them. First by talking to them with my mind. And then by carrying them back into the water. I've been chucking fish and stuff back into the ocean but they kept coming back faster than I could throw them back. For hours now. It's hopeless." He regarded his hands in defeat. "I can't stop them. I tried. And now, they're dying."

"Oh Daniel." I took one ravaged hand gently in mine. "Is that how you got hurt? Trying to return them to the ocean?" I looked closely at his wounds.

He nodded. "They're dying Leila. I can hear them. I can't get them out of my head. I don't understand what's happening. What's wrong with me?"

Before I could think of an answer that would make sense, Salamasina spoke from behind us, "Your mother had the same Gift. The ability to communicate with the ocean creatures. And to control them. Not all vasa loloa have it."

We both turned to look at her. Salamasina regarded us with sadness in her eyes. "Your Gift is strong Daniel. You will need training so you can control it. So that it doesn't overwhelm you. And so that you won't hurt anyone." She looked at the death around us. "Or any thing."

Daniel rose to his feet. There was a hint of hope in his voice. "Can you help me?"

She shook her head and hope fractured. " I am no telesā vasa loloa. You will need Tavake's help."

I leapt to my feet. "No. I can help him. I'm telesa." I turned to Daniel, "You can't trust any telesā sisterhood. I helped you the other night. We can figure this out together."

Neither of them looked very comforted by my assurance. Who could blame them? I sounded more confident than I felt. What did I know about oceans and talking to sea creatures anyway? Nothing. All I knew for sure was that Daniel shouldn't go anywhere near a Covenant Sisterhood.

In the hesitant pause that followed, Salamasina took charge. "Daylight is fast approaching. We need to clean up here and get Daniel home so I can tend to his wounds."

There wasn't much we could do for the dead marine life that littered the shore. Except make a pile of their bodies on the sand.

Salamasina and Daniel stepped back and watched as I summoned fire and set the pile ablaze. The smell of roasting flesh was overpowering and Daniel turned away, taut with some unnamable emotion. I forced the flames to intensify, wanting it all to be over faster. Salamasina went to stand beside him, an arm around his waist. The two of them stood there united as I did the only thing I was good at. Burn stuff.

As my core sang to the flames, I confronted the harsh reality. What could a fanua afi teach a vasa loloa? About control. About harmony with one's Gift. About the earth's elemental promise? About anything?

At some point, Daniel was going to need another Vasa Loloa. Where were we going to find one that didn't want to kill him? Or siphon out his powers?

I shoved the unwanted questions away and followed Daniel and Salamasina back up to the house.

The next day, I tried again to get back to the regular life I had been trying to live. I showed up to Dayna's muay thai class and the students greeted me warmly. Keahi was nowhere to be seen. Dayna shook her head when I asked about him, "He hasn't been back for over a week now. I got a text from him saying he wouldn't be helping with the classes anymore because he would be travelling for a while."

Keahi travelling? Had he joined Sarona? I tried to quell the fluttering of unease in the pit of my stomach. It wasn't my fault if he had chosen to take Sarona up on her offer. There's no way that I could have helped him. Not with him behaving the way he had. Not with the disastrous connection that we shared. I tried to put him out of my mind and went to meet with Mrs. Amani and catch up with the Center's activities. Everything was fine, except for Teuila.

"Her mother was released from hospital earlier this week and she moved back in with her boyfriend."

Stunned, I asked, "Not the same guy who knifed her?"

"The very same. Teuila didn't want to leave with her mother, but she insisted. I tried talking to her mother and getting her to change her mind, at least leave Teuila here. She's settled in so well and starting to open up to people and trust us. She loves the muay thai classes and enjoyed doing the fashion show with you so much. But her mother took her home."

I was so angry that my rage felt like a white-hot lance in my chest. Teuila deserved better than this. "Isn't there anything we can do?"

Mrs. Amani shook her head, "I share your frustration, but we have no legal grounds to stand on. Not here in Samoa. All we can do is be ready to help Teuila when she next needs it."

In other words, wait for her to get attacked again. My first instinct was to go visit Teuila at once but the way I was feeling, I knew I shouldn't. At least not until I calmed down because the way I was feeling – I wanted to knife someone myself.

All that day I couldn't shake my apprehension for Teuila, thinking about her long ago confessions about hiding in her room while her mother had drunken-fuelled parties bad enough that Teuila's fear would cause trees to fall on their house. I thought about how beautifully confident she looked on the night of the fashion show, how she had rallied our motley crew of models and how naturally she had modeled Simone's Rainforest Woman design. There had to be something I could do to help her now. I sat and watched the evening news with Simone but my thoughts were a thousand miles away – until a news item caught my eye. The reporter was interviewing the leader of a science expedition in Tonga. They had recovered a plutonium-operated battery device that had been sitting in the Tongan Trench for over thirty years – and then, someone had stolen it.

The camera zeroed in on the American being interviewed, "This is a security threat of massive proportions. We cannot emphasize enough, how important it is that the RTG be safely returned to us. If the protective casing is cracked or ruptured in any way then there is the possibility of leakage and fire damage. We don't wish people to be alarmed though. It is not a nuclear reactor and does not rely on fusion or fission processes. We are not talking about a nuclear bomb here."

An eager reporter interrupted, "Isn't it true that ingesting only one milligram of plutonium is enough to kill a person?"

The American sighed, obviously used to such dramatic statements. "Yes, that is true. But I highly doubt that anyone is going to walk up to an RTG and take a bite out of it. The alpha radiation emitted will not penetrate the skin and as long as nobody cracks open the RTG casket, then it will be fine."

Still not satisfied, the reporter tried again, "Can the plutonium in an RTG be used to make a nuclear weapon?"

"No. The RTG uses Pu-238. The same properties that make it a desirable fuel source make it useless in nuclear weapons. It very rarely may spontaneously fission. Pu-238 generates heat and so that makes it an unsuitable option for a thermonuclear weapon." He hesitated, "But, theoretically it could be used in a radiological or what they call a 'dirty' bomb."

"Can you explain that for our viewers, please?"

"It's a bomb that combines radioactive material with conventional explosives. The primary aim of such a weapon is to contaminate the area around the explosion with radioactive material, hence the term 'dirty'. But that's mere speculation."

And now the reporter was almost gleeful. "Isn't that the main concern here, with the missing RTG? That some terrorist group may have stolen it to make exactly the kind of dirty bomb that you're describing?"

The American looked exasperated, "That's all pure speculation and entirely unhelpful to the current situation. Suffice it to say, there's a NASA-owned battery device missing and we need it back." He stared directly into the camera for this, "The RTG may have sustained damage during its thirty plus years underwater. It could be leaking. If it's not safely contained then it could be a serious hazard. That is all."

The program cut to a commercial and almost immediately, my phone went. Daniel. "Did you see that on the news?" His voice was tense and low. "Salamasina is going ballistic over here. She's not making any sense. She says it's Sarona. She wants to put us on the first plane out of here. She thinks it's all connected somehow with Sarona wanting to get back at you. Crazy right?"

"Definitely crazy," I agreed. Plutonium and me. No connection whatsoever.

Ten minutes later, my phone went again. This time it was Mrs. Amani. "Leila, Teuila's missing. She's been gone since yesterday. Her mother just called me, thinking that maybe Teuila had come here. She's frantic with worry. I think Teuila may have run away from home." She hesitated, "Has she showed up at your house?"

"No, but I'll look out for her."

I grabbed my car keys and was headed out the door when the phone rang. Again. Simone raised an eyebrow at all the cellular activity. "You're unusually popular tonight. So many friends, I'm jealous."

But it wasn't a friend. A calm, cool, and collected voice spoke, "Hello Leila. This is Sarona. Listen very carefully. I'm calling from Tonga. I have a little friend of yours with me. Teuila. She has a most interesting ability, one I've never encountered before. And one that I'm very much looking forward to studying."

I caught my breath. "Don't you dare hurt her."

Sarona was ice. "Be quiet. You're not the one giving the orders here. Not anymore. Now, this is what you are going to do. Your mother left you something in her will besides the money that belonged to me. A particular bone carving. You will bring it to Tonga. There's a flight leaving in the morning. When you get to Nukualofa, I will phone you with further instructions. If you're not on that flight tomorrow, I will kill the girl. Perhaps I'll have Keahi set her on fire." A low, musical laugh. "That's right. He's here too. And I'm enjoying his company very much." Her tone sharpened, "Did you hear me, Leila?"

"Yes."

"Good. Oh, and bring your boyfriend with you too. He and I have unfinished business." The phone went dead. A second later it beeped as a photograph arrived in my inbox. I opened the image. It was Teuila. Standing against a rock face, facing the camera, unsmiling, with Sarona by her side. Sarona wasn't lying. She did have Teuila.

One of Grandmother Folger's favorite sayings had always been that a lady does not give in to her emotions, especially in times of trial. "When in the middle of a crisis, Leila, always remember, that is when you most need to focus, remain calm, and be at your most dignified." I thought about that as I called the airline after-hours number and booked two tickets to Tonga. And carefully walked back to my room, grabbed my backpack, and started packing a few essentials. *Yes, I would need my toothbrush. And a change of clothes. My face wash? Nah, Dad says soap will do for everything.* I was calm, focused, and even dignified. Grandmother Folger would have been proud of me. With a bag packed, I had to try to remember where I had put the box the lawyer had given me six months ago. So annoyed with my mother and the contents of her will, not to mention seriously freaked out by my encounter with Sarona, I had chucked the box in my suitcase without even opening it. I dug it up now and opened it. Disinterested and impassive, all my emotions locked away behind calm, dignified walls. In the box was a chunky oblong bone carving engraved with ornate designs. It was as long as my forearm and about the same width as my closed fist. Clearly this was not a necklace. I studied it closer. The carving did not seem to be complete. One end of it curved inward as if missing an interlocking piece. I packed it away into my backpack and took a moment finally, to think about this new development and try to make sense of it. I needed to tell Daniel about this but first, so many questions whipped and writhed in my brain like eels caught in a trap.

What was this bone carving for and why did Sarona want it? Why Tonga? Why take Teuila all the way over there and why make me follow? What did she have in store for me and Daniel? I had no illusions – I knew there would be no fair trades conducted. The only thing I was one hundred percent sure of was that Sarona wanted me dead. I wondered, how did she find out about Teuila's unusual Gift? Even I had barely sensed it. And come to think of it, how had Sarona known about Keahi and his Gift? I had only told two people about Keahi and Teuila. I had confided in Daniel.

And Jason. But Jason wouldn't have told Sarona anything. He wouldn't have told anybody about our conversations. Except maybe his fiancé. The girl who had swept him off his feet.

The truth slammed me then. Sudden and violent. In that sickening moment, I knew with perfect clarity where I had seen that look before. The one that Jason always had when he talked about Lesina. When he looked at her. When she walked into a room. *No, please no.* With all my heart I wished for it not to be true. The heart that loved Jason like the big brother I never had.

I leapt to my feet and opened my desk drawer where I kept my important things. Like pictures of my dad. I searched through photographs of us together, standing at the finish line of a fun run. With fishing rods on a grey beach. Where was it? And then I found it. The picture that Grandmother Folger had sent me last year – of a striking woman gazing at the camera, defying it to capture her beauty, holding a baby on her lap with careless ease. And beside her, a sandy-haired, brown-eyed man who stared at that beautiful woman with the same expression that Jason gave Lesina. Complete and utter longing. *It's not difficult to brew a love potion if you have all the ingredients and the telesā know-how.* I wanted to vomit. Instead, I ran to the Jeep and revved it to a roar out the front gate as I went in search of the truth.

At Jason's house, I had to bang on the front door for what seemed like an eternity before he finally opened it. The look on his face frightened me. He was a man bereft. Lost. His eyes barely flickered in recognition. "Hi Leila."

"What's wrong? What's happened?"

"I don't know." He opened the door wide.

I followed him in. "Where's Lesina? I need to talk to her."

"Lesina's gone. She's left me."

It is a terrible thing to see a broken man. To hear the emptiness in his voice. And feel the depth of confusion in him as he struggles to make sense of his pain. "I can't understand it. Everything was going so well. We had scheduled a trip home to California so she could meet my family. And then I find this. What does she mean, 'ask Leila.' What is this all about?" He showed me the brief note. As cutting in its simplicity as it was telling.

I can't be with you anymore. I'm sorry. I'm not the girl you think I am. I never was and I never can be. Ask Leila to explain what I mean when I tell you – that I am telesā and we do not love.

I looked at Jason with my heart in my eyes. A thousand stars died and a millennium of perfect moments fragmented for him with these words. "I'm so sorry. If I had known sooner, I swear I would have told you. I would have done something or said something. Anything to stop this from happening."

He was bewildered. "I don't get it. How could she be telesā? And if she was, why did she keep it a secret from me? I love her. I wouldn't have let that stop me from wanting to spend the rest of my life with her."

I took a deep breath, "Jason, telesā are known for many things and their skill with plant medicines is one of them. A long time ago, Nafanua used a very special concoction on my father, a love potion if you will. I don't know much about such things, but I think it is used to cloud the senses, warp one's judgment, and cast a man into an infatuated state. Nafanua used one on my father. When I first met Daniel, Salamasina worried that I had used a love potion on him. I think that Lesina used one on you."

His eyes flashed dangerously. "No, that's impossible. I love her. I know my feelings, and I'm telling you that I love Lesina and her love for me is real." He came to an abrupt halt, as if aware of how hollow his words sounded as we sat there in his desolate house confronted by her letter of farewell. "I don't believe you. I won't believe you."

I was gentle, "How else do you explain how quickly you two moved from falling in love to being engaged and planning forever together? It was all too fast, too rushed, too impossible."

And now he spoke with anger. "You've never liked her. You don't know her like I do. I can't believe that of her. I won't. Maybe you should leave."

"You're hurting, Jason, and I understand that." I stood to go. "You should know. I've heard from my mother's sister who tried to kill us all last year." Quickly I summarized the situation for him. "I think Lesina is working for Sarona. Tomorrow, I'm going to Tonga. And when I see Lesina, I'm going to make her pay for what she's done to you."

And with those final words, I left his house. Tears blurred my vision and I had to pull the Jeep over to the side of the road so I could stop my crying enough to safely drive to Daniel's house. One look at my face and he had me in his arms. "Leila? What's wrong."

In the safety of his arms, I cried. For Jason. For the unfairness of a world where a good man with a sincere and generous heart could have the misfortune to have loved not one but two telesā in a single lifetime. And then to be betrayed in the worst possible way like this? I poured everything out to Daniel.

He held me and listened, and when I was done, he tried to comfort me. "This is not your fault. This is Sarona's doing. All of it."

I asked, "I hate to ask you this, but I promised you I would always walk with you and not keep things from you – will you go with me to Tonga?"

He gave me a sardonic expression, "You couldn't stop me from going, even if you tried."

Salamasina hated our plan. Of course. She argued, pleaded, and reasoned with him, but Daniel did not waver. "This is something Leila and I have to do. Together." So Salamasina said she was going with us. That was when Daniel put his foot down and the son became the authority figure. "No Mama. I won't allow you to come. I am vasa loloa and Leila is fanua afi. We can defend ourselves and protect each other."

I showed Salamasina the bone carving that Sarona wanted, hoping she would know of its significance. "Do you think it's a piece of the Covenant Bone you told us about in the legend?"

She shook her head, "I have no idea. My mother Tavake would know. She is the only telesā who knows what the Bone is supposed to look like."

It was getting late, and our flight to Nukualofa was at nine in the morning. I said good night to Salamasina, and Daniel walked me to the car, where I clung to his strength one more time. "I hate myself for saying this – but I'm scared. Not so much for me, but for all of us and what might happen. I'm scared that we won't save Teuila, that we won't be strong enough for whatever Sarona has prepared. I'm just scared."

He raised up my face so he could look me in the eyes, "So am I. But I know that as long as we're together on this, everything will be alright. We will endure." The kiss he gave me was slow and tender and bittersweet. What if this was the last time I would kiss Daniel within reach of the sound of the Samoan ocean?

Early the next morning, I had one more huge obstacle to clear before I could even think about getting on a plane for Tonga to face off against a telesā matagi and her assorted team of Gifted ones. I had to explain to Simone where I was going and why. It didn't feel right to lie to him but I also didn't want to put his life in danger by revealing too much, so I was deliberately vague. Simone listened to my rather nebulous explanation of my and Daniel's trip to Tonga, with a raised eyebrow.

"So let me get this straight. You and Daniel are flying to an undisclosed island location in Tonga, for an unknown period of time, to deal with some unmentionable problem that may or not involve danger? Is that it?"

I was relieved at how succinct it sounded. "Yes! That's it." I smiled.

He frowned. "You two aren't running off to get married, are you?"

I exclaimed, "No. Of course not."

"You better not be. Not in those clothes. And not without me to design your wedding dress."

I rolled my eyes. "Nobody is getting married."

"Right." A pensive look, "This possible danger that you mentioned, would it have anything to do with the fact that you can set parts of your body on fire and not get burnt?"

I winced, "Yeah, kind of. I just can't get into too much detail about it because the fewer people who know about it, the fewer people will get hurt. If that makes any sense."

"Okay. You go to Tonga with Daniel. And be careful, alright? I kind of like having you around."

"I'll be careful." A grin, "And yes, I know you would miss me desperately if I didn't come back."

I was halfway out the door when Simone called out to me, "Oh, Leila, just one thing more."

I turned back and met a super sober and concerned expression, "If something bad does happen and you don't make it back?" A deep breath, "Can I please have your Louboutin shoes?"

Simone's farewell kept me smiling all the way to the airport with Daniel. Until I saw a familiar face standing in the check-in line.

"Jason, what are you doing here?" I demanded.

He gave us a tight smile, "I'm going with you to Tonga. If what you say is true, then Lesina will be there with Sarona, and I need to talk to her."

"This is not a good idea. This trip could be very dangerous for all of us. And what makes you think that Lesina will talk to you?"

Daniel nudged me warningly and gave me *be quiet* eyes from behind Jason's back. It wouldn't have mattered anyway because nothing was going to sway Jason from this trip. "I'm going to Tonga – with or without you Leila, so deal with it."

The hour and a half flight to Nukualofa gave me time to 'deal with it.' It also gave Daniel time to give me a whispered lecture about crossing the boundaries of friendship. "He's having a hard enough time dealing with this as it is.He doesn't need you getting on his case. Let him be."

"But this is stupid. It's obvious that Lesina has been using him all along. To get to me, to spy on him – whatever. She used him and betrayed him and he still wants to chase after her so they can talk?"

"Haven't you ever done something stupid for love?" He was teasing, but his eyes were deadly serious and that shut me up immediately. I didn't say it, but in my heart I cried. Because I was pretty sure that Lesina had used a love potion on Jason – which meant that whatever he was feeling, it couldn't possibly be real love. Could it?

Once we were off the plane and through Customs in Nukualofa, the reality of what we were here for started to sink in. The town was beautiful – a smaller, slower-paced version of Apia but exuberant with color and an abundance of friendliness from the locals. "So where to now?" asked Jason as we stood and watched traffic go by. Slowly.

"I don't know. Sarona said she would call me with instructions. I guess we just have to wait."

We found a little café to sit in out of the sun but we didn't have to wait for long. All of us were startled when the phone rang. "Hello?"

"Welcome to the friendly islands of Tonga. I hear you brought not one but TWO boyfriends with you. How lovely." Her next words confirmed all my fears about Jason's fiancé and the woman who had befriended Simone, making herself an integral part of our lives over the last few months. "I'm sure that Lesina will be happy to see her fiancé's love for her is so powerful that it has brought him all the way here."

I didn't want to hear any more about Lesina. Because her name was second on my incinerate list. "Is Teuila alright?"

"That depends. Did you bring the Bone?"

"Yes. What do you want me to do now?"

"You'll need to charter a sea plane. Tonga has one hundred and seventy islands and I want you to go to one called Tofua. There is a large crater lake in the center where the seaplane will land. Go there and wait for my phone call." She laughed coldly, "I hope you're prepared to rough it. Tofua is uninhabited."

I ended the call, and the other two looked at me expectantly. "So what are we supposed to do?"

"Charter a seaplane and fly to an uninhabited island called Tofua." Quickly I googled our destination, trying to get as many clues as possible for what could be in store for us.

"What does Google – the source of all wisdom – say about Tofua?" asked Daniel.

"It's small – only fifty-six square kilometers – and it's one of Tonga's live volcanoes."

All three of us thought of the same thing at once. Jason voiced it first, "But that doesn't make sense. That makes it an ideal location for Leila, her powers will be amplified with the proximity of a volcano. Sarona knows that. Why would she want you anywhere near an active volcano?"

I kept reading the geographical description. "She also knows that I'm useless in water. There's a four kilometer wide caldera right next to the volcano, occupied by a freshwater crater lake that's about 250 meters deep. Salamasina warned us that Sarona could have vasa loloa on her side. Maybe she's planning to drown me."

It wasn't a convincing joke and neither of them thought it was funny. For a few minutes no one spoke, and then Daniel took charge. "Come on. We'll need to get a few supplies before we fly out. It's past midday already so I'm guessing that we'll be spending at least one night on this island."

We got directions to a place we could charter a plane and then bought a few essentials before going to the dock where our ride waited. It was tiny. Barely enough room for the three of us and the pilot. I felt sick just looking at it bobbing there on the ocean. We sat in single row seats and I gripped Daniel's shoulder tightly as the plane took off with a stomach-dropping leap. *Please don't let us crash. Please don't let us crash.* Flying was never a pleasant experience for me, and squished into an airborne sardine can was even worse. Xavier the pilot was French and regaled us with stories of his twenty years spent living in Tonga 'the most beautiful islands in the world' and pointed out sights of interest. I didn't look at any of them because I had my eyes tightly shut the whole trip. Not until he said, "There she is – Tofua." Then I opened my eyes and looked down.

The island was tiny – a flat-topped volcanic center with a steep and rocky shoreline all the way around. Xavier yelled over the engines to point out a cluster of desolate structures. "That's Hokula, an abandoned settlement where people used to live before they moved to the adjacent Kotu Island. A lot of Tofua's slopes are planted with kava, and villagers from Kotu will come to tend the plantations and harvest the kava."

We came into view of a stunning expanse of blue-black in the center of the island. Beside it, billows of smoke and steam issued from a volcanic cone. "I'm taking it down now. Hang on everyone."

I shut my eyes again while Xavier landed the plane on the lake and I kept them shut until we had come to a complete stop. The only motion was a gentle rocking of the craft on water. Daniel's voice was encouraging, "Hey, we're here. Come on, I'll help you out."

Feeling a little queasy, I allowed him to half lift me from my seat. Hands on my waist, he swung me out of the seaplane and settled me on dry land. Immovable, solid, familiar, beloved land. I resisted the urge to drop to my knees and kiss it in celebratory gratitude that we were still alive. I had learned something new today. Me and seaplanes don't go together.

Xavier was still talking a mile a minute about the view, "Isn't it amazing here? Nothing else like it on earth."

I looked around and had to agree that it was breathtaking. In a very rugged, desolate, and wild sort of way. The lake stretched forever and the looming volcanic peak stared down at us with foreboding. To our right was a cliff drop to the booming ocean below. There was nothing else here but sky, earth, and air. No people, no town, no houses, cars … nothing. His charter concluded, Xavier asked, "So when do you want me to come back and get you?"

For one ridiculous moment I wanted to beg him to take me back right now. *Don't leave us here!* But then I gave myself a mental shake. Don't be ridiculous, Leila. Teuila needed my help. And Sarona – whatever she was up to – needed to be stopped. And Lesina? She needed to get the stuffing flamed out of her. With those motivating thoughts, I was able to smile when Daniel asked the pilot to "come back in two days or sooner if we call you." We stood and watched as Xavier took his plane to the sky again, leaving us truly alone on Tofua island.

Or maybe not truly alone – because somewhere out there, Sarona was waiting for us.

We took a vote about what we should do next. I wanted to sit right there next to our bags, put up a fire wall of protection around us and wait for Sarona to show up. Daniel and Jason wanted to scope out the island, 'evaluate the terrain' and 'establish Sarona's location.' Much to my disgust, I was outvoted. And what exacerbated my disgust was the fact that both of them had regressed to thinking they were special ops soldiers in a wilderness scenario. Or at least that's what their conversation sounded like to me.

"We need to assess the terrain, identify the ideal location for an encounter with Sarona and her troops," was Jason's bright idea.

Daniel's wasn't much better. "I agree, but first we should check out if Sarona's here and see if we can find any weaknesses in her location."Somebody didn't play enough army games when they were little. I sat down on my backpack and wished they would just get on with it. Mosquitoes were having a party checking out the new blood on the island, and standing around being a blood cocktail was really beginning to annoy me. And then all special ops conversations were suspended. Because Sarona and her telesā arrived.

I saw them first and scrambled to my feet. Two women I did not know emerged from the trees about fifty meters away. Even from this distance I could see they were twins. Thick, wiry black hair that fell past their shoulders, dark eyes, and unsmiling red lips. Both wore fitted blue shift dresses that clearly showed the tattoo patterns on their arms and legs. I knew they were telesā. I could sense it. But what kind? Each of them walked along the edges of the caldera, keeping their distance until they stood at parallel ends of the cliff. Waiting. Watching. Both Jason and Daniel moved to stand in front of me, and I resisted the urge to shove them out of the way. If anyone needed shielding, it would be the two of them. But it was very thoughtful of them and I really shouldn't be complaining. I peered around Daniel's shoulder in time to see Sarona walk out from the shaded forest. And walking beside her was Teuila. Alive and well. And smiling?

She saw me at the same time and her face lit up with – surprise? "Leila! What are you doing here?"

She ran lightly towards me and I tensed, waiting for the trick, the attack, for Sarona to do something awful. But nothing happened. I pushed past Daniel and Jason, ignored their warning, and met Teuila halfway across the caldera. A fierce hug. "Are you alright? I've been so worried about you."

She laughed. "Yes, I'm great. Did you get my message? I have so much to tell you, so many good things."

I interrupted her chatter, still keeping a careful eye on Sarona, who hadn't moved from her position by the trees. "Wait a minute. What's going on here. What are you doing with Sarona? Aren't you her prisoner?"

Confusion clouded her eyes, "No. Why would I be her prisoner? Lesina invited me here. Sarona's amazing. Do you know that telesā are real? It's true. And I'm one of them. And so is Lesina. Sarona and her sisters have asked me to join them, and Sarona is going to teach me how to control my Gift with plants and trees. I never have to go back and stay with my mother again."

"Teuila, your mother is very worried about you. She thinks that you've run away, that you might be hurt somewhere. I've come to take you home."

Her smile died and she took a step backwards. "I don't want to go back there. My mother wants me to live with that man again. I won't do it. Sarona has offered me a better life and I'm taking it. My home is with her and the telesā."

Now Sarona acted. She laughed with confident ease, standing there in her trademark vivid green. She called out to me, "She speaks truth, Leila. In her old life, she was a victim without a voice, without a choice. With me, she will be strong and ferocious in her power and beauty. She will speak with the voice of the trees. Why would she choose her old life over that kind of power?"

Eyes narrowed, I tensed and quietly called for fire to be ready and waiting. Something was not right here. I felt Jason and Daniel come up behind me, strength and support. I called out to Sarona, "Why did you tell me she had been forced here? Why did you bring us here?"

Her reply was mocking, "For a joyous reunion. We are family, are we not? And the family that plays together, stays together." Three more people joined Sarona now from the forest and stood in a row beside her. A dark, lean form – Keahi. Even from this distance, my fire core leapt to see him. I wondered, could he feel it too? There was another telesā I did not know – striking in vivid red with a single streak of white through her black hair. And then Lesina. Hesitant – she refused to meet our gaze. Seeing her was like a dagger thrust targeted at Jason. I felt him recoil beside me. And I ached on his behalf for the pain he surely must be feeling. With her team arrayed beside her, Sarona continued, "Did you bring the Bone?"

"Yes. But it was meant as a trade for Teuila's freedom." I turned to the young girl in front of me, whispered, "Teuila, you don't know Sarona like I do. She's evil, I can't think of any other word to describe her. Her sisterhood is not the place for you. Come back with me to Samoa and I can train you to use your Gift. I can help you."

"Can you kill my mother's boyfriend for me?" She demanded. "Can you make sure my mother never works as a prostitute again and never brings home men who hurt me? Can you do all those things?" She paused, and her eyes flashed as she backed away from me, "No, I don't think you can. I choose Sarona. I choose freedom." She walked away and stood with the other telesā arraigned against us.

Sarona called out. "I'm sorry that particular reunion didn't work out like you wanted."

I ignored her and directed my venom at another. "Keahi, this isn't right, bringing a child like Teuila into this. She had friends who cared about her back at the Center." He remained impassive, and I tried another line of appeal, "Sarona can't help you with your fire."

He smiled that hateful leering grin. "That's where you're wrong." He slid his arms around Sarona's waist and kissed her on the mouth. For a blurred moment, their bodies were joined as one and then a flash of lightning lit up the clear sky above us. Sarona stepped out of the embrace and lightning channeled through Keahi, lighting him up like a match. Sparks, cinders, flames. Keahi was alight. Exultant and triumphant. My heart sank. I could feel his power through my own links to fanua afi and his control had grown a little. Which meant his capability for destruction had intensified. A lot. The odds were slowly shifting in this battle and I didn't like it. Yes, Daniel was vasa loloa but he was new to his Gift and had little or no experience with controlling it. I could not count on his ocean power today. It was too soon for him.

Sarona was impatient. "Enough of this. Give me the Bone."

Daniel moved to stand by my side and took my hand in his. A smile, a reminder. *As long as we are together, we can endure anything.* Jason stood at our flank, numb and silent. Daniel asked, "What will happen if we give it to you?"

Sarona's reply was swift, "Then I won't kill your girlfriend slowly. I'll take her out quick and clean." She shouted, "Now!"

Everything that happened next seemed to move in slow motion. With my core link to fanua afi, I felt Keahi combust a flame cannon, even before I saw it. But it was too fast for me to block, or avoid. A raging ball of fire burst from his hands and hit me full force in the chest. One instant I had air and the next I was gasping as it was forced from me. Fire was everywhere. Instinctively, my body flamed but too late, I was knocked off my feet and thrown twenty meters back. Over the edge of the cliff. I was flying. Then I was falling. And then, I was drowning. Black water pulled me, churned me, tossed me. *Swim to the light, Leila.* I broke free from the ocean's clutches and drew in huge, gasping breaths. My first and only thoughts were for Daniel. *Where is he? What are they doing to him?*

F O U R T E E N

Neither Daniel nor Jason could react fast enough as Keahi's maelstrom of fire barreled into Leila and took her over the edge of the cliff.

"No!" Daniel shouted. He spun round to run after Leila, to dive into the wild surf below, but too late, Sarona had him encircled by a whip wire of lightning. He froze in place, with the crackling energy only a hairsbreadth from his flesh.

"Not so fast. I've got plans for your girlfriend that don't include you." A flick of her wrist and Jason was blasted backwards with a direct lightning bolt hit. "You too, surfer boy. You're not going anywhere." She did not see Lesina flinch as Jason skidded along the graveled ground and came to a jarring halt against a cluster of rocks.

A stunned Teuila shouted, "What are you doing? Stop it."

"Silence girl." Sarona snapped, before issuing a command for the twin sisters who stood sentry on the cliffside. "Summon it now. Before she can recover and reach land. Hurry."

The two women in blue moved to clasp hands. A deep breath, eyes closed, wind whipping through their hair. Their tattoos glowed with an iridescent cobalt hue as they sang in unison. "What are they doing Elena?" a fearful Teuila asked the telesā dressed in red.

"They are reciting the chant of the octopus, Ko e lave Kia Feke."

The song intensified, and there was a dreadful hush of anticipation. Still nothing. Sarona was furious with the delay. "Dammit, where is it? You assured me that you could summon it. Look, the girl is swimming to the rocks now. You must be quick before she reaches land."

Daniel's heart leapt at her words. Leila was alive. She was swimming to safety. And once she touched land, she would be unstoppable. None of them would be able to hurt her. There was still hope.

Across the caldera, Jason stirred and slowly lifted his head. Noting his movement, Sarona barked out a command to Lesina. "Watch that one. Better yet, go restrain him."

Lesina walked to where Jason lay, a whispered command, and a coil of lightning was in her hands. But she paused and into that moment, Jason spoke, "You're telesā matagi."

Casting a glance at Sarona who was caught up with studying the ocean, Lesina nodded and knelt beside him. A curt command. "You better sit up. It will be less painful for you if you are upright when I put these chains on you."

There was blood trickling from a gash on his forehead, and he winced as he sat up. But he did not try to struggle as she carefully wound the livid wire around his body. Every time it brushed against his skin, it stung with volts of electrical energy and each time he flinched, her hands shook even more. She whispered, "Why did you come here? I meant what I said in my note. Everything between us was a lie."

There was only certainty in Jason's voice, "Maybe for you. But not for me. My love for you is the truest thing I've ever known."

He cried out in pain as Lesina tugged at the wire viciously, and the smell of singed flesh filled the air, "Stop saying that. I drugged you with a telesā elixir designed to induce feelings of euphoric happiness, and a state of obsession mimicking those emotions aroused when one believes they are in love. That's all love really is. A chemical reaction. All I did was give you the right mix of chemicals every day."

Jason gritted his teeth as live electricity cut deeper with her every word. "When did you stop giving me the elixir then?"

"A week ago."

"So how do you explain my feelings of euphoria and excitement when I saw you walk out of that forest? How do you explain why, when you're torturing me right now, all I want to do is kiss you and bring back that smile I love so much?"

Lesina sunk her face into her hands, released the lightning wire, sobbed. "Stop it. Please stop it. I can't do this. I am telesā, covenanted to Sarona."

Jason raised a gentle hand to her cheek, tenderly capturing a runaway tear. "This is not who you are Lesina. The woman I first met on a busy day in her office who laughed at my lame jokes and offered to give me directions to the National Park? That's who you are. The woman I fell in love with and then, after only two weeks, knew I wanted to spend the rest of my life with? I don't know who was crazier – the person who proposed or the person who said yes." A Jason trademark grin. "That's who you are. The woman who has defined joy for me."

And then Lesina's tears were flowing freely. "No, I'm not that woman. I'm sorry I betrayed you and Leila. All of you. I'm sorry I hurt you. I don't love you like that. I'm not that woman, Jason."

"But you could be. And I would wait for as long as it took." He placed a lingering, delicate kiss on her lips. For one fragile moment, Lesina and Jason held perfection in their hands. And then it was gone.

An outraged exclamation, "What are you doing?" Someone dragged them apart, throwing Lesina on the ground. It was Elena, her lip curled in derision. "You would choose this man over your Covenant? Turn against your Covenant Keeper, and for what?" She spat on the ground in disgust. "I knew you were not worthy for this cause. The only reason Sarona chose you is because you are the daughter of her sister Fotu and she thought you would want vengeance against the girl who killed your mother. Yet, here you are believing this man's lies. Your Gift is weak and you are weak." Elena beckoned and a rush of air answered her call, wrapping itself like a vice around Lesina's throat. Tighter and tighter.

"Leave her alone." Jason scrabbled for the first weapon he could find. A rock. He threw it with determined accuracy and the missile glanced against Elena's shoulder. She fell back and the air coils around Lesina's neck loosened. She coughed and gasped for air. Jason went to her and helped her to stand. "Are you alright?"

And then Sarona was there. "What's happening here? I told you to restrain him." Her eyes quickly assessed the situation. Irritation. "Must I do everything myself?"Lesina scrambled to intervene. "Wait. I'll take care of it, make sure he doesn't get in the way again. Leave him to me."

It was too late. "He's going to be more trouble than he's worth. He's served his purpose." She pointed an unwavering hand at Jason and hit him with a single concentrated burst of lightning, directly in the chest. Through the heart. It sounded almost like a gunshot. His eyes widened slightly, as if surprised, and then he dropped to his knees, swayed, and fell.

Sarona did not wait to see the consequences of her attack. She stalked away to study the ocean. Lesina stumbled to kneel beside the man who loved her. Who had believed she could be more, love more, give more. Jason stared with sightless eyes at an unfeeling sky. There was a coin-sized hole through his chest. He was dead.

At the cliffside, Keahi stood beside Sarona and the chanting sisters. Sarona beckoned to Daniel and her lightning ropes tightened, cut, and dragged him along the ground until he lay at her feet. "Come see as your beloved is consumed by the greatest terror of the ocean."

Daniel ignored the pain, his gaze transfixed on Leila as she swam with sure strokes towards an outcropping of rocks. It seemed as if she would make it to safety and then the water bubbled and boiled around her. Sarona exulted, "There it is." A giant snakelike tentacle emerged, gleaming orange-red as it lashed the water.

Daniel shouted a warning, "Look out behind you!"

Leila paused, looked back – just in time to see a monstrous writhing bundle of tentacles as a creature reared up out of the sea depths. It towered above her. Its gigantic eyes were two beacons of whiteness against the bulbous head, and its orange skin glowed with cobalt blue markings. The patterns of a vasa loloa tattoo. Daniel could make out the full bulk of the behemoth splayed along the surface of the water – over forty feet long. But all Leila could see was the gaping, yawning chasm of its beaked jaws as they opened and shut with terrifying precision. For a moment, she was frozen in place and then she switched to a frenzied backstroke, unwilling to take her eyes off the creature that threatened her but fighting to reach safety.

Daniel asked in horror, "What is that thing?"

Sarona took pleasure in answering. "It's a colossal squid. The largest known invertebrate on earth. No one's ever seen one this big before. It is the feke tenifa of Tongan legend. See its body markings? They mark it as a creature of the telesā vasa loloa."

Teuila ran up and grabbed onto Sarona's arm, "You never said anything about hurting my friends. Please stop this."

Sarona smiled, not unkindly. "My dear child, let this be your first telesā lesson. All those who do not stand with us? Stand against us and must be eliminated, by whatever means necessary." She clapped her hands with glee and gave the kill command to the sisters, "Hine and Hiva, end this now."

The sisters intensified their chanting and below them, the squid – mythical beast incarnate – responded to their direction. One tentacle dipped into the water, curled around Leila's waist and lifted her in one swift movement, up out of the water. Her scream was agonizing. The limbs of a colossal squid are lined with teeth and razor sharp hooks, some swiveling and others three-pointed – teeth that cut into Leila's flesh with crippling force. She kicked and struggled to get free but the pressure only increased and again came that gut-wrenching scream.

Sarona's delight was palpable. "Finally, after months of planning, vengeance is mine." She addressed the sky, the forest, the earth, "Do you know how long I have waited for this moment? All the effort that went into getting you fanua afi here at the mercy of the vasa loloa Feke? Oh, it's so rewarding to see a mastermind of a plan succeed."

Yes, Sarona had invested a great deal of thought and effort into this moment. But there was one thing she had not taken into account. One key factor she had not anticipated. Because Sarona did not know that Daniel was vasa loloa.

Daniel's fury was a torrent within him as the squid savaged the one he loved. Leila was slumped over now, a limp rag doll in the clutches of the feke tenifa as it writhed and twisted, shaking her back and forth like a kitten in the jaws of a mad dog. Blind now to pain, Daniel tore free from the lightning coils, ran and dived off the cliff into the water below. A surprised Sarona raised an eyebrow, "And so he sacrifices himself for the one he loves. How sweet. No matter. Now we will have the feke tenifa kill both of them."

Keahi threw her a sharp glance, "You said we needed to get the Bone from her, that we needed to gather the three pieces of the Covenant Bone so we could unite the different telesā gifts. You never said anything about killing her." Uncertainty dimmed his flames and they spluttered and died.

Sarona scoffed at his wavering. "Oh please, we want the same things. Unlimited power. Do you think that you're going to get it if you have to share fanua afi with her? She already made it clear that she's not interested in being partners with you." Her lip curled with disdain at his scarred body. "Why don't you go and find some clothes to cover that up?"

Keahi turned away.

Far below them, Daniel surfaced and began swimming towards the colossal monster that held Leila captive. He had no grand plan or strategy in place, just a crushing need to help Leila, to save her. Or die trying. As he swam, the ocean heeded his desperation. His tattoos began to flame with that indigo fire. White surf churned all about him and then the water raised him up on a swirling torrent. He now towered above the colossal squid and panic warred with fear. The fear of losing Leila. Remembering that day with her in the mountain pool, he focused his breathing, and tried to visualize what he wanted the ocean to do. It responded. Thick ropes of water snaked their way around the two lead tentacles, attempted to restrain them. It wasn't a good idea. The squid thrashed angrily, emitting a high-pitched screech that had everyone covering their ears. The violent movement only increased Leila's suffering as she was buffeted about. It seemed Daniel would have to try harder than that.

Again he beckoned, and this time a swell of water came rushing towards the squid, carrying with it rock from the cliff shoreline that slammed into the creature's body, rolling it to one side and dislodging its hold on Leila. She fell to the water below. Daniel hoped she was conscious but he didn't have time to worry about her because the squid had finally figured out who was causing all the trouble. One of its many arms whipped behind Daniel and sent him flying through the air. He hit the water hard and it felt like he landed on cement paving. *Please don't let that cracking sound be my ribs...*He ached all over. And then he felt a suffocating clenching around his chest as the squid grabbed him. The tentacle felt like thick rubber tubing, only it was a tire that stabbed into his flesh with eager claws and then twisted.

It was Daniel's turn to scream.

Sarona and her team stared in shock as the battle raged between man and ocean beast. "He is vasa loloa? How can this be?" The twins were drenched in sweat, trying to maintain their control over the feke tenifa as its mind became a red-soaked frenzy of blood lust. For a moment, it seemed the feke tenifa would succeed as its whipping tentacle carried Daniel down towards the gaping chasm of its open mouth.

But then Teuila made her choice.

"Stop it!" she cried as she barreled into Hiva, dislodging her connection with her sister. She grabbed the older woman's hand and in a neat four-step combination that would have made Dayna proud, cuff – sweep – throw, and pin, she had Hiva flat on her back on the ground.

"You little fool," hissed Sarona. She blasted Teuila away from the fallen vasa loloa with a sudden rush of wind. "Quickly," she ordered Hine, "repair your mind link with your sister."

But it was too late. The momentary break in the connection caused the feke tenifa to pause, loosen its grip on Daniel. He took advantage of the lapse to squirm free, and dropped to the water below. Again a liquid platform raised him up. He searched for Leila, saw her stumbling, collapsing onto the rocky shore, battered and bruised. Alive. He generated a broiling whirlpool that began to spin with deadly concentration around the feke tenifa, confusing it, holding it in place.

Sarona saw that Leila had reached the shoreline, that Daniel was overcoming the feke tenifa, "No. You see what you've done?" she snarled at Teuila. She ripped an invisible choke rope from the air around them and wrapped it around Teuila's throat. Pulled tight. Teuila's face began to turn blue, her hands tried vainly to loosen the crushing grip around her neck. "You think because you have an unusual Gift that I won't kill you? How dare you defy me?"

Who knows what would have happened if Keahi had not stepped in. "Stop it, Sarona. This has gone way too far. She's just a kid. Leave her alone."

Sarona felt her alliance disintegrating. And she didn't like it. "Who asked you? I'm beginning to think it was a mistake to forsake the rules about male telesā." A thought, an instant of anger, and a wild gust of wind slammed into Keahi and shoved him over the edge of the cliff. "Oops. Did I do that?"

Keahi fell with an awkward splash and was immediately sucked into the vortex of water that Daniel had constructed about the feke tenifa. Choking, drowning, Keahi was spun about like a doll in a washer and then grabbed by one of the squid tentacles.

Daniel tried to communicate with the squid, as a creature of vasa loloa. He focused his thoughts, reached out – but all his mind encountered was a raging torrent of raw power. If Daniel hadn't been so new to his Gift, so inexperienced, perhaps he could have asserted some kind of mind control over the creature. But no, he would need a weapon to end this battle. He summoned a ferocious current that ripped with it coral shards from the ocean floor, rock chunks, and sand, combining them into lances of jagged power. With a sweep of his arms, a multitude of them rose up out of the swirling ocean. Daniel hurled them at the feke tenifa with all his strength, stabbing it in a shower of deadly blades. The squid screeched and writhed in an agony that slowly came to a shuddering stillness. The ocean calmed its churning fury as Daniel breathed a sigh of relief. Only then did he see Keahi, still caught in the squid's coils, still struggling to break free as the creature slowly began to slip beneath the waves.

Dammit. Daniel hesitated and then dived into the water. He swam to where Keahi was trapped, helped to free him, and then towed him back to shore, throwing him down onto the sand. Bloody and bruised from his battle with the feke tenifa, Daniel was exhausted, but his only thought was for Leila. She sat further up the shore, huddled in a wet heap. He knelt beside her, "Are you alright?"

She was trembling, her teeth chattering – from fear or shock, he didn't know. She didn't answer, only grabbed him in a desperate embrace. He soothed her, "It's over. It's alright. You're okay."

He released her and only then did he see the blood, the mangled flesh through ragged remnants of her shirt. She noted his horrified gaze, reassured him, "It's worse than it looks, honestly. Nothing that some of Salamasina's magic ointments can't fix." A wince as he helped her to her feet. "But I never want a squid to hug me again."

Daniel looked at the damage wrought by the feke tenifa and his whole frame tensed with rage. Abruptly, he turned away from Leila and walked across the sand to where Keahi still sat, trying to catch his breath. He looked up at Daniel's approach with a grateful smile, "You saved my life, thanks."

Daniel drew back his fist and slammed it into Keahi's face, knocking him to the ground, then knelt over him, pummeling his face, driven by a frenzy of emotion so consuming that he couldn't hear Leila's shouts, "That's enough, Daniel! Stop it." Not until she pulled him away did his rage begin to ease.

He stood over a dazed, bleeding Keahi, "I should have left you to die."

Daniel turned his back on the shore where the bulk of a dead feke tenifa bore witness to the power of vasa loloa and went to help Leila up the steep incline to the caldera above.

There was nothing but pain waiting for them at the top of the cliff. Sarona, Elena, and the vasa loloa sisters were gone. There was no sign of Teuila either. And across the caldera, Lesina sat beside a fallen figure in the shade of the trees.

Leila came to an abrupt halt at the sight. Fear and panic at war with hope. "What happened? Is he alright? Where's Teuila?"

Lesina's tear-stained face was answer enough as she shook her head in dissent. "Sarona took her. She fought against them, but it was no use."

Leila's breath caught in her chest. "No." She let go of Daniel's arm that supported her and limped to where Jason lay on the ground, his head cradled in Lesina's lap. She sank to her knees, disbelieving what confronted her. She felt for a pulse, listened for a heartbeat, for something, anything. Some sign that Jason wasn't gone. He couldn't be gone. "No. This can't be right. We have to get him to a hospital. They can save him. Fix him. What about CPR? Did you try that?"

Lesina stared at her, bleakly nodded. "Sarona's lightning bolt went right through his heart. There's nothing I could do."

Leila stifled a sob, "This is your fault. You killed him. He loved you and you killed him."

Lesina's eyes were dead and her words were low, "He was never meant to get hurt. I was only supposed to make him fall in love with me, trust me so I could get close to you and your friends."

Leila backed away, incredulous – her own guilt compounding her emotions. *You broke me, Leila. I loved you and it broke me. And then I met Lesina and it was like she put all the pieces back together again.* "He was never meant to get hurt?! Love hurts. But you wouldn't know anything about that, would you? You're a cold, heartless telesā *bitch!* I'm going to make you pay for this."

Her hands burst into ready flame but Daniel was quicker. He wrapped his arms around her, held her, cautioned her and soothed her with his calming strength. "No. That won't bring him back. Jason wouldn't want you to do this." She stood unbending in his arms. "There are more important things now. Sarona has taken Teuila. We need to get her back." He looked down at where Lesina wept over Jason's body. "She made a mistake. Can't you see that she's hurting too?"

And then Leila broke. Wilted. Cried. "I loved him, Daniel. He was my friend and I loved him."

For a while he held her as grief racked her and then with a sigh, he raised her face to his. "There will be time for mourning later. Teuila needs us now. And we need to stop Sarona, once and for all because I am not going to live the rest of my life looking over my shoulder, waiting for her to strike at us." A thought occurred to him and he turned to Lesina, "Why did they let you stay behind?"

"I refused to go. I'm bound to Sarona by Covenant and she knows I can't attack her. Neither can she hurt me without breaking our oath. She needs the added strength that my Gift gives her so she didn't fight me on my choice." A ghost of a smile, "She promised to eliminate me once she's finished with the two of you though, so I'm sure I'll see her later."

Daniel's face darkened, "You need to tell us where they've gone."

Lesina shook her head, "It's a trap. All of it. An elaborate trap with many layers and all of it with one purpose only." She nodded at Leila. "To kill you."

Leila frowned, "That's nothing new."

"The feke tenifa was only part of it. She has a back-up in her arsenal of tricks. Have you heard about the RTG plutonium battery they recovered from the Tongan Trench? She was working with the search team, giving them location co-ordinates that she got from the vasa loloa twins. And then once the team brought it to the surface, she had us steal the battery from the Americans." Lesina pointed to the volcano that towered to their left. "She's got the RTG up there."

Daniel asked the obvious question, "Why though? What does it have to do with Leila?"

Lesina bit her lip, hesitated, "She said to me once that the only way to destroy fire – is with fire."

Her words gave a chill to the air as all three of them conjured images of sky-bursting explosions and mushroom clouds. Leila rushed to dispel them, "I watched the television report on this. The lead science guy said that the plutonium in an RTG is not the kind they use for nuclear weapons."

Daniel argued, "Yeah, well I saw the same report and they also said that the radioactivity is deadly and the plutonium could be used to boost the destruction of a conventional explosive." *Or a volcano* ... were his unspoken words. He took Leila's hands in his, "Maybe Lesina is right. Whatever is up there is targeting you. You should stay here with her and I'll go up and get Teuila."

Leila's response was outraged. She pulled away from him, "No way. You've always said that we can handle anything as long as we are together. We're both going up to that volcano."

Daniel knew it was useless to argue with her. "Fine. But first I'm calling for the charter plane. It'll take a while for Xavier to get here and we need to be able to take Jason home."

Leila knelt beside the body of her friend for a moment, kissed his forehead, whispered, "I'll be back for you."

Over by their gear, Daniel was rifling for first aid supplies. He called out, "Come here, Leila. We need to bandage those injuries before we head out. You might get blood poisoning."

"You mean if Sarona doesn't blow me up with plutonium first?" Her sarcasm was met with a frown. "We don't have time for first aid right now, Daniel. Sarona already has a lead on us and I'm worried about Teuila."

"This will be quick." Daniel argued as he quickly washed the worst of the sand and blood from Leila's midriff and then bandaged the gored flesh. He studied his handiwork, "This should do for now until we can get you to a doctor."

Leila was impatient. "Can we go now?"

"Alright." He paused, "But first, promise me that you won't do anything crazy. Like rush in ahead and take the telesā on by yourself. Remember, we're in this together." Leila tried to look convincing as she agreed with him and they set out through the bush towards the volcano peak.

FIFTEEN

It was a rugged trail to the volcano and the sweltering heat and insistent mosquitoes made it even more difficult. My ocean-soaked clothes dried quickly, sticking to my skin, salty and uncomfortable. The wounds from the feke tenifa ached with a throbbing pain that only got worse the farther we walked. I tried not to let Daniel see how much they hurt though, because for sure he would then try to make me turn back. And I was not going back. Not now. Not with Jason dead and Sarona still out there.

It was a relief to break free of the bush and walk out onto the bare terrain of the volcano base. We were advancing to the highest point of the island and had an unobstructed view of our surroundings. To the right was a cavernous drop where a pool of dark water, heated by the volcanic activity, steamed and bubbled. Ahead of us, grey smoke billowed from the cone and I could taste the sulfur in the air. It was a barren, acrid spot but my core did a little hop and skip as it always did when it was near fanua afi's pulse points. Even the ache from my cuts seemed to fade a little as my body welcomed the hint of fire power. Daniel put a warning hand on mine. "Slow down, they could be waiting for us anywhere around here."

I was grateful for his touch. I still could not believe the power he had demonstrated as he fought the feke tenifa. Seeing him ablaze with cobalt energy, wielding the ocean with deadly ease had been an awe-inspiring sight. I glanced at the blood stains on his ripped shirt that hid bruising and markings similar to mine. The squid had hurt him as well, but his only thought had been for me and my injuries.

We walked hand in hand a few steps and then both saw her at the same time. Teuila.

A short distance up the cone edge was an awkward-shaped object – a steel base that supported, at its center, a raised circular platform. Jutting from it was a tall black cylinder with panels and wiring attached to it. And tied to the cylinder with crackling, seething ropes of electricity – was Teuila. I had never seen her look more like a very frightened, very powerless thirteen-year-old.

I started to run towards her, but Daniel held me back. "Wait. Look."

Carried on wings of air, Sarona and Elena surged up from behind the cone tip, hair blowing wildly in the wind, eyes bleeding white with energy, sparks at their fingertips. I was transfixed, even as they aimed at us. Daniel acted, whereas I just stood staring in a daze. He tackled me to the ground as a line of lightning razed past. I had all the air knocked out of me. And a sizeable chunk of muscle crushing me. I gasped for air while Daniel rolled us away from the lightning attacks and into the undergrowth. The sizzling, burning noise was deafening but over it I heard him say in my ear, "I think now would be a good time to flame, don't you?"

Flames. Yes, that's right. That was me. I shoved him off and summoned flames, welcoming their familiar burn. Flesh became molten lava, rich red and vibrant, veined with gold rivulets. With fire came a renewed sense of purpose. I stood and walked into the barrage of lightning strikes, accepting their gift of energy, adding it to my own. There was the rushing sound of water and from the right where the hot pool bubbled, came a coil of boiling liquid, snaking its way towards us. The vasa loloa twins. Daniel called out to me, "You go to Teuila. I got this."

I hesitated, unsure. Unwilling to leave him to face the two telesā alone. But he gave me that crooked smile and a light taunt, "I'll be fine. I'm a water god, remember?" And then the sculpted planes of his body were lighting up with their call to the water that powered him and I was reminded, yes, he was vasa loloa, son of the ocean.

I advanced towards Teuila and what had to be the RTG. A particularly feisty splurge of lightning tingled down my spine and I decided it was time to go on the offensive. I took careful aim and threw a mass of fire at the nearest airborne telesā. Elena. She dodged it clumsily and it clipped her on the shoulder, unbalancing her control of the wind that carried her. As she struggled to stay airborne, I hit her with another cannonball of flame. This time it blasted her right out of sight. I hoped it hurt. A lot.

It was time to face Sarona. She hung back at a distance while I moved with slow purpose towards Teuila. I kept a careful eye on the weather witch as I knelt to sever the electrical wires that bound Teuila to the RTG. Her face was drawn and pale. She whispered to me, "I'm sorry, Leila. I didn't know she was going to do those things to you."

I soothed her, "It's alright. I'm alright." I stilled my flames and helped her to stand. The lightning ropes had burned deep welts into her legs. "Can you walk?"

Sarona interrupted us, "Here, let me help her." A mighty gust of wind hit Teuila square in the chest, lifted her off her feet and blasted her fifty meters away. She crashed into kava plants and bushes with brutal impact and was still.

And then Sarona descended from her aerial perch and came to rest directly opposite me, with only the RTG separating us. "Finally, we are alone. It's time for me to put an end to this."

I gave her a bemused nod, summoning red heat to me again. "I'm fanua afi, a fire goddess. There's no way you can defeat me."

She gave me a knowing smile, "I'm not trying to. All this? The feke tenifa, even the matagi assault, these were mere diversions."

I didn't understand her. She knew it, and it gave her pleasure.

Sarona reached out her arms to the heavens and jagged fire rained from angry skies, directed into one crucible of energy – the RTG. The lightning spike seared through the outer casing of the battery and through its protective layers, and the entire unit hissed and sparked as it cracked open. "You see, Leila, I know there's only one thing that can kill a fire goddess. The stupidity of her self-sacrificing nature."

I stared at her in disbelief, "You're going to kill us all."

Sarona was triumphant, "No, I'm going to fly up on the wings of a conqueror and watch from a distance as you burn."

And then a shape came up from behind her. A boy whose body screamed with angry tattoos and the markings of a lifetime of abuse. Keahi.

He hooked one arm around her throat and growled against her ear, "I'm sorry but you're going to have to miss it." There was the glint of steel in the sunlight as he brought up his knife in the other hand and stabbed Sarona in the back.

Time missed a beat. Sarona's eyes widened and lush red lips parted in an *oh* of surprise. Keahi leaned into her back and ground the knife a little deeper. Blood pooled in her mouth, dripping to the ground as her head lolled forward. And then Keahi wrenched back the knife and released her. Sarona slumped to the ground.

A wave of horror brought nausea with it and I fought the urge to gag. "Why did you do that?"

Keahi knelt and used Sarona's black velvet hair to wipe the blade of his knife before answering. "A thank you would be nice right now. I just saved your life."

"No, you did that for you."

The arrogant smile and the Khal Drogo eyebrow were belied by the resolute look in his eyes, "Maybe I did it for both of us."

Before I could find any sense in his words, blue flames sprung up from the cracked battery in front of us. Keahi backed away and asked, "That does not look good. Please tell me you have some sort of fire goddess plan to get us all out of this?"

I looked back to where Daniel was subduing the vasa loloa sisters. He had one struggling in restraints of liquid silver and another captive in a foaming bubble. As if sensing my thoughts, he turned to look at me. I smiled. Through the smoky haze and air still acrid with the metal tang of lightning, he smiled back. He had not noticed the sparking battery.

In that moment, I knew what I had to do. What only I could do. In that moment, I understood Sarona's taunting words. I guess she would be the victor after all.

I nodded at Keahi. "Yes, I do have a plan. It involves us all running as fast as we can to get away from here. Take Teuila and go. Quickly."

Keahi needed no more encouragement. He ran to help Teuila to her feet and together the two of them began making their way down the hillside. Two fewer people who might try to stop me. I turned my head to seek out the one I loved. I needed to see him one last time. Imprint him in my mind to give me the strength to do what needed to be done. *Daniel.* I held on to the whisper of his name, enfolding it like a secret curled away in the innermost recesses of my heart. *I can face anything, as long as we are together.* I knew he would see this as a betrayal. *Daniel, please forgive me.*

With the strength that came with my fire, I lifted the RTG easily, careful to hug the cracked seam tightly against my chest. My heart. *Daniel.* Carrying the bulky mass, I took the few steps towards the rim of the cone precipice. Peering down was a daunting thing.

Whoa, that's deep. It wasn't a straight drop into the heart of the volcano. Rather, the cone sloped at a gradual angle and the rising clouds of noxious smoke obscured the rest. I couldn't tell how far a hike it would be until I hit the actual lava seam. I needed to hurry. I balanced the battery against my chest with one hand and half slid down the loosely graveled incline, righting myself with the other. *See, nothing to it. Just like surfing.* Against my will, memories of Jason popped into my mind. Laughing at me as I fell down. Again. *You should see yourself up there. You get this psycho serious look on your face and then it changes to complete panic just before you fall off. And when you come up out of the water, you're so mad. It's really cute!*

I hurried my pace, focusing on the distant glow of red, dimly visible through the smoke. The RTG was stinging against me, like taking a cheese grater to my skin. I wished I could move it away for a moment.

Wait a minute ... I was in lava form, I shouldn't be feeling stinging. Pain. I shouldn't be feeling anything. *Keep moving. Don't stop. Get this thing out of here.* Shaking off the edge of unease, I sped up. A shout startled me.

"Leila! No. What are you doing?" It was Daniel. He stood at the edge of the cone, calling down to me. "Don't do this."

I didn't want to look at him. I shouldn't have paused to meet his eyes. But I did. And it almost made me falter. Almost. Coughing and choking against the gaseous smoke, he half ran, half slid down the incline towards me. "I won't let you do this. Come back."

I waved my free hand and sent a rippling wall of flame barreling towards him. A thought, a flick of my wrist and it stopped directly in front of him, steady and immovable. Instinctively, he flinched back from the heat, shielding his face with his hands. "No. Please. I love you."

This time I didn't look back. Instead, I took one, two, three more paces and there it was. The gaping chasm of heaven. Or hell. Depending on how one looked at it. The cauldron of bubbling goldenrod and embered orange was mesmerizing. It coughed and churned unceasingly. Ropes of fire, swirls of ruby-encrusted gold.

I called back to the one I loved, unsure if he could hear me. "Don't worry about me. I'm a fire goddess, remember?"

And then I dived. With all the force and power of earth, I powered my body into the heart of the fiery furnace, holding my precious cargo of plutonium in a desperate embrace. The lava welcomed me, as I knew it would. I was a recalcitrant child returning home to her mother at last. Ecstasy. Exquisite in its embrace. Every piece of me delighted in sheer pleasure. The swirling current of fierce red buffeted me, trying to tear the RTG from my hands, but I refused to let go. *No. This is mine.*

Deeper. I knew I had to go deeper. I kicked and swam with one hand, forcing my body down deeper into the depths. The heart. *Pele. I am here. I am home.*

It was a struggle to remain in control. I hadn't anticipated how hard it would be to contain myself. To stay me. To keep my form. One with the volcano, and I was pulled on all sides as my molecules fought to join their sisters. *No. I must keep myself together. I cannot blend. I cannot lose myself. Complete your task.*

I needed to burn and rage and burn some more. Enough to eradicate every emaciating molecule of plutonium contained in the generator. I fought for control. And it was not an easy battle. The call of the earth was strong. A joyous delight to my very soul. I clung to that which had always given me strength. He who had called himself the other half of my soul. *I can be that for you, Leila. I can be the water that calms you. Soothes you. Gives you strength. Daniel.* I held on to the whisper of his name. His love. In the deepest innermost recesses of my soul. *Daniel. Please help me to do this. Don't let me fail.*

In my arms, the RTG blurred and began to melt into a congealing gloop, thick and sticky. Was I deep enough into the volcano? Was it hot enough? How could I be sure? Go further. Go in deeper. Push harder. Still I powered on. Going against the upward current, the raging maelstrom of liquid energy around me was intoxicating in its sheer power. I could no longer tell where I ended and the volcano began. I loved it. This is who I was meant to be. This is who I am.

And then it happened. The mess that was left of the RTG sparked. Glowed. Blue edged with gold. White diamonds of searing light cut through me. Pain. My every thought serrated with it. If I could, I would have screamed. Again and again. And every scream would have had his name written on it. *Daniel.*

Flashes.

You. Me. Us. Beside a midnight pool. Tears. Comfort.

On a green field under a diamante velvet night sky. Running. Laughing.

He sings his song to me. His tattoos speak their story, his body glistens with coconut oil. He is the noble Pacific warrior of every myth and legend. And he is mine.

Leila, you don't love someone because they're a dream of perfection. You love them because of the way they meet their challenges, how they strive to overcome. Because together you bring out the best in each other. I loved you before you burst into flame. You drive me crazy and not always in a good way.

I'll be your running partner, your designated driver, the guy who picks you up off the floor, I'll even be the guy who gets his eyebrows flamed just so I can give you my shirt the next time you burn all your clothes off. I'll be what you want me to – just don't shut me out.

You will give your life that man might live.

I'm fragmenting. Dying. It surprises me. I thought I was a fire goddess, that fire could never die. Who knew there could ever be such a thing as too much heat? Too much fire? Too much power. I can't hold on any longer. It hurts too much. There is not enough of me left to resist the call of my mother, fanua afi. She whispers, seductive and promising, "Let go. Give me your pain. Your sorrow. Give me your everything. Give me your body."

Daniel, I'm sorry.

I release my fragile hold on that which is Leila. And become one with earth. Fanua afi.

Darkness.

And somewhere, a woman laughs. She is not my mother earth. But she takes all that I am and she exults.

"Yes! Mine, you are mine."

S I X T E E N

Above ground everyone watches in awe as a plume of fire erupts from the cone, piercing the sky, making it bleed with color and light. Keahi and Teuila halt in their ragged dash down the hillside. Far below, Lesina is startled to her feet.

And Daniel?

Daniel's world shatters. *Leila.* Every piece of him screams her name. Water. Maybe water can save her. He summons it. From all its secret places. From the earth beneath his feet. Sucked from the seared air. Called down from the billowing cumulous clouds. Water from the distant sea. Telesā vasa loloa,son of the ocean, speaks. And elemental earth answers. Six massive tornado waterspouts – twisting columns of fury rake their way towards him. One engulfs him, raises him above the furnace that is Leila's volcano. He gazes down at the magma bubbles that rejoice in the return of telesā fanua afi, daughter of the earth as it streams upward, brims over the cone. Champagne celebrations, frothing red and gold, seeking release, pathways to party. And unless something is done, they will rage and flow downward to where Keahi and Teuila stumble and fall in their haste to escape, where Lesina holds Jason's body close. Daniel focuses, manipulates the raging columns of liquid power, and they carve chasmed pathways through centuries of black rock, tunneling with violent force, throwing up giant sprays of chipped rock fragments. A single thought and the vortexes begin to rip their way to the sea, leaving in their wake clear pathways that lead to the beckoning distant surf. At the ocean, the water tornadoes blend as one with the silver surf and only one remains, a platform for Daniel. The erupting lava delights to find easy routes along which to run and smoothly takes the five paths of least resistance. Away from the land. Away from the volcano that has taken the girl he loves.

The rivers of lava run in lazy flowing tides of crimson, slow and sinuous. At the cliff's edge, the flow hangs poised for one perfect moment of fiery hesitation and then it pours into the waiting ocean. Scarlet ropes of fire meet water and hover on the surface. Steam hisses. Billowing clouds of white tranquility. Water burns.

Daniel catches sight of the unusual shape that blurs in the nearest ravine, shifting and rolling in the rippling lava flow. Hope sparks. Can it be?

The water obeys his bidding. Fluid and supple, carrying him over enflamed earth as he races to catch up with the dark shape carried by the fast-flowing tide of lava. He reaches his quarry just as the ravine ends at the cliff side. Just as it falls far, far below. Arms out-flung, hair flowing, body limp as a ragdoll. It's a woman. A woman on fire. A falling star, a burnt out meteorite.

Leila?

The body splashes into the ocean. Daniel doesn't breathe. Doesn't think. He launches himself from the cliff-top, executing a dive of perfect grace. The water is hot. Boiling hot. Steam obscures his vision. But he does not need to look for her. He can sense her. With every melded molecule of hydrogen and oxygen he can feel her. And she is not breathing. Her heart is not beating.

He swims to her. Finds her. Swathed in grey silk water. All flames extinguished. *Leila.* It is an easy task to raise her up, raise them both up on a whitewater bed of foam that eases them towards the nearby shoreline. Black sand is the bed on which he gently lays her. She is what he never thought she could be. Burnt. Barely recognizable. Her skin is blistered and peeling. Flesh bloodied and lacerated, grimy with speckled black rock. He tries CPR, the long ago Boy Scout first aid course coming to startling life as he covers her mouth with his, as he counts and pumps with precision on her chest. Again and again he tries to breathe life into the one who has stolen all of his forevers. There are no tears. Only single-minded intensity. She cannot be dead because they are fatu-ma-le-ele-ele.

Heart and earth. *We can handle anything as long as we are together.*

Dimly he is aware of the tide washing in around them. And in the far-off distance, the flash of silver. Dolphins. He ignores them. So intent on his task that he does not see the woman until she is almost upon him.

"Daniel." Her voice is lyrical. The lilting caress of a feather-soft sea breeze. Again. More insistent. "Daniel."

This time he looks. Pausing to raise his face up to the silver light. It is too bright. He flinches, shields his eyes. Gradually makes out the dim outline. It is a woman coming up out of the ocean. Hauntingly familiar and yet unknown. Her form mists at the edges, hazy and blurred like a holographic image, colors and promises unrealized. She stands in the shallows, long hair trailing in the soft waves. Draped only in seaweed, her skin gleams with an eerie blue-green glow, catching starlight in a mélange of color, billowing clouds from burning water at her back. Is she real? What does she want? Daniel is wary. He stands, moving to shield Leila's inert form behind him and water responds to his apprehension, automatic coils of water whips clenched tightly in his hands. Fists ready.

She speaks again. "Bring her here. Into the water."

He ignores her command. "Who are you? What do you want?"

"I want to help you. Help the girl you love. Bring her into the water. Quickly, we don't have much time."

"Why do you want to help me?" His eyes narrow in suspicion. "Why should I trust you?"

The woman smiles, but there is only sadness in her eyes. "Because I saved your life a year ago. When Sarona and her sisters stabbed you and left you for dead in the ocean, I healed you." She hesitated. "More precisely, our ocean mother vasa loloa healed you."

Stunned, Daniel asks again. "Why? Who are you?"

"Once upon a time, a long time ago, I was your mother. My name was Moanasina."

Daniel reels. A tsunami of shock rages over him. "No, that can't be. My mother died. She drowned."

"Yes, she did. Moanasina chose to blend her Gift with the ocean that gave it to her. Without the man she loved, without her child, she returned to that which gave her happiness. The wild child gave herself to the ocean. Her body died but her spirit embraced vasa loloa.I am the embodiment of earth's water element."

He struggles to understand. "So you're *not* my mother?"

"No. Moanasina died all those many years ago."

"So why are you helping me? Why do you care what happens to us?"

The woman looks mystified. "Moanasina's love for you is strong. It … moves me." She shakes her head at him impatiently. "Now hurry, bring the girl to me."

He doesn't question it anymore. What is there to lose after all? Without Leila, he is nothing, has nothing. He kneels beside her, places a single kiss on her forehead. And remembers that first kiss so long ago. In the whispering shade of a mango tree when Leila was in his arms, soft, vulnerable, and trusting. When he had wished he could kiss her lips even though hundreds of curious eyes watched them from the block of classrooms. He remembers and he weeps. There is so much of her now that is bloodied flesh and cruelly raw that he barely dares touch her. With tender care, he carries her in his arms, tears glistening shards of glass on his cheek. He walks with sure strides into the ocean, her body hanging limply in his embrace, her fingers trailing in the white surf. He walks until the water is waist deep and he stands directly in front of the silver-tressed woman. Closer, and now he can see that her silver skin is tattooed boldly. Strident patterns down her arms, legs, and even her neck. And all of them smolder with that same blue luminosity as his pe'a, so much so that the ocean floor is lit up. The woman who was once Moanasina radiates with embered blue energy and Daniel's breath catches in his chest. What is this woman?

As if she can read his mind, she speaks. "Mermaid, water nymph, siren, naiad – history has given us many names."

She gazes at his face. Curious. Impassive. Detached. She reaches with a silver-scaled hand to caress his cheek. Her touch is cold, and Daniel flinches. The movement startles her and she takes a step backwards.

His voice is harsh. "What are you going to do with her? I don't want you to hurt her."

"This will hurt no one. Release her."

The woman guides his hands to lower Leila into the water, pressing firmly so that she is captive and completely submerged in the glowing ocean.

"Hold her underwater." Her command is abrupt.

"But she can't breathe." Even as he protests, the words die on his lips. *She's not breathing anyway, you fool.* He obeys, kneeling on the pebbled sand so he can cradle Leila in his arms in the water.

The woman begins to sing. Daniel does not understand her words, but he can feel their haunting beauty. The song begins soft and low at first and then builds to a piercing intensity. The melody tugs at the emotions. There is pain. Sadness. A hollow emptiness that then begins to fill with happiness. A joy that threatens to drown you. The water churns and spins about them. And then Leila is raised up into the air and suspended in a sphere of water that radiates blue light so bright that Daniel cannot look at it. And still the woman sings.

Just when Daniel decides that this is madness – the song stops. There is silence. An impossible silence, as if the ocean itself had just ceased to breathe. No waves, no roar of crashing surf on the reef, no gentle hum of patterned waves. Nothing. Just a silver-edged woman emanating cobalt energy, arms outstretched, head thrown back, face to the sky, and Leila's body suspended under the full-globed moon.

And then the sphere gently, gently lowers Leila back to the ocean, back to Daniel's waiting arms. She coughs, struggles to open her eyes, and then sinks back into her darkness. Daniel stares at her, disbelieving. Her body is bathed in moonlight and it is beautiful. The savage burns are gone. Her skin is smooth and gleams with newness. Her head rests on his shoulder, she is soft and pliable in his arms, still not conscious but she is breathing.

The description of joy eludes him. Relief. Happiness. Lightness. Joy. Gratitude. He asks, "I don't understand. How did you do that?"

"Water is life. It always has been. Vasa loloaare healers, and the ocean's gift is magnified a thousand fold when the moon is full." A frown. "But there are some wounds that vasa loloa cannot cure. Her body is restored but I can do nothing for her spirit, her mind, or her heart. You may lose her still."

Fear is a knife that cuts deep. "What do you mean? What's wrong with her?"

"She has not yet won her battle. She fights even now. And none can say when she will wake. I'm sorry."

"What should I do to help her? Tell me what I should do?"

"There is nothing you can do, nothing anyone can do. Except wait. Love her. And hope she returns." The woman turns and begins to walk away from them, deeper into the ocean. She takes the light with her. "No, wait. Come back. I want …" *I have so many questions I want to ask you. So much I want to tell you. Please. Don't leave me. Again.* "I want to say thank you."

She half turns her head to frown back at him. "Don't thank me yet, Daniel, son of the ocean. One day all of earth's telesā may live to bitterly regret this healing. Even you, Daniel. Especially you." And with that enigmatic statement, she shimmers, fades, and dives. There is a blinding flash of ocean light and she is gone.

Hospitals. Daniel hated them. They were so removed from what he had always associated with healing. Medicine for him was his grandmother's garden. Lush greenery and rich color. Gathering baskets of white ginger flowers beside a sparkling mountain stream. Salamasina grinding koko bean and ginger root. Her laughter as he made a face at the taste of her concoctions, "Fine, I'll put some more honey in it. You're such a big baby." The compassion in her touch as she massaged his dislocated collar bone with fragranced coconut oil. Healing was love. Touch. Comfort. Closeness.

Not this. The sour-faced nurse standing sentry at the ward entrance. The thick odor of disinfectant blanketing a sterile room. The constant drone and beep of monitors and the slow drip of an IV. The hushed tones of doctors as they held their clipboards close and their jealously guarded knowledge even closer. The needles, tubing, and wires.

And Leila. Lying so still on the bed. Unresponsive. Pale and lifeless. It had been three days since the volcano, three days since she had been in a coma – but already she seemed thinner. She was wasting away right there in front of him and there was nothing he could do about it. Frustration warred with guilt as Daniel clenched his fists tightly on the side railings of Leila's bed. If only he had moved faster, if only he had stopped her from doing her usual dumb-ass sacrifice move. Maybe he shouldn't have trusted that woman. What did he know about vasa loloa anyway? What if the ocean spirit woman had lied to him? What if this was her doing? Dammit, Leila please wake up. Please come back to me.

He had promised not to leave her side. To walk with her always. Especially when she walked through valleys shadowed with danger. A difficult covenant to keep, especially with Matile giving him evil looks as if she held him personally responsible for Leila's condition. And rightly so. He was the one who had failed to keep her safe. Tiredness threatened to drag him under. Salamasina brought him food and clothes. Words of comfort that did little to numb the fear that knifed at him.

Others visited daily and waited for Leila to awaken as well. Teuila, wracked with guilt, "It's all my fault. She was only trying to help me." A subdued Simone who wrung his hands and cried. "She was trying to say goodbye to me and I told her that if she didn't come back, I wanted to have her Louboutin shoes. I'm such a heartless, cold witch." Maleko and Sinalei, Rihanna, and Mariah came every day and brought flowers. Exuberant, hopeful bunches of color that Daniel knew Leila would smile for. If she would only come back from whatever distant shore she walked upon. Lesina came too. She brought the Bone with her.

"I got this from Sarona's campsite. She never told me why she wanted it. Something about a legend and Pele the volcano goddess. All I know for sure is that she was going to have us search for two more pieces." An awkward shrug. "This belongs to Leila. She should have it back." Lesina didn't stay long. She was busy making arrangements with Jason's parents for his body to be returned to America.

Keahi tried to visit Leila. But Daniel leapt to his feet as soon as he saw him enter. An angry whisper. "What are you doing here? You're part of the reason she's in here." At the other end of the room, a jug of water shattered with a thought. The silver liquid merged with glass shards, coiling into a garrote wire that twisted with lightning speed around Keahi's neck.

Keahi winced against the razor-sharp vice at his throat, but made no resistance against the attack. The two stared at each other for a long taut moment. As blood seeped. Keahi held up his hands appeasingly, "I'll leave then."

The days dragged into a week and still Leila showed no signs of improvement. Time was running out. Matile had finally been able to reach Leila's Uncle Thomas in America. He was sending a private plane to transport Leila back to a medical facility in the

United States, as soon as the doctors cleared her to travel. Daniel was sure there was no way they would allow some unknown Samoan boy to hitch a ride with the patient. Even if he was the vasa loloa ocean complement to her fanua afi earth self.

"You've got to wake up. I need you here. Not in faraway America. You promised me remember? You promised that we wouldn't be apart like that again. Skype just doesn't do it for me."

The doctor had said that talking to coma patients was helpful. That it could be their voice in the darkness. The light that called them home. And so, every day, and into the nights, Daniel sat and talked to Leila. "I've got a deep, dark shameful secret to tell you. Now that you're incapacitated and can't attack me. Maybe it will make you mad enough that you'll wake up?"

A hopeful pause in the deepening twilight. Nothing. No response. "Okay, here it goes. I kind of stalked you a bit when you first started at SamCo. After that debate in Ms. Sivani's class, the one where you went nuclear on me for no good reason at all, remember? After that class when I tried to talk to you and you told me to get lost, I couldn't stop thinking about you. I don't often get people hating me so viciously. So I asked Simone to go talk to you. You know, find out why you hated me so much and maybe try to put in a good word for me. The plan was for Simone to get me some inside info on the enemy, and for a while he was an excellent double agent, telling me everything I wanted to know about you and even stuff I never asked him! He kept telling me to 'be a man' and go talk to you myself but you gotta admit, you were kinda abrasive. A scary chick. Then Simone decided to be best friends with you and he stopped sharing info with me so I had to do my own stalking. That day you were on Hard Labor for skipping class? I wasn't supposed to be on prefect duty. I only switched with Manuia when I recognized your name on the detention list." A laugh, a smile, as memories ran away with him.

Massage was good for coma patients as well. Daniel asked Salamasina to bring a bottle of moso'oi fragranced coconut oil from home.

Late one evening, when the last stragglers were leaving after visiting hour, Daniel sat and massaged Leila's arms, and the heady perfume disguised the disinfectant, if only for a little while. Delicately he traced the patterns of her taulima. "I wish I could take you to our special place, Leila. Our secret mountain pool. When you get better, we're going to go there again. I've already decided that it's the place where I'm going to ask you to marry me. That's right. I said the M word. I've been doing a lot of thinking, sitting here every day waiting for you to wake up and I realized that when you find the person who makes you want to believe in forever? Then you should hold on to them and never let them go. And yeah, you should even marry them. I think you and I are going to have to face a lot of storms because of what we are. We should face them together. And make every day our forever. Because we don't know how many days we're going to get."

He didn't see her eyes open. He didn't know that she was listening to him. He didn't see her tremulous smile. Or the single tear that ran down her cheek. But he did hear her say, "Daniel Tahi, are you proposing to a girl who's asleep?"

"Leila?" He rose to his feet, careful joy on his face. "You're awake. You're back."

She laughed weakly, "Did I go somewhere?"

He took her in his arms, breathed kisses on her forehead, her cheek, her lips. "I thought I had lost you."

"What happened?"

"How much do you remember?"

"Not much." She winced, "It hurts to try and think. I remember getting on a plane for Tonga with you and Jason." A frown. "And that's it."

He held her hand. Maybe it was best that she not remember everything. At least not all at once. "Wait here." He got up and went to the door.

She frowned, "Where are you going? I just woke up and you're leaving?"

"I'm going to call the nurse. Tell them you're awake so they can check you. Make sure everything is alright."

The nurses came and bustled about with equipment and monitors. Said they couldn't do much until the doctors came in to do their rounds the next day. "In the meantime, she needs to rest. No activity. No excitement," they instructed severely. "Don't tire her with too much information either. She may be disoriented. Don't expect her to have complete memory recall right away. Take it slow."

After they left, Daniel said, "Everyone will want to know that you're awake. Shall I call them for you?"

"Not yet." She pleaded. "Don't call anyone yet. Come sit with me. Just let it be us for a little while longer."

He went back to sit on the bed. She clutched his hand again and asked fearfully, "Did it work? Did we save Teuila? Is everyone alright?"

Daniel nodded. Smiled. Reassured her, "Yes. We saved Teuila. And everyone is alright." He thought of Jason and tried not to show sorrow. There would be time in the days to come for Leila to remember Jason's death. Time to grieve.

Leila made room for him beside her and he put an arm around her as she leaned into his chest. Listening. "There it is. Your heartbeat. It's so strong. Soothing. It always reassures me. Calms me."

He grinned down at her, placed a kiss on her hair, breathed deeply of her scent. "This isn't the way I imagined our first time in the same bed together."

She answered with a shy smile, "I'd love to hear how you did imagine it."

"No way. We're not going there. The nurse said no excitement."

She gazed up at him, "Can you at least tell me again how you're going to propose to me one day? I was a little out of it and didn't catch all the details."

Daniel ran his fingers through his hair, ruffling at it in that embarrassed gesture she knew so well. "You weren't supposed to hear that."

"Why not?" She faked a horrified expression. "Was that proposal meant for some other girl?"

"No, you flamehead. But it was meant to be a surprise. A beautiful, romantic surprise proposal."

She snuggled closer into him. "I love surprises. Tell me it now so I can practice being surprised. Go on. I just woke up from the edge of death. I'm sure you're supposed to be super nice to people who just wake up from comas."

"Alright. But only because you're a recently awoken coma girl. That's all." Moonlight danced through the window as Daniel proceeded to tell her again, all about how he wanted to ask her to spend forever with him.

And Leila listened with a sleepy smile. And when he was finished, she asked, "What about the wedding? Where are we going to get married? Tell me the story."

A tropical breeze danced through the open window on a star-spangled Samoan night as Daniel told Leila a story of a wedding. "On the other side of the main island of Upolu, at the end of a weather-beaten track through the rainforest, there is a secluded beach that very few know of. It's a narrow strip of powder-white sand, fringed with rainforest and there's a river that meets the ocean there. The beach looks out to a small island, Nu'u I'a Sa. The Island of the Sacred Fish. We'll get married on that beach, just as the sun is setting. Mama will be there. Your aunt and uncle. A few of our friends. You'll be wearing a dress made by Simone. Of course."

With her eyes fighting to stay open, Leila laughed softly. "Of course."

Daniel continued, "But nothing too fancy. And definitely nothing with gold bodypaint. Just you in a simple, white elei dress and barefoot in the sand. With your hair down. Trailing with white ginger flowers."

"And how about you? What will you be wearing?"

A shrug, "I don't know. Clothes."

"A black lavalava and a white elei shirt. Like that night when you took me to dinner after the Culture Dance performance."

He kissed her hair. "Fine."

She interrupted. Again. "Can there be candles? All over the sand? And some floating ones in the water?"

He frowned. "Alright. But not too many. It will be a full moon and the stars will be out, more than enough light. Now stop interrupting my story."

"Sorry." She snuggled into him again. He ran his fingers through her hair and she sighed with contentment. Sleep was calling her.

His voice dropped to a low timbre, "So we'll be married on the beach and then everyone will congratulate us and go home. Immediately. And then we'll get into a canoe."

She mumbled, "Which will have flower petals all over it. And some candles on it."

He rolled his eyes, "Okay. Flowers and candles. And I'll paddle us to the little island where we will be completely alone. There's a small fale beach house there, overlooking the cove. It's got a bed and a mosquito net. A lantern."

Her eyes were closed but she was still with him, "And pie. Matile's pineapple pie. Ice cold vai tipolo lemonade."

He grinned, shaking his head at her, "Yes, there's food. I wouldn't dream of taking you on a honeymoon on a deserted island without any food."

A happy sigh. "Keep going. This is the best bit. This is where I finally get to love you in all the ways that I've dreamed about." She prompted, "And then?"

"And then Daniel and Leila live happily ever after." He teased, waiting for her to protest. But there was no response. He looked down. She was asleep in his arms. Daniel held her, watched her breathe. Gratitude. Joy. Peace.

Music seemed to be the only way to express what he was feeling. Soft and low, he sang to Leila in the moonlight. *As the river flows, gently to the sea, darling so we go, some things were meant to be. Take my hand. Take my whole life too. But I can't help falling in love with you.*

And slowly, slowly – with Leila safe in his arms, he fell asleep.

Perfect moments. They're rare, few and far between. Hold them close when you find them. They will give you strength when the storm comes.

The Bone that Lesina had returned sat on the bedside table.

Sometime in the night, the smile on Leila's face faded. It was replaced with an uneasy frown. She shifted in her sleep, whimpered as if caught in the clutches of a nightmare. The Bone began to glow. Emanate a fiery orange light. Leila's tattoos answered.

And then her eyes flickered open. They glowed with the intensity of a millennia of powerless fury. The woman who lay cradled in Daniel's arms smiled into the darkness and whispered softly,

"At last. I am free."

The End

An excerpt from the third book in the Telesā Trilogy
by
Lani Wendt Young

The Bone Bearer

❈

The Legend of Pele, the Fire Goddess – as told by the Telesā

Pele was born in the islands of Hawaii, an Ungifted daughter of Noalani – a legendary telesā fanua afi. Noalani was the Covenant Keeper for the ruling fanua afi in the Pacific and, as such, the holder of the Tangaloa Covenant Bone. Noalani hoped, watched, and waited for her daughter's Gift to manifest. But her hopes were in vain. Pele grew to womanhood and only demonstrated a whisper of fanua afi capabilities, barely a spark next to the raging fire that was her mother. According to the Telesā custom, Noalani should have sent her away. Given her to a good mother to raise so she could find a place in the world. As a healer, a wife, a mother. So she could find happiness. But Noalani loved her daughter too much. She could not bear to part with her and so she kept her with the Fanua Afi Sisterhood. In this, Noalani did her a great cruelty because Pele grew up a stranger amongst her own kind. As a child, Pele was scorned by her sisters. Pitied by her elders and mocked by her community, who knew that she was a fanua afi without fire.

Racked with guilt and sorrow for her daughter's pain, Noalani did the unthinkable. She gave the Tangaloa Bone to Pele and showed her how to use it to take the Gift – and thus the life – of one of the youngest and newest telesā fanua afi. An orphan child who "noone would miss."

"There my daughter. Now you have the Gift of fanua afi and you can walk proudly amongst your sisters. Put aside your sorrow. Embrace who you are. My daughter."

For a time, Pele was content to be the same as her sisters. But like a tree maggot, the hunger for power ate at her soul. She nurtured a growing hatred for her sisters, they who had scorned her, mocked her, pitied her. Her hatred drove her to do the unthinkable. She took the Tangaloa Bone without her mother's knowledge and secretly used it on another young girl in the village. And then another. The string of mysterious deaths had the whole island puzzled. Who was killing their daughters?

Suspicion grew in Noalani, a tree fern unfurling its leaves in the sun. She confronted her daughter. Noone knows exactly how it happened, but Pele stole her mother's Gift. And her life. The girl who had begun life as the weakest among them was now the strongest telesā fanua afi in Hawaii. She could have been the Covenant Keeper. There were none who dared to oppose her. But Pele did not want to belong to a family that had rejected her. She did not want to belong to a sisterhood. She wanted everyone to suffer for the years of pain she had endured. Vengeance was her enduring thirst.

And thus began the Time of Darkness in Pacific telesā history. Pele killed off all the telesā fanua afi one by one. But she was not content to stop there. She wanted to rid the world of every fanua afi in existence. She hunted them in Tonga, Samoa, Fiji, and Tahiti. And with each kill, her powers grew. She turned her attention to the other elements. Using the Tangaloa Bone, she then hunted the vasa loloa and matagi who dared to oppose her. It was a time of fear, suspicion, and distrust.

But Pele's unquenchable thirst for power proved to be her undoing. She stole so much of the Earth's raw power that a body of flesh and blood could no longer contain it. One crimson-spangled day, Pele erupted into flame and her body was no more. Her spirit fused with the very heart of the volcano she ignited and the earth's fierycore enveloped her and would not release her. She was bound forever to the earth from which she had stolen.

She lives still. In raging rivers of molten red lava. In shimmering bursts of cindered light. In the raging violence of earthquakes.

She is Pele, the Fire Goddess, and she festers beneath the surface of the earth. Brooding, innately powerful, but forever wanting that which she cannot have.

A body.

�֎

They say that the Pacific Council of telesā met after Pele's death. The Council agreed that the Covenant Bone must never be held by any single telesā again, the lure of its power too great. It must be protected from the powerseekers and instead secreted away for the time spoken of in prophecy, when the Bone would be used to bring together all telesā as one heart and one mind. The Bone was broken into three pieces and given to three chosen telesā to safeguard.

The elements of Air, Fire, and Water – forever separated.

Waiting for the coming of the Bone Bearer.

✖

In Samoa, the heat arrives before the fullness of the morning sun. Seeping in softly through the screened windows, wet in its humid embrace. Eight o'clock and sweat was already staining the uniform of the grim-faced nurse as she stood in the doorway, shaking her head at the couple that lay on the bed, entwined in each other's arms. Asleep.

Roughly she shook the boy first. He awoke instantly with a start. "What is it? Leila? Is she alright?"

Calm replaced the panic as he gazed at the girl asleep in his arms. Safe. Alive. And well. The nurse was not happy. "What are you doing in here? This is against hospital policy."

"Shh…" Daniel slowly arose from the bed, gently loosening from Leila's embrace. Still she slept. He gave the angry nurse a grin and walked her away from the bed, out into the hall. "What is? This? Patients having their family spend the night at the hospital with them?"

He nodded across the hall where other patients slept in a line of beds. And beside them on mats on the floor, slept their family, keeping them company. Because no self-respecting Samoan ever let a family member stay in hospital without someone to sleep alongside them.

The nurse frowned even more. "It's not right for you to be here all the time with her. Are you this girl's family? No you're not."

Daniel was about to say, 'Yes I am. She's my fiancée.' When a muffled gasp from the room interrupted them. He spun around. Leila was sitting up in the bed, looking at them with mingled fear and confusion. He smiled. Pale, rumpled, and wearing a dingy hospital gown – she was still the most beautiful girl he had ever seen.

"Hey you. You're awake." He went to hug her and she shrank back from his touch.

"Who are you? What is this place?" Her look of fear had him slowly releasing her. He sat beside her on the bed and spoke soft and slow. Calming.

"Babe, it's me, Daniel. You're in the hospital. Remember? You've been in a coma for a week and you woke up yesterday. I must have fallen asleep holding you last night." A reassuring smile. A nod at the sour nurse. "This nice nurse is here to check on you. Make sure everything is alright." He gave Leila a nudge with his shoulder and leant in close to whisper with a lighthearted tone, "She's been giving me a hard time about staying with you because I'm not family. I was about to tell her that we're closer than family. I'm your Vasa Loloa and you're my Fanua Afi."

But there was no answering smile on Leila's face. She shook her head, terror in her voice, her face, her body. "What are you talking about? I don't know you. Where's my Dad? I want my father. I don't know this place. Somebody help me! Get away from me."

Leila pushed against him, eyes wild with fear. Daniel stared in horror as she started thrashing and screaming, pulling at the wires and tubes that connected her to the monitors. The nurse shouted for help. Two more nurses came running in, pushing past Daniel, curt and efficient.

"Move. Out of the way." With quick precision two nurses restrained Leila while the other gave her a shot of something in her IV line. They soothed her with professional ease. "It's alright. We're here to help you. You're in a hospital, you've been sick and you're just a little confused. Calm down. No-one is going to hurt you."

Whatever they had given her worked quickly because in a few minutes Leila's body relaxed and she sank back onto the bed with a weary sigh. Her eyes were glazed and her speech slurred as she asked the nurses, "I want my Dad. Please can you get my Dad?"

"Of course we will. You just rest now and he will be here soon." said one. The other took Daniel to the side, "Where's her father? You better call him that she's awake and asking for him."

Daniel shrugged helplessly. He whispered, "I can't. Her father's dead. He died two years ago. She knows that already." He glanced at the drugged girl on the bed. "Well, she knew that before she got hurt. I don't understand. What's happening? She didn't know me."

"Shh…we'll talk outside. Come." A nurse took him outside into the hall. "The doctor warned you that she might have compromised brain function when she regained consciousness, didn't he?"

Daniel interrupted, "Yes but he said she might be a little confused. Disoriented. Not this. She has no clue who the hell I am! She looked at me like I was a complete stranger. Last night when she first woke up, she was different. She was fine. She knew me. She loved me. Dammit, what's going on?" His voice rose to a shout. He was battling for composure.

"Daniel? What is going on here?" The stern voice of disapproval startled him. "Why are you speaking with such disrespect to this nurse?"

He turned and wilted with relief. It was Salamasina, frowning at him. "Oh Mama, I'm so glad you're here."

He swept the old woman into a fierce hug. He was tired, hungry and beaten. "It's Leila." His voice caught and his grandmother instantly assumed the worst.

"Oh no, my son. I'm so sorry." The compassion on her face was genuine. Daniel rushed to correct her.

"No, no she's okay. Leila's awake Mama."

"That's wonderful news. I don't understand, what's the problem then?"

"She's awake but she doesn't know me. She can't remember anything about what happened and she doesn't recognize me." Shoulders slumped; he sank into a chair in the corridor, face in his hands.

"This is a foolish reaction don't you think?" Her lips pursed in disapproval as she sat beside him, an arm around him. "The important thing is that she is going to be alright. There will be plenty of time for you two to catch up. You must be patient my son. And remember, she will need you more than ever as she recuperates. Now is not the time to be discouraged. Or to be selfish."

A deep breath. "You're right, Mama. As always." A half-smile. "What matters is that Leila is awake. And she's going to be fine. Everything's going to be fine now."

"Yes, so maybe now you will consider getting some rest? You can't keep going like this. I'm going to take you home for a good meal and a sleep. You can come back tonight."

Together they stood and Salamasina took the opportunity to take her son in her arms. A rare moment to hold the boy that had always been her reason for living. She felt tears burn her eyes. Daniel pulled away.

"Thank you Mama for being here. And supporting me, I know you've never been happy about me and Leila."

"I don't think any mother ever thinks any girl is good enough for her son. Don't worry about my feelings. I only want you to be happy." She smiled up at him, seeing him as the little boy that he used to be. Daniel caught the glint of tears.

"Mama, what's wrong?"

"Nothing son. I was just remembering…when you were a little boy, you would hug me and promise me *I'm never going to grow up Mama. I'm going to be your little boy forever.*" Tears broke free. "Sometimes I wish you were that little boy again. And for always."

"Oh Mama, of course I love you. Even if I'm not your little boy anymore." He bent to kiss her forehead. "I'm just going to say goodbye, let her know that I'm leaving."

"Of course. Give me some time to go find her doctors. I want to see what they have to say about this latest development." One last quick hug and Daniel went into Leila's room where a nurse fussed with charts and meds.

She looked up as he walked in. "The drugs have calmed her a bit. We don't want her to be agitated though so please, just a quick visit. She's still trying to process everything, so no big revelations or any more information about anything alright? It will only add to the sensory overload. There will be plenty of time for that sort of thing in the days to come." She left him with that last warning.

Leila lay in the bed staring out the window.

"Leila?"

She turned to his voice. Slowly. She was crying and the look in her eyes caught and held him captive. They were the eyes of a child, lost and afraid. "Where's my Dad? Why isn't he here? I need him. He's the only one that loves me. The only one who understands me."

Three steps and he was kneeling at her bedside, holding her hand in his, choking on emotions. "I'm so sorry, he's been delayed. But I'm going to stay with you until he gets here." The lies tasted like broken coral in his mouth. "I'm going to stay right here. Right beside you."

She flinched at his nearness and carefully pulled her hand away from his. A wall shut down between them and her tone was polite. Distant. "Thank you. That's very nice of you." She wiped her face on the sleeve of her hospital gown in a vain attempt to hide the fact that she had been crying. And still wanted to cry buckets more. "I'm sure that I will be fine by myself until he gets here. You can go - Daniel. That is your name, right?"

He nodded, unwilling to trust himself to speak. To have her speak to him with the neutrality of a stranger hurt more than any pain he had ever experienced. "Yeah, that's right. I'm Daniel."

I'm Daniel Tahi. I know what your lips taste like. I know your favorite snack is Diet Coke and Doritos. I know that you're scared of needles but you were brave enough to get a malu tattoo. I know you roll your eyes when you think someone is an idiot. I know that you wish you were six inches shorter so you wouldn't be taller than most of the boys you've ever met. I know you would give your life for the people you love. I know I have your fire, your name tattooed on my heart.

I am Daniel Tahi. I am telesa vasa loloa.

I am yours.

And you can't remember who I am.

She seemed troubled by the look in his eyes. They stared at each other for what seemed like an eternity but couldn't have been longer than a few seconds. For one wild moment Daniel considered leaning closer and capturing her mouth with his. Forcing the memory of their past into her with his kiss.

But before he could do anything so stupid, there was a sound at the doorway. Keahi.

"Can I come in?"

Daniel pulled back, stood, feeling his every nerve tingle with the liquid ice of hatred that always seemed to well up whenever Keahi was in his vicinity. "No, you can't. I thought we agreed that you couldn't come anywhere near Leila." He flexed his fingers, aching to wrench water from all its hiding places and lasso it around Keahi's neck. Resisting, knowing that something like that would definitely be way too much for Leila to handle right now. Heck, she couldn't even remember who he was, let alone the minor detail that he could summon water and talk to fishes.

Daniel and Keahi faced off. The Hawaiian was still bandaged, an open button-down shirt revealing the swathes of white wrapping the full length of his torso. Daniel noted with some satisfaction that he also had a couple of band aids on this neck where he had last marked him with a water coil.

"Well?"

Keahi's response was low – muttered for Daniel's ears only. "I heard she was awake. I want to apologize. Can I talk to her? For just a minute?"

"Like hell. No. Get out."

That's when Leila peered from around Daniel's bulk, trying to get a glimpse of whoever he was talking to "Who is that?" She caught sight of the lean, lithe boy in the doorway. "Oh." An abrupt sound, soon followed by a greeting. "Hi. Did you want to see me?"

Keahi's smile was immediate. And laden with relief. "Yeah. I came by to see how you are. It's good to see you awake."

He took several steps inside the room and Daniel's eyes narrowed at him warningly. *Careful, don't push it.* Keahi ignored him, so intent was he on looking Leila up and down. A big smile. "Wow, you look great. I mean, you're skinnier and kinda washed out but you look way better than I thought you would. I mean after what happened to you…"

"Shut up, you idiot." Daniel's command was a whispered one but still clear enough for Leila to hear him. She frowned at him and immediately smiled again. At Keahi. A really big smile. *What the f...?*

"Thanks. My head hurts but yeah, I'm fine." Another smile. "Thanks for checking on me."

What's with all the smiling? Why is she so happy to see this freak that almost got her killed? Hello?!

Daniel interrupted. Brusquely. "I think you gotta go. The nurse said Leila isn't supposed to have visitors. Until she's stronger."

She frowned at him. "But you're in here." She looked back at Keahi. "I'm sorry, what's your name anyway?"

Keahi raised an eyebrow. *Not the bloody Khal Drogo eyebrow again...* He looked back and forth from Leila and then at Daniel. "Wait a minute. Are you kidding me?" He stopped, looked at Daniel for confirmation and then leaned in to whisper. "She doesn't remember anything?"

Daniel shook his head and Keahi continued, "How about you? She must remember you."

"Not yet." It hurt to even say the words.

Keahi grinned. "Aww shit, man that bites." He leaned against the doorway and for a minute, he looked sympathetic. "That's gotta hurt dude. How are you holding up?" Then the attempt at sympathy faded as a thought ran like wicked fire through him. "Wait, that means, she's technically not even in love with you anymore is she? How could she be? She doesn't even know who in hell you are." He laughed. Long and loud. "Guess I don't need to apologize for what she can't remember!"

Daniel spoke through gritted teeth. Hushed but deadly. "Get out. Before I throw you out that window."

Keahi's laughter ceased abruptly and his expression darkened as he leaned in close. "Yeah? You and what ocean?"

Every nerve, every muscle, every sinew in Daniel tensed taut and wired as he drew himself up to tower over Keahi. "I don't need any special powers to hurt you. Just like I don't need to leech fire off someone else to kick start my own gifts. You parasite."

Keahi seemed unmoved by Daniel's disdain. He smiled his ever-ready mocking grin "You just can't stand it, can you?"

"What?"

"You can't stand it that me and Leila share a bond that you never will."

Daniel flinched. "You share nothing. You've got no right to be here. Because of you, Sarona almost killed her."

Finally, Keahi lost his smile. "I got every right to be here. Because of me, Sarona is dead."

Leila interrupted, irritation coloring every word. "Excuse me, would one of you please tell me what's going on? What am I missing?"

Daniel answered her but with his fierce gaze still on the other boy. "Nothing's going on. I'm just telling Keahi that it's not a good idea for people to be here bothering you while you're still not better yet."

Keahi took a step closer to Daniel in deadly intent, "And I'm telling Daniel nicely, that at times like this, you need your best friends around you. Friends who you can relate to and connect with." A sly smile. "In all sorts of explosive ways."

Leila looked confused, "So you and me, we're close? We're friends?"

Keahi side-stepped Daniel and walked over to stand by Leila's bedside. "Oh yeah. We're best friends." He reached out with one hand and gently, slowly, tucked back a loose strand of her hair that covered the side of her face, then trailed a whisper soft caress on her cheek.

Daniel's voice was harsh, "Don't you touch her!"

It was too late.

Red patterns glowed on Keahi's skin, like coils of heated steel wire. Leila's eyes widened in disbelief. She shrunk away from his hand. And then her taulima armband seethed with an answering fiery burn. "What's happening?" The terror on her face spurred Daniel into action. He wrenched Keahi away from the bed, slamming him up against the wall, one forearm jammed at his throat.

"I said, don't touch her." Rage unlocked power. The tattoo that stamped the full length of his arm, sparked with iridescent blue fire and where it met with Keahi's neck markings – it hissed and smoked. As water burned.

Before Keahi could react, Leila made a muffled sob of terror. Both boys turned.. She sat bolt upright on the bed, staring at the evidence of their angry Gifts. Horror. "What are you?"

Panic unlocked power. The arterial current of fanua afi lit up her malu and her fingers sparked with cindered light. She held out her hands. Fear. "What am I?"

Keahi shook loose from Daniel's restraint. A triumphant smile at Leila. "I told you. We're friends." A sideways glance at Daniel's cold blue fury. "All of us. We're the same. We're telesa." Laughter. "There's a couple more of us out there. We're a team. Like the X-Men. Right Daniel?" His wry grin dared Daniel to contradict him.

But Daniel only had eyes for Leila. As molten tears glistened and ran down her face, a trail of ruby fire. As she looked helplessly at the strange sparks that lingered at the edges of her being. Regret consumed rage. He calmed the ocean within him. Walked to her and took her hands in his. With delicate precision, he summoned water from the jug on the bedside table, so that it rippled through the air with silken ease and lightly entangled about her fingers, stilling the hints of flame. He wiped away her tears with hands of water. Leila stared at him wide-eyed and questioning but somewhat soothed.

"I'm sorry we frightened you. Keahi's right. We are your friends. We care about you. Very much. And we're going to help you get through this. Help you to get your memory back."

Daniel placed a delicate kiss on her forehead before backing away. "We're going to leave you to rest now. I'll be back later." He spoke to Keahi. "Let's go."

Keahi didn't want to leave, but he felt like he had won the war, getting Daniel to admit that he had been right after all. He threw Leila his careless smile. "Later Leila. We'll work this out." He followed Daniel out into the corridor and together, the two of them walked out of the ward and towards the parking lot. Past a line of concrete water tanks.

Keahi shook his head as he walked, amazement coloring his words, "I gotta admit, I didn't think you had it in you - agreeing to help Leila together."

Daniel didn't answer. And so Keahi kept talking. "I can't believe that her memory got wiped. But then, she went through a lot that day. What she did? Taking out that plutonium battery like that? That took a lot of courage. She could have died. Wonder how long it will take for her to remember everything…"

And then Keahi wasn't talking anymore. Because Daniel had turned, grabbed him by the shoulders and threw him against a concrete tank. He gripped the back of Keahi's head and smashed his face into the tank wall. One, two, three times. Blood gushed from Keahi's nose and mouth. He swore. Spat out chipped tooth fragments. He broke free and spun around. Dazed and in pain, Keahi's training kicked in. He struck with a straight foot-thrust kick to Daniel's mid-section, knocking him off balance.

But Daniel had started this with the element of surprise –which goes a long way. So does the element of water. In answer to his command, water ripped through the top of the tank, spraying chunks of concrete into the air.

Before Keahi could execute another kick, a thick coil of water encircled him, yanked him off his feet and into the air. He struggled. Shouted. "What – are you scared to fight me fair? Let me outta this."

With outstretched hands, Daniel manipulated water, slamming Keahi into the concrete wall, again and again. He watched with impassive eyes as Keahi fought – and failed to get free. Pain. Ribs cracked. Flesh bruised. Blood smears stained the tank wall.

Finally, Daniel forced Keahi to a kneeling position beside him, still bound in ropes of liquid. Keahi stared up at him. He was a battered mess. But still defiant. He choked on bubbles of redness as he cursed again.

Daniel spoke. "When it comes to the girl I love, I don't care about fairness. I will do whatever it takes to keep her safe from you."

All of Daniel's tattoos burned with steel blue intensity. "Know this - we are not the same. We are not friends. There is no team. You are not her friend. You will stay away from her. Or I will kill you."

And then Daniel Tahi walked away.

Acknowledgments

I pay tribute to the generosity, commitment, and fortitude of those who work with survivors of domestic violence and sexual abuse – particularly in Samoa. I honor the strength and endurance of all those women and children who are daily survivors of horrible things. If you are one of them – I hope you will seek the help you need to change your situation. Please know that you are not alone and there is support available in your community. The first step is often to break the silence and talk about it.

If nothing else, I hope this book can get more of us talking about issues that we are, too often, far too quiet about.

It's not easy for a book written by a Samoan author to find a global voice. Thank you to all those readers who took a chance on the first 'Telesā' book and then were generous enough to share it – review it, blog it, tweet it, Facebook it, email it, harass their family and friends to read it. The Telesā series has the bestest readers in the world. I am in awe of your passion, enthusiasm, and fiery creativity as you have embraced this Pacific story. It is always a joy to connect with you, whether in person or in the virtual world.

This book could not have been written without the unparalleled imagination of my daughter Sade who spent many hours dreaming up Leila's adventures with me. Daniel would not be who he is without the creative input of my husband Darren. And there would be way more fantastically impossible things in the book if not for my son Jade who battled (often vainly) to have the story make more 'scientific sense.'

Usually, editing is a painful process – but not when you have an editor like Anna Thomson who makes me laugh even as she's pointing out inconsistencies and casting a doubtful eye on my overly fanciful leaps of the imagination. Thank you for taking on the Telesā books and refining them. There is no-one else I would entrust with my chaotic manuscript.

I owe much of the inspiration for the spiritual-environmental themes in the book to Zita Martel, the 'Nafanua of the Ocean.' Thank you for sharing your insight into the 'teine Sa' mythology.

Einjo! To Tim Baice and Sefa Lematua who generously acted as linguistic consultants so that Simone could take a feisty, witty lead role.

Thank you to Cam Wendt and the Pualele Club for allowing me to showcase the magnificent thrill of the traditional sport of outrigger canoeing. My apologies for any technical errors that may have crept in. (Perhaps like Simone, I was distracted by the paddlers.)

The character of Lesina Agiao was created with the help of Kutoli Tanielu and Leitu Peseta Filo.

Grateful awe to fashion designer extraordinaire, Lindah Lepou for making a guest appearance and inspiring Simone's Pacific Couture dreams.

Jordan Kwan, Faith Wulf, Ezra Taylor, and the 'Covenant Sisterhood' models – the team that brings the Telesā characters to life in color and on screen – you take our breath away.

The Telesā writing journey has taken me to meet some amazing vibrant Pacific women, especially my sister bloggers throughout Samoa, New Zealand, Australia, Hawaii, and the USA. Love and gratitude to the Brisbane Telesā Sisterhood for a book week that surpassed all others. Huge admiration for the women of PACIFICA NZ that continue to inspire so many of us. Thank you Sina Wendt Moore for not giving up on me!

I'm grateful for the friendship and example of many amazing independent authors who are so willing to share their publishing journeys and experiences with me. Thank you Elizabeth Hansen Reinhardt and the fabulous and fearless FP team. Thank you Jillian Dodd and the Destiny Makers.

Love and appreciation to all my family and friends who continue to support and encourage my writing journey. Especially my mother, Marita Wendt and my big sister Tanya Samu who generously try their hardest to ensure that I don't *look* like a hermit cave writer when I go out in public (because yeah, pajamas or sweats are just not a good look for a book event...)

I am grateful for the opportunity to be living my dream. It is a blessing to be an author, blogger and writer of Pacific stories.

Fa'afetai tele lava.

Lani

About the Author

Lani Wendt Young was born and raised in Samoa. She completed her tertiary education in the USA and New Zealand before returning to Samoa to teach high school English for ten years. She now lives in Auckland, NZ, with her husband and five children. Lani's award-winning short fiction has featured in collections published in Samoa, NZ, Australia and the United Kingdom.

CPSIA information can be obtained
at www.ICGtesting.com
Printed in the USA
FSHW022231070721
83034FS